# SEDUCTION BY LIGHT

# SEDUCTION BY LIGHT

Al Young

A SEYMOUR LAWRENCE BOOK

A Seymour Lawrence Book
Published by
Dell Publishing
a division of
The Bantam Doubleday Dell Publishing Group, Inc.
666 Fifth Avenue
New York, New York 10103

Portions of this novel, in somewhat different form, originally appeared in *Ploughshares*, *Quilt*, and *Seattle Review*.

Library of Congress Cataloging in Publication Data

Young, Al, 1939–
Seduction by light / Al Young
p.   cm.
ISBN 0-440-55003-3
I. Title.
PS3575.O683S4   1988
813'.54—dc19                                                        88-9665
                                                                                      CIP

Printed in the United States of America

November 1988

10 9 8 7 6 5 4 3 2 1

BG

*For Jerry Marsullo and Lee Phillips,*
*whose affectionate and abiding*
*encouragement sustained me while*
*this story unfolded*

*In memory of my mother,*
*Mary Nettie Bell Campbell Simmons;*
*born Pachuta, Mississippi, December 17, 1922;*
*died Detroit, Michigan, July 23, 1982*

The author is grateful to Seymour Lawrence for his vision, Carole Baron and Jane Rosenman for their understanding, patience, and editorial suggestions, and the Pamela Djerassi Foundation for its warmth, enthusiasm, and beneficence.

# SEDUCTION BY LIGHT

*"In Hollywood anything can happen, anything at all."*

—*Raymond Chandler,*
The Long Goodbye

*"This world is the movie of what everything is, it is one movie, made of the same stuff throughout, belonging to nobody, which is what everything is."*

—*Jack Kerouac,*
The Scripture of the Golden Eternity

*"Every shut eye ain't sleep; every good-bye ain't gone."*

—*Afro-American proverb*

# 1

Once you know your days are numbered, you dont waste too much time foolin around—not if you got any sense. Well, sense is still pretty much the only thing I ever had plenty of. It might not be common sense, but it's sense all the same. And it's what helped me start slowin down, straightenin up, and tryna put my own little fallin-down house in order.

It all seemed to start the night I woke up outta this beautiful dream about bein a little girl again in heaven and heard all this racket goin on out in backa me and Burley's ramshackle house in Santa Monica. Now, there was a time when Burley woulda leapt outta bed the minute we heard the disturbance and swaggered right straight to it. But wasnt no use of me wakin poor Burley up on accounta by that time of night he was so doped up until he didnt know right this minute from the year 3000 no more. He'd had his second stroke and was doin well to even be breathin, much less springin into action.

I wasnt exactly feelin like turnin cartwheels either, but I did pry myself outta bed, grab a flashlight, and tip thru the house to my sewin room at the back, the one with the window with the missin screen. I eased back the curtain and that's when I saw these two kids—well, technically, they were grown—monkeyin around with the latch on the garage door. Would you believe I stood there for the longest, I guess tryna figure out what they were up to? Then it dawned on me I better do somethin fast— either scare the rascals off or sic the police on em.

In less than half a minute I shot back to the bedroom and fished this funny-lookin snub-nose tear-gas pistol out the drawer where I keep my panties and bras and underthings. For some reason I'd gone and ordered that thing for $9.95 plus postage from an ad in the backa this conservative newspaper my employers, the Chryslers, subscribe to but never read. Somethin at the time musta told me I might be needin that extra little ounce of protection. I always knew I had a guardian angel, but the way things are today, even guardian angels got their work cut out for em. Next I went and dialed 911, the magic emergency number, and told the police I'd caught a coupla dudes in the act of breakin and enterin my property. That way, you see, I had all bases covered.

By the time I'd slipped back and heisted my sewin-room window real quiet, those jokers were still hunched over the garage lock, whisperin at one another. In fact, they'd somehow got the lock off and was tryna slide the door open. I got to my knees in the dark, cocked my tear-gas pistol, took dead aim, and just like somebody's wrote it out in a script for me, I said, "All right, hold it right there!"

Oh, you better believe they fell up against one another when they heard that!

"Hey!" I shouted. "I got me a peacemaker right here in hand with my finger on the trigger that says I can blow you suckers away faster'n you can get in and outta my garage!"

"No problem," one of em says. All I could make out is he was skinny compared to the other one. He blurt this out and threw up his hands. "We were about to leave. We—we thought somebody we knew lived here."

"You thought *what*?" I said. "You thought somebody lived in there?"

"Yeah," said the one with the big belly and the nervous mustache, "but we obviously made a mistake."

"You doggone right you made a mistake," I said. "And I'll be makin an obvious mistake myself when I pull this trigger and start blastin yall's thievish remains to Kingdom Come."

The one with the mustache said, "Calm down. Just take it easy, lady. We got the wrong place, that's all."

"Uh, yeah," said the skinny one. "Please dont shoot!" But while he was sayin this he made a fast move inside his jacket like he mighta been reachin for some kinda lethal weapon—a real gun, for all I knew. So that's when I made up my mind in one split second to either shoot, poot, or get off the pot. Let's face it, it mighta been years before I got another chance to test out my little ten-dollar purchase, and I wanted to find out for myself if it worked.

Well, it worked, all right. I squeezed off two shots, one right after the other, and the pellets went flyin straight out the barrel and exploded into pure tear gas that started stinkin and stingin up their eyes and mine so bad until I heard em drop whatever it was they was carryin when they turned tail and hustled up the driveway along the side of the house back toward the street.

I knew my bravery couldnt hold out much longer, so I slammed the window shut and was just catchin my breath when I heard not one but two police cars squeak up in front. All that blue and yellow-red light twirlin around in the bushes and trees —that was all we needed. Now the whole doggone neighborhood would be pourin out on their porches to stand around and watch. But so what? The worst thing to come outta this, I'm thinkin, was I might get on the *Six O'Clock News,* and even that could end up meanin money in my pocket.

Now I'm out there on the front porch in my sweatsuit—which is what I started wearin to bed after Burley took sick and our fuel bill started doublin and triplin—because when I got that outfit on, I'm ready for Freddy and anything else. Mind you, I also got this hairnet stretched all over my head, and suddenly I remem-

ber my face is still caked and smeared with Noxzema. What can
I tell you? I gave up tryna be cute a long time ago.

Actually, it tickled me to see the police'd done scooped up
both them thugs.

I stomped down the front steps with my tear-gas pistol still
smokin in my hand.

"You the one dialed?" a cop called out.

"Did it with my own trigger finger," I yelled back. "My, you
guys're quick!"

"Please tell us exactly what happened, ma'am."

I told all four cops exactly how it came down, the same as I'm
tellin you. They lollygagged around there and listened; then this
one officer that looked a tad like Billy Dee Williams, he hauled
out a notebook and asked my name.

"Mamie Franklin," I told him.

"Middle initial, please."

"Aint no middle initial—that's it."

"And this is your full legal name?"

"Far as I know, yes. Some of my friends who know me from
my show-biz days still call me Dame Mamie sometime, but—"

"You reside at this address?"

"Last I heard, yes."

"Alone?"

"No."

"Kindly explain."

Now, that's what I cant stand about the law. You give em an
inch and you know theyre gonna hound you for miles and miles.
I liked the looks of this young man tho, so I looked him in the
eye while I studied his aura, which I approved of, and I said,
"No, I live with my husband. He's an invalid and somethin like
this is definitely detrimental to his delicate condition."

"What's your husband's problem?"

"He's paralyzed . . . had a coupla strokes."

"Occupation?"

"Mine or his?"

That's when this handsome cop frowned and grinned at the

same time in such a boyish way that I knew he was okay to trust, for the time bein. "Whoever's working," he said.

"My husband's retired," I told him. My heart was startin to thunk around some. "He use to work for this cheese corporation up around San Jose, traveled all over; but I'm the one earnin the checks and signin em now."

"And what is it you do?"

Now, it was gettin cold out there with that nasty nighttime breeze whippin at us off the Pacific and I was tireda bein questioned when what they needed to be doin was cross-examinin the criminals themselves that caused us all to be standin around out there in the first place. But all I said was, "I'm employed by Mr. and Mrs. Carleton Chrysler of Beverly Hills."

"Oh, I see," said the cop, his eyes lightin up. "Domestic?"

"Yes, officer, that's right here in California, L.A. The Chryslers good friends of the mayor, too."

Not too sure how to take my remark, the cop went on and took down my work address, both phone numbers, then proceeded to quiz me about how come I'd called. After that the crooks, still red-eyed and snifflin from my tear gas, they started lyin and explainin how they were supposed to be pickin up this box of stuff from a friend's garage, and first one thing and another. Made me sick to hear em lyin like that, plus I'm freezin and my patience is runnin out.

A few people, quite naturally, was out there on their porches or peepin out their curtains and window shades at us, even tho it was past midnight. The whole spectacle was gettin on my nerves so much it wasnt funny.

"Please," I said, "dont think I'm bein uncooperative, but I still gotta get up and go to work in the mornin. And, yes, I'm willin to identify and press charges."

One pair of cops walked back in the yard with flashlights to see for themselves if the garage lock'd been picked like I said. They came back beamin and carryin somethin wrapped up in a piece of canvas. Then they bunched together, peeled back the canvas, and started jabberin real low. I had to kinda strain to make out what it was they'd found, but it looked to me like a pistol, sure enough. That's when my stomach froze, and that's when Fats and Skinny quit mumblin and givin me the finger and started shakin.

Actin kinda like they had enough to go on now, the police clamped handcuffs on both of em, threw one in one car and the other in another.

"Surely," I said to the handsome cop, "there's gotta be enough laws on the books to hold these birds for *somethin!*"

"Get a good night's sleep," he said. "Don't worry about a thing. We might have to send a detective around."

"A detective? What in the world for?"

"Routine—just to ask a few questions, get a fuller statement from you, check for fingerprints and other evidence, that sort of thing."

"All well and good," I said, "but I'm a workin woman."

"We'll keep that in mind."

"Officer, I mean, it's a shame. Decent, hardworkin folks like me tryna earn an honest livin and all the time gettin knocked in the head and ripped off by no-count scum and ruthless politicians."

"We do what we can," said the cop. "By the way, if you don't mind my asking . . . Where'd you come by that tear-gas revolver of yours?"

It tickled me when he said that. I held the little thing up to my nose and sniffed at the barrel. "I sent away for it. Why? Is it illegal or somethin?"

"No, no, nothing like that. It's just that I've never seen one quite like it before. Strikes me as being highly effective."

"Well, I believe it struck them thugs that way, too. Tell you, it takes somethin like this to get people up offa you sometime. Sure makes more sense than these whistles and canned sirens they be handin out now to women for protection. And if you wanna get realistic, people these days aint about to come to your rescue just cause you make some kinda noise to signal you in trouble. You gotta have some kinda backup."

And just when I was fixin to slip back into our nice warm house, who should I see come clickin on his light and pokin his old fat cathead out from under his raggedy shade but Sneaky Pete himself. His real name is Monroe, but Sneaky Pete's what I been callin him ever since I looked up and caught sighta him up there on his second floor with his binoculars checkin out me and my son Benjamin and Benjie's girlfriend while we were talkin and sayin good-bye in the driveway one Saturday mornin a month ago. Oh, I know him like I know the inside of my mouth. Soon as Burley taken sick, here come old Sneaky Pete grinnin at me and offerin his help. Remember when Mike Todd died and suddenly up pop Eddie Fisher all up in Elizabeth Taylor's face, consolin Liz and seein her around? Well, that's one of the good reasons I got for callin him Sneaky Pete and, hey, that's stuff you gotta watch.

# 2

The only reason I could see for Monroe trainin his giant binoculars on us that mornin was on accounta Benjie'd left his shiny eggshell-brown Rolls-Royce sedan parked out in the driveway. Psychic as I am, it dont take a mind reader to know what was goin on in Monroe's jellybean brain. Just what was Mamie Franklin's boy doin with a car like that? What happened to that little Fiat he use to get around in? And if he did have to go gettin uppity, wasnt a Cadillac plenty good enough? I mean, how about a little respect for tradition?

Brought up like I was to speak no evil, I'm usually not one to do much complainin. Mother Dear and Papa, they brought the five of us up to be strong, handy, and lastin so we could get done what had to be done, then go on about our business. Even though I turned out to be the oddball in the batch, I'm still tryna stick pretty much to the family philosophy, doin what I have to do without bitchin and pissin and moanin and belly-achin.

But in case you havent noticed, the devil done taken over this world. It's the devil's day, and I mean to tell you he is havin himself a ball, a real field day! And here we are right out in the middle of his playground. What we're livin in now is the Era of Low Blows. That's right, the Era of Low Blows. And if you dont believe it, just pause for a minute and take a good long look around. You dont need to look all that far, and you certainly dont need no special trainin or Ph.D. to see what's goin on. That's what scares the water outta me sometime. You got more people runnin and slippin around now with degrees and credentials and certificates than ever before, and yet you cant hardly buy gas for your car or heat your house—if you was lucky enough to get ahold of a house back in the days when the gettin was good. Then come to find out it aint no accident that the oil companies knockin down record profits, and everytime you look up some giant company's either merged with another big company or else taken over some little business that's just beginnin to feel its oats. Now, my eyesight might be failin, but aint nothin wrong yet with my sense of smell. You cant tell me the devil dont know what he's doin!

Bein blessed like I am with this special gift—even tho it does seem sometime like these powers of mine have a way of helpin everybody else more than they do me—I feel qualified to testify there's another side to all this mistreatment and bein dogged around. Mind you, there was a time when you couldna no more got me to run off at the mouth like this than you could a terrapin. When it came to my private affairs, I was about as tight-lipped as a New Jersey jukebox czar at a Senate investigation. But bein around show biz and movin amongst the so-call Beautiful People like I been doin now for a good piece of my life, I have loosened up a whole lot since I left home. Besides, like I say, there's this quiverin I can feel sometime. If you was to ask me where it's comin from, all I could tell you is it's comin from a location inside me there's no real name for. Like, I would have to say it's someplace between the part of me that dreams real deep and the part that's only halfway awake. Now, that might not exactly pinpoint where this quiverin be comin from, but that's where I feel it throbbin at the oddest times, tellin me my time might not be long.

I'm not askin anybody to believe any of this spooky stuff—not too many people do or was intended to—but for me myself the message is as clear as gatherin clouds. But you know what they say: No rain, no rainbow. So I know there's a lotta things I been savin up and puttin off that I'm gonna have to get said and done on the double.

When it comes to this hurryin stuff, tho, I'm like my friend Charlean Jackson, the live-in housekeeper right up the street there for Nixxy Privates, that wildcomedian with the nasty mouth. You know, the one that almost went up in smoke back here that time. You oughtta hear some of the stories Charlean tells about life around that place. She's probly the one needs to be puttin out a book. Charlean says she likes to take life one night at a time. She says if you can manage them nights, the days'll take care of themselves. Well, me, I'm to the place where it looks like one hour at a time is about the best I can do.

It wasnt always like that. At twenty, a minute seemed to me like half an hour. By the time I hit thirty, an hour had turned into, say, fifteen minutes. Then forty slipped up on me, and it felt like it was all I could do to get up, get dressed, turn around and catch my breath before it was time to get undressed again and go back to bed. Now the months just zoom away from me like ponies lined up at the startin gate. If I so much as pause for a few minutes, then everything comes pilin down on top of me the way that dirty laundry comes tumblin out the clothes chute at the Chryslers'. But I lay in there. I stay right with it. I like to take it real slow. One hour at a time, and first things first.

The first hour after I got back to bed, I couldnt sleep. Bein woke up in the middle of the night to catch somebody tryna break into your property wasnt the same as bein woke up by Burley layin over there cross the room in his little hospital bed, snufflin and stuff in his sleep. Little by little I'd gotten use to his sickness. I'd even gotten use to losin a little sleep here and a little sleep there, sittin up with him nights when he got real restless. The Chryslers, knowin how hard things was for me with a sick

man at home, they didnt mind my cuttin my coffee breaks and
lunchtimes short and makin up for it by takin myself a forty-five
minute nap in the middle of the afternoon. Fact, they even
upped my salary a little when Burley was taken sick, and that—
combined with what little money I pulled in givin psychic con-
sultations on the side—all that helped pay for the housekeeper I
had comin in to look and pick up after and to cook and do
around for Burley while I was at work. The situation use to
fascinate me sometime. I mean, there I was a domestic with a
domestic of my own. That wasnt how I wanted it, tho.

See, I tried to hem that little money up and keep it in the
family by hirin Maxine, this niece of mine that was just out from
back East. My sister Rose shipped Maxine out here to get her
away from this dope-addict boyfriend that was makin their life
miserable back there in Chicago, so I told Rose the child could
stay with me for a while and I'd get her enrolled in this nice little
community college right close by where I even take a course
every once in a while myself. But the way it turned out, Maxine
was too lazy and resentful for me to be around. She figured on
accounta we kinfolks she didnt have to mind me and didnt have
to do no work. That child wouldnt hit a lick at a snake. All she
did was antagonize poor Burley and lay around here and wait on
Saturday, when, like some kinda fool, I'd pay her. I might just as
well'd taken that money downtown and chunked it in the La
Brea Tar Pits. You practically had to turn the bed upside down
and shake her out of it in the mornin.

I finally had to cut Maxine loose and send her over to stay in
that cottage Chance rents out in backa his house. Chance Franklin. Why, just a few days ago I'd seen him on television in this
spot about how you should help conserve energy by carpoolin to
work and back. Well, there was Chance, sittin up there on the
backa this big parade-lookin float movin up the freeway,
crammed with goo-gobs of kids, got that old cigar clamped in his
teeth, that hat pushed back and bangin away at this upright,
singin, "Everything's cool . . . in the motor pool . . ." I could
tell he done gone back to dyein his hair, but I had to hand it to

old Chance, tho. Dont care how hard times get, Chance Franklin's gonna figger out him some kinda way to draw him a check. And Maxine seem to be actin a little better since she moved over there to his cottage. Got herself a job and started earnin some honest money. She was just more than I could handle. I already raised one child; half raised him anyway—Benjamin is legal age but he still got a lotta growin up to do—and that almost taken everything outta me. I cant be overseein nobody else's youngun.

Anyway, my mind is rollin on and on like that when I heard Burley actually laugh in his sleep. Now, that was a new one and it startled me so I had to snap on the lamp and take a peep at him across the room. He was sleepin, all right; got a grin on his face. As glad as I was about him bein spared all that police excitement, I still couldnt help wonderin what he coulda been dreamin.

Finally when it started to look like I might not ever get back to sleep that night with the thought of how I mighta been shot by those very intruders, I did what I always do when I need some serious calmin down in a hurry. I said my secret prayer; then I snapped on my big Sony radio cassette I keep right there on the nightstand with the drawer fulla tapes. It didnt take much rummagin around in the drawer to find the tape I was after—the music soundtrack from *Madame Rosa.* I popped that in, pulled my earphones on, clicked off the light, and buried my head way back up in the pillow. Oooh, lemme tell you, when the music come on in the dark and that lonesome violin started sendin tender little chills up my spine, I could picture Simone Signoret with her stout, pitiful self hunched over in her Paris apartment, tryna bear the burden of takin care of these other people's kids all by herself. I'd seen that picture three or four times, and there was somethin about the way the light from the window casts shadows on her face in this one scene that made me feel real peaceful inside in a sad kinda way.

Guess I musta felt like feelin sorry for myself because the music got me to cryin right away, and before I knew it I'd done cried myself on off to sleep.

# 3

It was like I'd sunk straight to the bottom of a dream. You know what that's like, dont you? For one split second you catch yourself hangin between bein asleep and awake and then, without anything resemblin a shift, you snap back to the middle of some scene, and it's impossible to tell which one is the real you. Sometime it gets so sweet and cozy and satisfyin out there in the dream world until I dont have any interest in wakin up. And sometime I ask myself: What if the dream kept rollin for a thousand years? You'd never know the difference.

In the part I'd dropped down in the middle of, I was back singin with Chance Franklin's band. The song was "You Go to My Head," and I'd reached my favorite part, the lines that talk about how, like a summer with a thousand Julys, you intoxicate my soul with your eyes. Oooh, I love singin that; it use to gimme goosebumps when it came time to project that verse. I would put everything I had into gettin that across. In the dream, Chance could feel the emotion I was puttin out, just as if I'd reached around to where he was, in backa me leadin the band, and grabbed him by the wrist.

Whoosh, I got swept up into the words so completely, the

music and the lyrics took on a life of their own. The singer, me, Mamie Franklin, disappeared. "You Go to My Head" was suddenly somethin you could taste and smell and feel and see like, well, like the bubbles in a glass of champagne poppin in the air and bein blown by some breeze across the smoky room and out the door of the club. From there I watched myself—that is, the Mamie that'd become the words and the sound—go sailin cross the street. There was a catch to it, tho. I didnt bother floatin cross the street in a straight line like you might expect; I just hauled off and rose clean up over all the cars and people on bicycles and motorcycles and trucks and stuff. Just like I was a helicopter made outta nothin, I lifted straight up off the sidewalk and went to reverberatin so strong when I hit the note that goes with the word "eyes" until I thought I would splinter into a zillion pieces.

Mind you, this was all happenin to me the same as I'm tellin you, and when I did come down, oh, I have to laugh . . . When I did come down it was the tenderest landin imaginable. There was Burley Cole, all decked out in a tuxedo, if you can believe it, which you couldnt get him to put on in the other reality even if you were to poke a pistol in his belly. First I saw him as a tiny speck of light down there on the ground; then as I got closer, I could see who he really was. I was tightenin up by then, gettin scared I might not be able to land okay. Burley stretched his arms up toward me, threw em wide open, and suddenly there I was slowin down like I had some kinda parachute attached to me made outta feathers and silk.

"What taken you so long?" he wanted to know.

"I had to make sure I had it straight," I told Burley, "before we blew all our precious, hard-earned money."

"So do you think you figured it out finally?"

"Sure did."

"What should I play?"

"You mean, What should *we* play, dont you? I'm puttin a thousand on this horse too."

"All right," said Burley, "a thousand for you and a thousand for me. You sure?"

"Just as sure as we're standin here."

Burley laughed that deep-down, love-crammed laugh of his I can still hear whenever I think about how much fun it use to be to make love with him.

Maybe I need to let you know here that until me and Burley got ahold of each other, makin love had stopped bein fun for me. Chance used sex a little bit like a lotta women still do. I mean, he somehow twisted it into somethin slick and political so he could feel like he was in control of things. Sometime with Chance, that first husband of mine, bless his heart, I would be burnin up to melt. Chance would know this good and well, and yet he'd hold back and take his own good time even touchin me. Or else, if he was mad with me about somethin, Chance would get all cruel with me in bed and make me feel lower than an earthworm, like some kinda bait he was about to drop in a can with the resta the worms to go fishin with. Aw, I dont even like to think about it!

Burley and me, all we ever did was that good-natured, friendly lovemakin. Even after he took sick, the first round of his illness anyway, we somehow figured out more ways to fool around with one another without it becomin too much of a strain on his heart.

"Okay," he said when we stepped up to the bet-placin window. "I hope you know what you talkin bout, Mamie, cause I plan to shut my eyes and plunk all this money down on a win-place-or-show bet."

"No," I told him, a little sad, just a tad, since that kinda bet woulda reflected how little confidence Burley had in my intuition. "Forget about win-place-or-show. Ben Franklin's gonna win this one hands down, or hooves down, or whatever you say."

Burley laughed again and said, "I can tell by the way your cheeks crinkle up and the way you grin when you say it that you'd practically lay down your life on this hunch."

"You got it, Mr. Burley!"

So that's what we did. We put the whole two grand on Ben
Franklin; smacked it down on the counter and just about scared
the cashier to death.

"Boy, you guys're either brave or far out, one!" he told us, all
big-eyed and shakin his bald head. "That's a thirty-five-to-one
shot."

"Accordin to the lights out there across the track," I said,
"the odds have gone up to forty to one."

"Well, all I can say is, I guess you know what youre doin."

"We dont know nothin!" Burley said, which was a funny
thing to say. Not funny ha-ha, but that didnt in no way stop the
three of us from laughin.

Then, like magic, the way it happens in dreams, a big crowd
popped up to cheer and scream and holler and carry on, the way
crowds're suppose to do at racetracks. And the minute the man
on the P.A. went, "And they're off!" Burley tried so hard to leap
clean outta his skin that he bumped me in the shoulder and
almost knocked me down.

It was a seven-horse race and they were runnin the full mile.
The track was muddier than I'd ever seen it, but the sun was
shinin down so hard you could almost see the dirt and turf dryin
up while you looked.

I cant remember all the other horses' names, but the favorite
was a French horse named Moulin Rouge, and that old song
went to slippin thru my head when I saw it on the program.
There were two other horses people were bettin heavy on too—
Saturday's Child and Copasetic, Jr. I got a big lump in my throat
watchin how long it was takin Ben to even get outta the gate.
Burley looked at me like he was fixin to dig a hole in the mud
and hide in it.

Since I had trouble listenin to the man call the race and
watchin the numbers flash on the toteboard at the same time, I
told Burley, "You can watch and tell me what's goin on. I'm too
wound up to look." Yet even while I was sayin this, there was a
parta me that was as calm as the clouds hangin over the track

that afternoon. I knew exactly what was gonna happen, even if I couldna told you *when* it was gonna take place.

Burley grabbed holda my arm and squeezed and squeezed while he hollered in my ear, "Uh-uhhh, Mamie, they comin outta the turn now and, whoa, whoa! I dont believe this shit, I dont believe it!"

"What's happenin, Burley?" I shouted. "Tell me, tell me!"

"No, ma'am," he said, "I want you to open your eyes and see this for your own self!"

And when I peeped, then let my eyes pop wide open, I could tell why the crowd was goin nuts. Old Ben was movin up the homestretch so fast it was like some giant invisible hand'd reached down from out the sky and was quietly pushin him along past all the others.

"Lookit that!" Burley screamed. "Just lookit! He bout to catch up with Moulin Rouge!"

The words had no sooner left Burley's mouth than Ben Franklin, that forty-to-one shot of ours, leapt right up there neck and neck with the horse from France. Then it was like all the sound clicked off and all the excitement that'd been keepin me from lookin or sayin a word simply cooled down and disappeared. It wasnt even like I was lookin at a horse race anymore; it was like I was seein the whole thing from the perspective of one of those flip books. You know, where you be flippin pages with drawins on em and see the picture go to movin.

Ben Franklin, who, accordin to the program, would turn two years old that very day, he shot up there so quick it was practically like I had decided to flick the pages across my thumb a little faster than I'd been doin, just to see what would happen. When the horses came across the finish line, I let my thumb come to a full stop so I could see for myself what was what. It was Ben Franklin by half a head, but the man on the sound system was sayin, "It's a photo finish, folks! A photo finish! Please save all tickets until the judges have studied the pictures."

Burley was tremblin and stutterin when he talked.

"M-M-Mamie," he said, "if this race d-dont t-t-turn out the w-w-way you—"

"Aw, hush!" I told him. "Wont nobody be able to talk to us in a coupla minutes."

Sure enough, the man came back on the loudspeaker, tellin us, "It's official. Ben Franklin's the winner! Moulin Rouge is second and Copasetic, Jr., third. Ladies and gentlemen, this has been one of the most remarkable races I have seen in my twenty-five years as a track announcer! Ben Franklin the winner and Joyce Azuela the jockey. They'll be stepping into the winner's circle in just a moment. Ben Franklin, ladies and gentlemen, paying eighty dollars on a two-dollar bet!"

Me and Burley hugged so hard I thought we were gonna come out the other side of one another.

"Mamie, you knew it all along, didnt you, didnt you?"

"Tell me, Burley. How could a horse named Ben Franklin lose? Especially when there's a woman ridin him? Old Ben is my man. Always has been."

"Shoot," Burley said, wipin away tears of joy, "you talk like you musta got it straight from the horse's mouth!"

"Somethin like that," I said in a soft voice. "Yessir, somethin just like that."

And then that off-the-wall dream stuff started up. By this I mean there I was, couldnt wait to get my hands on the money. We each had forty grand comin to us, and I was thinkin how even after the Internal Revenue nailed us right there at the window for their cut we would still have enough left over to do somethin strange and wonderful and wouldnt have to hold back, but do it whole hog! I was thinkin this when I started wakin up, and all I remember about that transition is that the dream went to movin and jumpin around a little on the turbulent side. I mean, the racetrack, me, Burley, the crowd, the jockeys, and the horses, everything—we were shakin quite as if some giant, like the one in "Jack and the Beanstalk," was comin back home to roost. It was like his footsteps had turned into stomps that were makin heaven itself jiggle and shake, but I do mean *shake*. The last thing I remember was lookin up at the sky and seein how the clouds had all turned green and it was rainin money.

It was one of those deals where you fight to go on dreamin and not have to click back into the wakin mode, but it was also a fight I knew I wasnt gonna win. Slowly I floated back up to the surface of things, floated to the skin of dreamin, you might say, and got a little shock when I realized where I was.

I was layin next to Burley. That's right. Someplace along the line, I had actually gotten up sleepwalker-style and shifted from my bed to his. This'd never happened before. He was as quiet as a blade of grass. I woke up with my hands stretched palms up in the air so I could catch some of that fallin money, I guess. Isnt it awful the way dreams can jack you around sometime?

But the weirdest thing, tho, was how much control it took for me to keep from throwin myself on topa Burley. There were times—and this was one of em—when I resented Burley's condition, when I felt like havin him all snaked up inside me the way we use to could do for hours. I use to love it when his arms'd be wrapped all around me like silk and there I was all snug in my cocoon, yet knowin full well the moment was close at hand when I'd be wrigglin and wingin my way loose and come up out of it the loveliest butterfly you ever wanna see.

While I was tryna stay quiet while I slid outta Burley's bed to make it back across the room to my own, a strange urge overtook me. Suddenly I slipped my hand down to his waist and went to thinkin about how we'd met.

I let my thoughts drift back to the casino. Las Vegas. I'd run my winnins on the nickel machine up to the limit, $7.50. Then I'd hit the quarter slots and then the dollar ones. Burley was standin there next to me, playin the dollar slots too—two at a time, in fact—when I made my first pull and somethin like two hundred of them things came tumblin down, he got right up in my face and said, "You wont believe this, but I been lookin for somebody like you all my life. You the one could change my luck."

I mean, it was such a lame come-on I still have trouble believin I went for it. We were both gettin away from our little scenes for the weekend—Burley from that cheese company stuff and me from worryin about Benjie and the lies I'd been tellin him and whatever happened to Mamie Franklin and first one thing and another there in L.A. As Marvin Gaye would say, *"L.A. . . . now, what I say?"*

Say what you will, I decided it wasnt worth it to dwell any longer on that wonderful night; it was too painful. And it clashed too much with the way things stood now. I smoothed my hand over Burley's warm, skinny waist, rememberin how meaty and paunchy he'd been before his health turned bad. Back then when that commercial would come on that asked, "Can you pinch more than an inch?" Burley would grab up a sizable chunka that spare tire of his and turn to me and say, "Pinch an inch? Hell, I can grab a slab!"

That's how he was. Burley's the only man I know—not that I've known all that many, mind you—who could be lovin on you so hard you felt like you were about to catch on fire, to bust out in flames like spontaneous combustion, and then in the middle of it he might even crack some joke, mumble somethin like, "Yeah, I can grab me a slab!" and the both of us'd be laughin while we shot off like a thousand roman candles in the starry black skies of a thousand Julys, every last one of em the Fourth.

And while I was strokin him, I put as much energy as I could into imaginin the two of us swimmin in pure white light so we would be totally protected from whatever it was that, deep down, I could feel playin around the edges of what I'd just dreamed. In many ways, it felt like a terrible somethin that sooner or later was bound to find someplace to haul off and happen.

It did my heart good to hear Burley let out a little low-pitch chuckle in his sleep—the second one that night—when he turned over again. I knew he was gettin what I was busy thinkin too. The message was sinkin in: All would be well. Now all I had to do was be careful about filterin out what was tiptoin thru the

opposite side of my mind: all that tremblin and shakin and tur-
bulence in the racetrack experience I'd just got thru dreamin. I
wasnt crazy about that aspect of things, but the more I thought
about it the better I felt.

Listen, how many times do you get to be plunked right smack
down in the middle of a scene where cash money is fallin out the
sky and your longest shot has sailed clean thru like light set free?
Dont tell me Old Ben himself didnt have anything to do with
this. Goin all the way back to when I was a little girl, he hasnt let
me down yet.

The thought of Benjamin Franklin, the real one—the man,
not the horse—was enough to clear all the fear outta me. I felt
the tension leavin my body, even if the lust didnt, while I got up
and went back to my own bed and eased back into the sleepy-
time state. And while sweet sleep was takin its own good time
slippin up on me again, I began to pick up little disconnected
flashes and bursts that were like pieces in a jigsaw puzzle except
made outta vibrations I could see inside myself that had another
Benjamin written all over em. I'm talkin now, of course, about
Benjie my son. Dont ask how, but I knew he and his girlfriend,
Tree, were curled up under the covers way out there in the
freeway distance, lovin one another like lemmings.

But dont get me wrong, I never would use any powers the
Lord gave me to violate anybody else's privacy. That stuff can
and will bounce back on you, you know. And I do believe in doin
unto others the way I expect them to do unto me.

# 4

Burley woke up in a pretty good mood for a change. On days like that, I didnt wanna leave him to go to work. When I told him about what'd happened the night before, this mischievous look crept up in his eyes and spread all over the parta his face that wasnt paralyzed.

I said, "What you suppose they coulda been after, tryna break in our garage like that?"

I was wheelin him from the bedroom thru the house, swervin around all the junk stacked up and piled all over the place.

He cocked his head to one side and said, "You know, Mamie, if there was such thing as a school for fools, I'da had me five or six Ph.D.s by now."

Since the kitchen was Burley's favorite mornin spot, I tried to keep it relatively cleared out. I say relatively, and yet there was still too much clutter even in there for the average person to put up with. Miz Wheelock, the housekeeper, was always grumblin about all the shelves fulla old magazines and books and balls of string and busted utensils and jars of nuts and bolts and whatnot.

"Yessir," said Burley, tuggin at the loose skin round his Adam's apple—one of his worrisome habits that set my teeth on edge—"I'da done had me at least half a dozen Ph.D.s, maybe even a few honorary degrees." He still slurred his words, only it wasnt half as bad as it use to be.

"Burley, I didnt ask you about no Ph.D.s and honorary degrees. I asked what you think them devilish burglars mighta been after out there in our garage."

"No tellin," he said. "Just no tellin."

He went to yankin at his throat skin again, but I reached over and taken his hands away and said, "How come you cant quit doin that? You know how much it vexes me."

Burley screwed up his face then and said, "What makes you think they had to be after somethin anyway?"

"I was lookin dead at em. Somethin about the way they carried themselves, the way they were actin. It was like . . . well, it was like there was nothin they wanted from the house itself, just the garage. I do believe they knew exactly what they were lookin for, Burley."

"Aw, you and your hunches and notions!"

I heard what Burley was sayin, but I could tell too that there was somethin he wasnt sayin, somethin the new look in his eyes and the tight little wrinkly knot in the middle of his handsome forehead was tryna say instead.

We were at the kitchen table now, right there by the window where Burley liked to sit and read the *Los Angeles Times* and look out into the yard. Fog was still rollin like tumbleweed clouds, but I knew the sun would be out by the time I booted Sweepea up thru traffic over to Beverly Hills.

"You might even have a bachelor's or master's yourself," he said, grinnin at me again.

"Burley, just what in the world are you mumblin about? I'm runnin late as it is, and I do not have time to be hangin around here playin guessin games. The police suppose to be sendin a detective around to do some more investigatin."

"Investigatin?" Burley folded his hands in his lap and gazed out the window. He was lookin so serious now, I couldnt tell whether he was studyin the sparrows lined up on the fence out there or the side of the garage. He twisted his neck around and looked at me real hard and said, "I wasnt just playin about that school for fools, either. Wouldnt nobody but a coupla fools keep draggin junk up into a house like we keep doin."

I was shocked—not by what Burley'd just declared, but by the fact that he'd said it at all. I couldnt agree more. Me, I'd been wantin to clean house and dust my broom years ago. Now, why was he just now gettin around to realizin how stupid we'd been carryin on?

And Burley Cole wasnt just talkin neither, I mean, about junk. Practically every inch of that house, plus the backyard and the garage, was crammed with stuff he'd been bringin in there from almost the day he moved in with me. Look like it wasnt nothin he could pass up. Auctions, garage sales, stuff he'd see advertised on supermarket and Laundromat bulletin boards or in the classifieds—he made it a point to check em all out, and he didnt hardly ever come away from any expedition emptyhanded. I mean, we had televisions, refrigerators, furniture, trunks, suitcases, file cabinets, car batteries, fish tanks, almost every kinda camera and photography equipment you could think of. And we had tape recorders, radios, tools, power mowers, lawn edgers, a small printin press, mattresses, bedsprings, ladders, air conditioners, encyclopedias, electric fans, vacuum cleaners, electric brooms, typewriters, old 78-r.p.m. record albums, boxes of ballpoint pens, crates of old foam rubber turnin yellow, store-display racks, sinks, fishin rods, wooden toilet seats, a water cooler, busted water heaters, a coupla outboard motors with no boat to hook em up to. We even had a gang of ski stuff, and the closest I ever got to skiin was the two, three times the Chryslers taken me to Aspen with em. And I wont ever forget that time we all went over to Switzerland where this smooth Frenchman got after me and wouldnt let up. From what Danielle Chrysler'd been tellin me, I'd expected the men over there to be some pretty cold "feesh," as she put it. But the point I'm makin now is that me and Burley had a little some of everything stored around our place. You see, some people get addicted to dope and some to drink, but Burley was addicted to deals. That man was the *original* junkie.

It was dreadful. Burley'd spent the first part of his life tryna get hold to a few dollars so he could buy somethin. The rest of it he spent tumblin and stirrin around in junk. It would get so bad sometime until the city'd be after us to get the yard cleared out; said the neighbors was callin up complainin; said we were violatin codes and statutes.

"Well," said Burley after he'd sat there a while. "I want that old trunk moved from out the garage."

"Which one? You forget there's about six or seven of em out there."

"The big one," he said. "That great big green army trunk, the one that use to belong to Kendall."

Kendall was Burley's only son who'd gotten messed up in Vietnam.

"Where you want it moved to?"

"Someplace safe."

"Someplace safe? It's been out there all this time and nothin's happened to it. How come youre so worried about it all of a sudden?"

"I would just feel better if it wasnt around, that's all."

"Oh, yeah? Then tell me, what's in the trunk?"

Burley mighta been sick and slow in his movements and the way he spoke but, lemme tell you, his mind was just as quick as it'd ever been. He just closed his eyes and got real quiet. Now, dont get me wrong. I loved that man and hated seein him in the shape he was in, but like my mother Ruby Franklin use to say— bless her soul—"Every shut eye aint sleep!" *Burley* rhymes with *squirrely*, you know, and there were times when I knew good and well that Burley was usin his condition to hide behind and do what he wanted to do, just the same as anybody else that's sick.

"What do you think we oughtta do with it?" I gave in and asked.

"Maybe Benjamin could help you move it to his place."

"Now, Burley, you know Benjie moves around too much to be

callin any place *his* place. C'mon, cant you tell me what's in that trunk? Who cares about that old beat-up thing, anyway?"

"Then maybe you could find a place for it up there at the Big House." Burley loosened up and laughed when he said this. He knew how much I hated him callin the Chryslers' home the Big House. "Yeah," he said. "That's the best idea yet. Why dont you clear it with Mr. Chrysler and have the thing hauled up there for safekeepin?"

"That's funny, Burley. As long as the roof's been leakin out there, I never knew we had anything much worth even protectin, much less hidin. You mean to tell me after all these years youre still keepin secrets from me?"

"Didnt say nothin about any secrets, Mamie. I was—I was givin some thought to what you said about last night, and that's my conclusion. See, I have a lotta old papers and pictures and souvenirs and things stored away in that trunk I wouldnt want to get lost or anything to happen to em."

"Oh," I said, "then why didnt you say so? I'll be sure and ask Mr. Chrysler about it first thing."

"First thing, when?"

"The first thing this mornin."

"Good. That makes me feel better."

That was when the tea kettle started whistlin, which made me notice the time on the stove clock. Seven ten. Miz Wheelock was runnin a little later than usual.

"What kinda tea you want this mornin, sugar?"

"The peppermint, thank you. Believe I need to lighten up some on that Constant Comment."

"No problem," I told him. "It was the caffeine and the acid the doctor say you need to cut out."

"Ah, but, you know, I still miss my coffee."

"Maybe so, but it means more to me to see you gettin better than to see your health and strength washed away in a silly cup of coffee. That's how I'm givin it up too—to set a good example."

Burley twisted his stiff neck to one side and said, "Betcha

anything you still help yourself to some when youre away from around me, when youre up there at the Big House, dont you?"

Thank goodness, I was saved by the bell and didnt have to go makin up some half lie. Miz Wheelock was here at last and now I could be on my way. On my way to get the door, I said to Burley, "You guys *are* back on good terms, arent you?"

"You mean about the soap battle? Oh, we finally got that worked out, I think. I'm lettin her watch *As the World Turns* on the Motorola in the bedroom while I look at *One Life to Live* on the big Sony in the livin room and have lunch."

"Well," I said, "maybe that's a decent solution, even tho I'm not all that thrilled about payin her to sit up and look at television."

"Aw, c'mon, Mamie, have a little heart. That's when she eats lunch and picks up the bedroom and cleans the bathroom."

"You really like that old woman, dont you?"

"She's all right in my book, but I'll tell you one thing. I'd like it better if you was here to watch my stories with me. It's more fun having somebody to wisecrack with."

"Well, bless your heart," I said and opened the door to let Miz Wheelock in.

"Mornin, Mamie," she said, lookin all bright-eyed with her glasses steamed up. "Can you help me bring somethin in from the car?"

Quite naturally I was a little put out when the woman didnt offer me no explanation why she was late, but all I said was, "Sure, Miz Wheelock. What is it?"

"Just a little portable television my grandchildren chipped in and got me for my birthday. We packed it back in the box so it oughtta be easy for the two of us to carry."

"But, Miz Wheelock," I said, "we already got seven TVs around here!"

"Oh, I know, Mamie, I know. But all of em but one is black and white. I have to see what the people really look like and what theyre wearin and how the rooms and houses is decorated when I catch my stories."

Wasnt nothin else to do but help my help lug that thing out
the trunk of that beat-up Cadillac of hers and drag it on up into
the house with all the rest of the merchandise. Sometime I think
what Burley and me shoulda gone into was the secondhand business.

# 5

After you struggle up Santa Monica thru all that thick stop-and-go traffic and racket, you make those turns and suddenly it's quiet. When you start seein more trees and tall hedges and high walls than you do people, then you know youre in Beverly Hills.

At the gate I had to turn off the radio just when they were gettin down into Vivaldi's *Four Seasons* which, for my money, is about the best thing he ever wrote. Didnt you love the way they worked that score into that picture *American Gigolo* where Richard Gere threw all them hundred-dollar shirts of his out across the bed when he was tryna make up his mind which one to wear on this date he had set up just before he meets Lauren Hutton?

I buzzed the gate and when it creaked open, I eased Sweepea —that's what Burley nicknamed my little Honda Civic—around thru the circular driveway to the side entrance. The Chryslers' big stockbroker Tudor isnt all that easy to see from the street because of the trees. That mornin the magnolias was in full bloom and the spicy fragrance of eucalyptus was like medicine to my nostrils. Burley use to call em Noxzema trees.

The minute I stepped inside, I could sense somethin was

funny—and I dont mean funny ha-ha. The whole downstairs
had an aura about it that wasnt sittin quite right with me. Now,
usually either Mr. Chrysler or Mrs. Chrysler, Danielle, met me
at the door with their tennies on, their tennis clothes, if it was
good weather. Otherwise, one or the other one'd be knockin
around in somethin casual, busy makin phone calls or readin a
script or somethin.

This particular mornin, tho, I had to let myself in. I knew
Danielle had been talkin about takin a midnight flight to France
over the weekend, and I'd even helped her pack, but she was so
hung over and jittery from the night before until I never thought
she'd actually make it. Danielle goin back home to France wasnt
any big thing. She liked to pick up all of a sudden on a moment's
notice, book a plane, and take off that same day, whenever she
got the urge. She might even sloop around over there for anywhere from two to three weeks before poppin back. Now, I
ought not be tellin this, but I been knowin for the longest that
Danielle's trips didnt necessarily have as much to do with bein
homesick as she made out like to Mr. Chrysler. Sick maybe, but
not homesick. But Mr. Chrysler didnt seem to mind, so it certainly wasnt any of my business.

First off, it wasnt smellin right in there. That sharp, sweet
eucalyptus-magnolia scent turned into stale smoke, stale per-
fume, and stale people odor after I shut the door behind me. I
stepped thru the vestibule and stuck my head in the door of the
small livin room. Mr. Chrysler and Danielle like to do their light
entertainin in the small livin room. Oh, every now and then they
threw a big formal party and would use the big livin room, but
basically it was pretty much for show, I guess on accounta its
size. It looked like a museum and it was parta my job to see that
it stayed immaculate for when the big stars and studio heads and
bankin executives came callin.

Now, the Chryslers have been known to stage some lively,
late-lastin parties, so when I hit the house after a long weekend
I'm ready for anything. This particular mornin I was so jumpy,

tho, that when I looked in the little livin room I practically wet my slacks.

Stretched out across one of the sofas—the round furry one over by the bookshelf—was a young blond woman with her mouth wide open, the same as her legs. And she was nekkid as a jaybird. It looked like somebody'd done flopped one of Mr. Chrysler's ski parkas on top of her for a blanket, but the thing'd slipped off and gotten all bunched around one leg. The other leg was propped up on the couch, and there was a pair of shiny drawers, purple as eggplant, layin on the rug all balled up.

This woman, I'd say, was Danielle's height—tall for a French-woman—with her toenails and fingernails painted black. Her eye mascara was smeared and she wore her hair in a kinda shaggy crewcut. She had a tan but all the same she put me in the mind of a bleached-out, fuzzy-headed raccoon. I say bleached-out for good reason; the hair on her head didnt match the hair curlin out from under her armpits and the resta her body.

I looked around for the resta her clothes but didnt see nothin but bottles and glasses and ashtrays need emptyin. Albums and cassettes was scattered all over the floor, and over by the stereo the old Monopoly board was still set up. When I saw that, I knew Mr. Chrysler musta been in on whatever'd gone on. That man loves to play Monopoly like a schoolkid loves playin hooky. And I'm here to tell you that he and certain friendsa his have been known to play with real money.

Well, after I stood there in the doorway gettin gooseflesh, I tiptoed in and eased around the child to this little corner desk where I knew it was blankets in the bottom drawer. By the Chryslers bein so big on their energy-savin kick, the house was always a little on the icy side and I figured she mighta done already caught cold. She certainly wasnt lookin so hot to me, but then again there arent too many grown people I've seen that look all that good while theyre sleep.

Just when I was fixin to cover her up, the woman commenced to sniffin and wigglin her nose like a bunny. Then she started yawnin with her eyes still shut. I went on and laid the blanket over her anyway.

"Oh, Carleton," she moaned, "what a snowstorm! Just snuggle up and let me wrap myself around you." And then she let out another yawn, this time with more of a groan in it.

I was close enough to her now to see all the little white crystal flecks caked up around her nostrils. Her red, runny nose looked kinda like an underripe strawberry that'd been dabbed in powdered sugar.

Actually, I'd seen worse carryins-on in their household before, but Danielle's about the only one I ever seen nekkid around there in broad daylight. Well, I said to myself, just hold on a minute. Hold on a minute and hold down your job. I left the woman layin there and hurried down the hall toward the kitchen foyer to get some hot water goin. Burley sure called that one right. I had to get my hands around a mug fulla hot coffee to feel even halfway right, more especially after what I'd done been thru since last night.

Well, who should I find in the foyer but Mr. Chrysler himself, slouched in a kitchen chair pulled up to the table. He was hunched over with his face buried in his Rams sweatshirt sleeves and lookin like he mighta spent the whole night sleepin facedown like that.

There I was again, mindin my own business, not botherin nobody, just starin at how the fluorescent ceilin light was reflectin off the topa his tan, bald head. I hated that light. I was always tellin Danielle and him how that fluorescent stuff wasnt no good for people. I'd figured this out for myself from the way that kinda light when I was under it for any length of time left me feelin drained and zapped. But when I happened to catch a research woman on the radio tellin about it, about how it might even turn out to be a contributin factor to cancer, that's when I sure enough got after the Chryslers to do somethin. And do you know, for all the health food and vitamins and bio feedback and Esalen and Rolfin and aikido and jiujitsu and who-knows-what-all

they spend good money on, they still wouldnt have that dangerous fluorescent lightin replaced?

Anyway, there Mr. Chrysler was slumped over the table with a
half-finished glassa apricot nectar, oblivious to the world, for all I
could tell. Now, what I really wanted to do was dissolve into thin
air and go back home to bed. Jesus, I was sleepy! Instead I shook
him by the shoulder and said, "Mr. Chrysler, Mr. Chrysler! You
all right?"

He bolted straight up, grabbed his head with both hands and
groaned. "Oh, Mamie, it's you. What are you doing here?"

"I work here, remember?"

"But I didn't think you'd be coming in today."

"Mr. Chrysler, I dont understand. You the one buzzed me
thru the gate, wasnt it?"

All at once he jerked his neck around to look at the intercom
system; then he stared at me real hard, then looked back at the
buttons and switches again. It was all so peculiar that it got me
to worryin I might be the one whose mind done snapped.

"Well," I said, "somebody had to press the button to open the
front gate. Mrs. Chrysler's still overseas, isnt she?"

Mr. Chrysler picked up his juice glass. That's when I noticed
how bad his hand was tremblin. He polished off the lasta his
leftover nectar in one gulp and said, "There should be some
more of this in the fridge, Mamie. Pour me another glass, would
you?"

I searched the refrigerator but all the nectar was gone, and I
couldnt find any in the beverage pantry, either. "Sorry, Mr.
Chrysler, but it looks like we're fresh out. Can I get you somethin else?"

He thought for a second and said, "Can you remember how to
make a Salty Dog?"

"Lemme see now . . . a Salty Dog. That the one you make
with grapefruit juice and vodka on the rocks?"

"That's it, precisely."

"And that's what you want me to fix?"

"Isn't it what I asked for?"

"Well, yes, but—"

"But what? Mamie, why do you stand there gawking at me?"

"No intendin to it, Mr. Chrysler, but . . . but . . . are you okay?"

"I'm fine, thank you. Why do you ask?"

"You worry me. You arent acting right and, if you dont mind my sayin so, you dont look so good either."

"I know, Mamie, I know! Please, just prepare the drink. I could use one."

"Mr. Chrysler, is anything the matter?"

"Oh, you know how I live," he said, rubbin his eyes and pushin his chair back. "Nothing's ever *all* right with me, now is it? But not to worry, not to worry. Nothing you need trouble yourself over."

I went on and pulled a fifth of Stolichnaya out the freezer and got to thawin out some frozen grapefruit juice. By the time I got around to saltin the ice, I could hear Mr. Chrysler in the next room, talkin real low with somebody else. Wasnt either one of em soundin too happy.

From the other side of the swingin door, I could hear Mr. Chrysler sayin, "Fiona, Fiona!" He was tryin not to shout, but his voice was gruff. "Would you please put some clothes on, for crying out loud!" After I heard him say that, I wasnt sure if I wanted to walk in on em or not, so I stood there behind the door with his doggone Salty Dog.

"Not until you apologize," I heard the woman say. She was cryin and tryna talk at the same time. She sounded British. "You owe me an apology, Carleton."

"Listen, I don't owe you a goddamn thing! You're the one who should be apologizing for your . . . your scandalous, outlandish behavior!"

"Carleton, how dare you! I'm simply unaccustomed to being treated this way. You have been absolutely beastly and I'm in no mood to quarrel again."

"Fifi, will you be reasonable for a change? All I ask is that you make yourself presentable. Get dressed and then we'll discuss matters."

"Why, you bloody bastard, you! Let go of me!"

I cleared my throat real loud and pushed the door open, sayin, "Excuse me, please. Mr. Chrysler . . . your drink."

He had his hands clamped to the woman's shoulders like he was fixin to start shakin her. Big tears was drippin down her cheeks. With all that heavy mascara smudgin up her face, she looked kinda like she'd been minin coal. When he seen me, Mr. Chrysler let go of her and reached for his drink, lookin sheepish. He was shakin so, tho, and I was so worried he might fumble and knock the glass out my hand that I figured it was time for me to shift into high domestic gear.

"Here," I said. "Why dont the both of you sit down and let me serve you. Miss, you care for some juice, some coffee, anything? Some Perrier, perhaps?"

Oh, I can be a regular Alfred Hitchcock when it comes to steppin around a sticky scene that calls for some careful, intelligent direction. After all, it was in my own best interest to keep every cat right there in the bag without lettin out even so much as a meow.

"Thank you, Mamie," Mr. Chrysler said. I could see he was relieved now that things were back on a formal kick and order was sorta semirestored. He pulled out a chair and motioned the blonde to be seated. "Uh, Mamie, I'd like you to meet Fiona Prince. Fiona, this is my good friend and housekeeper, Mamie Franklin. Mamie's been with us for years."

A long, goose-bumped arm came pokin out at me out from under the blanket. "Pleased to make your acquaintance," said Fiona. "Begging your pardon, but is it Mrs. Franklin or—?"

"Miz," I said, lookin down into her swollen green eyes. "Miz Franklin will do just fine. That's how they were addressin my mother back in Mississippi long before there was ever such thing as women's liberation."

"Bloody boring," Fiona snapped all of a sudden, "all that dismal lib rubbish!"

"Come again?" I said, not sure I'd heard her. Fiona had a way of swallowin her words, plus she was still busy snifflin, too. I handed the child a napkin to blow her drippy, aggravatin nose.

"Never mind, Fiona," Mr. Chrysler broke in. "Mamie, Fiona's from London. And I don't think she'll mind my telling you that she's enormously popular over there as a television performer—what we'd call here a hot TV property."

"Ah," I said, "and what brings you to the States?"

Fiona had seized the Salty Dog and got it up to her lips and was just about to answer me when Mr. Chrysler spoke up.

"We threw a little party for her last night," he said. "My partners and I seem to agree that Fifi here is, without question, megabuck material." He was lookin dead at her. "Under the circumstances, you don't mind my calling you Fifi, do you?"

That "under the circumstances" part kinda got to me. I had to strain to keep from crackin up. I mean, there she was at nine in the mornin, a thermal blanket wrapped around her and need to bathe, slurpin on this alcoholic beverage, with one plump titty hangin out, lookin like the sorriest version of "No Business Like Show Business" you ever wanna see.

All she said was, "Carry on, Carleton. You've engaged my attention."

"And, tell me, Miz Prince," I said, "do you sing or dance or act, or what?"

"I'm an actress."

"What kind?"

"Quite a serious one, thank you. I studied for two years at RADA, and I've—"

"Wait now," I said. "Back up a little. What's RADA?"

Mr. Chrysler said, "Mamie, that's an acronym for the Royal Academy of Dramatic Arts."

Fiona didnt like him hornin in like that. She shot him one of them subzero looks and said, "She asked *me*, Carleton, not you." Then she wiped her smutty face on the edge of that nice clean blanket, smearin it up with loose mascara. I felt like ballin up my fist and poppin her one right upside her skinny head.

All I said, tho, was, "Lemme give you your cue again, dear. What kinda actin you do?"

She sniffed and blinked her smudgy eyes at me. "All proper and legitimate, you know. I've done Shakespeare, Ibsen, Strindberg, Chekhov, Dickens, Pirandello, O'Casey, O'Neill, Beckett, Pinter, Osborne, Albee." Then, shiftin into a southern accent, she said, "Why, I've even played Maggie in Tennessee Williams's *Cat on a Hot Tin Roof* in repertory."

"My goodness!" I said, tryna be polite. "That's some range. I'm impressed. So, tell me, havent I seen you on some of those BBC dramas we get over here on the Oil Network?"

Mr. Chrysler started laughin. " 'The Oil Network,' " he chuckled. "Mamie picked that up from me. Actually, I must explain that even though Fifi's credentials as a thoroughly competent professional actress are impeccable, it's been as a marvelous *comedic* talent that she's excelled in British television." He hit that word *comedic* hard, stared at the both of us, then sat back, lookin relieved, kinda like he'd finally got his chance to put Fiona back in her place.

Fiona picked up the Salty Dog, threw back her head, and took a huge slug that made her turn red in the face. She slammed the glass down, looked at me, then turned to Mr. Chrysler and said, "Carleton, kindly fuck off, would you?"

It was all Mr. Chrysler could do to control himself. I could see that his jaws was tight and he was startin to tremble again. He got up out his chair, all disgusted, and shook up. "Mamie," he said, "I'll be in my upstairs study. I'd like a word with you alone —that is, whenever it's convenient."

After he'd gone, Fiona bust out cryin and wipin her eyes and messin up that blanket again. I tried to console her, but she wouldnt quit sobbin and mumblin stuff like, "Just a cruel, bleedin, 'opeless bastard, that's all 'e is." But she said all these things real peculiarlike, shiftin accents on me again. I wondered which play she was actin in now.

But somethin at the backa my inside mind was tellin me, *The same play youre in, Mamie, the same old raggedy production.*

It took some patience and coaxin and hand-holdin, but I finally got Fiona calmed down enough to get her to one of the
downstairs guest rooms and into a hot bath. She like to worried
me to death about findin her purse; said she had some pills in it
she needed to take.

"Dont trouble yourself over that, child," I told her. "I'll find
your purse. It's your clothes I'm worried about."

When I got upstairs to Mr. Chrysler's study, he was pacin the
floor, lookin the way he did when some deal went sour or some
phone call was late comin thru.

"Look, Mamie," he said and shut the door. "It's been a bad
night, a very bad night. Now, you know how much I respect your
intelligence, so I'm not about to insult that. You're probably
thinking I've gone bonkers."

"Well," I said, "somethin like that."

"Just wanted you to know that I'm as uncomfortable with this
situation as you are. But, believe me, it isn't as bad as it appears.
All I need is a couple of days to get things under control."

I just lowered my eyes and didnt say nothin.

"It's obvious what you're thinking," he went on, "so I'm going
to be straight with it. Fiona Prince is going to be a blazing star in
this country. You know why? Because she's talented, striking,
and totally original. But that's not the only reason she's going to
make it over here. She's going to become a superstar because I—
Carleton T. Chrysler—and the Chrysler Organization intend to
put a lot of money and promotion behind her, that's why. But, as
you can see, there are some problems to be ironed out."

"Well," I said, "I'd definitely say she was a little on the unruly
side."

Mr. Chrysler let out a nervous laugh. "Unruly is hardly the
word for it, Mamie. You know that's never posed a problem for
me. Taming wild, hot-tempered, unruly artists is one of my spe-
cialties. Fiona, however, has this condition."

"What kinda condition?"

"Doctors call it Tourette's syndrome. She's suffered with it all her life, but it can be medically controlled. It's only since she's been in the States that it's flared up to any extreme degree."

"How longs she been over here?"

"Not quite two weeks, but it's been hellish for everyone having dealings with her."

"Tourette's syndrome," I said, pronouncin the term real slow. "Never heard of that before. What in the world is it?"

"It seems to vary from victim to victim. Some get these tics and twitches and make odd noises such as snorting, barking, moaning—that sort of thing. Some are even driven to sudden outbursts of foul language, profanity. Fifi tells me that the worst aspect of it is the depression, a very profound depression."

"And how do they treat it?"

"There is a medicine that's prescribed for it, but apparently it can be as bad as the illness itself. Oh, Mamie, it's a dreadful malady and my partners aren't entirely convinced that the Organization should risk a big investment in her." Then a gleam came into the man's eye and he strutted over and banged the top of his desk and shouted, "But, damn it, Mamie! I *am* the Organization! I built TCO up from nothing and I stand to lose more money than anyone else! So if I say Fifi Prince is going to go over big, then, goddamit, that's all there is to it!"

All I did was narrow my eyes and try to remind him one more time. "Mr. Chrysler, you know how much I disapprove of profanity. You sure you might not be catchin this Tourette stuff from Fiona?"

"Sorry, Mamie. I've been operating under a monstrous strain for the past twenty-four hours."

"Then that makes two of us. Do you know somebody tried to break into our garage last night?"

The minute I said that, Mr. Chrysler's eyes lit right up, the same as if I'd just clicked on a switch. "They did?" he said, quietin down to the place where he was practically whisperin. "Who was it? Tell me, what happened?"

Now, even tho the Chrysler house had never been burglarized or broken into—not since I'd been workin for em—that man lived in fear that one day somebody or other was gonna somehow slip up on either him or Danielle and kidnap and hold em for ransom. He had microphones and secret cameras hid all over the house, and the whole estate was hooked into one of them private security computers where if anybody so much as jiggle the window the wrong way, then alarms go off over at headquarters and the patrolmen come racin to see what's the matter. Mr. Chrysler'd even gone out and bought a coupla these kidnap-proof attaché cases they make over in England with secret compartments, push buttons, a tape recorder, and a secret radio mike with knives and daggers and guns and stuff in it—one for him and one for Danielle—and that's what he toted to work everyday.

So I told him about the police comin and all, and asked could I store Burley's old trunk fulla valuable papers up there at the house for a while.

"For certain," he said, "for certain! I deplore that kind of thing. Bring the trunk and we'll secrete it away where no one will ever find it. Mamie, I—I was thinking . . ."

"Yes?"

"I was thinking that since we've both had impossible nights and it's such a slow day . . . There really isn't much to be done around here that can't wait until tomorrow, is there?"

"Monday's a heavy dirty-clothes day," I told him. "And Danielle asked me to Scotchgard the new easy chair and sofabed in her study."

"The laundry can wait," he said, lookin more serious than he needed to, "and so can Danielle's furniture. It'll be good to have the house to myself while I puzzle over what we're going to do about poor Fifi. In fact, I'll be working at home today."

"You think you can handle it, Mr. Chrysler?"

"I believe I can."

"Well, I promised Fiona I'd find her purse for her. I reckon that's her medication she keeps in there."

"Forget it, Mamie. I know where her purse is, and where her clothes are too. Go on . . . before I change my mind. You are herewith dismissed for the rest of the day." He looked at his watch. "As a matter of fact, why don't you just disappear until Wednesday? That ought to make both you and Burley happy, yes?"

We stood there for one of them minute-long seconds, lookin at one another. I could see he was havin a hard time lookin me in the eyes, so I put him out of his discomfort and said, "If that's the way you want it, what can I say? Thank you. I accept."

While he was goin into one of his slow, tired smiles, I started to tell him he could reach me at home if anything came up and he needed me. But, hey! Considerin what he would call "the circumstances," there wasnt no reason to go gettin too generous or actin too grateful. After all, who was it doin *who* a favor?

## 6

I dont know how much any of you know about Benjamin Franklin, but it just so happens I know plenty, probably more than it's
even healthy to know. I'm talkin about the original Ben Franklin
from way back in Colonial times, the man they use to teach us
about in school that went out kite-flyin and discovered lightnin
was electricity. Well, way back, musta been in the eighth grade, I
did a book report on him that pulled a B plus, which in those
days was considered pretty good. Mr. Puckett, my teacher, wasnt
exactly known for handin out no A's, didnt matter how good you
thought you were. I'll tell you, he was one mean sucker and
didnt stand for no foolishness. You go to actin up in his class and
he would be up in your chest in a minute! He's the one use to
would make you stand up in class and say, "Mr. Puckett, may I
please have a swat?" See, that way he figured he was gettin
around the regulations. Anybody go home tellin their folks he'd
swatted em on the behind, then he had it covered. "Well," he'd
explain to the parents, "the whole class was there and heard So-
and-so ask me if he could have a swat." Puckett was kinda fair-
minded about it, tho. The girls he'd just sorta tap kinda, unless
they'd gone and done somethin to really get him riled up, but

the boys—whew!—look like he'd try his best to knock the natural stew out of em!

Anyway, I never got swatted. In fact, lookin back, I can see now where he was actually a little soft on me. I guess that's because I had sense enough to do all my cuttin up in the halls or on the playground. In class I paid attention and minded my lesson. After I turned in my Ben Franklin report, tho, Mr. Puckett sent a note home to my folks that said, This girl is on the ball, or words to that effect. Funny how things go, isnt it? Insteada that bein the thing that made Mother Dear and Papa quit criticizin me so—more especially Papa—it turned out that they commenced to drivin me even harder to do good in school. Many's the time I've wondered how my life mighta gone if I'd gone ahead and stayed in school insteada droppin out in the eleventh grade and leavin Mississippi like I did.

There was somethin about Ben Franklin that got to me. I mean, they just dont hardly turn out men of that caliber anymore. Just think about it. The man didnt have too much schoolin himself, and yet he was probably one of the most brilliant men America's ever produced, white men, anyway. It's been plenty Negro geniuses of every persuasion, but look like this prejudice is so hard to penetrate until mosta them dont ever get over enough to get the kinda credit and recognition they deserve, not even from our own people. You take George Washington Carver, for example. Now, Henry Ford himself was crazy about that man—knew he wasnt nothin but a natural-born genius—yet and still when Dr. Carver would come to visit Ford at one of his houses up there in Michigan, he had to go round thru the back door. And if you think that's somethin, just wait till I tell you that Henry Ford finally went on and had a cabin built out in backa this particular residence of his so Dr. Carver wouldnt have to be in the main house when he stayed over. I love readin about all such as that, and it was that paper I wrote on Benjamin Franklin that got me interested in history.

Not only did Benjamin Franklin do some shrewd politickin and ambassadeerin to raise the money for the Revolutionary War

to run the British away from here, he also found time to do a
little some of everything else after he'd made a killin in the
printin business. The lightnin rod and the Franklin stove—if
he'd only just come up with those two, that woulda been
enough, I suspect, to go down in glory. But old Ben, see, he
didnt stop there. He went on and invented the harmonica, bifo-
cal eyeglasses, the electromagnet, smokeless stoves and furnaces
and chimneys, a letter-copyin machine, a clothes wringer, an
electric jack to turn meat while it roasted over a fire, a library
chair you could fold out into a stepladder, a three-wheel clock,
daylight-savins time. He was also the one that started public
libraries, a fire department, the U.S. Weather Bureau, the post
office, the first hospital in America, the way we print different
denominations of paper money. More than that, Franklin's the
one responsible for gettin all these Rotarians and Kiwanis and
Lions clubs started, for whatever that's worth. Plus he dabbled in
ship-building, botany, farmin, anthropology, foreign languages,
and put out a newspaper, *Poor Richard's Almanack*, wrote books
and songs, was the first political cartoonist we ever had over here,
was a Rosicrucian, and I havent even told you the half of it.

And now, are you ready for this? That man, as gifted as he
was, he wouldnt even take out no patents on any of the stuff he
came up with. No, sir! Didnt believe in it. Ben said his inventions was for the world to use and enjoy, the same as he'd been
usin and enjoyin other men's inventions. Now, that's somethin!
Nowdays it's done just about got to where a greedy dimwit hits
on some little puny, triflin, half-baked idea and—just before they
even got it worked out good—jump right up off the toilet and
rush out ready to get it patented, copyrighted, trademarked, and
world rights exclusive.

That only goes to show you how tight a grip the devil has got
on the world. I mean, okay, take where you build a car that you
know is subject to blow up on the drivers while theyre behind
the wheel, but you go head on and put that car out on the
market anyhow, figurin the lawsuits you might get tied up in
wont eat into company profits all that much. Now, if that isnt

evil, then you tell me what is. But that's the way this thing is goin now.

No, they just dont make em like Ben Franklin no more, not that same Ben Franklin that came to me in a deep trance nap I was havin one night when I was fifteen, sittin in the front-porch swing back home. It was one of them August nights, right after it's just turned dark, thick with gnats. I remember just before I slipped into this trance, all these lightnin bugs—what we call fireflies up here—come streamin and swarmin way off in the distance and commenced to flashin and dancin around in a circle out there over the cornfield. It was just like they knew what they were doin, and it was just like they wasnt doin it for nobody else but me. That's when I got this tinglin feelin and dropped off into my thoughts. And then it happened. I opened my eyes and there stood Benjamin Franklin himself—not the baldin Ben with his long hair combed back that we usually think of, but a much younger version; that one that musta charmed all them rich women in Paris, when he went over there on a little fund-raisin mission. There he was just as plain as day, standin over the swing, smilin down at me. He didnt say anything. He didnt need to; we understood one another perfectly. As a matter of fact, everything turned so mirror-clear and calm and quiet the moment I saw him standin there until it look like I could hear the grass growin in the dark and the whispery sound of feathers sproutin on fuzzy little baby birds cuddled up in nests underneath their mamas' breast.

And that's the very reason I named my boy after him. Since the *Franklin* was already there anyway, the *Benjamin* part was a shoo-in. And somethin else. That Franklin tag's been trailin in behind me all my life, look like. Even after I got it into my mind to slip off and leave home, who should I take up with but that slick, high-steppin, sweet-talkin, smooth-singin band leader that blew into Hattiesburg like a Texas tornado and swooped every one of us girls right off our feet! Who else but Chance Franklin? Oh, lemme tell you, Chance was puttin down some stuff hadnt nobody ever heard before. Why, that rascal, back in his day, was

the King Bee and the original Honeydripper, both! And the
ivories wasnt the only thing he could tickle. The only word I
know for it is magic—and, child, it like to got me killed.

Just like I coulda predicted, that Benjie of mine wasnt nowhere to be found when I really needed to see him. I called his
house and got some silly tape recordin he and Nomo musta
dreamed up, all this reggae thumpin and boomin in the background so steady until anybody call up there with any real business, why, they might fall asleep before the beep came on for em
to leave their message. How many times did I have to tell that
child that these are serious times we're into now? This old broth-
erhood junk, funny stuff and jive everybody use to be talkin—all
that went out the minute the money started gettin shaky, the
same as them costumes and hairdos, even out here in L.A. People aint laughin and jokin and playin no more. You wanna break
into the picture business nowdays, you gotta come on like
Dracula in a three-piece suit. And I also keep tellin Benjie and
his buddy Nomo that theyre gonna have to step it up some,
because they do not have that much time left. These kids that's
runnin the show round here now, theyre twenty-two, twenty-
five, twenty-nine years old—and theyre white! Theyre like little
old men and women that aint never had time for anything as
unproductive and time-consumin as a childhood. They started in
readin *Variety* and *Billboard* when they were nine; and before
they even enrolled in high school, some daddy or uncle or cousin
or somebody'd done promised em a summer job in the mail
room at the studio. The only way you can even halfway compete
with a situation like that, especially if youre black, is by learnin
how to do everything twice as good as they can, takin advantage
of every teen-einchy break come your way, and stayin outta debt
and off dope.

Then too, you have to stick right close to somethin outside the
business that's meaninful to you and that's for real. If you dont
look after these things, then it's curtains because all the resta this

posin and stylin and barbarianism that goes on here around the clock aint nothin but community theater.

That's what I keep tellin em, all right. But, you see, Benjie's got the jump on Nomo when it comes to understandin what I'm talkin about. That's on accounta Benjie—unlike poor pioneerin me—was practically born into the business from his mother's and father's side, both. After all, I mean, as good as Nathaniel and Ruby Franklin was to me, I pretty much raised myself; and why I thought this show-biz mess was anything worth complicatin my life with—well, that's one I'm still tryna piece together.

I started to drive by Benjie's new place over by Hollywood High but, halfway there, changed my mind and decided to go by the post office and check on the box I rent there. Since the check I get every month from Silvertone Communications had been runnin about a week and a half late on the average, I figured my timin might be right. It felt good bein off in the middle of the day, for a change, and not have to clutter up my weekend with errands like this.

Sure enough, I flipped thru the junk mail and advertisements crammed in my P.O. box and—praise the Lord!—there was the long, cream-colored envelope with the brown printin on it, only this time it was a tad fatter than usual. I stood there for a moment in the post office lobby, wonderin what could be in it. Then I tore off one end, blew the thing open and pulled out this typewritten letter with the check clipped to it:

Dear Mamie:

By my calculations, it's about time we set up a meeting to discuss some very important matters. I neither intend, nor can I afford, to continue with our present financial arrangement. Moreover, I no longer feel legally or morally committed to BF"s support now that he has come of age.

I'll be in Tokyo and Moscow on business until the middle of April. Please don't call my office or home, but leave a message with my private answering service. Simply let me know when you'll be available to talk and I'll work around your schedule.

Inasmuch as your birthday is coming up, I'm enclosing a
modest bonus that I trust will be put to good use.
                                    Kind regards,
                                    Harry


What is it about a letter like that can put your nerves on edge?
I mean, there I stood with the check in my hand made out for
seven hundred fifty dollars insteada the usual five hundred, and
yet here I was gettin madder by the minute. Course, it wasnt the
money. I was always glad to get that, and the couple hundred
dollars extra would come in handy for sure. Harry didnt have to
do that and he knew it. He was pretty good about puttin in some
kinda "bonus," as he called it, on both me and Benjie's birthday
and at Christmastime too. But that snide little lyin letter of his
—that's what I didnt appreciate. I coulda done without that.

I sat in my car and read the thing over again, and by the time
I'd gotten over to the Hughes Market on Beverly Boulevard I'd
figured out exactly what it was that irked me about Harry's letter. It was his attitude. The nerve of him referrin to Benjamin as
BF and tellin me how he couldnt no longer afford to send any
money. And of all people, who was Harry Silvertone to be talkin
about moral commitments? He certainly didnt get to be a tycoon
by bein no saint. As for this little "arrangement" of ours, there
never had been anything legal or illegal about it in the first place.
It was based on common decency, that's all. I thought we'd got
that straight twenty years ago. I mean, the very least a father
should do is help his child, dont you think? I coulda been bad-
mouthin Harry all over town if I wanted to, but I didnt. I was
reasonable and, if I must say so myself, a little on the charitable
side too. Now, all my life people been tellin me about how discretion is the better part of valor. Well, I got to thinkin that,
since I'd already just about run discretion into the ground,
maybe it was time to test out the valor some.

And wouldnt you know it? Just when I was climbin outta
Sweepea to run in that market to see if them rich Eyeranians
that shop there had left me any of those hot baked chickens I

liked, it started to rain. There I was without a shawl, umbrella, or a newspaper. I had to dash thru the parkin lot jammed with Mercedes, Cadillacs, Lincolns, and Porsches to keep my fresh-done hair from gettin wet.

# 7

It was still rainin when Mr. Chrysler called that Wednesday mornin before the alarm went off.

"Mamie," he said, "I thought I'd try and catch you before you started getting ready to come to work." He still didnt sound right, and I was almost afraid to do too much proddin.

All I said was, "How's it been goin?"

"Not bad, not bad," he said.

"Did you get the problem with Miss Prince squared away?"

"No problem, Mamie, no problem at all."

Now, just that alone told me to be quiet and let *him* do the talkin. Just as sure as Mr. Chrysler started doublin up on his answers, you could bet your bottom dollar he was stallin. Yet and still there he was on the telephone, and it wasnt even good and light out yet.

Finally, after I went down into my silence bag, he said, "I was, ah, I was thinking perhaps we could strike up a deal."

"What kinda deal, Mr. C.?" He liked it when I called him that. He liked it so much, in fact, until I made it a point to be careful not to wear it out.

"I know you were planning to come in today, but instead—

and only if you're agreeable to my proposal—I was wondering if you might be willing to take another day off and work all day Saturday, including Saturday night, and stay over."

"Stay over?"

"Yes, we'd be needing you Sunday morning as well, but you would be getting off by two."

Saturday was my birthday and I hated to give that up, even tho it'd been sweet having a minivacation in the middle of the week. I had been lettin Miz Wheelock do half days while I shopped and relaxed and knocked around. When I came home in the afternoon to be with Burley I took my time cleanin, cookin, sewin, and readin. Burley just flat-out liked havin me around those coupla days. I could tell it was doin him almost as much good as that physical therapist he saw once a week. Saturday I was plannin to bake myself a birthday cake and have Benjie over—if I could ever locate his behind—and maybe even invite his new girlfriend, Tree, and his buddy, Nomo, too. Oh, what the heck, if Charlean Jackson was free she could come over too. And now here Mr. Chrysler was askin me to come to work on my birthday. It wasnt so much I was still all that crazy about birthdays. Tell you the truth, I'd just as soon skip em now.

"What's up?" I asked.

"Oh, nothing much, nothing much."

"Mr. Chrysler, I have to make plans for somebody to come in and see after Burley if I'm gonna work on my—that is, if I'm gonna work Saturday and stay over."

"Yes, indeed," he said. "I understand totally. You see, I'm putting together a party for Danielle. She gets back Friday and—"

"How long's your guest list?"

"I've invited only a few people—thirty to forty. But you know how it is. Not everyone will show. You've always been a big hit at our gatherings, and if you could prepare some of your marvelous jambalaya and perhaps a simple paella, I'd be eternally grateful."

"Aw, go on with your flattery, now. You dont have to go butterin me up."

"So do we have a deal? Three days off with pay and I'll consider the weekend as overtime duty. What do you say, Mamie?"

"Now, Mr. Chrysler, you know there's no such thing as a simple paella. And that jambalaya of mine takes two days to make."

"Exactly. That's why I'm giving you ample notice."

I hesitated for as long as I figured he could stand it, then I said, "All right, you talked me into it. I'll be in tomorrow and you can count on me this weekend."

"Oh, Mamie, you've made me so happy! I know Danielle will be delighted too. You know how fond she is of you."

I hung up feelin like a perfect fool. Then again, I knew good and well that between the birthday money from Harry Silvertone and the extra earnins I'd be pickin up at the Chryslers' I'd be able to put a healthy down payment on that whirlpool bathtub I wanted to put in for Burley. I'd read where they worked wonders for people that'd had strokes. Actually, me and his sisters and one of his daughters was gonna chip in and get him a video recorder so he could tape his favorite shows and play em back when he felt like it, but I figured the whirlpool might be more worthwhile. Outta sight, outta mind—that's how I feel about all this television-watchin. Poor Burley. As good as all the women in his family been to him, I knew how much he was worryin and grievin about Kendall ever since that boy got so messed up behind that Agent Orange stuff over in Vietnam.

I was wonderin if Benjie would ever turn up again to help me haul that trunk of Kendall's.

That very mornin, since I didnt have to go back to work yet, I got on outta bed anyway, helped Burley get dressed, and baked a cake. It was one of my chocolate specials, and I do mean specials. Mama taught me how to make it when I was twelve. There's only been two other people I ever gave it out to, and that was Mae West and my friend Charlean Jackson. Both of em promised me they wouldnt divulge the secret of how I get it to come out so light.

"What's this?" Burley wanted to know when I brought the cake into the livin room after lunch with one lit candle stuck in the middle and set it down on the coffee table.

"What's it look like?"

"Looks like a birthday cake, but—" His hand shot up to his mouth. "Uh-uh," he said. "Mamie, dont tell me! Is it your birthday already? I thought it was—"

"Never mind," I said. "How about a piece?"

Burley studied the cake. His eyes lit up the way they use to do when I first met him at the gamin tables in Vegas. In fact, they lit up the way they did the time he told me I might as well know he loved me and we might as well move in together because he wanted to spend the rest of his life bein around me. The light in his eyes—for the moment, mind you—was shinin the very way it did in the old days, when we'd look at one another and I would know the dishes and everything else could wait because two people in that house—namely me and him—had somethin on our minds that could only be worked out by slidin outta our clothes and slippin into bed and turnin off the lights and payin a long, no-distance visit with each other.

"Well," he said, pickin up the pot of Constant Comment to pour himself some, "since you went to all that trouble, the least you can do is make a wish."

I hadnt even thought about that, but after he said it, I snuggled up beside him on the sofa, shut my eyes real tight, and started concentratin. Funny. All I got was static. I knew it was on accounta the problems my body was havin that I hadnt bothered goin in to see the doctor about yet. It didnt take long, tho, for me to get cleared enough to visualize me and Burley enjoyin one another for the rest of our lives, with him feelin good again and me always happy to see him. That's all I wished for, then I blew the candle out.

"I know youll get what you wished for," he said. "You always do."

I smiled and sliced him just a sliver of cake, since I knew how careful he had to be about keepin tracka his sugar intake. Then he wanted me to sit with him while he looked at *Search for Tomorrow* and *One Life to Live.* Aw, when it came to his "stories," that man was worse than my mama use to be, only with her it was a radio habit. Unless he happened to be in so much pain until he had to take the strong medication that knocked him out, he never missed them two programs.

So I sat there with him, even tryna make out like I was enjoyin myself. Serials, somehow, they dont do too much for me. My own life is all the soap opera I can handle. But bein in a kinda celebratin mood, I put up a good front and pretended like I was right in there with Burley when he would start laughin or gettin sad. Every once in a while, tho, when he'd be so engrossed watchin the screen until he forgot about me, I would cut my eyes and steal me a look at this man I'd been livin with common-law for seven years. The sad part was Burley still looked awful handsome and robust for a man in his condition. True, his hair had turned almost pure white after his second stroke, the one that put him in a wheelchair, and he slurred his words so bad he sometime sounded like he was drunk. But he still looked pretty good for the shape he was in. Oh, he'd put on some extra weight, but by him bein so tall and big-boned anyway, it wasnt all that noticeable. His hair and his mustache, along with his dark complexion, made him look distinguished. And Burley's face was still loose and jolly with them deep dimples I loved, and that Navajo-lookin forehead. There was still plenty light shinin outta his big round eyes the color of hot, fresh-poured coffee.

Sitting up there next to him, I felt contented about him bein in such a good mood for a change. Provided he wasnt feelin too poorly, Burley Cole could cheer me up and lift my spirits faster than anybody I'd ever met—with the possible exception of my mother, Ruby, or that sometime buddy of my son's, who went and changed his name a little while back to Nomo. Mind you, it's taken some gettin use to, all these youngsters up and changin their names, but I think Nomo picked him a pretty good one— Nomo Dudu.

Then all of a sudden, after the commercial come on, Burley

cranked his head around at me and started laughin. By me bein so busy studyin him on the sly and driftin off into my own thoughts, I'd forgot to pay attention to the television. I looked up and saw this famous actress—she's gettin on up in years now —who use to be a regular dinner guest back in the days when I was keepin house for Harry Silvertone. Now all this actress was doin on the TV screen was wringin out a slip and a paira panties in her bathroom face bowl bubbled up with suds. Of course she was grinnin into the camera and then, in a tight soft-focus close-up, she was tellin us, "In my busy, hectic life as a career woman, I simply cannot afford to waste precious time being misled by false advertising. That's why I only use Lux for all delicate lingerie and fine washables. So take it from a professional . . . On Lux you can rely."

"I musta missed somethin," I told Burley. "What's so funny about that?"

"Wh-what's funny," he said, "is when you stop and think about it. I mean, what in the world does she ever have to wash, anyway? Some drawers and a handkerchief every once in a while, *maybe.* Hell, I mean, *heck,* Mamie, that's how come *you* got a job, so they can have somebody to cook and clean up after em— and wash their drawers out for em."

I must declare that for as long as Burley'd been hit with that commercial, there he was just now gettin around to findin it funny. He kept right on laughin, tho, and flopped back on the couch. Tears was streamin down his cheeks. And then it was like somethin'd got caught in his throat. Just as suddenly as he'd started laughin, he stopped. He went to feelin on his good arm with his bad arm and I watched his neck jerk back. My whole body commenced to breakin out in gooseflesh.

"What's the matter?" I said. "Some cake get caught in your windpipe?" Right away I was rememberin this chart tellin you what to do in case of chokin that I'd been studyin for years in a little rib joint we use to eat at over on West Adams Boulevard. They got it posted right there up over the counter.

"Mamie," he whispered, "I d-dont feel so good. Think maybe I need to lay down."

I eased Burley down across the couch so he could rest his head on a cushion. He started clutchin his chest. When I pressed the backa my hand to his forehead, it felt too warm and sticky. Oh, Lord, I went to feelin this hot and cold lightnin flashin all thru me, and my heart was boomin like summer thunder.

"Burley," I said, still tryna act calm. "Burley, sweetheart, tell me, does it feel like youre comin down with another attack?"

"Dont feel right, Mamie," he said. Then he went to tremblin and groanin.

I got down on my knees on the rug and threw my arms around him. That's when I heard him suck in his breath. "Burley," I said, "you just stay right here and breathe as slow as you can. I'll call Dr. Winslow and find out what we oughtta—"

"No," he said. I couldnt hardly hear him. "Doctor cant do me no good. I—"

"Then let me just call the paramedic ambulance. Theyre right up the street and can be here in a minute."

"No," he whispered. "No, no, no! Dont want you callin nobody. I—I just want you to . . . listen."

"But, Burley, this is serious. You arent even in your right mind. I cant let you—"

"Shhh! Please! I *know* what's goin on. I have to . . . have to tell you somethin before, before—"

"Before what? Quick, tell me!"

"Before it all drains out."

"Before *what* all drains out? Youre makin no sense!"

"It's . . . it's openin up, Mamie . . . openin up fast . . . s-s-so lemme just tell you . . ."

By then I was so scared and stuffed up with tears I couldnt hardly see. I snuggled my face down against the collar of Burley's robe until my ear was pressed smack up to his lips. Even at that, it still wasnt easy to make out his words. I felt like I was about to melt. One parta me wanted to get up and race to the phone, while the other part was fillin up with this—well, this warm, powerful feelin. It was like, if I tried hard enough, I could almost remember what hadnt even happened yet. What I was feelin was like a throb burnin its way up into my throat, and it was keepin me glued to the floor down there on my knees, clingin to Burley and so choked up I thought I would faint. And there was this voice kept ricochetin around inside my head, bouncin off the hollows of my skull, goin, *Let him go, Mamie; let the man go. Burley's gotta be somewhere, and youre holdin him back.*

He groaned some more; then he cupped his hand around one side of my face and said, "I swear it feels like . . . feels like it's all about to slip away . . . down the drain . . . Aint much more time now . . . Just promise . . . please, promise me . . . Say youll promise—"

"Promise what? Anything you say."

"I cant talk much longer . . . It's blowin, it's blowin, it's blowin thru my window . . . like a breeze . . . blowin me away. You see . . . aint no real words to . . . Kendall, Mamie, Kendall!"

"What about Kendall?"

"I can . . . I can almost . . ."

I could see Burley's mind was snappin, snappin fast as he mumbled on. Then a strange thing happened. He taken his hand away from my cheek and draped his arm over my shoulder. I could feel his fingers growin weaker and weaker as he tried to hold on to me.

Wasnt nothin I could think of to say now, so I just held him the best I could and whimpered. Then I heard him clear his throat and suddenly he was speakin to me again in his regular old voice. He didnt whisper and he didnt slur and he didnt even stammer. I raised up and taken a good look at Burley.

"And Mamie," he said, with his eyes still shut. "Dont give up on Benjamin. Please dont give up on him. Help the boy out. You got the power. It aint gon be easy for either of you, but you got the power. Stick it out. I'll . . . I'll do what I can too."

Now, I knew exactly what Burley meant by that, but when I went to tell him he neednt worry, I was so choked up I musta sounded like a little baby tryna babble with a mouthfulla pabulum.

Burley's lips curled up. He was strainin to smile. "Dont forget," he said in a low, deep voice. "Kendall . . . Benjamin . . . Zaccharetti . . . Dont let Zaccharetti fool you for a minute . . . Dont forget . . . you got the power . . . Stick it out."

All at once he smiled, sure enough. Not only that, he opened his eyes and looked at me and said, "H-happy birthday, sugar." I was so hypnotized when he did that until it felt like I could see straight thru his pupils and clean up into his soul. All them scary feelins and notions that's had me all tied up in knots, they faded away. I caught myself growin light in the head and even relieved in a guilty sorta way. In fact, for a split second there it crossed my mind that Burley might be fixin to tell me everything was gonna turn out all right, after all, that he was feelin better now and all he needed was a nap. In that same split second I saw him wakin up from his nap all refreshed, and I would be out in the kitchen gettin dinner for us. I leaned into Burley and kissed him on the mouth.

Then the moment unsplit itself and I heard him whisper, slurrin this time, sayin, "Dont worry, honey, we'll . . . we'll be in touch. I feel so light . . . like I'm about to float, so . . . my shepherd . . . not want . . . He leadeth me . . . m-maketh me to lie down . . . in green pastures . . . I love . . . love you, Mamie, oh, Mama . . . This feelin, this . . . this . . . this . . ."

Burley's lips quit movin and his face went blank like the screen in a theater when the film snaps in the projector. His chest quit heavin, but his eyes stayed open. A hot chill shot thru me and I broke out in a cold sweat. I reached over to push the poor man's eyes shut. His face was still warm but didnt feel right. I pried his arm from around my back; then I fell out across Burley's emptied-out body for a lifetime, look like.

Somehow, tho, I remember the calm that came over me after I got thru cryin. Honest to God, I could still feel Burley in the room and all over the house. Felt like he was walkin around, yet at the same time I knew he was up there someplace way up over me. And even tho I couldnt hear him sayin anything, I had this sensation he was out there feelin as sorry and confused about what'd just happened as I did.

Not knowin anything better to do, I finished recitin the Twenty-third Psalm for Burley; then I got up and wobbled to the telephone. I'd no sooner hung up from callin Dr. Winslow—dont ask me how come—than the doorbell rang.

When I opened the door, there was a fat man in a raincoat with a hat on. Without stoppin to think, I threw myself in his arms and went on cryin.

"Mrs. Franklin?" he said, lookin like he was fixin to keel over backward.

"He was such a beautiful man," I blubbered out. "All these evil people still walkin around, and Burley had to up and die on me! I'm the one that shoulda died, not him, not Burley!"

"I beg your pardon," the fat man said. "This is the Franklin residence, isn't it?"

"Yes, yes, yes. You got the right place. Wh-who are you?"

The man had to struggle to do it—on accounta I had him in such a tight clench, I guess—but he did manage to get his hands inside his coat and pull out a wallet. I let go and moved back when he flashed his little silver badge all up in my face.

"Mrs. Franklin," he said, lookin kinda sheepish now. "I'm Inspector Beaumont of the Santa Monica Police Department. As I understand it, there's been a burglary attempt and two men are being held in custody."

"A burglary?" I said. "That was days ago! Where've you people been? Now there's been a death!"

Inspector Beaumont whisked off his hat and his mouth dropped wide open. "I—I'm afraid I don't understand. Are you saying someone's been murdered?"

"No," I cried, "that aint what I said. Somebody's died, that's all. Somebody real close to me just now died and—"

I couldnt believe my eyes and ears, and I couldnt hold myself

in any longer either. Tears commenced to pourin outta me like
stormy weather. I fell right back up against the fat inspector and
mashed my face into his soggy, dog-smellin raincoat and cried
like there wasnt no tomorrow.

# 8

After they came and collected the body, I sat there in the kitchen—sat right there in the dark, I mean—for the longest, tryna get my thoughts together. But if my life'd been at stake, I couldna focused on any one thing, no matter how hard I tried. Sadness was cruisin all thru me; there wasnt anything else to call it. Sadness. You hear people say that word all the time, especially in songs and in stories, but the real sadness isnt anything like the sadness you always hear about.

The real sadness has somethin kinda glad about it. As crazy as that might sound, it's true and this is what I mean. The sadness I was feelin because Burley had died didnt, truthfully, not when I zeroed right in on it, have all that much to do with Burley. Nope, it had more to do with me than it did with him. I was the one with the problem. Burley, bless his soul, was gone; he was free. He was just the way Martin Luther King preached about in that famous sermon of his, where he quotes that powerful old spiritual: "Free at last! Free at last! Great God-a-Mighty, we are free at last!" Everytime they run that old tape over radio or over TV, I get goosebumps all over from listenin to Dr. King deliver that.

The goosebumps wouldnt go away this time. All I was doin was thinkin about what it must be like to really and finally be free at last. It had me feelin glad and sad at the same time, and that's the kinda sadness I'm talkin about. Here I was, still had to worry about eatin right and keepin a roof over my head and makin a livin and livin long enough to see Benjie out on his own. I still had a job to fool with, all that junk of Burley's to get rid of, a car that wasnt gettin any younger, and taxes to worry about. Burley could tell the Internal Revenue to kiss his natural you-know-what. He didnt have to worry about a thing, and he sure didnt have to worry about me.

But there I sat, feelin sorry for myself in some odd way, feelin like it was unfair for him to be gone and for me to still be there to carry on. It was like a bad dream. I missed him; I missed the man. Even tho I could still feel him swooshin all around me, I missed not bein able to reach out and grab him by the flesh and say, "Whacha know good, Robin Hood?" Or anything. That's what we forget while we're still walkin around talkin trash and processin information; we forget that when that life oozes outta the body, that's it! Sure, I thought I understood that, because it sounds so easy to grasp, but when I saw rigor mortis start to set in on Burley—and it starts happenin faster than you expect—that threw me for another loop.

It occurred to me that I needed to get somethin to eat, but somehow that didnt seem right. It was no time to be eatin; all of this was too solemn. For twenty minutes I let that kinda thinkin take over, but pretty soon my stomach started makin itself heard, and I knew I'd better get up and heat some soup or somethin. Then I got stuck thinkin about all the different food there was in the house, right on down to what was left of that chocolate cake. Then I got to thinkin about Mr. Chrysler and Danielle and all that jambalaya and paella I was gonna have to fix.

After that, it was a case of somebody bein glued to their seat while pictures and smells burglarized their senses. Chicken and rice and garlic and olive oil and saffron and sausage and thyme and shrimp and clams and bacon and onions and crab and ham and parsley and pepper and butter and tomato and cayenne and celery and all those wonderful aromas and that heat and even the way the onions made me cry and cry—all of it just seemed like the perfect thing to be doin at that moment.

Before I knew it, I'd written up my list, fixed up my face in the bathroom mirror, pulled on my coat, and was startin up Sweepea. As bad as I thought I oughtta feel at the time, doin somethin as triflin as that when here Burley was dead—for some reason, I figured it might turn out to be just the thing I needed to keep my mind off his death. You know, there are certain things so serious that the best thing you can do is not take em too seriously.

Everything I was workin with, every bit of the ingredients, started takin on some special significance while I let myself disappear inside of em. No, I wasnt losin my mind; I was just tryna hold on the best I could. Mother Dear use to tell me that sometime, especially when youre troubled, the best thing to do is to stay right with yourself. "Just stay right with yourself, Mamie," she'd tell me. And it usually works. The only reason I say *usually* is that mosta the time I forget to try it. But the sadness I was tryna hold back that night pushed me into rememberin *every*thing.

Choppin onions was maybe the purest example of what I'm talkin about. I thought about Mother Dear a lot while I was choppin. A lotta her philosophy came from around-the-house stuff like fixin food and keepin things together, and while I was choppin, tryna recall what it was she use to say about an onion and how it was like life, it hit me how we're all kinda like onions the way we shed our skins and shed our years and keep on diggin down to where we can get at the center of things. Maybe I'm only talkin about myself, but that's never kept me from bitin my tongue.

When the tears came pourin and tricklin down my face, I didnt even bother reachin for a Kleenex or a paper towel or anything to wipe em away. It was humorous, really, with the onions—it seemed like I musta chopped fifteen or twenty of them things—with the onions causin the tears to flow that wanted to be flowin in the first place. I even had to let loose with some pitiful laughin right in the middle of all that. I was thinkin about how my whole life I hadnt been nothin but a fool.

My folks and friends all told me I was a fool for leavin there from outta Hattiesburg with Chance Franklin, that they always figured me for bein smarter than that. And I *know* I was a fool for droppin outta show biz when I did to have Benjie. That'd been the first time, tho, that these visitations began to happen on a regular basis. I'm talkin about my psychic abilities and how all that went to openin up. The longer I kept singin, the more I realized about my ability to heal people, just by directin what I was singin at em. The first time it happened—while I was beltin out "Happy Birthday" to a man—I'd only been vaguely aware of my powers. It was up there in Oakland at Slim Jenkins's Club and the man out in the audience whose birthday it was had come up to me afterwards and said, "Mamie, I dont know what it was you put into that birthday song you sung for me, but when you got finished singin I felt like I could walk clean up the wall and thru the roof. Whatever you did, thank you, thank you!"

After this happened enough times that I got to be conscious of it, my own ideas about what I was doin started changin too. Music, I began to figure out, wasnt exactly what we mostly think it is: entertainment. There was somethin medicinal about it too, somethin that didnt go with the kinda life I'd been leadin with it.

When I drifted outta music and called myself breakin into actin, I found I wasnt crazy about that, either. I mean, the parts they grudgingly let us play wasnt exactly encouragin. You remember back here when that kid Levar Burton couldnt get a role playin anything in Hollywood after he got thru starrin in *Roots,* one of the biggest-grossin TV pictures ever. Then along came Steve McQueen, I believe it was, who had his scriptwriters change a role that'd been originally written for a dog, for the dog that was gonna play Steve's pet. He had em rewrite the part for

Levar Burton to play it. Tell you, I was so got off with after I read this I clipped it from out the paper. Then, when I came across it later, I reread the thing and busted out laughin. "You know," I told my pal Charlean Jackson, "in the old days, plenty of us woulda been tickled to even get the chance to play the damn dog."

Dont go gettin me wrong now. I never had anything against Stepin Fetchit or Clarence Muse or Butterfly McQueen or Willie Best or Mantan Moreland or Hattie McDaniel or any of those old movie performers. After all, a gig is a gig! Those were great comedic actors and they played their stuff to the hilt. In some of those old Stepin Fetchit pictures you can almost see the brother winkin at you as he wipes his hand cross his mouth and whines in that slow, molasses voice of his, "Well, boss, I'se gwine to de big ribbuh boat up yonder in heahbun!" But I just didnt happen to be all wrapped up and gung-ho to play those kinda roles. Even when I did play maids—and that's mostly what I played—I had to strain to try to bring a little dignity to the role. I havent spent all that much time figurin it out, but you must admit that there's irony, as my boy Benjie might put it, to my startin off playin domestics and then endin up bein one in real life.

Sometimes when I'm out there by Mann's Chinese Theatre on the Hollywood Walk of Fame and lookin down at my feet while they step on all the stars and names of all those immortals, I find it hard to believe when I was young I wanted to have a star down there with my name next to it, wanted it so bad I woulda done pretty much anything to make it come true. Now when I go walkin out there on Hollywood or Vine, I wonder what it all signifies. I mean, the other day I was checkin em out as I stepped along: Smiley Burnett, Arturo Toscanini, Buster Crabbe, Fay Wray, Susan Hayward, Ida Lupino, Mario Lanza, Rin Tin Tin, Dale Evans, Bela Lugosi, Mickey Rooney, Hedy Lamarr, Lon Chaney, Errol Flynn, Simone Signoret, Ruth Gordon, Billie Dove (that's the one Billie Holiday named herself after), Basil Rathbone, Boris Karloff, Buster Keaton, Roscoe "Fatty"

Arbuckle (who I still believe was framed), Jayne Mansfield, Sal
Mineo, Sidney Poitier, Leo Gorcey, Vivien Leigh, Don Ameche,
Mickey Mouse, Johnny Weissmuller, Pier Angeli, Spike Jones,
Mae West, W. C. Fields, Piper Laurie . . .

The longer I thought about the whole thing, the slower I
caught myself walkin, until finally I stopped right where they'd
finally laid in a star for Billie Holiday herself not all that long
ago, except this was the first time I'd seen it. And you know
what I asked myself? I thought, *Well, Mamie, how would* you
*feel with people walkin all over you day and night? And spittin on*
*you and droppin ice cream on you and gettin dog-do all over you*
*and mashin out cigarettes on you?* Then I remembered about
what it took to get yourself one of those stars—three thousand
dollars. That's what it said in *Jet,* and I always read that thing
from cover to cover every week, goin all the way back to when
they use to have stuff on me in there.

While I got my jambalaya into production, that so-called
Walk of Fame loomed up so big in my mind until I actually said
out loud to myself, said, "What is *that* ?" And when I tried to
imagine Burley Cole's name down there glitterin next to a star,
then the whole thing got put in perspective fast. This immortal-
ity thing everybody's so hung up on sure takes on some strange
forms. I never really understood it all the way. I want people to
remember me too, but I want em rememberin me in their hearts
the way I was already rememberin Burley. If the truth were
known, and I wouldnt lie to you, I'd already been doin a lotta
rememberin about Burley long before he got out of his body. You
do that when somebody is sick for as long as he was—just a little
under five years. Burley was the most uncomplicated man I ever
got involved with, plus he had a knack for makin me feel good,
for makin me laugh, and he never held a grudge about anything.
Sure, we'd have our little fights and spats like everybody else,
except with Burley the mess would be buried and forgotten as
soon as it happened. He'd put in his time on the job, helped out
his family, done the best he could, and made out his will and his
insurance to Kendall and me.

I pretended like I was fixin the jambalaya and the paella for him because Burley was crazy about that stuff. And I could almost feel him leanin over my shoulder, watchin me slice and stir and mix and sauté and whatnot. He was good for sayin off-the-wall stuff too, stuff that kinda irritated you at first but then, when you let it sink in and realized he was tryna express affection, you wanted to hug him for it.

"Oh, boy!" he told me one time while I was fixin up a big batcha coquilles St. Jacques—you know, scallops baked in sauce. "Mmm-mmm, that smells so good. Be sure and make plenty of em so that nice round belly and these beautiful hips of yours dont get too deflated."

For a split second, I thought I could feel him standin right behind me with his hands wrapped around my waist, sayin somethin dumb like that into my ear and then lickin the backa my neck and kissin it. When I spun around, tho, and didnt see anybody there it shook me up so much I almost cut my little finger off with that sharp cleaver of ours. But, you know, I swear I could feel Burley breathin down my neck.

Once I got everything pretty much together and was sittin at the kitchen table, all proud of myself and how good the food smelled while it simmered away, the gloom set in again. I knew I was gonna have to call somebody soon. The only person I could think of that might be up at three in the mornin for sure would be Kendall, only I didnt have a phone number for him. The best I could hope was that the news would somehow trickle out to him, or else maybe Benjie would know how to reach him. Benjie had a big test in the mornin on film history, so I wasnt about to disturb his sleep. And it was still a shade on the early side to be callin up anybody in the family such as my sister Rose in Chicago at that hour. But what if I was to telephone Charlean? She was probably out there at the house by herself, I thought, since Nixxy was outta town, and live-in means what it says.

I sat there with my hand on the phone for so long, tryna make up my mind what to do, until finally the urge to ring up anybody floated clean outta my mind. You ever do that? I felt all wrong about it at first. After all, there had been a death, and death is serious. You oughtta be able to call the White House or the Kremlin when somebody's died on you and say, "Oh, I'm sorry, I know it's late, but my husband just died and I'm kinda, well, you know, out of it. I had to talk with somebody." And they should be understandin and chitchat with you just to be kind. But the longer I sat there, the less I felt like talkin to anybody. I decided to just get real quiet and close my eyes and calm down before I dozed off on the couch, and I *would* be sleepin on the sofa, since it wouldna felt right goin completely to bed.

After I quieted down and got my thoughts focused, it was clear what I needed, and that was to get outta the house and be close to somebody who'd understand. Charlean Jackson kept poppin up when I shut my eyes. I could see her just as plain in my mind, so I decided to concentrate on one thing: seein if I could send how I was feelin out there to where she was. And how do you do that? You just put your whole mind on somethin, picture it strongly, and insteada actin like it's somethin that's gonna happen, you act like it's already happened.

In my imagination, Charlean was lyin in her bedroom there at Nixxy Privates' house deep into slumber. I could even see her curled up on her side and I could hear her snorin a little, not much, tho. When I shut everything else outta my mind and hung right on to that picture of Charlean, all the time thinkin, *Charlean, Charlean, this is Mamie and I need you, girl. I need you to call me. Just pick up the phone there by your bed and call me, Charlean!*

Soon I was dozin off, myself. Time to catch a nap, I thought and got up to check on the food and start puttin some of it in the spare fridge we had. Tomorrow I'd have Danielle send Rodrigo the gardener or somebody over to come pick it up for the party.

Finally, just when I'd gotten the jambalaya and the paella all squared away, had flossed and brushed my teeth and washed my face, and was stretching out on the couch and pullin the quilt up over me to snooze, the phone started ringin. I'd dragged it over there by the sofa and put it on the floor, just in case.

"Hello."

"Mamie? . . ."

I could hear all the yawnin she was holdin back.

"Mamie, this is Charlean and . . . and I dont even know why I'm callin you. But I was havin this dream and—hey, are you all right?"

"No, no, I'm not all right."

"What's goin on? I dont be gettin up callin people at three in the mornin."

"Charlean, Burley died!" There was nothin else to do but blurt it all out.

"When?"

"This afternoon."

"Honey, why didnt you call me? Who's there with you?"

"No one."

"Are you crazy?"

"Yes."

"Do you want me to drive over and stay with you?"

"No, I wouldnt mind stayin . . . I mean, would it be okay if I stayed up there with you for the resta the night?"

"Are you in any shape to drive?"

"Uh, I dont really know."

"I'll put on my clothes and come pick you up. Oh, Mamie, I'm shattered. I'm soooo sorry to hear that. You must be goin outta your mind. Hold on and pack your toothbrush or whatever you need. No, dont even bother with that; Nixxy's got everything you could ever need right up here."

"I was just about to grab a nap on the couch."

"Well, just stay put; I'll be right there."

"What made you call me, Charlean?"

"I dont know. I really dont know."

"Will it really be all right? I mean, this wont get you in trouble with Nixxy, will it?"

"Get me in trouble with him! Girl, Nixxy Privates *is* trouble!"

"Is he there?"

"He started out the night here, but I think he mighta gotten up and gone over to Fifi's."

"Fifi?"

"Fiona Prince."

"Yeah, sounds like they both need to go someplace and sit down. I'll be right over."

Charlean was so kind to be doin this that it moved me to tears. I couldnt help myself.

"Mamie," she said, "youre gonna cry yourself sick if you aint careful. Save some of your tears so we can do some cryin together, please!"

"Charlean, do you think I can keep it together until tomorrow?"

"Keep what together, dear?"

"Myself, plus all the stuff that has to be done—contactin people, notifyin businesses, explainin to the Chryslers, findin Burley's son, arrangin for the funeral and—"

"Hold it, hold it!" Charlean said. "Youre carryin on like there isnt gonna be any tomorrow."

"That's how it feels to me right now."

"Well, dont go gettin aheada yourself. Not only will there be a tomorrow, but next week is practically at the front door ready to ring the bell."

"Charlean, youre so sweet to do this."

"Wait, you gotta let me get off the phone so I *can* do it."

After hangin up, I sat there on the couch feelin paralyzed. It was a nice kinda paralyzed, tho. That's when I got the idea of playin each day, every hour, every moment as if it just might be my last. I got up to go get dressed myself and heard somethin fall off the bookshelf as I walked thru the livin room. It didnt surprise me when I went over to where the sound had come from and found a book layin on the floor. It was *The Autobiography of Benjamin Franklin*. I picked it up and held it a second before puttin it back on that part of the shelf where I keep all my history books and stuff about him, and I could feel electricity cracklin in the air as I tapped it in place so it lined up even with the other books.

# 9

But you know as well as I do that there will always be some type of tomorrow, and plenty more besides. We might not be here to enjoy and rejoice in em all, but that's never been known to stop em from comin.

"Old Shakespeare," I was tellin Benjie between cryin bouts, "he sure got that part right, didnt he?"

"Shakespeare? What on earth are you talking about, Mom?"

We were on the Pasadena Freeway, on our way back from Burley's funeral, and Benjie was drivin. Charlean Jackson was ridin with us, hunched up right behind me in the backseat. She leaned forward and rested her hand on Benjie's shoulder and said, "Let your mother say what she got to say, son. These havent been the easiest of times for her."

I balled my handkerchief up in my hand and said, "You know that part in *Macbeth* where he go to hittin on that riff about tomorrow and tomorrow and tomorrow? Well, I was just thinkin about that, that's all." Thinkin back, I guess it was a pretty odd thing to be bringin up just then, but for some reason it'd popped in my head and I'd let it on out.

"He was a wonderful, understanding man," Benjie said, never takin his eyes off the road.

"Never knew you was on such buddy-buddy terms with William Shakespeare," Charlean said.

"No," Benjie told her, cockin his head to one side, "I mean Burley Cole. In many ways he was like the father I never had. I don't think I'll ever forget the advice he gave me when I was worried I'd never make it through film school at UCLA."

Now, this was a new one on me and I just had to know what Burley had told Benjie. "And what was that?" I asked.

Benjie eased the Rolls into a right lane to let some raggedy Plymouth that'd been tailgatin him struggle past. I had to hand it to my boy for bein so cool when he coulda just stepped on the gas and give that trashy car a real run for its money if he'd wanted to.

"Oh, it's nothing to talk about, really," he said. "As I recall, we'd gone to a Lakers-Celtics game and during halftime I'd told Burley what a hard time I was having staying on top of all the homework and assignments they were throwing at us."

"And what'd Burley say?" I asked.

"Well," said Benjie, "it was funny, just peculiar, coming as it did from him. And paradoxically, it was also totally characteristic of Burley's perceptiveness."

Charlean sat straight up and started breathin thru her nose all hard. I could tell she was a little got off with. "Now, hold on a doggone minute!" she said. "Your mother and me here, we aint no English majors. We just plain, simple, down-to-earth Americans. So would you kindly try and talk *to* us and not *at* us? All we wanna know is what it was Burley told you that was so important at the time, all right? Shoot, you sound just like my oldest boy, Murray, after I busted my back gettin him thru school and turn around and ask him a simple question and get some type of dissertation throwed up in my face."

"All right, all right," said Benjie. "All Burley said was, 'Aint no use in askin the cow to pour you a glass of milk,' that's all."

"Well, all right, then," said Charlean. "Now you talkin!"

"Listen," I told Benjie, "Burley cared more about you and your gettin an education than youll ever know."

"Aw, I always knew that, Mom."

"You sure didnt act like it mosta the time. In fact, durin the last days we didnt hardly see that much of you at all."

"That's not true. I was—"

"Just a minute now," said Charlean. "Need I remind everybody that the poor man hasnt even been all that long put in the ground good, and here we go carryin on like buzzards. Please—a little bit more respect for the deceased if you dont mind."

"I'm sorry," I said. Tears was slippin outta my eyes again, even tho I was tryin my best to look at what was happenin from a whole different angle. I knew good and well that people dont die the way we like to picture em as dyin; you know, just dead, gone, finished, and that's that. I mean, hadnt I been out there myself, ramblin around in the ether long enough to know better? If my gift hadnt taught me death wasnt like that, then what good was it? Folks run around here scared and worryin about dyin when mosta the time they be dead inside themselves, sleep anyway, and dont even know it. And then too, most people dont have any idea how much is goin on right close in around em and up under their noses—things which, because they cant see em, they dont even believe exist. Now, as long as I'd been crossin paths and dealin with the unseen, there I was feelin like the bottom'd dropped outta my world. Just snufflin and grievin like everybody else at the funeral, and cryin my heart out.

We all got quiet and didnt say anything for a good halfa mile. Then Charlean scooted forward in her seat and put her arms around me from behind and kissed me on the cheek. I could feel the soft hair of her huge wig hat brushin up against the side of my watery face.

"Save your tears, honey," she whispered, " 'cause you sure gonna need em." Then she spoke up, I guess so Benjie could hear what she needed to say. "Mamie, I cant think of too many women anymore that woulda stuck with and done for a sick man the way you did for Burley. I was sittin right there lookin at his ex–old lady and the resta his family while the service was goin on. Made me mad to see them breakin out in hysterics and shoutin all them amens when here you was the one nursed and seen after him thru both his strokes."

"It wasnt quite that bad, Charlean," I whimpered. "His daughters kept in touch and showed their concern."

"All right, well, see, I didnt know that. But what about all the rest of em? Wasnt that Burley's son propped up there next to his mama?"

Benjie glanced back at Charlean, annoyed. "But youve got to understand about Kendall," he told her. "You see, he's out of it."

"Out of it?" Charlean shouted. "What kinda excuse is that? Everybody's out of it. I'm out of it; youre out of it; every—"

"No, no," said Benjie. "Kendall's never been the same since they started giving him those treatments down at the V.A. hospital."

"What treatments?"

"From what we can discern," said Benjie, "they must be administering shock treatment and flooding him with Thorazine. He used to be bristling with a wild, infectious energy—even if it was on the negative side—and now he's virtually a vegetable. The ultimate corporate punishment. Kendall got himself shipped over there thinking he was fighting for us, fighting to protect his country and, really, all he was fighting for was the continuance of multinational capitalism at its most moribund—I mean, at its deadest and most desperate stage. And you see how society rewarded his patriotism."

Charlean cut her eyes at Benjie, then looked at me. "There he go again," she said, "except this time he dont sound like Murray. This time he remind me of Dexter Shank, my old boss out in Bel Air. Went and got hisself blacklisted, talkin that same stuff this boy is talkin."

"McCarthyism," said Benjie. "We studied that. It must've been awful. All those lives, careers and talent—down the drain, for nothing! And you actually knew Dexter Shank? He was one of the finest screenwriters around during that era."

"One of the best," said Charlean, "and one of the most careless men I ever knew."

"Careless?" said Benjie. "How do you mean?"

"With all that vocabulary you got, you dont know what careless mean?"

"Mrs. Jackson, come on, give me a break."

"Benjie," I said, "Charlean's just havin some fun with you."

"Well, it isn't always that easy to tell."

"When I say Dexter Shank was careless," she went on, "I mean exactly what I say. He was a happy-go-lucky kind of a fella who said whatever was on his mind and did whatever he wanted whenever he felt like it. That was his downfall. He liked us to call him Dexter—none of this Mr. Shank stuff. He was for the underdog, and he liked women and liquor, and he read too much. Dexter had a way of gettin the class struggle mixed up with the ass struggle—if youll excuse my language, Mamie. That was his downfall."

I could tell Benjie didnt know what to make of how Charlean was carryin on all of a sudden, but I had my own ideas.

"Well," he said finally, "I just hope those days never come back, even though I know witch-hunting tends to be recurrent in American life."

Charlean laughed. "Child," she said, "you aint never gon find out from readin no book what them days was like. See, they like to make out like it was all politics, but a whole lotta that blacklistin dookey wasnt nothin but personal and professional malice. And malice is the name of this picture business—malice and money. If they was to hire me to teach one of those movie-history courses, I'd level with them students the same as I'm doin with you. And, remember, I go back almost as far as popcorn. You listenin to me?"

I had to dry my eyes and chuckle some my own self when I saw Charlean winkin at me on the sly. I thought, well, at least she was still here in the world, along with Benjie and a few others, to help me stave off some of my loneliness.

"Blacklisted," said Charlean, "that's what they done to Dexter all right. Lost everything he had—his home, his livelihood, even his health. All I lost was a pretty good job, but I aint forgot for a minute what blacklistin really mean. Shoot, you been blacklisted from the moment they yanked you outta your mama's womb."

Benjie just shook his head and kept on drivin. Wasnt much use in me sayin anything. All I did was kick off my high heels and look thru the windshield at all that Los Angeles still comin our way. It was hard to believe that I'd wasted so many precious years foolin around this town only to end up still feelin like a stranger.

"Just be glad," said Charlean. "Be glad, boy, you got people in your life like me and your mother to school you in some of the fine points they might not be gettin across in them picture-show classes of yours. It's people in this town that'd sell they grandmama and grandpapa to make some money and see they name on the silver screen. Burley, he wasnt like that. He was . . . he was . . . he was a good man. He was too real for this town."

Now it was Charlean's turn to cry. Like with everything else she did, Charlean didnt hold back a drop. Tears started pourin outta her like summer sweat. This time when she leaned over the car seat to hug and start nudgin up against me again, I could smell the brandy on her breath.

I dont go to church much anymore—only at Easter and Christmastime—but there's a church in my heart I slip into now and then. The message I get whensoever I turn inside is always the same: There's somethin bigger than me or the world or the whole universe that I'll have to be answerin to by and by.

Now, that *by and by* can do you in if you play it cheap. It's somethin youre bound to live out in stages. Livin out the first *by* can take a long time. But it's that second *by* you gotta watch, and I'll tell you why. That sucker is tricky because it has a way of sneakin up on you without seemin to take as long as the first *by* took. Next thing you know, it's time to get ready to say bye-bye.

I sailed past that first *by* a long time ago and, lemme tell you, sometime the pain from sufferin over a long haul can bring you to the place where the only chance you stand of winnin the war is to lose the battle. Me, I've already lost so many little battles until it looked like the best thing for me to do after Burley died was to slow down and do some inventory. That's what I had to do. I didnt just stop; I clean shut down. Turned off all the switches, pulled out every plug, and put the world on hold. Well, almost. There was still a few details I had to take care of, not to mention some dusty corners that needed sweepin.

As long as Mother Dear's been gone from this earth, I can still feel her smilin out at me when I talk like this. I never could much see it until I got half grown and ran away from home, but Ruby Franklin was a real sincere, jolly kinda person. She was comical and she was deep. By comical, I dont mean to say she was anything like any of these people you gotta put up with nowadays who only *think* theyre funny; all these old nasty-mouth comedians that'd stand on their heads and turn their heinies inside out if they thought it would get a laugh. Mother Dear was more along the order of your true humorist, what they use to call a wit. She was beautiful at comin up with stuff that could make you smile and cry at the same time. That's because the things she'd say would be so real and hit so close to home until, even tho it made you feel like cryin sometime, you just naturally had to break out grinnin, too. When I think about how hard life musta been for her back there in the Dark Ages, I have to hand it to Mother Dear for bein able to laugh at all.

Nathaniel Franklin, my father, was a big man, like Burley, and he was known for bein one of the most successful dairy farmers in Forrest County. For years they kept tryna get him to come up to Jefferson City, Missouri, to teach at the colored A&M college there. Mother Dear was all for it, but Daddy's attitude was a smidgin on the icy side. I can remember him sayin, "You cant sit on the bucket and draw water at the same time." Beside, he said, we couldnt live off what little salary they wanna pay him up there.

I was the youngest of Ruby and Nathaniel's five children, all girls, except for the eldest, Maurice, who I never got to know too well. Maurice was killed in action over in Korea and sometime I think that was the biggest cause of Daddy turnin so sour by the time the rest of us had come of age. Rose, the next youngest, moved up to Chicago, but Alice and Jolene, well, they did what was expected of em; married, had kids, and stayed in the South. We're all still in touch. I was the one with a headfulla dreams and peculiar ideas. It's hard now to remember exactly what I was like, but I can tell you I always did wanna be somebody.

What I do remember—even before I went into first grade— was bein in love with pictures of people in movies, newspapers and magazines, and the way they sounded over the radio or on records. I loved the idea of bein in so many places at one time, havin your face or your body or your voice hit so many thousands of people at the same time. For me that seemed amazin and the only sensible way to go. I couldnt wait to get grown so I could become one of those people everybody felt like they knew because they'd already seen or heard so much of em.

I guess it all started out with me singin in the Sunday-school choir and actin in plays the school would put on. But even at that, if you was to ask me why I wanted to get into this business as bad as I did, I dont believe I could answer that to anybody's satisfaction, least of all my own. I did have a favorite uncle, tho, on my mother's side—Uncle Yut. His real name was Eliott, but we all called him Yut. He was a natural showman. Uncle Yut was a big-eyed beanpole of a man, with a deep, gruff voice. He could use that voice to say the table blessin and make it into somethin so entertainin and pretty until it was not to be believed. You could put Yut up on a platform or a wooden box—I doubt if he ever played on a real stage in a theater in his life—and he would just know in his bones and fingernails how to steal the show. He could tell a story, crack jokes, sing, dance, and give a sermon or make a speech better than most big-money showfolks can do nowadays. Uncle Yut could pick up chairs and stools and things with his teeth just like Lockjaw Jackson, plus he was smart. In fact, it turned out he was a little too smart for his own good because he went up there to Chicago and got arrested and done time for sellin lucky incense and goofer dust and all that kinda mojo and hoodoo stuff. Mail fraud, they called it, on accounta he was advertisin in places like *Jive* and *Tan Confessions* to reach the down-home colored trade. But Yut managed to sock away a lotta money before the law caught up with him, and when he got outta jail he started him up a bowlin alley and, last I heard, has been straight ever since.

I plumb admired Uncle Yut when I was a little girl, just as I admired Chance Franklin later on, and all the performers I thought was talented and sophisticated that passed thru our little parta the world. I got it in my head I was gonna turn out to be a star of some kind too, didnt matter what kind. I wanted to get out there and thrill folks by showin em how astoundin it was to be alive, to even exist. Mother Dear always talked about how we coulda been born a pig or a chicken or a swamp frog or a worm or a mosquito. But we were born humans, which means God musta intended us to be special. Well, that left me with plenty to roll over in my mind. I wasnt gonna stop until I'd let the world see how special and outstandin I was.

Bright lights and hoopla attracted me so much until my school work suffered. I was spendin my time studyin what was generally considered to be foolishness. I learned to sing, learned to dance, learned to walk correctly and speak correctly; and I learned how to make a good impression and charm people. Fact of business, I never did have to concentrate all that hard on bein charmin, since I was born Southern and well-bred, not to mention brown-skin and comely-featured. I guess you might say I was blessed with more than a little advantage over the average woman.

Not to toot my own horn, but I never was one to bite my tongue either. After all, if you dont stand up and holler, youre bound to be overlooked. Taken me a long time to learn that. Even now when some old picture I played in turns up on TV, I cant help rememberin how dumb and shy I use to be. I still suspect that if I'd been more outgoin and outspoken and fol-lowed up on my hunches back then, I mighta gone on to get bigger and better roles in movies and built a fabulous career for myself.

Oh, I never was no ravishin runaway beauty like Lena Horne, and I didnt have Dorothy Dandridge's good looks either—to say nothin of all that good hair—but I was definitely more than cute. You know, there still arent that many backwoods and grassroots colored gals who got as far as I did just on talent and mother wit. Sure, Josephine Baker and Eartha Kitt, they brought it off and taken it on out with style. But you see what they had to do first, dont you? Had to go way overseas, both of em, and make a big splash with foreigners before these old drowsy, prejudiced people over here would even give em credit or any kinda real break. You think things'll ever change?

Poor Lena with that pretty coppertone colorin of hers. I was awful young at the time, but I still havent forgot when she was over there at M-G-M and they kept pastin her in pictures like *Panama Hattie* and *As Thousands Cheer*. All they'd do was let her come on glitterin real slinky and glamorous and sexy to perform some song. Look like they was determined to keep the woman from doin any true actin. And then they came out with *Cabin in the Sky* and *Stormy Weather*, two pictures I never will forget. None of us had ever seen anything like that before—I know I hadnt—where you had Negro performers on the screen from beginnin to end.

I remember how a whole gang of us, family mostly, we taken up a whole row in that teen-einchy theater back there in Hattiesburg, the Grand Lux. I sat there next to Mother Dear that Saturday night and everytime Mother Dear shed a tear, I'd get all choked up too. Daddy wouldnt go. He just didnt believe movies did anybody much good. He was like that about picture shows and liquor. Far as Daddy was concerned, drinkin and movies was bad for you—somethin for white folks to fool with and ruin themselves. "Watch and see," he was always tellin us. "In your lifetime youll see how the powers that be wont be satisfied until they got everybody hemmed up in town drunk, eatin light bread and store-bought food, listenin to the radio and lookin at pictures. And when that happens, then yall can forget it. If you think these big-business rascals is bad now, just wait and see how they do people after they get thru takin over *everything.* Tell you, this world wont hardly be fit to live in." But to this day, I wish he had of gone and looked at *Stormy Weather.*

As if Bill Bojangles and Lena wasnt enough, there was Fats Waller, Ada Brown, Dooley Wilson, the Nicholas Brothers and old Cab Calloway himself, throwin that blow-hair of his around and doin his "Hi-De-Ho" white–zoot suit numbers all over the screen. The white folks downstairs was enjoyin it as much as we was. Uncle Yut wasnt the only one to come jitterbuggin out of the theater, only he was singin his own version of "Stormy Weather" that had all of us snigglin and crackin up:

> Dont know why
> Aint no porkchops on the fire,
> Starvation . . .
> It's overtakin the nation;
> Be's hungry all the time,
> All the time . . .

Anyway, after I saw Lena Horne in *Stormy Weather* I was as good as gone to Hollywood, California, wherever that was. I knew it was gonna require some time, years maybe, for me to get myself ready and find my way there. But I also knew, young as I was, about the mother of invention and the way of the will.

Even tho I knew I had no business goin back to work so soon, it seemed a whole lot healthier than crawlin around that cooped-up house of mine, receivin visitor after visitor, openin and cryin over condolence cards and telegrams, and answerin the telephone. I could feel Burley everywhere; yet and still it only felt like half a home. Benjie moved in with me those few days I taken off and tried his best to cheer me up. We got to where we could communicate, as people say now, with one another again. Oh, people was as nice as they could be. Even old Sneaky Pete,

would you believe—Monroe from across the street—dropped
over and said he'd be glad to mow the yard, do any repairs I
needed, or just keep an eye on the place when I wasnt there. But
I was lonesome. Look like it took forever for a night to creep by.
I'd get so far down into my thoughts and scariness and guilt and
regrets until I was wakin up mornins tireder than when I went to
bed. So when a dream came to me where I saw myself gettin
busy and feelin needed again, I snatched the hint and went on
back to work.

That mornin I was busy makin my way from the dinin room
to the kitchen, carryin a heavy stacka the Chryslers' best china to
start washin by hand when I glanced out the kitchen window by
the sink and seen this man's face grinnin in at me. It scared the
daylights outta me and I jumped. Lucky I had sense enough to
pile mosta the saucers on top of a big servin plate; otherwise I
mighta lost all of em. As it was, only the top two slipped. And
what a sound it made! Two delicate little pieces of the finest
china over a hundred years old hit the kitchen floor and splat-
tered into a thousand pieces. Wasnt no way I was gonna be able
to get around this. Already I could see Danielle and Mr. Chrysler
dockin me for two weeks' back pay. I mean, this was heirloom
stuff that'd been around his family for generations.

Somehow I made it to the sink counter, set the load down,
and looked out the window to see who it was made me shiver like
that. This time I let out a long breath and caught myself lookin
Nomo Dudu dead in the face, with all them awful-lookin
dreadlocks of his stickin out every which way. Before I even
stopped to wonder what in the world he was doin on the property, I wanted to kill him for scarin me like that and makin me
drop that china, with his big old doofus self. Then, to add insult
to injury, the rascal had the nerve to go to wavin at me.

Not stoppin to think, I waved back, then I twisted the latch
and pushed the window open to find out what he was doin.
That's when I saw Benjamin comin up along the path at the
backa the house right behind him. They was carryin that old
army trunk of Kendall's. I broke out laughin. Couldnt help my-

self. They looked like Laurel and Hardy in that old picture where they was haulin this old piano uphill, the same as Benjie and Nomo was haulin this trunk, and get halfway to where they're goin and let the doggone piano slip right outta their hands. I'll never forget the sighta that upright tumblin and bashin over the side of this hill and crashin. Oh, and the racket it made!

"How'd yall get in here in the first place?" I shouted at em.

"Aw, Miz Franklin," said Nomo, "aint you even gonna say hello or good afternoon or anything cordial?"

Benjie said, "Hi, Mom. Surprised to see us?"

Wasnt nobody else home but Danielle, and I could hear her racin down the stairs, callin my name and mumblin in French.

"You two mighta just now cost me my job," I yelled out the window.

"How's that?" said Nomo, still grinnin. I still wanted to light into him for what he'd made me do.

"Mom, you can't be serious. We're only dropping the trunk off."

"Mamie, Mamie!" I could hear Danielle callin. "Zat terrible noize! Are you okeh?"

"All I wanna know," said Nomo, "is where do you want us to put this thing?"

"Yeah," said Benjie, "I got the heavy end coming up that incline!"

Danielle rushed into the kitchen in jeans and a sweatshirt, with one of them Christian Dior scarves tied so tight around her head you mighta thought she was bald underneath. Not one stranda reddish-brown was showin, and she was all outta breath. But one look at her dark eyes scannin the floor was enough to tell me she'd figured out right away what'd happened.

"Just a second," I hollered to the boys. "I'll be right out."

I shut the window and turned to Danielle. "I know what youre thinkin," I said, "but let me explain."

She was shakin her head and smilin. "You dont have to explain," she said. "I can see for myself."

"All I can tell you, Danielle, is I'm sorry—sorry from the bottom of my heart!"

She stood there with her little hands on her big hips, lookin from the mess on the floor up to me and back down again. Then she did somethin I never much thought about till now. She walked over to the fridge, kicked some of the broken plate pieces outta her way, yanked open the door and grabbed a bottle of Dom Perignon champagne. I mean, she snatched the bottle right out the icebox and pressed it up against her cheek like she was cuddlin a baby.

"Oh, I cannot help myself," she said, laughin, all glad-eyed. She coulda been rememberin somethin in French, some old joke, maybe. Then she started wavin the bottle around like it was a magic wand. "Voilà," she said. "Voilà, life is so wondairful at times, so beautiful. See how things work themselves out, don't you think? Voilà!"

I was tryin my best to work up some kinda sickly little smile, just to be sociable, you understand. But I still couldnt help feelin sheepish and foolish. It musta showed in my face because Danielle wouldnt quit shakin her head and tellin me to relax. "Here," I told her, "I'll get the broom and dustpan. Have this cleaned up in no time."

"No hurry," she said, "no hurry at all. Relax, Mamie. I never liked zose dishes. Zey are ugly, ugly! Such bad taste! I told Carleton when we first married how sore zey made my eyes and what terrible taste the Chryslair family had to keep passing zem from generation to generation." She plucked a clean dish towel out of a drawer and wrapped it around the bottle.

"Well," I said, followin her to the sink, "it mighta been ugly —I'll grant you that—but I still figure I'm gonna be docked for a month's salary, at *least*, once Mr. Chrysler finds out who broke em."

"Nonsense!" she said. "How is he to find out if no one tells him? You leave it to me, okeh? I know zat man. I know what to say."

Danielle was gigglin. She turned her head away and squinched

her eyes while she worked her thumbs up along the cork of the
Dom Perignon. It popped out real smooth and hard and hit the
ceilin and landed in a bowl of fruit down at the other end of the
counter.

"Magnifique!" she cried. "I should play for ze Lake-airs, yes?"

"Youre sure a heck of a lot better at openin that stuff than I
ever was."

Champagne was foamin and tricklin all down Danielle's wrist
and fingers and soakin up the towel. While she was lickin some
off the back of her hand, I saw her eyes grow big.

"Anything the matter?" I asked.

She drew in her breath and pointed at the window where
Chance was standin, flashin one of his nonchalant, award-win-
nin, show-biz grins. Scroonched up right behind him was Nomo
and Benjie.

"Ah," she said, slappin one hand to her heart. "Your handsome son Benjie. But who are his friends?"

"That's my ex-husband and a frienda my son's."

"S'*merveilleux!*" she groaned. "Pairfect timing! Let them
come and celebrate with us."

# 10

It didnt feel right, the five of us all hangin round the kitchen, slurpin up champagne like that. I use to could put away some liquor back in my salad days; but along about the time I drifted outta the business and tried to settle down, my whole system changed and I had to cut the juice aloose. Chance was the one taught me to drink, and now I could see that even tho he'd gotten up in years and gray in the head he could still hold his own when it came to the sauce.

"Miz Chrysler," he said, smackin his juicy lips, "this is awfully good."

"By all means, then," Danielle told him, "help yourself to some more."

Oh, they were gettin on my nerves, the two of em, sittin up there at that tight little table. I was far enough away, sweepin up the pieces, that I could see their knees touch under the table every once in a while. Danielle's face was flushed and tiny little beads of sweat was breakin out on Chance's forehead. Look like they couldnt keep their eyes off one another. What both of em needed was somebody to slap em upside the head and say, "Grow up."

Anyway, I finally joined em at the table and even started sippin me some Dom Perignon.

"So this is where you work," said Nomo. He and Benjie was kinda half leanin, half sittin on the edge of the counter by the sink. "Nice spread. Nice spread, indeed." He turned to Benjie, who was lookin embarrassed. "Tell you, man, after I get my hit, this is just the kinda layout I intend to invest in. Might even go lookin for the very architect that designed this one."

Benjie said, "Nomo, the way the economy's going now, we'll be lucky to even find work, much less get a hit."

"That's the way you see it," said Nomo. "Me, I'm positive and optimistic. How I look at it is somebody's gotta get a hit, so it might as well be me."

Chance reared back in his chair and twisted his head around to where he could see Nomo. "You young bloods can talk about hits until youre green in the face, but I'm here to tell you hits are few and far between. What you need to do is develop your art, your craft. Get your skills and act down and *maybe*, with a helluva lotta luck and the right connections, youll land some work."

"Aw, Chance," said Nomo, takin a big gulp of his drink like it was Sprite or ginger ale. "See, there you and Benjie go, jumpin off that same old supercautious bridge. You gotta think, Hey, I got what it takes. I'm star material. Things gonna work out my way."

"And what happens," said Chance, "after you up and get this so-called hit?"

"Invest the proceeds," said Nomo, "then go out and get me another hit."

Chance laughed way down in his throat and turned back to Danielle. He was probably a little got off with about me bein at the table now, so he had to split his actin time projectin to the both of us. "These youngsters," he said. "You cant tell em anything. I been in this business longer than both of em put together and still cant get em to see anything."

"M'sieur Franklin," said Danielle, "how long have you been in entertainment?"

"Long enough to know it's the pits—and you can call me Chance."

"The pits," said Danielle, turnin to me. "What is the pits?"

"He aint talkin about where the orchestra sits," said Nomo. "I can also tell you how long he's been around. When they built the first stage, Chance Franklin helped saw the boards and hold the hammer."

"M'sieur Franklin, ah, Chance—tell me why it is you seem so familiar? I feel as if I have known you for a long time, but I cannot understand why."

For no particular reason, my belly got to quakin when I saw Chance slip into his glory. I let out a laugh. I knew it was partly the champagne and partly the way Danielle was slumpin cross the table when she said this, lookin so deep and sincere until if I hadnt already known the answer to her question I mighta thought she was comin on to Chance.

As for Chance, the old goat picked his cue right up. He settled back and twiddled the corner of his thick mustache and said, "You know me from television."

"Television?" Danielle looked tickled.

"Yes, that car-pool announcement."

"I do not know zis car-pool announcement."

"Oh, yes, you do." Chance whipped a cellophane-wrapped cigar from his denim shirt pocket, clamped it between his teeth, and wiggled his eyebrows like Groucho Marx. "Quit being fuel-ish," he sang, "and acting the fool . . . Everything's cool in the motor pool."

"Aha!" said Danielle, springin from her chair. "I knew it, I knew it! I knew I knew you! You sing and play ze piano so lively —and on zat freeway with all zat traffique. Wondairful, wondairful!"

She shot to the fridge to drag out another Dom Perignon.

"I never did tell you," I said to Chance, "but I get a kick outta that spot too. It seems to be pretty popular."

"Well, you know," he said, "just tryna keep my hand in. I didnt make much up-front money since it was public service and all like that, but my agent used it to dredge up some other work."

"Like what?" I asked.

"Well," he began in a voice loud enough for everybody in the kitchen to hear, and anybody upstairs too. "Last month I shot one for the United Negro College Fund and—"

"A mind is a terrible thing to lose," Nomo broke in. "Isnt that the truth? I lost mine years ago."

Benjie said, "I believe the line is 'A mind is a terrible thing to waste.' "

"Either way," said Nomo, "my mind is gone, thank God."

"Thank God?" I said. "Is that anything to be thankful for?"

Nomo winked at me and said, "In this society it is. I feel sorry for anybody got some sense and tryna function over here in North America."

Just then Danielle popped open the other bottle. This time Nomo caught the cork as it sailed through the air.

"Good catch," said Benjie.

"I been tryna tell yall, you gotta go with the flow and stay in the know."

Danielle poured us all another round and said, "Here is to everyone getting ze most out of zis grand production, zis show we call life. Zat is my toast."

"And let me butter the toast," said Nomo, hoistin his glass. "Here's to everybody gettin the role they want."

"And what role do you want to play?" said Danielle.

"The comic role, mademoiselle. I want it said of Nomo Dudu that he's the funniest man in the western world. Not one of the funniest, but the funniest."

"Ah," said Danielle. "I should have known—a comedian."

"You guessed right. Got an audition comin up at the Comedy Store on Sunset Strip next Monday. Wish me luck."

"Are you ready for it?" I asked.

"Gettin there."

"You must be happy," I said.

"Happy as a sissy in a C.C. Camp."

"C'mon," said Chance. "You arent even old enough to know about the Depression and the Conservation Corps."

"Maybe not," said Nomo, "but you forget the Depression is back and these are conservative times, are they not? Depressin times, too."

"And you?" said Danielle, turnin to Benjie.

"Me?"

"Yes, what role do you choose in zis big production of life?"

Benjie stretched out his long arms and looked up at the ceilin. "I suppose what interests me most," he said, "would be scripting the show."

"I see," said Danielle, "a write-air. You would be ze write-air. You tell us what to do and say, but yes."

"Listen," said Nomo. "You know how you can tell the Polish starlet, dont you?"

"Polish starlet?" I said. "What on earth are you talkin about?" I was feelin bubbly and chucklin even before he'd hit the punch line.

Nomo knocked back half of his new drink in one swallow and said, "Yeah, you know, you can always tell the Polish starlet because she's the one that sleeps around with writers."

Danielle just about choked she was laughin so hard. "I get it, I get it!" she said. "Sleeps around with write-airs. Oh, zat is so cruel. Forgive me, Benjie, but it's so outrageous and true!"

Benjie didnt seem to mind bein the butt of Nomo's little joke, but I couldnt help noticin how he kept lookin at his watch and how antsy he was.

"Hey, Nomo," he said, "I have to pick Tree up by five if we're gonna have dinner and make that show. We better find out where to stash this trunk."

"Oh, yes," said Nomo, "the trunk, the trunk. What's in that doggone thing, anyway?"

"Not much," I said. "Burley was attached to it. I promised him I'd store it someplace where it would be safe. Mr. Chrysler said it'd be okay to leave it downstairs in the basement storage room."

"Which one?" said Danielle.

"The one off the screenin room," I told her.

"Here," she said, motionin to Benjie and Nomo, "I'll lead ze way. It can be tricky. Zere are four storage areas. Where is zis trunk?"

Nomo pointed and said, "Eet eez out zere on ze porch."

Danielle stopped dead in her tracks, got red in the face, and gave Nomo a look that'd freeze a polar bear. Chance looked at me and I looked at him and we both looked at Benjie who was grittin his teeth.

"Why you make fun of ze way I talk, eh?"

Nomo threw up his hands like he was askin for a truce. "I'm sorry, I'm sorry," he said, tryna smooth things over with a weak-eyed smirk. "Didnt mean anything by it. When I'm around anybody that talks a certain way, seems like I just pick it up after a while and start imitatin em. I cant help myself."

Chance got up outta his chair and walked over to Nomo. He reached for Nomo's head and grabbed a danglin rope of hair. "This just might turn out to be part of the problem," he said to the rest of us. "Now, if you were to unravel some of these knots in your hair, it just might loosen up your brain some."

"Ouch!" said Nomo. "Ease up, Chance. I already said I was sorry. I'm sorry, mademoiselle."

"*Madame*," said Danielle. "Madame Chryslair. I accept your apology, but I also understand ze motivations and impulse of a born mimique. You should study languages. Zey would be easy for you."

"Naw," said Chance, "he needs to learn English first."

And with that, Chance let go of Nomo and, as smooth as baby oil, dropped his arm around Danielle's shoulder. "Here," he said, "lead the way and we'll put that trunk in storage."

"It's all right, Chance," Benjie said, still fidgety. "We got it covered, me and Nomo. Sit down and enjoy the rest of your champagne."

With nobody left but me to play to, Chance quieted down and even tried to soothe me some.

"Your losin Burley like that," he said. "I know youll be a long time gettin over it."

"It's rough," I said. "I still feel rocky, like I'm walkin into quicksand or somethin. You catch what I mean?"

I took a big swallow from my glass and noticed how much it was startin to taste like soda pop. Bein around Chance always made me a little edgy. I couldnt help rememberin all those years we'd spent on the road when I was singin with his band. Oh, that man treated me so low-down, chasin after every floozie that would grin and blink her eyes at him! I had to give the devil his due, tho. Chance did get us to Hollywood, like he always said he would. Got us to Hollywood and straight into pictures. Not quite the way I thought it was gonna be, but the tune did change from "California, Here I Come" to "California, Here I Am." I finished up my second glass and Chance poured me another.

"Personally," he said, lookin at me sideways, "I was glad when you guys hooked up and settled down together. I think it was good for the both of you. Benjie got him a pretty good father; you got yourself a decent man that cared about you; and Burley—" He trailed off to pick up his glass and put it back down. "At least Burley got away from all them gangsters."

"Chance, I dont think I like it when you talk like that."

He sat straight up and stared me in the eye. "The part about the gangsters, that's what you dislike, isn't it? Just callin a spade a spade, Mamie. Face it, the feds have been after Frank Zaccharetti for years. Okay, so they finally nailed him on nickel-and-dime stuff. Income tax and some lightweight counterfeit charge, wasnt it? But that little eighteen months he got is just about up. They cant hold a slippery rascal like that, not for long. He's got too many connections. He's too powerful. Hell, he's too rich."

"Listen," I said, "Burley had nothin to do with any of that. All he did was travel and work for Zee's Cheese Products. He was strictly legit."

"Mamie, I never said Burley wasnt on the up-and-up."

"Then what *are* you sayin?"

"All I said was it's a good thing Burley got hold of a good woman like you and retired, that's all."

Then it got real quiet, so quiet we could hear Danielle and the guys still clompin around in the basement. I could hear her and Nomo laughin. The champagne was goin straight to my poor tired head, I knew, but it was too late now. I upended my glass again, studied how Chance was lookin at me now, and thought about how I use to could gobble down liquor, ice cubes and all.

"You still lookin good, Mamie," Chance said outta nowhere.

"What makes you say that?"

"Because it's true, that's why. You always were attractive and you always will be. Is it a crime to say so?"

"Oh, I dont know. That might depend on who's sayin it, I suppose."

"Well, I'm the one sayin it. You know, I'm a changed man now. I've had a little time to slow down and look back. I can take time out to smell the flowers now. I still feel bad about some of the things that went down, back when we were tryin to stay together."

"You think we ever tried all that hard?"

He looked away and made a clickin sound with his tongue. He still looked pretty good himself, for a man pushin sixty. Whoever his dentist was, he sure did do a first-rate job of outfittin Chance's mouth with a handsome set of choppers. He'd managed to keep his belly pretty flat too. And I was glad he'd quit dyein and conkin his hair and was lettin it grow out gray and dignified.

"All right," he said, "I know I didnt try as hard as I would if we were to start all over again. But you tried. You gave it all you had, didnt you?"

"Look, can we talk about somethin else?"

"I think about those days, Mamie, I actually do. I was proud, I was vain, I was cocky. Your mama use to call me a hog on ice."

"She called you a few other things too."

He smiled and went right on. "If I hadnt been so busy tryna

make this deal and make that deal, runnin from one gig to the
next, then maybe—"

"It wasnt only the gigs, Chance."

"All right, okay. I know I was wrong and hard to put up with.
I drank too much, I ran around, I didnt appreciate the good
thing I had, I—"

"What is this, a confessional? Chance Franklin, I am not a
priest. Please knock it off. That's all ancient history. That's like
talkin about what if Queen Isabella and King Ferdinand hadnt
ponied up the money for Columbus to stumble upon America.
It's too late now. Time to move on to somethin else. I was just
too dumb and green back in those days to be foolin around with
the likes of a travelin bandleader. But all that's like a dream now,
a bad dream I had back in the Dark Ages. I harbor no malice
against you. Quite frankly, I'm more interested in livin long
enough to see Benjamin thru and helpin get him on his feet."

Well, Chance stayed quiet for a minute and fiddled with the
cigar again. Finally, he took a sip of his drink and cleared his
throat. I thought I saw his eyes waterin up, but that mighta only
been my imagination.

"Benjie," he said, "he's really serious about this script-writin,
isnt he?"

"Serious as he can be. And talented too. He and Nomo got
somebody interested right now in doin one of his ideas for television. Speakin of which, werent you sayin somethin about doin
some more commercials?"

Chance's face lit back up. I knew I'd hit the right button. He
hadnt changed *that* much.

"Oh, yeah," he said. "I might land a little part in a thirty-
second spot for Pan Am."

"Pan Am? You mean the airline?"

"None other than," he said, beamin like a bulb. "You know
that guy that's been runnin around lookin like Bogart? Well,
they got him signed for this. He's hunched over the piano in a
white dinner jacket, holdin a drink, sayin, 'Play it again, Sam.'
But the kicker is, this couple flies a Pan Am jet to the real

Casablanca and pops into this joint and finds him there. You followin me?"

"Sure am," I said. "And guess who's at the piano, knockin out 'As Time Goes By,' right?"

Chance leaned across the table and touched my hand. "You got it, Mamie, you got it! Youre lookin right at him, the new Dooley Wilson."

"When did you shoot that?"

"Well, I havent yet. I only auditioned for it last week. Some people heard some of my old records on that nostalgia FM station after they saw the car-pool commercial. They figure I'd be a natural."

"So it isnt definite yet."

"Not yet, but I feel pretty good about it. Things are on the upswing again. What I'm tryna do now is find one of these hip, all-around white kids to team up with and make a new record. Somebody like, say, Ry Cooder or Scott Hamilton or maybe even—"

"You wastin your precious breath on me," I told him. "I never heard tell of either of them people. But it does sound like things're pickin up for you again."

"Isnt it peculiar how it goes?" he said. By now he had the champagne bottle in his hands and was peelin the edge of the wet label off with his thumbnail. "You roll along and roll along till you either run outta steam or luck. Then turn around and here the public comes lookin for you."

Chance always could make me laugh. I downed what I thought was gonna be my last glass and we both just sat there lookin dumb, listenin to Benjie and them clack back up the steps.

Suddenly Chance bent over and said real soft, "You told that boy the truth about his father yet?"

"I'm about to," I said. "Everything's comin right down to the wire."

"Well, dont let the wire catch fire."

I couldnt figure out what he meant by that. Besides, I was in no shape to figure out much of anything by the time Danielle jumped back up in my face and said, "Everybody, zey are ready for another round?"

# 11

That night, half looped, I soaked in a hot bath at the Chrysler house and thought about everything me and Danielle had talked about after the men'd gone. Nomo and Benjie had to make it to a rock concert at the Hollywood Bowl. Tree, Benjie's new girl-friend, was goin with em. I hadnt met her but, even so, somethin told me she was a real mess. That's just one of the problems with bein too sensitive to stuff you havent come face-to-face with yet.

Danielle, with her sweet self, had talked me outta tryna drive myself home. She thought I needed more time off work to get over Burley. The big idea she and Carleton had worked out was for me to spend a coupla weeks restin at their little beach house out in Malibu. I was game.

Layin back in her double-size tub with all them fancy suds bubblin up around my chin, I couldnt keep my mind off Chance rushin off to warm up for his gig at Crime and Punishment. Accordin to him—which you have to take with a few grains of salt—the place was fast gettin to be one of the hottest new spots on the Strip. I remembered seein a picture of the owner, too. Natasha Somethin-or-other. She wasnt bad-lookin for somebody with two teenage kids. In fact, her American husband had been a pretty close frienda Harry Silvertone's before they up and fell out over all those pitiful Palestinian refugees was massacred at that camp over there in Lebanon.

I tried to picture Chance playin his boogie-woogies and jump numbers and blues and "My Funny Valentine" and "The Look of Love" and "You Are the Sunshine of My Life" and "Where Is the Love?" and "Quiet Nights" and other bossa nova numbers at the Crime and Punishment, with that sloe-eyed Russian boss of his slinkin around in the background. Sometime I even wondered what life must look like from inside Chance Franklin's head. Like, how did he script and direct his own memory movie? Interestin man, but not for me. All the same, I coulda done without all that touchy-touch and mashin knees under the table he and Danielle'd been doin.

I wasnt crazy about bein in that huge house all by myself, but Mr. Chrysler was in Vegas on business, and late that afternoon Danielle got a call from this woman with a German name that makes pictures in Italy. I caught two or three of her things on videocassette once, and the one I remember best was about this high-tone society woman that gets stranded on a desert island with this no-class Communist. It was pretty good. Anyway, this woman, whatever her name was, invited Danielle out to this last-minute dinner party, and you know Danielle. She loves company.

After my bath my appetite started comin back. I went down and fixed me some scrambled eggs and English muffin with jam, one of my favorite meals anytime of day. Then I built a little fire in the guest bedroom I was stayin in and turned in early, tired to the marrow of my bones. I curled up in bed with a *National Geographic* and looked at some pictures of Russia and read a little bit about how crazy they are over there about cold boiled potatoes and all that vodka.

Mind you, it was the first time I ever had anything to do with a waterbed except make one up. You ever attempted to get comfortable enough to do any kinda serious readin in one of them things? Just when I was ready to get up and go look in Danielle's

medicine chest to see if she had any Dramamine, sleep started to
slip up on me. I was so woozy from the champagne and so tired
that all I did was snap off the readin lamp and stretch out under
the covers to look at the fire and the shapes and shadows it was
makin on the furniture and walls. Ah, it was so restful. Before I
knew it, I'd floated out clean and was gone bye-bye.

"What made you do it? What made you do that, Mamie?"
All in my sleep, look like, I kept hearin somebody talkin at me.
"Why, Mamie, why? I need to know why?"
The dream had its arms round my waist, huggin me from
behind. I was deep off into it and it wouldnt let go. Seem like I
was sittin by myself in a little boat tied up by the bank of some
creek back home in Mississippi. Just a-sittin and a-rockin, like
that song goes I use to sing with Chance's band. Just me in this
boat with a light breeze blowin all around and the sunshine
comin and goin the way sunshine'll do right before a squall
comes up. Felt like I was maybe thirty-some years younger, wigglin and wagglin, out there in that boat, waitin on somethin, but
I couldnt tell you what.
And there's trees lined up all along the creek bank. At one
point it got to be so vivid and *with* me until I catch myself gettin
this glad-all-over feelin when I look up at the leaves real close
and study the way the sun is hittin em. See, the light wasnt
exactly hittin em when you stopped and studied it. The sun just
kinda traveled out to where the leaf was and shimmered all
around it; then the leaf sends out this invisible feeler, like a
message ray or somethin, and suck up the light around it, drink it
up, sip on it like you would a glassa buttermilk.
Had me hypnotized. Leaves would warm up and glow; then
they would cool down and darken. They looked like tiny jewels
flashin off and on, all the time swishin and whisperin to me,
sayin, "Mamie, why? Mamie, why?" over and over.
Then the rustlin died down and the trees go away—at least
that's what I remember it felt like. And when I look down I see
the boat's gone too, even tho I could still feel myself bein rocked

and swayed, swayed and rocked, to and fro. Now there's no boat, no creek bank, no creek. Only me and this ebb and flow, with the sun playin tricks on my skin, except for that chill from the breeze, from deep inside the icewater breeze. It wouldnt quit mutterin and carryin on.

Next thing, *snap!* From outta somewhere came this real loud pop, supersonic loud. So loud you couldnt even hear it. You felt it rattlin the bones down under your nerves; your blood bubbled. It woke me up. I sat up on that wobbly water-filled mattress just in time to catch my breath and rub the sleep out my eyes.

I took time starin all around the bedroom, checkin out everything in the dark. The fire'd done burnt down mostly to reddish-orange embers, the color of the sun in the dream just before the trees stood still. The room was fulla that sweet, woodsy fireplace smell. A softer version of that *pop!* hit the insides of my ear and I had to laugh. I realized it was the burnin coals that'd caused that noise. That's when it all fell in place. All I'd been doin was dreamin on a doggone waterbed. I wanted to float back up the dream chimney like tender smoke and sun in that boat a little longer.

Just when I'd got halfway cozy and toasty again and was on the verge of dozin back off, that voice came rubbin up against my ears again—only this time it didnt sound like it was comin from way off in no distance.

"Mamie, I have to talk to you. Dont be afraid. Please, it's me; it's only me."

One second before, I'd been warm and comfy under that big, soft comforter fluffed up with down feathers from more Red Chinese geese than I could count sheep. And now here I was feelin like somebody'd just opened the door to some giant refrigerator. The whole bedroom was gettin blasted with icy polar-bear air. I actually broke out shiverin.

This time I decided not to sit up, not right away, not just yet. I kept the comforter pulled up over me and raised my head. I twisted it around just enough to see if the readin lamp was still there.

I clicked on the light and *boom-boom-BOOM!, boom-boom-BOOM!* My heart was poundin up against my chest like it was some prizefighter's fist I had balled up inside me that was tryin to punch its way thru, tryin its best to bust out.

Then I saw it. I saw it with my own eyes; yet I still didnt wanna believe it. I mean, hearin things and seein things is nothin new to me but, I must confess, what I saw standin there at the foot of the bed that night was too dramatic for even a low-keyed psychic like me. I like things kept on the quiet side, you know, toned down. Never did go in for dime-store magic or any of that flashy stuff, special effects.

But if, as they say, seein is believin, then I had to buy it. I didnt have any choice but to go for it because the thing was right there in front of me and it didnt seem to matter how much I shuddered and blinked and swallowed and hoped it would go away. Whatever it was, it was glimmerin sure enough, sort of lightin up and dimmin and then comin on real shiny again like my dream leaves I'd just woke up from. It kept flickerin like this at first, gettin on my nerves.

Finally I got up the courage to sit back up in bed and reach for the Bible I knew was in the bed-lamp table drawer. I held the good book up in fronta that thing the same as you'd hold a cross in front of a vampire. I did it real slow and, with all the strength still left in me, I concentrated on shootin out beams of white light and godly thoughts all around me. You can do that, you know, if you practice it right. I shut my eyes as tight as I could while my light was generatin, and I asked the Lord to forgive me for all the sinnin I'd already done, all the sinnin I was doin right now, and all the sinnin I was probably gonna do.

When I opened my eyes, the only thing that'd changed was I could see the image in fronta me real sharp; it was a whole lot clearer than it'd been before. It was like I'd done somethin to make it solidify. Jesus, I was scared!

"Wh-what's goin on?" I shouted.

"Mamie," it said, callin my name again in that faraway voice. "Mamie, dont you see what youre doin to me?"

"What I'm doin to you! Who are you? What are you? And what in the world are you doin here?"

"All right, then," he said, "I'll make you a promise. I wont harm you. I *cant* harm you. Watch . . ."

I'll be doggoned if that thing didnt move up alongside the bed to where I was layin and reach out its hand and place it on my jaw. Well, anyway, I thought it was a hand and I thought it was my jaw, but somehow there really wasnt no connection. At least I didnt feel anything. The only way I can explain it would be to say it was quite a bit like bein touched by light from a movie projector. And when you got right down to it, the whole experience was somethin like bein in a theater that's set up to show off some newfangled, fancy, overwhelmin technical advance in motion pictures. Like, imagine a system that's more realistic than Cinerama, 3-D, Magnavision, Wide Screen or Dolby Stereo or Quadraphonic Sound. It was like somebody'd figured out how to get the characters and actors to walk straight off the screen and down the aisle right up into your face.

I mean, it didnt matter that you couldnt technically feel em when they touched you; the sheer ingenuity of it was what blew you outta your seat!

*O Lord,* I prayed, *be gentle with me. I know I have never been normal in anybody's eyes. I know I was born both blessed and cursed. But, Lord, if I am finally losin my mind, then please dont let me drop and shatter like a fragile plate. Just let me nut out gradually; let it happen by degrees . . .*

Never once did I take my eyes off the figure in fronta me. I took a gang of deep breaths, tho. The deeper I breathed, the more my heart slowed down and the sharper the image beside me got. Oh, I tell you it was frightenin! But all the same, it was flat outta one of those worlds I'd always managed—in my lucid, message-gettin moments—to keep a coupla toes in, if not a whole foot.

My heart slowed down.

I blinked again and focused my eyes, tuned my ears.

This tight blur of light moved to the foot of the bed. And

that's when I saw who it sure enough resembled. It resembled, it favored, it looked like—well, it was Burley Cole. Yes, Burley himself, and he was comin thru bright and clear, every bit as clear as if he was bein broadcast live and direct over some local cable hookup. The only difference was he look to me to be as big as life. No, he wasnt exactly wall-to-wall and treetop-tall, but what there was of him seemed for real. Burley was real enough to me then to needle me into wonderin somethin: How come I'd never felt about any of the other men I'd lived with—includin my only official husband—like I did about him?

I gulped again when he lit down on the edge of the waterbed —which he couldnt make rock—and looked right at me. "Say, Mamie, what was wrong with that king-size mattress I went to all that trouble to set up at our place? I went back to the house to contact you, and now here you turn up in some strange white folks' bed!"

Now that I was beginnin to get use to how the stuff worked, I wanted to crawl over and hug Burley with all my might, but I couldn't. I was still havin trouble even breathin.

# 12

I was scared to look too close at what was happenin and scared to blink. Either way I thought the hallucination I was havin might break down and disappear. So I stayed put while Burley ranted on.

"You know, it aint the easiest thing in the world to find somebody when theyre not home."

"B-but I thought ghosts—I mean, uh, I thought spirits was suppose to be able to go anywhere at all."

"As usual, you arent listenin to me, Mamie. I didnt say anything about going places, did I?"

"You said it was hard to find me because I was up here in Beverly Hills insteada down there in Santa Monica."

"Well, yeah, and it's a trick to it I havent quite got the hang of yet."

"A trick to *what*, Burley? I'm not followin you."

"It's a trick to pickin up on people wherever they are, especially people you know. See, youre suppose to be able to run thru here and check on old So-and-So and see how he's been doin. I'm just now startin to kinda learn how you do that, but it's gonna take a lotta hard work."

Tears was tryna boil up in my eyes. I had to will em away. I felt like I was back in the fourth grade and Miz Rucker was askin me to name the capital of Iceland. My mouth'd fall open and nothin would come out because I couldnt even think of the name of the place, much less pronounce it.

Finally I did manage to say, "I know this might sound peculiar, Burley, but there's somethin I just gotta ask."

"Aint nothin peculiar to me anymore, honey."

"I can believe it! But tell me, and please dont think I'm makin fun, but—exactly where are you?"

"Where am I?" Burley looked perplexed.

"Yes, where are you now? Like, where are you comin from just now? You said there was this trick about findin people, and stuff. Now, where do you be comin from in the first place when you set out to locate somebody out—out—well, out here where I am?"

Burley fell on his back and started rollin and laughin all over the bed, which still didnt wobble. It wobbled when I moved, but not for Burley. He laughed so hard and so long I got concerned about Danielle comin back from her dinner party and hearin us up there carryin on like that. I was so glad to have him back, sort of, until worryin over somethin as triflin as that seemed kinda sick under the circumstances. At least I wasnt about to risk scarin him off by askin him to pipe down.

"Mamie," he said, gettin control of himself, "that's the funniest thing I've heard in a long time."

"Well, I'm glad I can still cheer you up."

"No, you dont understand. I spent all that time over there on Earth worried about dyin and worried about people I cared about that died. That's one of the things I wanted to talk with you about."

I couldnt say anything. It was like my throat'd froze up.

"I can see you still terrified of me," he went on. "I been tryna prove to you I cant do you no harm. Look, I was the one always doubtin all that spooky talk, and you were the one suppose to believe in it. Always gettin messages from people that'd passed on, and tellin folks's futures and readin they minds. Now here I am tellin you to relax, that dyin aint no real big thing, and you backin off from me like I'm some kinda skid-row thug."

That still didnt help. I panicked. What if I never got my voice back? What if I had to lay there in that guest-room bed forever, paralyzed like some invalid? What if anybody else popped in and saw the way I was lookin right then?

"Here," said Burley, "I'll try it again."

"Try what?"

"This . . ." He curled right up next to me on the same side of the bed he woulda normally been sleepin on if he was alive. All this light was swarmin all over the covers and me. Burley wrapped his glowin arms around me and pushed his shiny face up alongside mine. Still, I couldnt feel anything except a new sorta tinglin warmth that started someplace down around my lower intestine and fluttered on up to just above my belly, to my solar plexus. That's about the closest I come to touchin the man, the spirit, whatever he was. Now, when I closed my eyes—which I did automatically when Burley took me in his arms—I felt like I could feel his body heat movin into mine. The longer he held me, the stronger that feelin got. But, I dont know, it's hard to talk about, and I already knew there wouldnt be too many people I was gonna be able to tell any of this to.

But he got me to cool down some by doin that. He sat up in bed and leaned on one elbow, the way he use to would do before his health got rotten. I looked into his face and for the first time noticed he was younger-lookin than I'd ever known him to be, even younger than that night we met at Harrah's. I was more confused than ever. Did I dare open my mouth again to see if anything would come out? Mother Dear woulda said, "A dog that'll *carry* a bone will *bring* you one."

"Well," I said. "Can you answer my question?"

"Baby, that's what's so funny about it. I havent gone any-where."

"Huh?"

"I aint gone no place! I'm still right here. It's kinda like I

moved next door. But, see, there's this partition, not a real partition that you can bump up against or anything, but some sorta
time wall. That's all I know to call it. We're in different worlds."

"I'll say!"

"No, I'm on a whole different time than you."

"You mean, like Daylight Savins or something like that?"

"Youre way off there. I have to slip over here to see how much
time in Earth hours done gone by. I'm still not comfortable. It's
like I been floatin around in this limbo since I got here. There's
voices that keep callin to me, tellin me I got to move on, tellin
me I aint reached my destination yet."

"Do they have wings and fly around pluckin on harps?"

"I havent seen no angels yet. I did see you, tho."

"Where? When?"

"That afternoon I, uh, died. I was sorry it had to be on your
birthday."

"Well, under the circumstances, I never held it against you."

"It was like this hole opened up in the middle of my forehead
and light started pourin into it, light that ran clean thru my head
to the backa my head, the part where the neck connect with the
skull. Light was blowin around thru there and somethin said,
'Here you go, Burley Cole. Jump in and make your getaway. Just
jump right into that stream of light and it'll take you on out real
clean and natural.' I did what the voice told me and pretty soon
there I was movin up that tunnel, lookin back at what I was
leavin behind."

"Wh-what did you see, Burley? How'd it feel?"

"It felt like a relief, but I felt so bad. I wanted you to know I
wasnt in no pain, that you shouldnt cry over me. But when I
looked back and saw my body laid out there on the couch and
you pressin my eyes shut with your fingers and cryin and cryin
and sayin, 'Thou preparest a table before me in the presence of
mine enemies,' I was movin out in a hurry; floatin all up around
the ceilin, pushin on thru, tootin on the roof, blowin on out thru
the rain and up above the rain into the light that was so bright I
couldnt hardly stand it. Then I forced myself to come back down

for another look. You were huggin on this man in a trench coat and still cryin, cryin, cryin, and moanin."

"I—I didnt want you to go," I said, no longer able to will back the tears. They were inchin down my cheeks now. "I want you to be back here—with me—with me and Benjie. Since youve been away it's been like a train station that's been shut down."

"A train station?"

"Dont know why I said that. It's like a place that use to be warm and busy and friendly and useful and purposeful, and all like that. Now it's just a place where I go to get some rest and air out my sad thoughts."

"I know," he said.

"You do?"

"Sure, I watched you for the first few days."

"You mean, there at the house?"

"Uh-huh. Watched you mopin around and pickin over our stuff and callin everybody, and receivin visitors."

I turned around. "You saw all that and you didnt say anything?"

"Like, what was I supposed to say?"

"Oh, I dont know—anything. The kinda stuff youre sayin now, I guess."

"Sugar, I was as sad as you were."

"But why?"

"Because you were so busted up and heartbroken. Dont you know how much it hurts when you hurt somebody you love deep down? Besides, I hadnt gotten my moves together yet. I didnt really know how to do anything except hang around and look."

I tried to touch Burley's face and kiss him, but about the best I could do was smooth the light where the image of his face was pulsatin and then kiss at the spot where his beautiful mouth seemed to be. I squeezed my eyes shut, partly to make the tears quit fallin and also to see if the kissin and touchin felt realer, like it had a few moments ago. It did. Tell you, right then and there I wouldna minded goin blind if it'd meant bein next to Burley again and feelin his presence all the time.

"So," I asked, "what do you do all day?"

"I cant answer that."

"How come?"

"There arent any days."

"Just one long night, huh?"

"No, Mamie, that's the part I dont understand yet. I thought
I'd be seein a lotta other people I knew—my mother and father,
Ruthie my sister, my grandmother Josie, and all the buddies who
got away before me, and them I lost in the war. I aint seen none
of em!"

"You sure youre in the right place?"

"What you mean by that?"

"I mean, everybody else coulda gone one place and you went
to another. It must happen all the time, dont you think?"

"Well, I thought about that too. I never was exactly what
you'd call retarded, you understand. There's no days, no nights; I
dont need sleep and rest and even tho I look out there and see
food I want and stuff I'd like to drink, I find I can get along well
and good without it. But I dont feel right. I'm lonely, so lonely
you couldnt even grasp it. It's a loneliness like I'm the only one
in this world where I live, the only one on this planet or whatever it is—this space, I guess."

"Burley, that's hard to believe. You mean you havent run into
a soul out there you can talk with?"

"Well, that's another thing I needed to ask you. You been
foolin around with this kinda hocus-pocus ever since I've known
you. Cant you try your powers and get me in touch with somebody out here I can relate to?"

"Oh, sweetheart!" I couldnt help myself. I started cryin again.
"I cant believe this is happenin to you. Of course I'll send out
some feelers, be happy to find out whatever I can. But I'm all
mixed up. I mean, there you are dead and here I am livin—
theoretically speakin, anyway—and youre comin to me to help
you find out where all the other dead people went."

"That's right," Burley said, his belly startin to tremble again.
Sure enough, he went into another one of them unbelievable

laughin fits. Got me to laughin, too. "That's right," he said again and again. "Crazy, aint it? I mean, it doesnt make any type of sense, does it? I cant figure it out to save my life!"

"Have you *heard* anybody, Burley? You said somethin about voices a little while back. What kinda voices?"

"Dont know yet. It's like it's either somebody or somebodies in behind me all the time. They keep comin at me and I keep sidesteppin em."

"Why?"

"So I can come back here and see what *you* doin."

"Did you go to the funeral?"

"Thought it was one of the pitifulest, most movin things I ever sat still for in my life. It was a beautiful service, Mamie. And everybody was so real when they stopped at the casket and bent over to take a last look at me or say somethin. And you wouldnt believe some of the things I heard people sayin."

"Like what?" I was laughin so hard now I didnt wanna stop.

"Like, well, Miz Wheelock, she leaned close in over the body and whispered, 'Dont worry, Burley. Every night when I say my prayers I'll sum up what's been goin on in the soaps so you can keep up.'"

"She actually said that? I dont believe it!"

Burley sat up and held his hand like a Boy Scout. "Said it just as sure as I'm livin."

"Sweetie, I wouldnt place no big bets on it. But it would be just like Miz Wheelock to be runnin her mouth about *General Hospital* and you layin up there dead."

"How long you plan to hang around here, Mamie?"

"Here in the flesh?"

"Nah, round here in Beverly Hills."

"Oh, just until . . ." My train of thought went to gettin away from me. Burley was fadin on me. It was like the light shimmerin round his edges was goin outta focus, and all that pulsatin was slowin way down. "Burley, what's goin on? It's like I'm losin you."

"Dont worry," he said, his voice droppin some. "It's one of

them, uh, I guess you call em spirits. That man is botherin me again."

"What man?"

"Funny-lookin man. Dont ask me who it is. Ever since I got in this condition, he's been one of the ones tryna hem me up and drag me off."

"Well, then, why dont you listen to the man and find out what he's tryna tell you. It might be important."

"Baby," Burley said, soundin all sad, "I aint ready to travel no place yet. I like it around here."

Suddenly all I could cling to was Burley's voice, which was gettin harder to make out. The resta him had evaporated. The only light in the room now was the little bit that flickered from the fireplace. And pretty soon the cracklin noise from the burnin embers even drowned out his whispers more and more until it was as if none of what I'd seen and heard had ever taken place.

Had I only been dreamin deeper than usual, or what?

You tell me.

# 13

By the time I got woke up good and washed and dressed and served Carleton and Danielle Chrysler their breakfast, the memory of what'd happened up in the bedroom that night came curlin up around me full strength like ropes of smoke bindin me to a cross. It was the doggonedest feelin I'd ever had. Breakin into other levels of seein things wasnt new to me, but holdin a drawn-out conversation with a ghost was. Anybody can have visions of spirits and things to come if they quiet down and go beyond their everyday thoughts. We all got that ability, even tho most people dont bother usin it or developin it. But to talk with the dead and argue with the dead and laugh with the dead— well, that's a whole other ballgame, and what I was havin trouble believin was that I'd actually arrived at the point where I could handle it a little bit. I felt kinda like I was movin from the minor leagues into the majors at lightnin speed. Sure, it scared me some, yet I knew somehow I was turnin a corner and a whole new chapter was startin in whatever was left of my life.

I looked at Mr. and Miz Chrysler while I was pourin coffee, and I listened to them arguin over stocks and bonds and investments and Dow-Jones this and money market that. Mr. Chrysler was even sayin how he was thinkin about drawin some of their money outta Switzerland and movin it down to Spain because the Swiss was gettin so fulla holes they'd leak out information to the Internal Revenue over here. And I was rememberin Burley and all that junk at our house and thinkin, *Well, once you leave this Earth is it gonna matter one bit that you spent all your time stackin up assets and wheelin and dealin?*

"Mamie," said Danielle, "you slept well, yes? You look a little angelique today."

"I do?"

"But of course. No more hangover. You dreamed it all away in ze night?"

"I feel much better, Danielle, thank you."

Mr. Chrysler had a gleam in his eye. "Mamie," he said, "what do you think about the gardener?"

"The gardener? I think Rodrigo and his guys have been doin a pretty fair job. Why?"

"Oh, Danielle and I are interviewing. A lot of our friends are switching over now from Mexicans to Japanese."

"Why's that, Mr. Chrysler?"

"Because," said Danielle, "zey are cheapaire and do excellent work."

"I was over at Harry Silvertone's the other day," Mr. Chrysler said, "and I couldn't help but admire how much neater and crisper than ours his grounds looked. We talked about it. Harry agreed that the Japanese seem to have a genius when it comes to gardening, and they're so industrious. No weeds, no neglected plants, and not a drop of wasted time or effort. He doesn't have to supervise his gardeners the way I do Rodrigo; they know what there is to be done and they do it beautifully."

"You saw Mr. Silvertone?" I said.

"Sure, he's just back from Japan where he's been putting together a combination movie-TV package that threatens to set the whole industry on its ear. That Silvertone, I'll tell you, he and the Japanese have a thing or two in common. Their genius for packaging, for one thing."

"Yes," said Danielle, "but he cannot make zese cars and elec-troniques like ze Japanese."

"Not to worry," Mr. Chrysler said. "He's still a brilliant pres-ence in our business. We all owe Harry a thing or two."

*And Harry Silvertone owes me a thing or two,* I was thinkin, but all I said was, "I happen to like Rodrigo, and I think we should give him a chance."

"You know how I trust your gut feelings in these delicate matters, Mamie. That goes for Danielle as well."

"Then, with your permission, Mr. Chrysler, I'd like to speak with Rodrigo, tell him the score, and maybe get him to under-stand that youre thinkin about bringin in a new set of groundkeepers. Isnt that fair enough?"

"Fair and square. Danielle, you agree?"

"Let Mamie take care of it, yes."

All along I kept kinda lookin around for Burley to pop back up. If ghosts could mow grass, I sure wouldnt waste no time gettin him back out there to do ours. Here the Chryslers was worried about that Yosemite Park of a yard of theirs, and all I could think about was how the weeds and crabgrass was takin over my little puny yard at home. Maybe I could strike up some kinda deal with Rodrigo and his staff.

"And, Mamie," Mr. Chrysler said outta the blue. "It might interest you to know that Harry and I have worked out all but the fine details of a deal that might very well result in a box-office smash."

"How's that, sir?"

"Remember Fifi?—Fiona Prince, the comedian?"

"Oh, yes. How could I ever forget her?"

"Well, we're thinking of pairing her up with Nixxy Privates in a far-out comedy that'll have us walking up the aisles when we clean up at the Academy Awards."

"Oh," I said, "what's the picture gonna be about?"

"Ahem, that's one of the fine details we've yet to resolve, but never you fret. Just the idea of getting the two of them together should be enough to get the bankers all hot and bothered, don't you think?"

"Ah, zees Fifi," said Danielle, "she is sooo neurotique. It is nothing of my business, but—"

"No, no!" Mr. Chrysler insisted. "It's perfect, perfect! Now all we have to do is find the right writer, get a funny-as-hell script, a hot supporting cast, and we're home free, *free!* We think it's the most bankable idea since *Gone With the Wind.*"

"Well," I said, "I wish you luck."

"There's luck and there's bucks," he said, "and with your generous blessings, Mamie, Harry and I will have both. Oh, it's bound to put TCO right up there with the best of them!"

And that's the picture business for you—the only business I know of where you can raise more big money countin your chickens before they hatch than you can after they done got thru layin eggs. Someplace off in the backa my shook-up mind, I thought I could see Burley Cole yankin on his Adam's apple and nudgin me with his bony elbow, goin, "And I thought the cheese business was fulla holes and rats!"

"Mamie," Mr. Chrysler said, "you go ahead and speak to Rodrigo and report back to me when you get a chance. If he and his gang can shape up, fine. If not, I intend to bring the Japanese in. These are hard times, you know. We're going to have to start trimming the fat and cutting back around this household."

I looked at Danielle. She was gigglin. "Does zat mean you are going on another diet, Carleton?"

She might not've been the only one thought it was funny, but she was the only one laughed. Me, I had sense enough to hold back mine until I'd carried their plates back into the kitchen.

It wasnt long after that I got another one of those snippy little lyin letters from Harry Silvertone himself sayin he had to see me right away, and would I come to his office after hours over in Celluloid City. That was on a Saturday mornin when I picked up my mail at the post office. That very afternoon, while I was on the phone to this high-class junk man, tryna to work some kinda transaction whereby he would come out and haul some of the junk away from the house, who should turn up at my door but Charlean Jackson all gussied up and talkin a mile a minute. Motor Mouth, Burley use to call her.

"Girl, why dont you come shoppin with me? It's been forever, look like, since we got together and gossiped."

I told her okay, and off we went, lookin crazy in our blue jeans and boots. For some reason, I was feelin pretty good that day, kinda like I was ready for anything to come down. Whatever it was, I could handle it. It's days like that, you know, when you feel your health is bouncin back, even tho privately I knew I'd better get to a doctor soon and line up a check-up for myself.

"Hey, Charlean," I said as we were headin into the Hollywood Ranch Market. "Stand back a second so I can read what that T-shirt you got on say." It vexes me to see people wearin these doggone T-shirts with messages all over em, and sometime the message is so long you have to stop and concentrate to take it all in. I dont wear em myself, but I know plenty women that do, and get paranoid and antsy when some men go to starin at their peaches too hard.

But Charlean never was shy about much of anything. Right away she flung open the lapels of her denim jacket and thrust her heavy chest right out at me. Spelled out in white across her dark blue T-shirt was:

> The Brain—is wider than the Sky—
> For—put them side by side—
> The one the other will contain
> With ease—and You—beside—
>
> —Emily Dickinson

Charlean started radiatin—oh, I could see the light around her face gettin shinier—and she said, "How you like it?"

"Well," I said, "it is a little on the deep side. Where'd you get it?"

"Believe it or not, Nixxy himself gave me this shirt for a present last week. He's big on T-shirts. At first I wasnt gonna wear it, but then I turned around and said why not? You see all these youngsters sloppin round in em, some of em not even sure what it is they broadcastin."

"So who's Emily Dickinson?"

"Oh, she was one strange white lady. I did some readin up on her, and I do mean *strange*! Wrote all these poems and things and didnt believe in publishin nothin. After she died they went rummagin thru her stuff and come up with close to two thousand of these things she'd jotted down. She wasnt much for goin places or doin stuff. Didnt even, to my knowledge, have a boyfriend. Just laid up there in the family house and got her own kinda religion and took notes. I'm gettin to be one of her biggest fans. You know, Mamie, if I had it to do all over again, I believe I might opt for layin up someplace and takin it real slow."

"I know what you mean, I think."

"Now, where you wanna start?"

"Start what?"

"Shoppin."

"You sound as if you have an itinerary. I thought we were just gonna do somethin simple." You made out like we were just gonna grocery shop here at the Hollywood Ranch Market."

"Well, yeah, and I'll carry the groceries back to the house and then we can whip on over to Baldwin Hills."

"What's at Baldwin Hills?"

"More stores, dummy! Mamie, dont you feel in the mood to just let go a little? You got to do it, girl! You been grievin over Burley much too long now."

"Maybe not as much as you think."

"Oh?"

I jerked loose a coupla carts for us and off we went to the Land of Oz. Hollywood Ranch Market is still Oz to me after all these years, even tho it's done got way too much publicity and, like everything else, it's on the way down. But what I still like about it is you never know who you liable to run into while you roamin the aisles. One night, after I first got to California, I rolled my shoppin cart smack into Veronica Lake's. Now, I know that's nothin special since there's people all over New York, where she lives, that see her all the time. But she just happened to be visitin L.A. that week and, I swear, we ended up sittin down havin some late-night doughnuts and a coupla coffees.

"Veronica," I told her, "you and Fredric March and Susan Hayward and them outdid yourselves in *I Married a Witch*."

"Oh, you liked it, did you?"

"Hey, I know theyre on the verge of parlayin that flick into a TV series and all, but I wanted you to know you were tops."

"René Clair has to take some of the credit. He's some kind of director."

"And youre some actress. Would you sign my napkin?"

"Certainly, be delighted."

I would linger over incidents like that for weeks and weeks in the early days, but as time rolled by I found myself runnin into so many famous people—or, like that no-singin Bob Dylan use to put it—people that was famous long ago. Braggin is definitely not my style, but if I was to draw up a list of people I've run into grocery shoppin down there thru the years you'd find me mentionin people like Sonny Tufts, Mario Lanza, Doodles Weaver, Joan Blondell, Linda Ronstadt (with her hair up in curlers tied over with a scarf), Eddie Fisher, Steve Allen, Scatman Crothers, Slim Gaillard, Shelley Winters, Frank Lovejoy, Brian Donleavy, Betty Grable, Rhonda Fleming, Cyd Charisse, Arlene Dahl, Frank Zappa, Aldo Ray, Dorothy McGuire, Linda Darnell, Melvyn Douglas, Marlo Thomas, Lee Van Cleef, Walter Slezak, Sterling Hayden, Diana Rigg, and I could go on and on. Sometime they'd be strollin around the market, got shades on or some old funny hat that's suppose to be a disguise, yet you could see right off how they were tryna *act* like they didnt wanna be recognized, sort of, when in fact they wanted you to know they thought they was somebody.

"Charlean," I said finally, "are you shoppin for yourself or for Nixxy?"

"Both."

"All right, let's grocery shop and get that over with. Then I can decide if I can afford to put in any more time."

"What's the matter, Mamie? You got a date?"

"Benjie and his girlfriend say theyre takin me out."

"Where?"

"They havent told me yet."

"Then why dont the three of yall have dinner at the house?"

"Which house?"

"The big house—at Nixxy's. He's back east on a publicity tour. You know about that remake theyre doin of *Birth of a Nation,* dont you?"

"Read all about it in *People* magazine."

We got behind our carts and off we pushed, moseyin up and down the supermarket aisles like chumps and sleepwalkers. Charlean had quite a long list and, for some reason, insisted on lettin me know how she felt about every item and product she checked off. After twenty minutes my feet was killin me. I needed to sit down. Never have been crazy about shoppin. The Chryslers leave me in charge of stockin their kitchen and bar, plus I also take care of the bathroom supplies and general cleanin stuff. But the way it works is different from what poor Charlean gotta go thru. I draw up my list and phone it in to the Ariola Brothers Market and then Vic or Lou bag and box it all up for us real nice. All I have to do is drive down and let them load the car. I'm not much for this physical involvement, where you literally stand up there readin and analyzin all the data and lies they print on cans and bottles and packages. But Charlean, seem like she took pride in the savvy she'd built up over the years. She was what you call a sharp, attentive shopper, somethin like Mother Dear.

"You remember Johnnie Mae Keyes and her husband Fletcher?" she said. "I introduced em to you and Burley back in 1972 at the Hollywood Fundraisin Benefit for SNCC, back when Negroes was halfway still in style. Well, Will Frisbee just fired the both of em. Found out they was shoppin double on him."

"How's that?"

"You know . . . everything they was buyin for him, they'd turn around and buy one for themselves. It was embarrassin for everybody. Will's wife—she does the bills—finally figured it out and that's all it took to set their asses in orbit. Isnt it amazin how smart people can set themselves up so stupid?"

"Nope. You forget. The smarter you are, the harder you smart when you fall."

"Now, that's pretty good, Mamie. See, I can drop a line like that on Nixxy and, next thing you know, he'll be usin it in his act."

"Is he like that?"

"Lemme tell you, theyre all like that. Nixxy'll be sittin up shootin the breeze with me and laughin over things I say, and then turn around and steal whole stories and sayins and paste em right in his shows. But I'm gonna fix him."

"How?"

"You'll see. I got an idea that's only halfway worked out, but once I get it straight I'll pop it on you and see what you think . . . Hey, check this out—frozen toasted cheese sandwiches! Now, how decadent can you get?"

"Listen, they got peanut butter and jelly put up in the same jar."

"I know, they been done had that out. But if a fool cant melt some cheese on a slice of bread, then what can he do? Honest to Pete, next they'll be packagin up frozen ice water."

"Hmm," said Charlean, scannin the label on the Frozen Toastie package. "Listen at what all they put in here to hold this thing together—"

"Sorry, Charlean, but I'm gettin hungry. Let's finish up and go grab a bite someplace."

"I know just the place," she said.

*   *   *

We ended up at this little croissant joint on La Cienaga called the Railroad Croissant. Somebody musta been impressed with that café on Sunset that's actually set up in an old train coach, so they went and did the same thing, except with croissants as the draw.

"Do you think theyll ever quit?" I asked, sippin my coffee.

"Quit what, honey?"

"Runnin a good thing into the ground. I mean, the croissant's a tasty little invention, but who needs all this?"

"Girl," said Charlean, "I get so sicka these theme deals I dont know what to do. Take the chocolate-chip cookie. Nice, right? I use to bake a whole gang of em myself—and could put em away too—and it wasnt no real big deal. But Famous Amos came along with his high-price cookies; then all the copycats moved into that market. So now you cant even get a halfway decent chocolate-chip cookie for under fifty, sixty cents."

"That's what I mean. They get a choke hold on any kinda idea and do it to death. It's nice to see a Negro make a little money, tho, isnt it?"

"I reckon. Say, Mamie, when that boy finally drags his behind back over here, tell him I'm havin the plain with a bowl of split pea. I gotta hobble to the ladies' room."

The minute Charlean ducked out, the young man popped up at the table, ready to take our orders. Oh, lemme tell you, he was a cutie! Looked enough like Lionel Ritchie to make me do a double-take. It's odd, but I hadnt checked him out too close the first time when he brought our menus. I was too busy runnin my mouth with Charlean. But now I slowed down and taken a good look. He was trim and brown skin and smooth-lookin, with a squeezable behind, and he had a twinkle in his eye that was devilish and mannish, both. He looked to be around twenty-two and, Lord help me, the child was activatin somethin locked up way down inside me that hadnt been activated in quite that way since I dont know when. A warm quiverin started spreadin in my belly, then shimmered on up along my spine. I tried to keep the waiter from seein how I was reactin to him, but these young men, oh, these young men! I haven't run into one yet that was good-lookin and didnt know it. And I could tell right off he wasnt gay or one of those switch-hitters passin for hetero. L.A. is fulla them types—ready to go either way, dependin on who's handin out the money, or who's drivin the Jaguar. Altho, come to think about it, Jaguars dont be cuttin much ice the way they use to; it's too many common people sportin em now. But I could tell this youngster wasnt your common L.A. prettyboy; he was the real thing, the genuine article—a young man who just naturally lit up when he entered the presence of a real woman.

Please dont ask what came over me. I cant rightfully say. It wasnt just lustful-heartedness. I know. Because there was somethin about the light in his eyes that drew out some of the higher instincts in me. For maybe a flash of a second, I could read way deep up into him. And there was somethin shinin there, a little lit-up passageway that was like a corridor you could walk down that didnt come to a stop. And along this corridor was rows and rows of doors waitin to be knocked on. I could tell he was lookin for somethin you couldnt buy or negotiate, and he needed it so bad it was pullin him a touch over to the daffy side. Of course there was nothin about the way he looked or dressed that might signal any of this. In his neat white shirt and creased pants, his black hair snuggled up in little ringlets around his slender head, and those eyes, those innocent big brown eyes, he looked handsome and intelligent—that's all. Oh, yes, and friendly, awful friendly.

He grabbed his order pad from his back pocket and clicked his shiny ballpoint pen; then he looked at it all hard and scribbled on the pad.

"What's the matter?" I asked. "Runnin out of ink?"

"Not hardly," he said. "Not with this new cartridge. There's plenty, but it's hard to get it to flow sometime. The real problem is, it's a better digital watch than it is a pen. You can't win."

"Wrong," I said, hopin I wasnt lookin too moony. "You can too win. Besides, time is on your side."

At that, he blinked at me and scratched his head with the tip of his pen-watch. "Uh, my name is Theo and I'm your waiter and—well, have you had enough time to study the menu?"

"Sure, we're ready to order. My friend wants the No-Frills Croissant and a bowl of split-pea soup . . . and I'll have . . . You can bring me the Crossover Croissant and a Dr. Brown Celery Soda."

"Fine, and will you both be having coffee?"

"None for her, but I'd like some."

"Would you like that now or later?"

"Later, but—"

"Yes?"

"Theo, may I ask you a question?"

"Certainly."

"What's in the Crossover Croissant?"

"It's filled with natural cream cheese—no gummy additives— and flakes of tangy Nova smoked salmon. It happens to be my personal favorite."

"I'll bet you say that to all the customers, no matter what they order."

"No, as a matter of fact, I don't."

He smiled and I just about blew every bit of what little cool I had left.

"Theo?" I said as he turned to fetch our orders.

"Yes?"

"Are you . . . that is, do you work here everyday?"

"Monday, Tuesday, Wednesday, Thursday, and Friday. We're closed weekends. Is there anything else?"

"No," I said. "No, I really didnt mean to get personal."

"Think nothing of it," he said, pausin at last to take a good long look at me. "Anything even vaguely personal is refreshing around here." He looked straight into my eyes and cleared his throat. "I'll be back shortly with a lunch befitting the both of you."

I didnt tell Charlean how handsome I thought Theo was. In fact, I caught myself studyin how she was reactin to him while he served and brought us the tab. She'd taken a likin to him, all right—I could tell that much. But it didnt surprise me a drop to feel this chill washin over me while we was standin at the cash register, settlin up. It was a chill that put me in the mind of bein in a warm place, mindin your own business, when from outta nowhere you catch yourself in a draft, just like you yourself personally—and nobody else—was bein cooled by refrigeration.

"Whew!" I whispered.

"What's wrong?" asked Charlean.

"Oh, nothin."

That nothin, I knew, was quite somethin! It was sure enough nothin all right, yet I knew Burley himself couldnt be too far away. And now you too know what one of my biggest weaknesses is. Aw, lemme tell you, the devil got somethin up his sleeve to tempt everybody, dont care how cautious and vigilant they think they are.

"I'm tellin you, girl," Charlean went on. "You gotta learn to be good to yourself, just as good to yourself as you were to Burley. Let yourself go. Aint nothin the matter with *lookin*. If you dont look, then how you gonna see?" Then she pulled back her jacket lapels again and, lookin down, moved her finger along the letterin on her T-shirt. "Remember what Emily Dickinson said . . . 'The brain is wider than the sky.'"

"*Some* brains, maybe," I said, "but right now, mine feels like it's a puddle."

"Well, then, you better get to splashin! Look, let's drive over to Baldwin Hills and—"

"I'm sorry, Charlean, but can I have a rain check? I need to go home and lie down."

"Too much excitement?"

"I dont know. But I would like to catch a few winks, especially if we're all comin over to Nixxy's tonight."

Charlean looked vexed, but finally she said, "All right, Mamie. I'll run you back to the People's Republic of Santa Monica, but I want you to rest up good because tonight I intend to wine and dine and entertain you guys beyond the bounds of decency."

\* \* \*

By the time I'd got thru listenin to the soundtrack from *Chariots of Fire* and was snoozin along pretty good, the enemy, the telephone, had to go and ruin it all. It rang and rang and rang. The trouble was rememberin where I'd stashed the dog-gone thing. Just before he moved on, Burley had sent me out to Radio Shack to buy one of them new cordless phones. Ordi-narily, I kept it by the bed or the couch or someplace else sensi-ble, dependin on what I was doin at the moment. But this time I had to stumble around, still half asleep, tryna locate it strictly by where the ring was comin from. Then the ringin stopped. I figured I'd just forget the whole deal and go on back to bed. Nappin in the middle of a Saturday afternoon is a luxury I rarely got to enjoy. But when the thing got to ringin again, I popped out the sack and followed the sound straight into the bathroom, where I'd left it. So, like a fool, I plopped myself down on the stool lid and said, "Hello, Chrysler residence."

"Huh? Mamie? I thought I was callin your house."

"Oh, you are, Charlean. I'm still a little out of it, that's all."

"Oh, I'm sorry. Did I wake you up?"

"Never mind. What's up?"

"What's up is it's all off for tonight."

"All off? What happened?"

"I got back here, and who should I find in the middle of a poker party but Nixxy himself and a gang of his buddies."

"But I thought you said he was on the East Coast."

"He was, but he say he got to feelin homesick and lucky at the same time. So he cancelled some TV slots in Philly and flew back here to put a game together."

"You mean, just like that?"

"It's all par around this house, Mamie. I have to stick around and wait on em till seven; then I'm punchin out. You feel up to doin anything else tonight?"

"Like what?"

"Oh, takin in a movie maybe?"

"That's about the last thing I feel like doin."

"Well, I hope this abrupt change in plans hasnt messed up your evenin."

"No, no, it hasnt."

"Mamie, are you okay?"

"Call back in a few days and I'll tell you."

"I'll do that. You take good care of yourself. Bye."

I hung up feelin funny, even tho, when I thought about it, somethin musta told me all along that Charlean's big dinner night wasnt gonna play the way she'd scripted it. As a matter of fact, I hadnt even bothered callin Benjie and Tree. And to top things off, they hadnt even bothered callin me. What was wrong with that boy? I knocked myself out, scufflin and lookin after him, makin sure he gets all the right breaks and meets all the right people and—well, what can I say? Time's got a way of gainin on you. That old song about time bein so old and love so brief, and love bein pure gold and time a thief—that says it all. And I dont think there's any reason for me to speak low when I go to talkin like this. It's a killer, this thing called time, but it's also the mother of us all. You know about mothers, dont you? We hang in there and hang in there, no matter how ridiculous things get.

# ◆◆◆ 14 ◆◆◆

And you do get tired, tired of time. Sometime when they run that old picture *One Touch of Venus* over TV late at night, I'll get in a few Z's early in the evenin just so I can stay up and look at Ava Gardner, the way she looked then, prancin around in that white gown of hers. But the part I'm crazy about is the song "Speak Low." That's right on the money, so help me Kurt Weill! I use to would perform that song when I was singin in Chance's band. We had a real sweet, dreamy, Dinah Washington-kinda arrangement of it that'd make even the worrisomest drunk pipe down and listen.

The last thing I ever wanted was to be left in that house by myself. And, I swear, the house itself musta felt that way too because it would start creakin and poppin and carryin on the minute I'd even start thinkin about Burley. Oh, I knew Burley was just layin up there in the ether, bidin his time, waitin for another ripe opportunity to put in a new appearance, but when youre a woman alone in a house that's use to havin a man in it too, that can be a whole other experience. Sometime it's all you can do to keep from puttin on your clothes, walkin out into the street and knockin at the door of the closest house with a light on, and sayin, "Look here, can I please come in? I'm lonely!"

And wouldnt it be a beautiful world if you could bring somethin like that off, and not have people look at you like you was crazy? Picture it: "Well, you come right on in, child, and pull up a chair. You can even stay the night if you like. We got an extra bed. We know what you must be goin thru. We been thru it ourselves."

But, of course, that's not how it is.

Back when Burley was still well, we'd finish dinner, watch a little TV, then maybe talk and fool around with the newspaper. He liked to have a beer or two and work the crossword puzzle. Or else he'd get absorbed circlin ads in the classified about some new junk somebody wanted to sell or trade. I'd either work on a quilt I was sewin or get off into some article or book. I still like to read. I'll read anything. My education, you see, got cut somewhat short after I left home to go on the road, and I been doin my best to try and make up for it ever since. Got that from my daddy.

You'd never know it from the plain way he talked, but Papa was big on readin too. He never was a preacher or anything like that—in fact, he didnt even like preachers—yet he was always thumbin thru our Bible. Papa could just about recite anything from that book by heart. He could also tell you about history and politics and philosophy and science—that is, if and when he taken a mind to, when he wasnt too busy tryna win all the crop and livestock prizes at the colored county fairs. It was Papa's contention that books wasnt the only things around worth readin.

"You take Dr. Carver," he use to would say. "Dr. Carver didnt learn everything he knew about the peanut from no book. He got out there down on his knees in the dirt and was patient and understandin and he talked to them peanuts; and the peanuts, they would talk back—and Dr. Carver listened. He went right to the source. He learnt how to read the peanuts, the soil, the sunshine, the rain, the weather—the whole Creation. Dr. Carver loved them peanuts, and you know what the peanuts did? They read his thoughts and loved him right back."

Well, now, who in their right mind could argue with that?

Those first few nights alone, I sat around that house and walked the floor and prowled and monkeyed around with practically everything we had, waitin for Burley to turn up again. I could sense him out there, but I couldnt really see him. Then it dawned on me, if I didnt watch out, I just might wind up in one of them looney bins alongside a lotta the performers and smart people I'd bumped up against down thru the years. Either that, or else go and do somethin genuinely stupid I might later regret.

Oh, you go thru so many changes!

I kept callin Benjamin. That boy of mine'd been real sweet, touchin even, the way he comforted me after Burley died. We were gonna do this together and do that together. But after he and Tree stood me up on that dinner they'd made a big deal outta treatin me to, I grew cool on Benjie. Days slipped by, and not a word! He'd even gone and unplugged his silly answerin machine, so when I called up there the phone would just ring. It still beats me how a mother and son can be livin in the same town—more or less—and still be as outta touch with one another as we was. It made me wanna cry, and that's what I done. I started cryin for everything and everybody in the world.

Now, if you ever been on a cryin jag like that, then you know what I'm talkin about. Everything—and I do mean everything—is subject to sadness and futility. I imagine that musta been the same frame of mind Solomon was in when he finally curled up in a corner someplace and started in on his rough draft of Ecclesiastes. Sure, it's people around now, scholars, will leap at the chance to pounce on you and tell you it wasnt Solomon wrote that "all is vanity" stuff, and that's all well and good. But whosoever wrote it had to have some experience behind em—and I mean a whole lot of it—to come up with anything that *stayed* wrote the way that piece did.

And I'm here to tell you, Solomon definitely knew whereof he spoke, or spake. I'd get on my cryin kick and run back thru all those changes he himself musta gone thru. Dont forget, I might not be all that old in calendar years—I'm still in my forties—but I have packed more livin miles into the moment than the average woman. And the longer your memory, the more blues you find yourself carryin around. It's actually possible in one lifetime to do so much and to get caught up in so many of your own illusions and lies and half lies until it can finally come down to sun versus moon versus moonlight. I can see you all out there wonderin, What in the world is Mamie Franklin tryna tell us? Well, all I mean is this: Where do you begin when you start tellin your story and rememberin as you go along? Do you start with the source of light itself, the sun? Or do you start with what the sun touches, the moon? Or do you only deal with what the moonlight touches?

Oh, I'm gettin way out there tonight! Excuse me. My point is simple. Ecclesiastes is only one side of the record. Like with everything else in this realm of things, there's a flip side need listenin to, too.

Anyway, I decided to let my quilt go for the night. Been workin on that thing since Jimmy Carter was President. I'd just got thru takin my lecithin and zinc and my dolomite tablets and was settin all my cryin and thinkin and worryin aside to curl up in bed. Aw, I was so tired and frazzled I figured when I did finally pass out I might not ever have to wake up again. Burley'd been gone for months, yet I still kept to my side of the bed. Call me superstitious or anything you like, but that was one of the little ways I kinda kept up his memory. And just when I got settled down good, and all my thoughts and half dreams was gettin rhymed up right, then there go the phone—*RRrriinnggg! RRrrriiing!*

It startled me so when it went off, I couldnt help knockin the dumb thing to the floor while I was wrestlin myself across our king-size bed to answer.

"Hi, Mom, are you okay?"

"Benjamin! What's the matter? You dont sound right."

"It's Tree."

"Tree?"

"Theresa—my new girlfriend, remember?"

"What about her?"

"She's got the car. . . . She and Nomo, they—"

"Excuse me for bein so foggy, son, but it's late at night over here in Santa Monica. I was just on the verge of leavin this world."

"What? Hey, don't go scaring me again! What do you mean by that?"

"Well, here you are comin straight at me clean outta nowhere about Nomo and Tree—stuff I cant make hide nor hair of. I havent seen you or heard from you in days. I dont know where you are or what youre doin. Last I heard, we were suppose to be goin out to dinner, and then—zero! And me, your poor mother . . . You finally call up and you dont say, 'How's it goin?' or 'Hello, dog!' or 'Kiss my ass!' or anything, except somethin about Nomo and Tree and—"

"Wait a second, hold on, Mom. You're getting carried away!"

*Gettin carried away*—Benjie'd been usin that line on me since he was ten years old.

"All right," he said, "let's start all over. Are you okay?"

"Oh . . . I guess you could say I'm doin pretty good for the shape I'm in."

"I'm sorry about that broken dinner date. But there's a reason for that. You see—"

"Please, dont come plasterin me with reasons. All you had to do was call and say yall couldnt make it."

"Yes, you're right, there. You're absolutely right, and we were wrong."

I was tired. The ruby red numbers of the digital clock radio was flashin across the room in the dark and makin my already achin head hurt more. Charlean was right. At some point you gotta relax and let go.

"So what's all this about your friends?" I said. "Tell me, what is it that's got you upset?"

I heard his sigh mix in with the static on the line, and then,

"Tree and Nomo drove out to the Hollywood Bowl to catch Men at Work and the Tina Turner Review. Well, that show's been over for a couple of hours now, and they haven't shown up yet."

"Were they suppose to come right back?"

"Not exactly. We didn't make a contract, but she's usually pretty good about keeping in touch with me, particularly when she's out with that machine."

"You mean the Rolls?"

"Of course."

"And Nomo?"

"Aw, c'mon, Mom—Nomo is Nomo. You know how crazy and unreliable he is. I don't even let him drive the thing if I can help it."

"But I thought he was one of the people went in with you on it."

"Is that what he told you?"

"No, I just assumed that by the both of you bein such close buddies—"

"We aren't always that close. Not when it comes to ponying up actual monthly rent money, we aren't."

"Then what is it youre sayin?"

"Oh, Mom," he sighed. "For somebody who's supposed to be psychic—some of the time at least—you certainly have a way of letting me down."

"Lettin you down? Benjie, what *are* you talkin about?"

"Mom, isn't there any way you can tell . . . well, you know. Do you have any inkling about what's going on with Nomo and Tree?" Then he started coughin and fumblin for words.

"You arent comin down with another cold, are you?"

"No," he told me right quick. "I just seem to have this tickle in my throat. You know they had the smog alert up today?"

"Yes, dear, I heard it on the news. But let's get this straight. Youre askin me to use what little powers I got left to tell you where Nomo and Tree are, and what theyre doin, right?"

"I guess that's what I'm saying."

Right then and there, I had to laugh. You see, Benjamin Tous-
saint Franklin—my one and only child who'd been to good
schools and could express himself in other languages besides English—here he was playin dumb with me, his own mother. Of all
the people to run games on, I'd be the last one in the world for
him to try to fool.

The minute I started laughin, that's when he said, "Glad you
find me amusing, Mom. I suppose you do need some cheering
up. Sorry I've been so delinquent. It's been rough. You know
how much it takes out of you when you're trying to close one of
these network deals."

"Yes, I do," I said, feelin like havin some fun. "But to get back
to what you was askin, I got a hunch everything's gonna work
out just fine with your friends and that worrisome Rolls-Royce
that's got you tied up in knots."

"Mom, it isn't the car I'm worried about, it's . . . it's—"

"Oh, dont worry. Dont worry about a thing. Nomo and that
girl of yours, they probably got caught in a traffic snarl, that's all
—after the concert. They should be pullin back up at your place
any minute now. But, listen, I have to warn you about somethin."

"What's that, Mom?"

"Beware of evil expectations."

"Not sure I follow you."

"Think about it. Just as sure as youre growin suspicious about
the two of *them* bein out so late together, then you can rest
assured that all youre doin is plantin a seed that's gonna grow
into some kinda fruit that's bound to turn out strange."

And the minute I said that, I knew it wasnt fair. It'd taken a
long time for Benjamin to come around to believin in anything
he couldnt see or touch. Lately, very lately, he was startin to get
interested in stuff I'd been tellin him about from back when he
was practically a baby, hard-to-prove mystical stuff. Comin right
down to it, Burley was the first real person—real to Benjie, that
is—who had ever died. This fact alone was helpin to change my
boy's outlook a little.

After he got quiet again for a long time, Benjie told me: "If you don't mind my saying so, Mom . . . I find what you just said highly disturbing."

"All right, then—since we're on the subject of *highly disturbing*—would it ever occur to you how much it affects me that you cant even find a few minutes to call up and see about me? I'm here knockin myself out, tryin my best to carry on, and—"

"Aw, Mom, I get the message. I'll be by tomorrow morning bright and early."

"To do what, if I might ask?"

"To see you, what else?"

"Listen," I said, "tomorrow's Wednesday, my day off."

"I know, Mom, that's why I—"

"Ordinarily I'd be here, but tomorrow I have an appointment, an important appointment."

"Oh . . . you having your hair done again?"

"No, this is somethin else."

"What?"

"It's . . . it's personal."

"I see. Doctor's appointment, eh? That's good, Mom. You could use a check-up. You've been complaining too much lately about your health. Will you be finished in time for lunch?"

"Let's not count on it, Benjie. Why dont you just get back to me if youre free in the afternoon."

"That'll be tough. Nomo and I are supposed to see this big producer out in Burbank about our script. What time should I—? Oh . . . hold on a minute, would you?"

"What's goin on?"

". . . I think I just heard the car pull up in the driveway. Yeah, yeah . . . here they are now."

"Nomo and Tree?"

"Yes, it's them, all right. Mom, I gotta run. Hey, I love you."

"You do?"

"Of course I do. You know that."

It made me feel glad all down to my feet to hear him tell me that, even if he didnt mean it. He knew exactly what I needed to

hear. When he was actin right, Benjamin was downright irresist-
ible.

"Well, I'm glad," I said. "Dont stay up too late gettin reac-
quainted, hear?" Just then I heard Tree and Nomo mumblin
somethin in the background. "Good night, son. It's good to hear
from you."

"Night, Mom."

"And, Benjie . . ."

"Yes?"

"God bless you."

"Oh, yeah, sure, Mom. Talk to you tomorrow. Keep your
fingers crossed for us, okay?"

"I'll do that."

After I hung up the phone and rolled back over in bed, it felt
kinda soothin to know I hadnt actually lied to Benjamin. Sometime it's best to let people think what they wanna think. After
all, that's pretty much what they gonna end up doin anyway.

# 15

Harry Silvertone maintained a number of offices around the area, but the one where he'd set up the meetin with me was at his Tower-of-Babble office. I call it that because it's situated way up at the top of that Celluloid Studios Tower out in Celluloid City. Goin up there was a trip in itself.

It felt a little bit like old times. There I was in my finest clothes: a beautiful lavender skirt I'd bought in Geneva, a print blouse Danielle had brought me back from France, my soft eggplant-color Gucci pumps that I'd saved up to buy myself, and a rich burgundy head scarf. I dont go in much for jewelry, but I even wore the silver earrings Burley gave me for Christmas to celebrate the first year we'd spent together. Oh, I was threaded out!

When I pulled up in Sweepea at the studio gate, the tight-faced guard leaned out his booth window and took off his cap and smiled.

"Yes, ma'am!" he said, givin me and the car both a good lookin-over.

"Mamie Franklin," I told him, "here to see Mr. Silvertone."

"Just a moment," he grinned. He run his finger down a list

and checked somethin off with a pencil. "Miss Franklin for a ten
o'clock appointment with Mr. Silvertone . . . Right!" Then he
handed me a yellow slip of paper. "Here's your pass," he said.
"Place this on your dashboard. You'll be parking in the visitors'
lot."

"I thank you," I said, revvin the engine.

"My pleasure, ma'am. Enjoy your day."

It took some maneuverin, but I took my time findin the visitors' lot. I got a kick outta inchin along, checkin out all the
prestige parkin places with names painted on em. Most of em
was the names of executives and other people who worked there
that I didnt know from Adam's off-ox, but every now and then—
while I was easin over them speed bumps—I'd see a name I
knew:  AYKROYD,  PRESSMAN,  DUVALL,  STREEP,
PAKULA, GOTTLIEB, MOUNT, PRIVATES. Just before I
turned to pull into the visitors' lot, there was a crew of workmen
busy erasin somebody's name off one of the spaces. I knew what
that was all about too. Chances were a hundred to one some
poor clown had messed up and was bein put in what they call
turnaround, which is exactly what it sounds like. It's like you
walk into a project thru a revolvin door, then next thing you
know, you find yourself comin right back out, even if you dont
particularly wanna. By the time the sun set, I knew it'd be a
different name was gonna be stenciled there, and the paint
would be completely dry.

But the thing about the Tower that tickle me is the way it's
set up accordin to status. When I walked in on the ground floor,
the snippy little receptionist in a brown guard suit taken one look
at me and I could tell she didnt mean me no earthly good.

"Yes," she said, "may I help you?"

"The name is Franklin, and I have an appointment with Mr.
Silvertone."

"Mr. Silvertone, eh? Um, what's the nature of your appointment?"

I couldnt believe it. "The nature of my business," I said, "is
hardly any of your business. Just check your sheet, if you will."

See, I dont take no stuff off them kinda people. Never did and never will. She got all swole up and flushed, but she done like I told her and pressed a button.

"Miss Franklin is here to see Mr. Silvertone," she said into the intercom.

"Have her take the elevator up as far as it goes," a female voice came blattin back. "Someone will see her from there to his office."

Oh, I was fit to be tied! I took a piece of paper out my purse and went thru the motions of copyin this busybody's name and badge number down.

"What do you think you're doing?" she wanna know.

"Just catchin up on my references," I said, smilin. "Just in case I might need em."

She huffed up again and said, "Well, while you're busy taking notes, perhaps you'll be kind enough to put your name on the sign-in sheet."

"Be delighted, Miz Borowski."

"Bo-rahv-skee!" she corrected me right quick. "The double-u is pronounced like a vee, and it's *Miss-es,* if you don't mind!"

"Then do forgive me, *Mrs.* Bo-rahv-skee. Now, if you will kindly direct me to the elevator . . ."

She pointed halfheartedly to where a small bunch of people was waitin, tryna act like she was bein polite. But I could tell my little performance had shook her up some. What she didnt know was I go back to a time when colored people couldnt hardly even get on a studio lot unless they was dressed up in some kinda janitorial or maid's uniform.

But, you see, that's the way the Tower is set up. On the ground floor, you find yourself dealin strictly with ground-floor types, lunch-meat people, and the higher up you go the more important the folks become—or think they done become, anyway. Like, take while I was in the elevator, waiting for my floor to light up. There I was, squeezed in amongst all them men and women, some of em clutchin clipboards and file folders and ma-nila envelopes to their chests, others just standin there with their

attaché cases and leather grips. Everybody was sizin up everybody else, on the sly, naturally.

By the time we stopped at the eighth floor, mosta the women
had gotten off, all but one. That left me and her and several
expensive-lookin men. Then she got off at twelve with two of the
men. So there I was with these three executive types and, as you
might expect, each of em was scrutinizin me and cuttin their
eyes at one another, startin to get friendly. One of em—a tall tan
man in a turtleneck and herringbone-tweed jacket with leather
elbow patches—was lookin at me directly. His salt-and-pepper
hair was all styled out, and I'm up there tryna decide if he might
be one of the brand new picture or TV stars I hadnt caught up
with yet.

At floor fourteen, the elevator emptied out except for me and
him. All at once he reached and pressed the last button—the
fifteenth floor. Then he turned to me—I mean, got right up in
my face—set his three-hundred-dollar briefcase down, and
flashed his toothiest grin. I happen to know how much a genuine
leather briefcase like that cost, since I'd been halfway thinkin
about buyin Benjie one for Christmas.

"Let me see," this monkey said. "Didn't we work together a
couple of years ago on a Gary Coleman special?"

"Not that I know of," I said. "You an actor?"

"Heavens, no!" he laughed, and you could tell he was proud.
"I direct. But I once did bit parts early in my career. I was an
assistant director on the Coleman project."

"Well, all I know about Gary Coleman is he plays Arnold on
*Diff'rent Strokes*, right?"

"Right, right. And you?"

"And me, what?"

"Your name?"

"Mamie Franklin," I told him as the elevator stopped and the
doors was openin.

"Mamie Franklin . . . Mamie Franklin," he said, knittin his
bushy brows and rollin his bloodshot blue eyes. "I can't quite
place you yet, but I'm certain we must have worked together."

"Does the name Carleton Chrysler mean anything to you?"

His face lit right up then and he said, "Carleton? Of course. Why, we're meeting next week to go over some ideas for a feature he's planning."

"Is that the movie starrin Nixxy Privates and Fiona Prince?"

He looked around as if I'd let out some deep secret wasnt nobody else suppose to hear. "Yes, that's the one. Tell me, uh— how do you happen to know about it?"

"I'm his consultant," I said, nonchalant.

"You are?"

"Sure."

He walked off the elevator and he handed me his card. "Angelo's my name, Angelo Zelli."

"Pretty name," I said.

"Oh, do you think so? It certainly covers the spectrum, the alphabetical spectrum. Do you have a card?"

"No," I said, "I *am* a card."

"Indeed," he said as he stepped back to take me all in before headin off in the opposite direction. "So you are, so you are."


When I told the glamorous receptionist my name and who I was there to see, she sat me down on a cozy lean-back sofa and said, "Can I get you anything to drink?"

"Like what?" I asked.

"Oh, coffee, decaf, tea, a spot of champagne, or some Perrier, perhaps."

Champagne sounded awful good, but I knew better. I requested a Perrier and had hardly gotten partway thru it when who should sit down on the sofa across from me but Joan Rivers and a coupla men who both looked like lawyers. They sat there chattin real low and chucklin and carryin on. Me, I was real careful to appear as if I was mindin my own business, even tho my ears was perked up to catch anything they let spill out. Runnin thru my mind, however, was that crack she made on the Johnny Carson show one time about how she was so hard-up and lonely until when the phone went off in the middle of the night and somebody on the other end startin breathin real heavy and talkin all dirty, she said, "Wait a minute while I get a cigarette."

That's when I broke out laughin and all them Perrier bubbles went down my windpipe the wrong way. Joan snatched a tissue out her purse and got right up and handed it to me.

"Here, honey," she said in her raspy, breakneck voice. "Looks like you might could use this."

"Thank you," I said. "Youre Joan Rivers, arent you?"

"That's who I was when I came up here, but if it takes them much longer before they get to me I might be Rapunzel before I get out."

While I was blowin my nose and mullin that one over, the receptionist came back in and said, "Mr. Silvertone is ready to see you now. I'll escort you up to his office."

"Just show me where it is," I said. "I dont think I'll be needin any escort."

"But you don't understand, Miss Franklin," she said, holdin up a key. "Mr. Silvertone's office is on one of the upper floors. The public elevators don't go up that far. I'll have to let you up privately."

Joan, overhearin all this, said, "Take it, darling, take it! I think I could shimmy up a greased flagpole if I knew Harry Silvertone was perched at the top." Then she turned to her male audience of two and did a belly laugh. "And he usually is."

Even tho I was still coughin and splutterin, I reached out and squeezed her hands and thanked her the best I could.

"My pleasure, honey," Joan said. "Just hope you get the contract." And before I could get anything else out, she looked around theatrically and, droppin her voice, added, "Hey, can we talk? Just between us, Harry's about the only producer I know in this town who, when he fishes a buck out of his wallet, George Washington starts going, 'Ouch! I need sunglasses! This light is killing my eyes!' "

# ~16~

Harry was still talkin on the phone when the receptionist led me into his office. As a matter of fact, he was sittin behind the desk with his back to us, jabberin away.

"Listen, Irving," he was sayin, "I'm not really all that smart, but I sure as hell've been around a lot longer than anybody else, including you. So if you want to go with the contract you're drawing up with Paramount, you better wrap it up in mistletoe . . . that way you can kiss your ten mill good-bye! . . . Okay, so, say you change your mind, then call me back. But, hey, you better do it before Thursday . . . How's that? . . . Oh, Thursday this here enthusiast of antique cinema intends to be no place else but at Mann's Chinese Theatre . . . Irving, big fella, you mean you truly don't know? . . . That's the trouble with you—you gotta start keeping up . . . Yeah, gotcha, terrific, ten o'clock, okay. I won't exactly be waiting with bated breath, but I'll be here."

*Blam!*

Harry hadnt changed much since I'd seen him last, a coupla years ago. He still loved slammin down receivers. Truthfully, he didnt so much slam em as threw em back down on the hook,

kinda like you might toss somethin in the wastebasket or the
garbage, only with *oomph,* you know, and a lotta satisfaction.

He swiveled around in his chair real fast to face us. I could tell
he'd already pulled his smile into place before goin into the spin.
It was his no-skin-off-my-nose smile that was prepared to wink
and agree and go along with anything you might say, yet it never
promised a thing. There isnt too much I dont know about Harry
Silvertone, except maybe how much he's worth. And dont nobody know that for sure but Harry himself. I wont say he's tight-
lipped about his business, but everytime he sends me a check it's
got *Research Consultant* typed at the bottom. Sometime I wondered what kinda research consultin the Internal Revenue coulda
thought I was conductin all those years for Silvertone Communications. Whenever I asked Harry about it, he always told me not
to worry, that he wasnt usin my Social Security number or anything, and that it was all handled thru his European branch
anyway, which was based over in this little postage stamp–size
country called Liechtenstein.

"Mamie!" he broke out all of a sudden. "Dame Mamie the
Magnificent!" He dismissed the slinky receptionist with a wave
of his hand and waited until she was good and gone before he
got to his feet, stepped around the desk, and grabbed me up in
his short, thick arms.

I even squeezed the rascal back a little, tryna make out like I
was cordial, while all along there was one thought kept nippin at
me: Why in the world is he actin so affectionate and glad to see
me, and just who in the world was he tryna impress?

"Harry," I said, wigglin away some but holdin on to both his
sweaty hands in case he tried to move back in and start kissin on
me again. That way I could rassle him back against the desk if I
had to, even tho it might mean knockin over all them framed
pictures of his legal children by those four women he married. In
the first place, I dont much trust nobody that's got their family
pictures turned so they face the public on the other side of the
desk insteada the very one they suppose to mean somethin to.
And in the second place, I didnt go for Harry playin kissy-face

with me the way he do his starlets and female leads whenever there was a photographer around. This wasnt no talk show; I wasnt no cute or coquettish guest; and he sure as the dickens wasnt no David Letterman.

"How you been, Harry?" I let myself ask all polite.

"Not as well as you, lady," he said. "I can tell you that much right now. My, but you're lovely!"

When I checked out his neat white hair—which he still had plenty of—that didnt have a speck of brown or black in it anymore, I knew he musta quit abusin that Grecian Formula dye and was just lettin nature run its course. And his shiny suntan stood out against the fresh white linen suit and soft gray shirt he was sportin. His toasty knit tie was knot-perfect and them soft mocha-color shoes looked like theyd been molded to his feet.

"You aint no slouch yourself, Harry," I said. "You always could wear some rags. You sure you wasnt born wearin a suit?"

"Of course I was—a birthday suit."

"Well, lovely or not," I said, "I'm still me, and if you dont mind, I would like to get right down to business."

"I see your sense of timing hasn't rusted a bit, Mamie. Sit and let's chat. You know, you're the only one who ever worked for me that got as many raises as you did."

I pulled a cushiony chair right up to the desk and said, "You know I was worth every nickel I asked for, dont you?"

Harry plopped back down in his swivel seat and pushed a little dish of peppermint candies my way. "Care for one?"

"No, thanks," I said. "If I have one, I'll end up eatin all of em. You wouldn't have any Constant Comment, would you?"

"Constant Comment! Coming right up!" He hit the intercom. "Denise, you think you could round up a pot of Constant Comment for Mrs. Franklin here, and some hot water for me?"

"Hot water?" I asked.

"Yes, I had to cut out the caffeine too."

"But why hot water?"

"You remember the Duke?"

"John Wayne? Sure. He'd be President of the United States by now if he hadnt passed away."

"No, I'm talking about Edward Kennedy Ellington—real royalty. He was a hot-water drinker. We used to have dinner when he was scoring the soundtrack for *Anatomy of a Murder* for Hitchcock. They shot that show up in Michigan, you know. I was vacationing there at the time and started visiting the set. Well, Duke had given up coffee after he realized what he really liked was the hotness, not the caffeine. So all these Upper Peninsula waiters in this restaurant we'd go to would dance around the table between courses, saying, 'More hot water, Mr. Ellington?' I didn't think about it much until my doctor advised me to get off that French Roast that was holding me together."

"Very interestin, Harry. I always knew Duke stayed in a lotta hot water, but I wasnt aware he imbibed it too. But can we discuss our business now?"

"*Cosa nostra?* Yes, of course. No problem, love. Where shall we begin?"

"How about with act one, scene one?"

"Marvelous, Mamie. You know, I was just thinking maybe—" Just then the buzzer went off on the intercom. "Yes!"

"Mr. Silvertone," I heard the receptionist say, "sorry to interrupt again, but our Australian distributor, Cyrus Whipple, would like a few words with you. It sounds rather urgent."

"Denise, please tell Mr. Whipple I'll ring him back in an hour."

"But he's phoning from Hong Kong, sir, and insists it's the last opportunity he'll have to speak with you before he departs for Beijing."

"Excuse me, Mamie," said Harry, lookin up with all them wrinkles of concern bunched up in his forehead. "I have to take this."

I waved him to go head on. Really, I didn't mind because it would give me a chance to rehearse in my throbbin head again all what I was plannin to say.

He was still swivelin around in his chair and runnin up the bill when Denise rolled in the cart with the tea and hot water. She poured me a cup and disappeared. The minute I held that Constant Comment up to my nose, one sniff and all I could think about was Burley Cole. I swallowed a sip and had to go feelin around in my pocketbook for a tissue to wipe my eyes. Luckily, Harry still had his back to me.

I tell you, these men, these aggravatin men—the Chances, the Harrys, the Burleys, the Benjamins, and all the rest of em—sometime I wonder what it is about em that cause me to even bother gettin upset and ticked off anymore. What a waste of precious energy!

While I was waitin and nursin my tea, I got to lookin at all them pictures of his kids propped up there on the desk. There was five in all. The oldest boy and girl was grown, then came two teenagers—both of em girls—and a cute little boy looked to be around twelve. All-American kids, they were. The youngest was redheaded, and I knew that came from his mother's side. The ones in the middle, the teenage girls, both had blond hair and blue eyes. They looked to be a coupla years apart, fifteen and seventeen, maybe. The oldest boy looked like Harry's first wife, Sylvia. I knew her. They were busy bustin up right around the time I started workin for him. Sylvia was one of your bright, go-get-em Jewish women from the old school. She wasnt badlookin, either; kinda put you in the mind of Barbara Stanwyck, as I recall, once she got all that Estée Lauder and Elizabeth Arden and Helena Rubinstein blendin right. Their little girl, tho—I cant hold it back—she'd grown up to look a lot like Harry, which is to say she also favored Benjamin, especially around the cheeks and nose. Now, I'm not sayin that's bad, not at all. Marcia—I believe that was her name—she was dark-haired and perky, got that pouty, innocent Mediterranean look, almost like she could have a trickle of Negro in her, a little spook; some Italian or Spanish or North African or Ethiopian, or somethin. That Jewish blood, you know, is as strong as ours. They been everyplace and done everything, just like black people, except it's a peculiar strain in their features that allows em to pass for white. I wondered what would happen if Benjie should happen to run up on Marcia somewhere and peg her right off as somebody that looked like him.

All such stuff as that and how Harry and me got hooked up long enough to have Benjamin was plowin thru my thoughts when I started registerin Harry's voice, which had turned nasty for some reason.

"Whipple," he was sayin, "you tell that schmuck we never had any kind of agreement down on paper. He'll never get a quarter outta me! I assiduously explained what I wanted was a sassy, brassy Broadway-type musical. So he ends up mailing me a treatment for something that might go over on public television, but it sure as hell wouldn't put any asses in the seats in Woodland Hills or Milwaukee! Writers! I loathe the sonsabitches! They think they're the whole show! He can sue if he wants, but he won't have a pegleg to stand on! Yeah, call me at home tomorrow night."

*Blam!*

So there we were at last, face-to-face, and I was determined not to let Harry wiggle outta anything else.

"Harry," I said, "this is it! This is one flat deal we're gonna wind up. It's been draggin on for too long now."

"I'm listening, Mamie. What do you want?"

"I want my son—not our son, but my son—I want him to get the right breaks in this business. He's about to wind up his master's degree in film at UCLA. Benjamin's a good writer, one of the best I ever read, and I'm not just sayin that because I'm his mother. But as his mother, I wanna see him make a success of himself out here in this giggle jungle. He's black and he's good. I know that's goin against him in this business, but I think you need to cut the crust off your heart and plunge right down into what's left."

Harry sat back and slapped his hand to his heart. "You don't know what you're saying, Dame Mamie. The doctors in Moscow, a lot of whom are women, they told me . . . Oh, forget it."

"They told you what?"

"They told me how to keep from having a heart attack. They gave me a good going-over after I collapsed in the hotel over there. When you talk about my heart, you're hitting me where it's at."

"All I'm hittin you with, Harry, is the bottom line. I been pretty good about holdin up my part. For twenty years I've kept my mouth shut. Benjie himself doesnt even know who his father is."

"So what've you been telling him?"

"Told him his daddy was dead."

"Mamie!"

"That's right. He was a fella I had a one-night stand with while I was on the road in New York."

Harry's eyes was so big you mighta thought to look at him that somebody'd either shot him up with some new kinda dope or else he'd grabbed ahold of a hot wire. "Hasn't he been curious, Mamie? I mean, hasn't Benjie asked you about the guy's name and his family and how he died?"

I must confess that I myself had trouble believin I'd been bringin off this big masquerade all that time, and I knew the story and fine details so well by now and had lived em for so long until I halfway believed the lie my own self.

We stared across the desk at one another so hard for what passed for a moment, but was actually years, twenty years. What got me mad was the fact it'd taken Harry all this long to even show any interest in how I'd been protectin his own son from knowin who his real daddy was all this time. If it's true, like they say, that the truth can set you free—and aint no reason in the world for me to dispute that anymore—then it's likewise so, if you wanna know the truth, that a lie, especially the deep lie I'd been tied up in with Benjamin, can imprison you, the same as if somebody was to slam you in a cell behind steel bars.

I could feel the room movin and the light shimmerin; it was all pulsatin like a heartbeat or them two dots between the hour and the minute on a digital clock. The whole world, look like, it was waxin and wanin, comin and goin from someplace deep inside, and if I hadnt been use to experiencin other-worldly states and stuff, I mighta thought I was losin it. Somethin funny was hangin in the air, which felt hot, and my eyes got to jigglin like they were on the lookout for somethin that was on the verge of happenin. Somethin in the air, you know, the way oily rags left out in the sun or in a hot room will all of a sudden catch on fire . . . That's how it felt, like some type of spontaneous combustion was fixin to take place. I had to shut my eyes real tight. In the middle of my forehead I felt a burnin sensation and, when I concentrated, I saw a picture. At first it was like a color photograph of these orange and white flames; then when I studied it up close the flames started movin and wavin and dancin, until I felt a cold sheet of air wrap itself around me. That's when I opened my eyes and saw Harry frownin at me while he undid the top button of his shirt and loosened his tie.

"Mamie," he was sayin. "Mamie, hon, are you okay? Don't you feel well?"

"I'm—I'm fine, Harry, just fine. I just, I just—"

"What's the matter?"

And then, *wham*! To this day, I couldnt tell you if it was ten seconds that'd gone by or ten minutes, but when I tilted my head to one side, off to Harry's right, it took all the control I could muster to keep from gaspin out loud.

There in the easy chair, glitterin like neon, was Burley himself all over again. I blinked my eyes, hopin with all my might that he'd up and go away, but he didnt. Not by a long shot. He sat right there with the same grin spread all over his face that he use to get while he was lookin at *I Love Lucy* or *Sanford and Son*. Burley looked dead at me and crossed his legs, plus he had the nerve to lean back and—would you believe it?—actually winked at me.

Harry, he got up and walked around to where I was sittin and pressed the backa his hand against my forehead.

"Well," he said, "you certainly don't seem to be running a fever. But what the hell's going on? You're acting awfully strange. Do you even realize—? Oh, Mamie, I know I've been terrible about all this. That's the very reason I asked you to come here. It's high time we settled up. I mean, I can't possibly make up for all the discomfort and humiliation and suffering you've endured. However—"

"You can sit back down, Harry," I said. "All I have to ask of you is simple and clear, and cut and dried."

Quite naturally, uppermost in my mind was the question of whether Harry could see Burley. I wasnt sure.

"Look," I said, "would you mind movin that chair over here so I can prop my feet up?"

Harry cut his eyes from me to the chair and said, "No, not at all. If it makes you feel more comfortable, here you go."

Evidently he didnt have the faintest idea what I was goin thru. I felt like I could breathe easy then. I sat back and watched Harry push Burley's chair up close to mine. All the while, Burley was hoistin his legs and snigglin.

When I propped my feet up on the chair and they went clean thru Burley, I knew then and there that I was the one with the problem.

"Relax, Mamie," I heard Burley say. "I wouldnt miss this for the world."

After I realized Harry wasnt a bit more aware of what I was seein and hearin than Denise and the other women out there typin and chattin and movin around the reception area, I made up my mind I was gonna act my way thru this conference of ours without lettin on how nervous and distracted it was makin me. The only thing I know to compare it with would be the way you might feel if you were tryna keep up a real-life conversation with somebody and follow what's happenin on a TV show at the same time. Any way you go about it, it's hard to bring off without the two halves of your brain bumpin up against one another.

"Really, Harry," I said, regainin my cool, "I'll be all right. Some of this tea musta gone down the wrong pipe, that's all." I coughed some to demonstrate. "But you can relax."

"Are you sure?"

"Yes, yes. Please dont worry. I know youve got hundreds of things on your mind, so I'll be brief."

"Mamie, it's been so long since we've talked. Take your time. I want you to tell me what's on your mind."

"There's nothin on my mind but you—well, you and Benjamin."

Harry sat back in his chair, but I could tell he was still on edge. Burley by now looked to be thoroughly at ease. I mean, he was the picture of relaxation. In fact, there was somethin different about the way he looked now. He looked happier than when I'd last laid eyes on him that night up at the Chrysler house; his face seemed more serene, and there was even somethin different about the way he glowed. It's hard to describe. He looked mellower around the edges, and the color of his skin and clothes struck me as bein richer and more alive, if youll excuse the expression. What was vexin me was that, of all the times for him to pop up, he would have to go and pick this one. I was glad to be makin contact with Burley again, kinda. But I could also see right off where his uninvited presence just might end up bein a nuisance.

"Are you still with me, Mamie?" I heard Harry askin.

"Bear with me, please. I'm a little bit scattered today. I dont think we need to run the history of all this into the ground. You know the score, and I know the score. After all, we *were* the ones that got together that night and created this situation."

"That night?" said Harry. "What are you talking about? As I recall, what happened between us took place in the full light of day."

"The full light of day? You got to be kiddin. It was New Year's Eve, Harry. Have you forgot? You were gonna drive me home, then pick up some starlet—I forget her name—and drop by a party Marlon Brando was throwin."

"Yes, and then what? Refresh my memory."

"You changed your mind. You said, 'I hate parties, and New Year's parties I loathe. So if I feel that way, why should I go?

Let's have our own party, Mamie, right here. Let's herald in the New Year with some real feeling for a change.' "

"I—I said that?"

"You sure did. And you meant it too."

I glanced over to see how Burley was takin all this, and lemme tell you, he was sprawled all over that easy chair, had his chin down on his chest and his eyes was shut and his legs crossed, just like he was some courtroom judge done dozed off in the middle of a case. I couldnt tell if he was listenin or sleepin, or what. In all my years of playin in the ether, it never crossed my mind that ghosts might slip off into naps the same as ordinary people. Burley use to would nod off like that, dont care what was goin on or how many folks might be around. He'd do it when he was bored, and he'd do it when he wasnt particularly crazy about what was bein said. Come to think about it, he faded out a whole lot after he had his first stroke and didnt have much energy to spare.

"I'd like you to sit down and talk with Benjamin," I said. "Accept him or not, he's your own flesh and blood, and he's a good boy. In fact, he's what you might call extraordinary."

"How so?"

"He's always been an A student, ever since grade school. He's about to get his master's degree at UCLA, and his specialty is screenwritin. He and a buddy of his have collaborated on a script theyre doin their best to peddle right now. And I happen to think it's got all the makins of a dynamite sitcom."

Harry propped his elbows up on the desk and tapped his fingers together. "What's it about?" he asked, real cool like the big-time producer he was.

"It's about a down-and-out comic who's lookin for a break, but who in the meantime is holdin down a day job conductin tours on a studio lot."

"Hmm," said Harry, his eyebrows knittin every which way. "Sounds interesting. But, tell me—this comedian, is he black?"

"This comedian, Harry, is what we use to call a comedienne—and she just happens to be a preppy young white girl who's made up her mind she's gonna make it in the entertainment world

without any help from her influential folks or their connections.
Anyway, that's the fantasy element they hit on."

This said, I saw Harry's eyes light up. He quit tappin the tips
of his fingers together, flipped out a file card, and sat there with
his pen all ready to start jottin. "Tell me more," he said, "please
do. You have my full attention. I like the idea a lot. And you say
Benjamin came up with this?"

"That's right—Benjie and his pal, Nomo. It's a natural sitcom
if there ever was one, dont you think? Check it out. Comedy's a
staple, and stuff about show-biz behind-the-scenes is always in. I
dont see how this pilot of theirs can miss."

I shoulda been an agent. For years I been knowin that, but
there's only so much anybody can do, and right now my main
preoccupation was to straighten out all the mess I'd done made
in the first part of my lifetime. But if I'd known what I know
now when I first started out I dont think I woulda stayed and
stuck around this triflin, thievin, self-promotin business.

"Now, let me see if I'm hearing you, Mamie." Harry was sayin
this while he leaned forward and looked me hard in the eye,
which you better believe was taxin me plenty, since I had to go
on actin like we the only ones there.

I met his stare okay, but the minute I started talkin, here
come Burley up outta his catnap, stretchin and yawnin—pullin
all that distractin stuff.

"So," Harry went on, "what is it you want?"

"What I want, Harry, is for you to come clean with Benjamin.
I cant go on livin this lie. It's important that he knows the truth.
Anything can happen to me; then he'd be here all by himself,
thinkin he doesnt have a father or any next of kin. I just think
it's your responsibility to lay the cards out there on the table."

"You forget, Mamie. I haven't exactly been irresponsible or
neglectful of the kid. You've gotten your checks all these years. I
cared enough to help support him and support him generously,
at that."

"And that's true. I know that's true. But I think you gotta do

better than that. I got your letter about makin new arrangements, now that you dont legally have to stake him anymore."

"And what did you think?"

"I was kinda got off with when I first read it. Then after I
thought about it some, I told myself, The man's right. It really is
time for us to sit down and talk about this. Now I'm askin you to
get together with Benjamin and explain to him how the whole
thing went down."

Just then I peeped over and saw Burley sit straight up and fold
his arms cross his chest and glare over at Harry like he was fixin
to shoot the man a look that was gonna send him up in flames.
Actually, that mighta been just what the doctor ordered, since
Harry by then had turned so pale and weak-eyed until he looked
like somethin that'd been stored in the freezer and needed a
good thawin out.

"That's . . . that's a tough one, Dame Mamie. It isn't going
to be easy."

Harry just sat there fidgetin with his cup. I kept my eyes glued
on him, but he still wouldnt look at me. I could tell he'da rather
been anyplace but there. He kept lookin at the phones, waitin
for one of em to ring so he could pick it up and get off the hook.
But I hung in there. I wasnt about to let him duck outta this
one.

You see, deep down I know Benjie'd always sensed there was
somethin fishy about the line I'd been feedin him about his
daddy, and I couldnt blame him. Chance and Burley both had
gotten after me for stayin locked up in this deal. Burley was the
worst. He thought I was raisin Benjamin all wrong by puttin him
in all them fancy, upper-crust schools and raisin him like he was
some Bel Air white kid. Burley figured somewhere down the line
it was gonna screw Benjie up, but I didnt see it that way. I
figured that in this prejudiced society—crazy and cruel as it is—
Benjie was gonna need all the tools and resources and trainin he
could get. Then, after he got to be of age, he could decide for
himself which way he wanted to go. It was the teenage years that
scared me the most. That's when kids in this parta the world

start slippin and slidin into every kinda devilment you can imagine. Up there at that high school in my neighborhood, they got all the usual dope—marijuana, heroin, cocaine and Quaaludes—plus they got stuff so sophisticated I had to check books out the library to read up on it. They got pimps up there recruitin loose girls and they got porno people lookin for models, and crooks that's into trainin kids to be professional shoplifters and boosters, and the latest scam is the microchip gangsters. They teach the bright computer smarties how to steal big money by pushin a few buttons.

"No," I heard Burley say under his breath, "it wont be easy. But it wasnt easy for George Washington or Thomas Jefferson either." Then he looked over and winked at me.

And I knew what that wink meant. It meant Burley hadnt forgot the stuff I'd told him about the father of our country who had somethin like sixty children by slave women—accordin to Arnold Toynbee. See, it took an Englishman to point that out. I must say this for old George, tho. He provided for his outside kids. He saw to it they got trained in the right skills for the time, and it's said he died of a bug he'd picked up from one of them African women. And I know you all must know about Thomas Jefferson and that colored hot-and-heavy of his named Sally Hemmings.

"Mamie," said Harry, "if you want to tell Benjamin about all this, that's fine with me. I'm simply not up to it. I'm willing to do almost anything else but that."

"Well, I can tell you one thing—I'm serious. If you cant get up the gumption to fill Benjie in, I can."

"And whatever you tell him," Harry said, "it'll be public knowledge in no time."

"I know that's all youre worried about," I said. "But that's the chance we take. My bet is Benjie will be cooler about this than mosta the people on your staff would be if you asked em to clam up."

I had sense enough to know my son wasnt hardly gonna get an even break in this swamp, but I did do the best I could to try and route him around some of the thickest thickets—at least the ones I knew about—and, far as I was concerned, it was Harry's turn now to put forth some effort.

"Tell you what," Harry said finally. "I'll meet and talk with the boy."

"You will?" I was strainin not to sound like it was any big thing, but it wasnt easy to believe I'd heard Harry right. It wasnt easy either to believe Burley when he leaped up out his seat, did a little shimmy, then jumped up on the desk, did a coupla spins and laid down—I mean, stretched himself right out across the desk—and laughed, laughed in Harry's face. You talk about somebody bein beside themself—it was all I could do to keep from splittin in two.

Burley was winkin at me and pokin his hands in Harry's chest when the man sat back and pressed his fingers together again. It was like some huge load of lead had been lifted from his britches or someplace. He reached for a pencil and said, "I mean what I say, Mamie. You know me well enough by now to know I won't say it if I don't mean it."

"Earl Long," I said.

"Earl Long?" he said. "How's that, Mamie? I think I missed something."

"Earl Long was Huey Long's little brother."

"So?"

"I always thought you was somethin like Earl Long."

Harry threw up his hands like he was at wits' end and said, "So how come all of a sudden everybody's a writer? Okay, give me the punch line, Mamie, real slow."

"No punch line," I said. "Earl Long was the one use to say dont write what you can say; dont say what you can wink; and dont wink what you can—"

"Cut it out, cut it out! I'm not that bad. Honest, I'll set up an afternoon or a whole evening with Benjamin and we'll . . . well, we'll chat about things and . . . and maybe he can let me, uh, see that script of his."

Burley spun around my way and said, "Well, now, aint he the proud papa?"

Before I could check myself, the first thing shot outta my mouth was, "You arent bullshittin me now, are you, Harry?"

"Not on your life."

"Take precaution when you say that. Dont forget, it's real life youre puttin on the line."

While Burley was busy gettin out the way—I reckon the fool still didnt realize most people could see clean thru him—Harry got up and walked around the desk and swung his arms around me again. There was a lotta emotion mixed up in the mumblin and stammerin we did at one another. But when I felt him tryna get fresh and poke his old slippery tongue in my mouth, the way he use to when I was workin for him, I started hawkin like I was fixin to cough up a big gob of spit. That was just enough to make the sucker jump back and stay back.

Me and Harry, we talked over a few more details, and Burley up and cakewalked, yes, *cakewalked* around the office. I couldnt get over it, all that dippin and shimmyin and cavortin that people quit doin when my grandaddy was a boy. Meanwhile, I got it straight with Harry who was to check back with who and when so we could nail down a time for this big meetin to take place. Then I let my guard down a little and let Harry gimme a proper kiss on the cheek.

On the way out, with Burley still at my side, I slowed down in the reception area and noticed Joan Rivers and her pals were nowhere in sight. I figured they musta wisecracked thru their appointment and gone on about their business.

"That Joan," I told Burley, "she was somethin else. Betcha her and her pals're laughin and jokin all the way to the bank."

But, like Joan and them, Burley was gone too: literally vanished into hot air. I stuck my hand out and fanned around me, then realized I was all by myself again, standin there in the here and now, tickled, with my head still spinnin, on the very top level of the Tower of Bibel.

# 17

You all must know by now my feelins about the devil, and I do mean everything I say. But, all the same, I'm a flesh-and-blood human woman too and, like I say, the devil is out there settin up his stuff twenty-four hours of the day and night, and schemin up on tomorrow besides. With all that energy flowin around, you just know some of it's *got* to trickle your way. Mosta the time I'm pretty good about resistin old Satan's pull, but every once in a while even somebody like myself, who certainly knows better, has to let go and let the law of gravity do its thing. I always try to keep a coupla things in mind, tho. *Evil* spelled backwards is *live,* right? Now, spell *lived* backwards and tell me what you get.

I was feelin so good about the prospect of Harry and Benjie finally gettin together, I felt like celebratin, like doin somethin special, bustin loose a little like Charlean's been hintin at. Anyway, somethin got ahold of me. It was powerful enough to cause me to drive by the Railroad Croissant to see if that good-lookin young man, Theo, was free to come out to my place for dinner on the weekend. I mean, it taken a lotta nerve—and it wasnt like me to do anything like that—but just on a hunch, I went and did it.

"Maybe you could drop by late Saturday afternoon," I told him. "I have a lotta old belongins I need to get rid of."

"Like what?" he wanted to know.

"You name it, I got it—typewriters, record players, luggage, clothes, calculators, air conditioners, heaters, fans, car parts, books, lamps, filin cabinets, radios, televisions, drapes and curtains, rugs, bookshelves, fish tanks, vacuum cleaners, picture frames, tape recorders, cameras—"

"Hold up!" he said. "You mean to tell me you have all such items as this stored in your home and you . . . you plan to give them away?" Theo was eager to get back to his tables, but he dawdled there by the cash register and, lookin around, let his husky voice drop way down low and said, "Tell me, is it, you know, like, is it hot?"

"Theo, do I look like a lady who'd be dealin in stolen goods? What do you take me for—a fence of some kind?"

"No, no, I don't mean that at all. I happen to find the whole idea preposterous, so preposterous in fact that I can't wait to see it with my own eyes."

"Then I can plan on seein you there?"

Theo rubbed his chin and a funny light came into his eyes. Oh, dont you just love that unchecked, head-over-heels innocence young people project?

"See you Saturday," he said, "but I might have to leave early."

"Oh," I said, tryna sound casual, "you got a date, huh?"

"Nope, a class."

"On a Saturday night? What kinda class?"

"It's an art class. I'm trying to learn how to draw, and there's this woman who teaches at her home. It's great! It's the highlight of my week."

"You wanna be some kinda artist, eh?"

"Oh, I don't know about the artist part; I'm just one of those guys who was always good at drawing. Even in kindergarten I could do it better than the other kids, but I never developed it formally. I did it by instinct, you know, and now I'd like to develop some technical skills. This teacher, she's excellent. And after a week of waiting tables, I find it relaxing to kick back and get into something completely different."

"Theo," I told him. "I knew you were different, from the minute I laid eyes on you, but youre gonna have to tell me all about your drawin and stuff. Here's my address and phone number. You'll be comin by in the afternoon, right?

Theo looked at the note I handed him and tucked it in his shirt pocket. "I'll be there, Miz Franklin, but I have to get back to work now. The boss is watchin me, I'm afraid."

"The boss?" I said, lookin around. "Which one is he?"

"She's right behind you," he said, rollin his eyes.

I knew Theo musta been referrin to the chubby black-haired woman in owl-lookin glasses who was workin the cash register.

"See you Saturday, then," I said, and all but bolted for the door. It'd been so long since I'd pulled anything like that until I practically felt like if anybody else but Theo so much as peeped at me I might just up and turn to stone—or maybe melt into putty.

# 18

*Silly Putty* is the name of the first picture I ever played in. I say *played in,* but, really, it was a lotta hard work, even tho, lookin back, my part was pretty simple. Simpleminded might be more like it. When it comes to black actors gettin juicy parts, Hollywood hasnt changed all that much since I first got there back in the latish fifties. The situation's about the same now as it was then. Oh, there was a period back there for a while when it mighta looked to the public like anything black was gonna make money, no matter what. Black stuff was hot and would keep on bein hot from here to eternity. But that wasnt nothin but an illusion—just like it's an illusion to think we can keep on washin all that chemical detergent down the kitchen sink without it bubblin up into the water supply and comin back and cleanin us out. Somewhere down the line, the bubble's gotta burst—it's *got* to!

Now, the illusion I was operatin under when I first hit California with Chance's band was pumped so fulla bubbles I figured they couldnt do anything but grow bigger and bigger on into infinity. Of course, I wasnt free or white, but I *was* twenty-one. Far as I was concerned, the sky was still the limit. Any minute I was expectin the phone to ring and some voice to come on the line, sayin, "Mamie Franklin? This is Mr. Just Rewards and we have your million dollars. How do you want it—in twenties, hundreds, or thousand-dollar bills?" Naturally, I'da told him to haul it up to our little hotel room in twenties, just to make it seem like the money wasnt ever gonna run out.

The way I happened to land a part at all in *Silly Putty* seems to be the way most things come about in my patchwork life— that is, by bein in the wrong place but at the right time, and with the right stuff. Now, that might sound easy enough, but try bringin it off deliberately and it's hard to make work. A fluke, that's what it was. But in show biz if you tack enough flukes together, then you can maybe get a big break goin for yourself. And, of course, after enough breaks pile up, then you got yourself a career.

I wasnt thinkin like that. I wasnt even lookin to get into pictures. Me and Chance was on the verge of goin our separate ways at the time, but I was still singin with the band, which by then had been chopped down from ten to seven pieces, and we were all pretty nervous. For one thing, it looked like the kinda music we were into—standards and jump, with a jazzy, bluesy edge—was on the way out. We'd carved out a halfway decent livin for ourselves, workin what they called the Chitlin Circuit and stickin pretty much to colored theaters when we could get big-city bookins. That was the meat and potatoes. The bread-and-butter gigs were what kept us alive, and by that I mean we spent mosta our time in these dingy clubs and dives and joints. That's what I mean by all the wrong places—little out-of-the-way places in factory towns and all out in the country. But we hit some of the happenin places, too: Gary, Indiana; Toledo, Ohio; Pittsburgh, Omaha, East St. Louis, Birmingham; Jackson, Mississippi; Lake Charles, Louisiana; St. Pete, Florida; Oklahoma City, Tucson, Oakland, Portland, Buffalo, Denver, Seattle, Muscle Shoals, Inkster, Michigan; Corapolis, Pennsylvania; Pine Bluff, Arkansas; Baltimore, Milwaukee, Galveston; Gulfport, Memphis, Norfolk, Hartford, San Jose.

I can still tell you, to this day, practically anything you wanna know about all such places as that, from the perspective of an entertainer passin thru, anyway. But Los Angeles, that was a big thing in them days—and it's an even bigger thing now than it was then to play this town, more especially now that halfa New York is out here.

At the time—and this is goin back some, *too* far back, in fact —I was puttin all my heartache and soul into every song I did with the Inklings. Chance had cussed me out because I'd found out he was—excuse my language—he was fuckin everything female that wasn't cripple or spastic, and I'm still not all that sure about the spastic ones. It was a woman on crutches use to turn up every time we worked Minneapolis and she trembled and stuttered somethin pitiful. And do you know, even now, I wonder how come Chance always gave her a whole lot more than the time of day everytime she would slip backstage to get his so-called autograph. Oh, I bet he really signed the hell out of that one. Even now, I can see him whippin out his trusty pen.

That's pretty much the trip I was on with Chance—and I mean it was a real *angry* trip—right around when Harry Silvertone caught me by myself backstage one night while we were workin a little joint over in West L.A. called Rooster's. This was back in the fifties when show biz was startin to open up a little, even tho Republicans were still sittin on all the money, and on the surface everything corny seemed to be what was still in style. I been watchin this thing go around and turn around long enough now to be able to even offer a modest, homemade observation. When the scene starts to gettin heavily conservative and *repressed,* as people like to put it now, then you can pretty much bet your boodie that the opposite is what youre gonna see breakin loose in the business. Dont ask me why. Show biz, it seems, is just that way. You'll keep hearin, for instance, that jazz is dead. But under Ike and them, you had some of your finest jazz, to my ears anyway, and it's never been better since.

That was around the time when acts started to get breaks that never woulda had a crack at serious recognition if it hadna been for the times. I'm talkin about acts like, you take, say, Mort Sahl and Phyllis Diller and Moms Mabley and Lenny Bruce and Johnny Mathis. Now, who'da thought anybody soundin like a nanny goat wouldve made it as big as that boy Mathis did? We use to catch him when we popped thru New York, and Chance would drop downstairs there at Birdland on the off night to see what the bebop people were up to, and there'd be Johnny Mathis, sittin in with the most uncommercial groups you ever heard, doin jazz standards and ballads and stuff. Or you take this woman came outta San Francisco that did folksongs—and that was a phase when folk people were pickin up some mighty fat checks—Odetta. Now, I liked her a lot, yet I couldnt understand what all the fuss was about. There we were with one of the hottest little dance and back-up bands in the world—and me out in front of it, singin my insides out! And what was goin over with the public? Somebody standin up there with a guitar, or with maybe just a bass for rhythm, and makin out just fabulous! That's when this Kingston Trio got into the act, and old Sonny Terry and Brownie McGee were workin all the time. And I havent even mentioned these outrageous people like Little Richard and Bo Diddley and Screamin Jay Hawkins, or the incredible Nina Simone, or this fella named Ray Charles, who was just then comin on like gangbusters.

It was one excitin time to be in the business, even tho my favorite was, is, and will always be Dinah Washington. That's who I use to kinda model myself after, stylistically, that is, was Dinah. Say what you will about Lady D., her singin and her music was for real, as real as goin by the drycleaners after you get off work Friday to get your clothes out so you can party on the weekend and slide by church Sunday mornin.

Anyway, there I was, workin in L.A. at Rooster's with Chance Franklin and the Inklings, knowing good and well that the music was changin and that my relationship with Chance was changin fast. Even with a hot record out, we just werent gettin as many gigs as we use to because the club and theater owners werent crazy about bookin any seven-piece units when they could get

Sonny Till and the Orioles or Clarence "Frog Man" Henry, or
Ruth Brown and a quartet, or the Bill Doggett Trio—before
they hit it big with "Honky Tonk, Parts 1 & 2"—for a half or a
third of what Chance Franklin and the Inklings had to ask for to
keep our unit together.

The truth is that me and Chance had quit talkin to one another. On the bus, I'd hang around the fellas at the back that
played tonk and some of the other card games. For money. I
could play me some tonk in those days! And even tho my winnins were averagin seventy-five, eighty, even a hundred dollars a
week, card playin, I did that on the quiet, you see; just slipped
that little money in my pocket and didnt tell Chance about it.
So I'd been buildin me up a nice nest egg. But it got to the place
where the fellas werent all that eager to see me comin down the
aisle to sit in on one of their games. They liked to drink, as
musicians sometimes do, and I could handle a shot of Cutty Sark
or a nip of Tanqueray myself, at that point in my life. But I'd
found out a long time ago that alcohol and protocol didnt always
mix. That is, when you got somethin important to take care of—
like pickin up a little money at cards—the last thing in the world
you need is some chemical messin with your brain and percep-
tion and throwin your timin off.

Well, the night Harry Silvertone happened to be sittin out
front at Rooster's—the only white person, outside of another
couple at the back, weekend beatniks—I'd pretty much made up
my mind I was gonna leave Chance. I didnt know exactly how or
when I was gonna do it, but I'd had it. And I was kinda pissed
off with myself for hangin around and lettin Chance continue to
show his ass on me like that. I couldnt figure out if it was the
money holdin me in place, or was it that underneath it all I still
loved that low-down bastard.

I think the truth fell someplace in between, the way truth
usually does. For the first time since I'd been with Chance and
the Inklings, we had a kinda brisk single out called "Foolin with
a Fool." Me and the bass player had written it one afternoon on
the bus between St. Pete, Florida, and Atlanta. I'd been beatin

Happy Lucas so regularly at tonk—and all the rest of the boys, to come right out and tell it—until the minute any one of em would get to talkin about startin up a fresh game, I would say, "Yall must think you foolin with a fool!" And, do you know, it stuck.

So me and Happy got to bouncin off one another—musically, that is—one afternoon. I started singin a line, like that first verse, that goes, "They say the more things change/Well, the more they stay the same./Well, puttin me through these changes,/Baby, seems to be your game." And all like that until you get to the release where I sing, "I know you still think/ You're foolin with a fool."

We got into that thing so deep that by the time we stepped off the bus in Atlanta, Chance wanted to make a record of it right then and there. He didnt even know what I was singin *about*, that the song was actually about what was goin on between him and me, yet he was enough of a musician to know a hit when he heard one. So he worked up an arrangement of it; we recorded it the next time we hit Chicago; and the thing came out and started gettin played over the radio.

So there we were, with a single that was movin. And it was *my* name gettin a lotta prominent play for a change. That's what brought this young talent agent named Harry Silvertone down to Rooster's one night over on Central Avenue to catch the show. In those days, Harry was considered a little bit way-out because he was always tuned in to what was gonna be the comin thing. He was signin all these funny little acts most people in the business would overlook. But Harry knew what he was doin.

So after he sat out there in that packed room and listened to me sing my heart out, crammin all my emotions and frustrations into those songs, since I didnt have any other outlet for the way I was feelin inside, Harry came backstage and began to tell me how much he liked me and my singin and all. Chance saw him back there chattin with me and his mouth got poked out because Chance thought *he* was the one should be gettin the attention.

I'll tell you, you just werent gonna get anywhere bein anybody's vocalist! Not in those days!

"You ever thought about makin pictures?" Harry asked me.

"Pictures?" I said. "You mean, like, the movies?"

"That's what I'm talking about."

"Are you in the motion-picture business?"

"Not yet, but I sure as hell expect to be someday. Right now I'm agenting. I'm starting to build up a good track record for getting clients of mine into films. And I'd sure like to see what I could do with you."

"How much percentage do you take?"

"Standard. Fifteen. But I'm lean and hungry still. You go with me and I'll *earn* that fifteen percent. I'll work my tush off for you."

As you know, I tend to go by how I feel about a person, and Harry Silvertone felt right for me. But there was a whole lot I had to think over before I could make any commitment like that. For months I'd been on the verge of quittin Chance, filin for divorce and goin my own way. But there was somethin holding me back from doin it straight out. Maybe gettin my own agent, I thought, was the way to do it, to move out into takin care of myself.

There was this one problem, tho. You see, even back then I was startin to get tireda show biz. It's a tirin way to make a livin, at least in the band business. We were on the road all the time. We usually ended up stayin in these miserable hotels that catered to colored, especially in the South and in the small, out-of-the-way towns. It looked like we spent most of our time on the road, cramped up in that bus—and then it got to be a van—lookin at the scenery drift past. A lotta times we'd no sooner get thru windin up one show than it was time to pack up and drive like crazy to the next gig two hundred miles up the road. It seemed like I was always tired from not gettin enough sleep. I wasnt like some of the other musicians, tho. Stayin liquored up or doped up just wasnt my style. Chance could put away a lotta whiskey, and I have even known him to fool with that benzedrine and crack open Vick's Inhalers and soak the insides in wine from time to time. But Chance was also the kinda person could get up first thing in the afternoon and eat pork chops with mash potatoes and turnip greens and cornbread, plus eat a quart of ice cream and drink three cups of strong coffee. He could do that and wouldnt gain a pound; he just seemed to burn it all off with that high energy of his. Evil energy, I use to think. It kept him from turnin into an alcoholic. I really believe that.

"What you got in mind?" I asked Harry Silvertone.

"Well," he said, "they're about to shoot a picture over at Fox that's got a night-club scene in it. These two detectives track their villain to a club here in L.A. and catch him while he's in his cups, enjoying himself with all this money he's swindled."

"And—"

"So, why can't it be a club where you happen to be singing with Chance Franklin and the Inklings? That'll get you up there on the screen, and once people get a gander at you—because you're naturally photogenic in a real-looking way—I don't think I'd have any trouble picking up other bit parts for you. The situation for Negroes in the picture business is getting better than it used to be."

"You really think so, Mr. Silvertone?"

"Please," he said, "call me Harry. I feel like I've known you for years and years. And yes, I do believe Negro actors and performers are going to have an easier time of it from now on. After all, it can't really get any worse, can it?"

"I suppose you got a point there."

"What do you say? You interested in talking about this some more? You're a talented woman, Mamie. You're a marvelous singer, but I think you have acting ability too."

"But, Harry, youve never seen me act."

"Doesn't matter. I can tell. Being able to put a song across the way you do—that's a form of acting too, wouldn't you say?"

"Hmm, I suppose so."

"Of course it is. You've got the feeling for it. I can tell you're a natural."

"I'll think about it."

"Here's my card. Give me a call. You won't be sorry. I know you're under contract to Chance Franklin at the moment, right?"

"Nothin on paper."

A little sparkle came into Harry's voice when I told him this. "Oh, really?" he said. "Now, that's promising. I'll talk to him about the night-club scene picture possibility."

"I can have a word with him, if you like."

Harry came over and stood real close to me and mashed out his cigarette and took off his glasses. "People used to tell me I was maybe too much of a softie for this business. What I really am is sensitive."

"Why are you tellin me things?" I asked. There wasnt anybody back in the dressin room except the two of us. The band was still out front, doin a jump number for dancin.

"Mamie," Harry said, "I'm telling you this because my radar tells me you and the leader of this band aren't exactly hitting it off these days. Now, how keen is my radar?"

"Right on target," I laughed.

"I thought so. Let me talk with Chance. I have a feeling Twentieth Century-Fox will be knocking at your door before the summer's over."

Harry gave me a special look I knew better than to look at too close. At the time I had no way of knowin how familiar that devilish gleam in his eye would get to be. And sometime I wonder, did he?

Two weeks later, in the middle of August, we got the call, went over, and shot the sequence. I even got a chance to frown a little bit in the middle of the song I was singin. Just when one of the detectives was pullin his gun and about to close in on the crook, they edited the thing so I was down to that part of "Body and Soul" where I'm singin how "there's no use pretendin,/It looks like the endin"—and then I got to do like the director told me. I moved back from the mike and got this big look of scary surprise on my face. That was a parta the story.

So now when they show *Silly Putty* on TV and you see me and the fellas up there on the bandstand at the Bon Vivant Club, youll know the little story behind the story. And it wasnt long after this that I got up the nerve to kiss Chance Franklin goodbye and started makin my own crazy moves.

# 19

Saturday morning got off to a wild start when Benjie pulled up with Tree just as I was settlin down into my delicious state of mind. I cant think of any other way to put it. I was out there in my garden, down on my knees and workin in the dirt, not interested in seein or listenin to anybody. When I'm busy gardenin, I wanna be by myself. That's where the happiness starts bubblin up from, from deep down inside nobody but me. How do you explain that? I come from people who were always workin and scratchin in the dirt, and that's exactly what I thought I was runnin away from when I left Mississippi with Chance. And now here I am, lifetimes later, back pokin in the earth—and *diggin* it, as the expression use to go.

I remember my mother use to would say garlic always came up sweeter if you mashed and bruised up the cloves a little bit before you planted em. I'd decided to get out there in the backyard that mornin and test that out for myself. I even went her one further; I'd always heard too that if you got you some olive pits, you could plant them out there with your garlic and that'd help sweeten em too. Well, I figured, why not?

I'd just got thru settin out the lasta my garlic when I heard what sounded like tires squishin in the driveway, which was still wet from where I'd hosed it down that mornin. Now, I say it sounded like tires because it isn't always easy to hear the motor in a Rolls, more especially if it's runnin real low. But, sure enough, when I got up from my plantin and walked round to the side of the house to have a look, who should I see but Benjie and Tree.

"Hi, Mom."

"Mornin, Benjie."

I watched while he walked around to the other side to open the door for Tree. This amused me because most young women nowadays get a little bit funny about men openin and holdin doors open for em. I mean, it's the women now that hold the men's coats for em and light their cigarettes. But not Tree. Not on your life. Tree, I noticed, ever since Benjie started bringin her around a few months ago, she likes bein waited on and fussed over and looked after and attended to. Dont get me wrong, she's got a good heart and she's one of the cutest things you'd ever wanna see—and that's sayin plenty around this town, where good looks aint no real big thing. But Theresa Valenzuela, somewhere along the line, probably in the crib, had got it into her head that she was somethin special and she kinda wanted you to act like it too when you saw her comin. After all, by the time she was thirteen, her mother had her signed with a modelin agency. You can go thru the old Sears and Monkey Ward catalogs from a few years back and see her picture in the lingerie section, just as big, posin and modelin trainin bras and panties and nightgowns and stuff.

Tree sat right there and let Benjie open the door for her, then stepped out, in her dark leather pants and her big knit sweater, balancin somethin. I didnt think it was cold enough to merit such heavy clothes, but Tree's always grumblin about it bein too cold or chilly, no matter where she goes.

"Good morning, Mamie," she yelled in that sweet voice of hers.

"Hello, darlin," I said. "You two are up mighty early for night owls. What's up?"

She and Benjie both took turns huggin on me; then Benjie said, "Mom, we brought you something." He handed me the bag, which felt like a pie or a cake or somethin in a pan, with the bag slid over it sideways.

I could smell the most scrumptious aroma leakin out of the bag. "What is it?"

"Something Tree fixed," Benjie said.

"No, it isn't either," Tree said, correctin him right quick. "It's something my mother and I made especially for you."

"Really?" I said, touched deep down. "You and your mom baked whatever this is just for me?"

Tree got that naughty-little-girl look in her face—the look, I'll bet, that charms everybody she meets—and said, "Well, we made some for Benjamin too. But I was thinking about both of you while we were baking."

I started slidin the aluminum pan outta the bag, and the two of em just about had a fit.

"Oh, no!" Tree cried. "Not now. Wait until we're gone. You promise?"

"But when can I open it?" I said, disappointed.

"When you're having lunch or, better yet, after dinner. It's really an after-dinner delicacy, maybe with some coffee."

Benjie was smilin so broadly until I couldnt help askin if he'd already had some.

"Sure did, Mom, and it's magnificent."

"Magnificent, eh?"

"That's right." Then I watched him get excited all of a sudden. When Benjie starts gettin excited, he takes these big deep breaths and starts gulpin for air, except nobody but people who know him well would notice it much. "Mom," he said, lookin and soundin like he use to in the fourth grade. "Guess what?"

"Son, I'm not exactly in a guessin mood this mornin."

"But Mamie," said Tree, "you're gonna enjoy this bit of news!"

"Hey," Benjie said, givin Tree a playful little glance of annoyance. "Don't go stealing my big moment right out from under me. Mom, Nomo clicked on the telephone answering machine this morning, and there was a call on it from Silvertone Communications!"

"How's that?" I said, feelin my blood start to race.

"Silvertone Communications!" said Benjie, practically pantin like a puppy dog. "You know about Harry Silvertone, don't you?"

I didnt know how to react, even tho I knew I'd have to say somethin right quick, in a split second, if I didnt want em to think I was some kinda ninny. "Sure," I said. "That's that big producer, isnt it?"

"Precisely," said Benjie. "Precisely, precisely! And I'm supposed to call him back early next week." Benjie reached and placed both hands on my shoulders. "What do you suppose that means, Mom?"

"Hard to tell," I said. "Did you and Nomo send out a copy of your script to Silvertone Communications?"

"Not that I know of," said Benjie. "We've mostly been hitting these little indie-prods and leaning on the networks and cable outfits. Malcolm Aaron, my screenwriting prof, asked me for a couple of extra copies to show around to friends. He thinks it's a bankable script. Maybe someone *he* knows is connected with Silvertone."

"Well, all I can say is I'm happy for you, Benjie. I hope somethin comes of it. But you know this business. Like they say, it's apples and oranges."

"Plums and sour grapes," Tree put in, screwin up her face. "That'd be more like it."

"But, Mom," Benjie went on. "Could you maybe give all this a bit of special attention?"

"How do you mean, special attention?"

"I mean, you're psychic and all. Perhaps you could concentrate on all of this intensely, give it your best shot, and see what you can find out about our prospects. Or maybe you could just give it some of those blessings I've heard you discuss so much."

"Now, since when have you taken any interest in this sort of thing, Benjamin Franklin?"

Even Tree had to laugh before she said, "Mamie, he couldn't wait to get over here to tell you. 'My mom's a great psychic,' he kept telling me. 'She'll know what this is all about.' " Tree's black eyes were as big and shiny as quarters. "Isn't this exciting? And wouldn't it be wonderful if they wanted to see Benjie and Nomo's script?"

"Mom"—Benjie broke in before I could get out a word—"I just have a feeling that this is the tip of the iceberg. There's something strange going on here, I can feel it. Why would Silvertone Communications be calling me?"

"Calling you and Nomo," said Tree.

"No," said Benjie, "you're wrong there. The message was clearly and exclusively intended for me. There was no mention whatever of Nomo in the way it was worded."

"Well," I said, feelin like Orson Welles as Harry Lime musta felt. You know, when he played that double agent in *The Third Man*. "Silvertone, that's a biggie. Itll be interestin to see what they want."

"Just give it your best shot, Mom. Okay?"

"I'm still not sure what it is you want me to do, Benjamin."

Tree smiled her pearliest and touched me on the arm. "All at once," she said, "Benjamin's become a convert to divination and ESP and telekinesis and karma—"

"And all the other phenomena he used to pooh-pooh, right?"

"Something like that," said Tree with a wink.

"Well, thanks, Mom. We have to get going."

"Get going? You just now got here."

"I know," he said. "We just wanted to share the good news with you and drop off Tree's surprise."

"Benjie's dropping me off in Venice," said Tree. "I'm having brunch with my friend Nicole. You remember Nicole, don't you?"

"How can I forget her," I said. "She's in the paper every Sunday in those Macy's ads." Nicole Adams had gone to high school with Tree, and she was one of the skinniest women I have ever seen. Kinda put you in the mind of Olive Oyl, the original Olive Oyl in the funny papers, not Shelley Duvall in the movie.

"Yes," said Tree, "Nikki's really moving up fast."

"Nikki?" I said. "Is that her nickname?"

Tree laughed and said, "That's what we called her back at Hollywood High. We had this little club, six girls. And we would all chip in and buy these *expensive* European fashion magazines, mostly French. She didn't start all this 'Nicole' stuff until she got her first modeling job."

Benjie was gettin that mischievous look I kinda like. "Listen," he said, "I don't see you flaunting the name 'Tree' around either. It's Theresa all the way."

"Hmm," I said. "Tree Valenzuela. Actually, that wouldnt sound bad. It's different."

The way Tree looked at me all of a sudden, all sincere and serious, made me sorry I'd said that. "Do you really think so?" she said. "Because I'll do it. Hmm, Tree Valenzuela." She liked that, I could tell. "Benjie," she said, "what do you think?"

All Benjie did was look at his watch and motion toward the car. "Let's talk about it on the way to Venice," he said.

While we were huggin one another, I looked over Benjie's shoulders and, for the first time, noticed how the backseat of the Rolls was piled up high with videocassettes. Since we were standin right next to the car, I could see they were all in the same blue, yellow, and red boxes.

"Benjie," I asked, "what in the world are you gonna do with all those tapes?"

"Oh," he said, "that's a batch of films Nomo and I will have to study for this new project we're planning."

"Youve got a new project already?" I said, surprised. "Why, you two are gettin to be a regular team."

"He's into diversionary tactics," Tree said, grinnin. "His master's film is driving him crazy, so he's distracting himself with other ideas. I told him he needs to have someone who isn't from the film world look at it, just to see if it makes any sense."

"Come," Benjie said, taking Tree's hand, "we really must go. Bye, Mom."

In a minute I was wavin em off as they purred down the driveway. "Give me a ring, Benjie," I hollered as they were pullin out into the street.

"I'll call tonight," he yelled back.

"No, not tonight. No, tomorrow mornin's fine. And make it a little on the late side, hear?"

It's funny how a car can make you look so entirely different. Like, theres Benjie and Tree were—neither of em with a steady job—and both of em up there in that Rolls-Royce, lookin like Prince Charles and Princess Diana, except handsomer and prettier. I was still wonderin, tho, how come Benjie had to go and say what he did about those tapes stacked up in the backseat. They all looked identical to me, like they were copies of the same picture. For a long time, tho, it'd been gettin so that without my glasses I couldnt be sure of anything I saw anymore. But I wasnt *about* to go to wearin em while I was gardenin. Not yet.

"Mrs. Franklin, could you please call Emilio Sobrante. I'm Rodrigo's cousin . . . Rodrigo Ortiz, the gardener for the Chrysler household. I am the one he told you about who is in the hauling and salvage business. Rodrigo tells me you might have a lot of things for sale. Please give me a call at 555-9961. That's in East L.A. The best time to reach me is in the daytime during regular business hours."

I scribbled down the number and waited for the beep before the next call.

*Click.*

There's always those people who're gonna hang up without sayin anything. The Chryslers got this new answerin machine where you dont waste any time with that kinda junk. Theirs will scan the messages electronically and eliminate all the dead space and hangups so that all you get are the true back-to-back messages. And next they'll be comin out with one that edits down all that dumb jabberin, too. The trouble is I'm too sometimey about

these answerin machines. Burley had two or three of em piled up
with the resta the junk in the house, and every now and then I
like to hook one up just to see if I like it enough to wanna have
one permanently. That day I wasnt takin any chances on missin
a call from Theo, since I was fixin us a special dinner for later on
that evenin. So if he got it in his plans to cancel or anything, I
wanted to know in advance. Fixin big meals at my house was
somethin I'd got out of the habit of way back when Burley first
taken sick.

"Good morning, Mrs. Franklin. It's around ten, Saturday
morning, and this is Inspector Beaumont of the Santa Monica
P.D. I'll be telephoning you again when I go back on duty Monday, but if you could call the department and let me know your
schedule, I'd certainly appreciate it. I'd like to have another look
around your garage when it's convenient. I think I might have a
lead on what was going on there."

I froze on that one. Oh, I stopped the tape and went in the
telephone drawer and got his card out, but the last thing in the
world I wanted to be doin was callin the police, even if I *was*
curious about what mighta been behind what'd happened that
night. Maybe that sounds strange, but when it comes to the law,
I'm like my daddy. I never did like to have too much to do with
em. Somethin told me the best move to make on this would be
to go on about my business and let Inspector Beaumont catch up
with *me*. No sense in gettin *too* cooperative, if you know what I
mean.

"Oh, hey, Miz Franklin. This is Nomo. Has Benjie been there
yet? He's supposed to meet me over here in the Valley after he
drops Tree off. Tell him I'm runnin late, but not to worry.
Thanks. Yeah, hey, how're you doin? Bye."

Typical Nomo. Anyway, it was too late.

"Mamie? Hi, hon, this is Charlean. Gimme a ring when you
get a minute. I'm at Mr. P.'s all weekend."

"Mamie, if you wanna drop over to the Crime and Punishment this weekend—maybe Sunday night for the early set—I'll
leave your name at the door and you can sign for everything and

I'll pick up the tab. Be nice to see you there. I enjoyed our little
talk up at the Chryslers' the other day. We oughtta talk like that
more often. By the way, Mrs. Chrysler, she—"

*Bloop!*

Chance got cut off because I had the machine set on thirty
seconds; that's all the time I figured anybody needed to make
their statement. I sat there with my pencil poised while the tape
rolled on.

". . . Yeah, Mamie, this is Chance calling back. I see you put
the hook on me, ha, ha. Anyway, the Chryslers have been over to
see me twice now. And Mrs. Chrysler's even come by herself.
Try to come down, okay? If not tomorrow, then anytime. Just let
me know and I'll set you up for a comp. Bye. Oh, I forgot. You
need to come talk to that niece of yours, Maxine. Bye."

And that's what kept me from hookin up an answerin machine. It was sweet to not have to catch back up with calls I'd
missed while I was out or away. Besides, when people called and
didnt get an answer, they had to hang up, right? Now, didnt that
make sense? Wasnt that the way it was supposed to be in the first
place? Then why would I wanna go and be a sittin duck? What I
hated was havin to call people back.

So wasnt it the smart thing to leave well enough alone? All the
same, I decided to leave it hooked up for the resta the day since I
*really* didnt care to be interrupted anymore. Not until late Sunday mornin.

# 20

That's what I love about time: the way it works and keeps on workin and workin, all down thru, well, infinity, I guess you could say. There I was, puttin this meal together, which really wasnt all that fancy, just a little coq au vin with some asparagus tips and wild rice with homemade rolls, a tossed green salad. And —yum, yum, yum!—Tree's not-to-be-believed lemon-kiwi pie for dessert. There I was puttin this meal together, concentratin on first one thing, then the other, when all of a sudden it was time to get dressed and get my face and hair all orchestrated. The older I get, the crazier in love I get about this time thing. When I was a young girl, like back when I first fell in love with Chance, all I ever did was count the days and the hours and the minutes and the seconds that kept me from bein smack up next to him. Wishin my life away—that's what I was doin. Now that I know how precious every one of these seconds is, you dont catch me wishin nothin away. I like to take it slower than slow.

So by the time the doorbell rang and it was Theo standin there in his corduroy jacket and shirt and tie and pressed blue jeans, it was all I could do to keep from cacklin out loud because I could feel deep down inside my solar plexus exactly how the evenin was gonna go. No, I didnt know the details of it, but the outline seemed to have little wavy swirls of light pulsin out of it, the same as if you were to grab ahold of a beautiful thought, lay it out in the sun, and watch it materialize, throbbin all the while like it was made outta fireflies.

"Hi, Miz Franklin," he said, all self-conscious, and handed me a fifth of wine in a paper bag twisted all around it. "I hope I haven't inconvenienced you by turning up twenty minutes late."

"No problem at all," I said. "That gave me the extra time I needed to get my act intact. But come on in, come on in!"

For a second I wondered if I was soundin like Carleton Chrysler when he got nervous and started talkin double. It didnt take much lookin, tho, to see that Theo was actually kinda shy, once you got him outta that restaurant, which, I would imagine, must be somethin like actin in a play or performin on a stage. I mean, you got your entrance and exit memorized; you know the way the script's supposed to go; you know the role youre playin, and —well, it was like he'd wandered into a whole different movie being shot on another set on the other side of the studio lot.

Before I knew it, there he was, all the way up in the house, walkin around and lookin and peerin at stuff, tryin to act like none of it was fazin him much.

"Ahem," I heard him go, clearin his throat. "I see youve got quite a selection of luggage and attaché cases and portfolios, and the like."

"Yeah," I said, "my late husband was fascinated by things you carry stuff in. I dont know what that was about—do you?"

Theo gave me a tough little smile. "Maybe he'd expected to fill them all with interesting contents."

"Perhaps," I said, "but what you need to know about Burley Cole is that he couldnt pass up a bargain, or a deal of *any* kind."

"But, but—"

From the fridge, where I stepped to get us somethin to drink, I could see the flabbergasted look on Theo's face. His head went to jerkin around and his whole body, look like, it was tremblin as he checked out the piles and stacks and mounds and tangles and

jumbles of junk heaped up all in the hallways and parta the dinin
room and—to just flat out tell it—all over the house. All of a
sudden, I caught myself seein it from a new perspective. And
you know what? I couldnt hardly believe it either—and I'd been
livin with Burley's accumulations for a decade, near bout.
Nothin like havin somebody new in the picture to help you see
your own self in a fresh light. And when you start reachin a
certain number of decades in your development, like I have,
then sometime what it takes to open your eyes—not to mention
your nose and your pores—is somebody that was just comin into
the world around the same time as when you were gettin to
where you could qualify as grown. Or maybe even a little
younger. I remember our friend Art Blakey, the drummer, use to
say, "I intend to stick with the youngsters; it keeps the mind
active."

Well, lemme tell you, my mind was gettin more active by the
minute.

"Would you like a nice chilled glass of Chardonnay before
dinner?" I asked Theo.

"No, thank you," he said. "Since I'll have to be leaving right
after to drive across town to my drawing class, perhaps it would
be best if I stuck with something nonalcoholic."

"I had a hunch you might be a fan of this sparklin apple
cider."

When I held up the bottle of Martinelli's, that tight smile of
Theo's started loosenin a little. He reminded me of Benjie when
I'd treat him to some kiwi fruit sprinkled with fresh lime juice
after a meal. "Oh," Theo cried, "I love that stuff!"

And that's how it went for a while. I walked around in behind
Theo while he oo'd and ahh'd and studied the merchandise and
looked at me every once in a while as if I was suppose to say,
"You like that? Then take it—it's yours." Which is pretty much
what I was plannin to do with some of that debris, but only
when the time was right. That's the basic difference between the
way I was when I was Theo's age and the way I later became. I
dont have to gush anything out anymore; I take my time and

ease on into makin my moves, *only* when the moment is ripe.
And that's what you do; you ripen into know-how, or better yet,
know-when.

"You said you had a lot of cameras, Miz Franklin?"

"That's correct," I said. "Follow me. I'll have to show you
where they are because theyre all packed away to keep the dust
off."

I could tell Theo was havin trouble believin what I was tellin
him. But I led him down the hall to a laundry hamper, which I
opened and, pointin, said, "There you go."

"I—I can't believe this is happening!" was all Theo could say.
"There are cameras and cameras and cameras tangled up in here
like one of those swimsuit displays at a department store!"

"Yeah, well, like I told you at the restaurant, I got a little bit
of everything."

"Do you mind if I—?"

"Hey, knock yourself out!" I said. "I have to check on these
rolls. As soon as theyre ready, we'll be able to sit down and have
dinner. I hope you dont mind eatin early."

"Oh, not at all. Thank you, Miz Franklin."

"I remembered your art class at your teacher's home. So I
want you to be able to enjoy your food without rushin or strainin
to be polite."

"I appreciate that."

"And, Theo—"

"Yes, Miz Franklin?"

"It's all right for you to call me Mamie."

"It is?"

"Sure. I feel like I'm around home folks with you. Where you
from, anyway?"

Theo was busy unsnappin the case from some old 35mm German camera that'd been made back when the Nazis was runnin
the show over there. I remember Burley talkin about what a
good price he'd get for it if he ever decided to sell it. Theo
looked up and blinked at me funny. "Toronto," he said without
too much feelin to it, almost like he was a baby learnin to talk

and he was pointin at somebody's foot and goin, "shoe." Or else pointin at the map and goin, "Toronto."

"Toronto, Canada?"

"One and the same, yes."

"How'd you get way out here in L.A. ?"

By then Theo was so involved with the camera he was foolin with that I'd already made up my mind to offer it to him before he left. Without lookin up at me, he said, "My folks were like everybody else. They moved to the West Coast, to British Columbia, to get in on all of the opportunities that were opening up out there at the time."

"And both your folks are colored?"

"As colored as they can be. Say, this is some camera you've got here. I don't suppose you know where it's from or how old it is?"

"That camera, Theo—if it's the one I think it is—is older than either one of us. I think it was manufactured in 1935, or thereabouts, in Germany, and it's still supposed to be superior to mosta what theyre makin today."

"Really?"

"Yes, that's what they tell me. My late husband use to fool around with it and take pictures. Take a close look. There might even be some film still left in it right now."

"You know what?" said Theo after he'd looked it over. "I do believe there are a few shots left in it. Do you mind if I take a picture of you, just to see what the action's like?"

Right away I set down the dish of asparagus I was about to bring to the table, rested one hand on my hip and lifted the other up behind my head, classic movie style, and smiled right into the shutter.

"Hold it," said Theo, just like he thought he had to say that.

Dont you love the slow, slidin click a camera makes when it's snappin a picture? Like it's done soaked up all that shadow and light, wrapped up that pattern all upside down, and burnt it into the film so neat and complete that there's nothin left for it to do but to make that wonderful sound, that special, solemn, clean, slaphappy click that always puts me in the mind of the bathroom door bein latched on one of them old trains we use to ride goin cross country on some of those long hauls when I first started singin with Chance and them, when bands were still in and the money wasnt anything to sneeze at.

Then, after he'd got thru takin the picture, Theo did somethin that caught me so off guard I didnt know whether to stand there frozen in my tracks or to run over and throw my arms around him as tight as I could.

"Miz Franklin," he said. "I mean, Mamie—"

"What is it, Theo?"

"Do we have to have dinner now?"

"No, I suppose I can keep it warm in the oven a little bit longer. Why?"

"Because just now, just when I took your picture . . ."

"Yes?"

Theo put the camera back up to his eye again and moved it around the room like there was some special shot he was after, some angle he didnt have quite right yet. "This is hard to explain," he said, smilin at me now full tilt, no tremblin, no reservation, no thinkin out aheada time what he was about to say, none of that. Somethin had changed. I could feel it in the air, just as sure as I could feel the heat from the stove still burnin in the Pyrex dish of rice I was fixin to spoon into a servin bowl.

"While I was photographing you," he went on, "I could feel something about you I must have known all along, going back to when we met at the Cross . . ."

"The Cross?"

"The Railroad Croissant."

Oh, Lord, I stood up there, fidgetin with the potholder, actin like I'm just this older woman, this aunt or somebody, hangin on to his every word like he's on the verge of askin me somethin terribly profound and important and I'd better pay close attention so I'll know what to tell him for an answer at the end.

"Why, Mamie," he said. "Mamie, I think youre quite a striking woman."

"Thank you, Theo. That's kind of you to say so."

"No," he said, puttin the damn camera down at last and walkin across the dinin room toward me. "I'm not being kind at all. Far from it. I—I don't even know why I'm saying all this."

"Because you want to," I told him. "Youre sayin it, Theo, because you want and need to say it."

"Exactly," he said, barely loud enough for me to hear him this time. Then he said somethin else, only I couldnt make it out because it'd all turned into whispers and low rumblin. The air in the room was movin away from me. I dont know how to describe it. The air, it started movin in the opposite direction, away from how it was suppose to move into my nostrils and mouth for me to breathe. I started feelin light-headed and, for a minute, thought I was gonna faint. But in the center of my stomach there was this merry-go-round tingle, you know, the way you feel all glad and Christmasy when you know Saturday or Sunday's comin and the whole family's goin out to the state fair, or someplace, and you know it'll be nothin but fun.

Suddenly the air and the light, both of em started to back up and blank out. Was I blackin out, or what? I didnt know. I couldnt tell. All I could feel was his face hot up next to mine like that heat from the stove and the slippery taste of his lips against mine, his mustache ticklin me up under my nose, and his whole young body mashin up again mine, and me barely able to stand on my own two feet, my legs startin to wobble the way they did when I was standin on the moon of Mississippi made outta clouds and sinkin down cheese that night in the cemetery. It was easy breathin nothin but sweat and heat and aftershave. Mouth to mouth, tongue to lip, chin to nose—everything came crammin together all soft and sharp like the focus of a hug made outta light.

## ~21~

We weren't about to sit down to dinner, and that was that. I couldnt tell whether it was Theo who'd worked this out before he'd got to my house or whether it might've been my thinkin so hard about the possibility until there was nothin left for the idea to do but manifest. Whichever way it was, I didnt too much mind. I mean, you can fix a dinner anytime, but to actually be in on what was flashin and sizzlin between the two of us at that moment, hey, that was somethin I had to give a few moments of special consideration, preferably in a relaxed position.

Now, I have always found it funny the way people can jabber and yak and chitchat and carry on until you get down to brass tacks and basics. Then there isnt all that much to say, is there? My theory is this: That a long time ago, we used to didnt talk at all, and yet we understood one another more or less perfectly, probably better than we do now with all the computers and word processors and satellites and lie detectors and push-button telephones and answerin machines we got.

Be that as it may, the whole thing was feelin like instantaneous mental and physical telepathy, both. The moment I felt Theo's heart pumpin thru his coat, all up beside mine I knew he

was gonna have to come outta that corduroy jacket, and maybe
that shirt and those blue jeans too, just like I might have to do a
little sheddin myself. But there was the ever-so-slightest hesita-
tion on my part to push or tug at anything just then.

Slowly I was startin to breathe again. I wanted to say somethin
to this youngster, this young man who was probably only a couple years older than Benjie, but I didnt know what. My over-
mind—the one that sits on top of my real mind—it started to
flood over with all that stuff it specializes in, like: What if he's
got a venereal disease? He looks pretty enough to be bisexual,
and what if he is? And what if he's gone and picked up AIDS,
which there's plenty of around here in L.A.? Or what if Benjie or
Tree should come by while I'm up to this? Or . . . or—and this
one I didnt even wanna bring up, not even in my own mind—
but what about Burley? *Oh no, Mamie,* I warned myself. *Dont
even be thinkin anything like that. Just let go and ease into the
only reality there is; ooze into the right-nowness of this hungrifyin
aroma of food cooked with love by your own two hands and the
way the light's started to die out thru and beyond the dinin-room
window where you can peep out the corner of your eyes about to
cry over the prettiest sky risin up from down by the ocean, where
the beach'll go crazy when it turns night soon. A sky all bright
match-flame yellow with fast whispers of white shinin thru the
blue and tangerine edges around it.*

Maybe that doesnt make the best of sense, but I dont care. It
was a moment like all moments, which is the same as saying like
no moment that ever came before it or after, and I could feel all
that alternatin current, like they were talkin about on the radio,
and synapses in my brain go to poppin and cracklin.

"Theo," I said. At least I think I said it. Maybe I only whispered it or thought I'd said it, because at first he didnt answer.
Then I remember locatin my voice down in my choked-up
throat and I said loud enough for me to hear it this time:
"Theo," I said, "Theo, Theo, Theo, Theo, oh, baby . . ."

I could feel him feelin a little shook-up; could feel the wobbly
energy racin thru his arms while he grabbed me tighter, and I

knew I didnt wanna let go of him. You know how it can be sometime, dont you? The smell of all that love and starvation and frustration from so many old days when you *thought* you'd got used to doin without that touch and yet, oh, oh, oh, I dont know how to put it. It was puttin me away the way the right song at the right time can. And that's when I let my mind make itself up that it wasnt gonna do anything sudden or painful, nothin that didnt feel right in tune with the moment.

"We might feel better," I heard myself sayin, "if we got off our feet."

"Yes," he said. "I know you're right."

And just like we mighta been holdin up glasses of champagne sparklin in moonlight, we toasted one another; we drank to that, except with kisses. No clinks.

Even if you was to hypnotize me, to put me into one of those trances where my whole over-mind gets a freeze put on it, you couldnt dredge back up from me what happened after that, I dont think. Honest, it was like a jump cut, but slow—I do know that much. I remember pullin the curtains in my Mamie-fragranced bedroom and the way he stood there, checkin me, only thinkin about somethin else, I could tell, while I slid outta my clothes. When I'd gotten down to my slip, Theo sat on the corner of the bed, up there by the pillow, which I do recall thinkin was odd, and he leaned forward and put his knuckles to his lips and, like he was more me than I was myself, I could feel him thinkin, *She's got good legs for a woman her age . . . If only her tummy didnt pooch out so much . . . But the love floating around the rest of her . . . those warm, round titties, that natural womanly behind of hers that wants so much to be in front, to be confronted . . . This love that's written all over her, all up and down her insides and outsides . . .*

Maybe I only imagined it, but I would swear I felt him thinkin all this.

All the while, the girl in me—the one I thought had died on a bed of grass in the country graveyard that Indian-summer night

outside Hattiesburg, October, where Chance had walked me after turnin off the motor of his old DeSoto and taken me by the
hand, and I thought my pretty blue dress with the teeny-weeny
white polka dots was never gonna be wearable again, the way he
was crushin and mashin and sweatin on me before I slipped
clean out of it, the way you slip out of a cocoon when the time is
ripe and find yourself twitchin and strugglin a little before you fly
free, and next thing you know, youre up and gone on about your
natural business—the girl in me rose up inside my sweet, rich
blood, and I could feel her spirit hummin in my veins, pressin up
against every bone in my body, ready to fly back out.

When I bent to pull the covers back, Theo realized he was
gonna have to get down and get with it. I slid in between the
cool and satiny sheets I hadnt too long ago bought when me and
Charlean'd gone shoppin.

Sometime there's no explainin the connection; it's simply the
right one, that's all. This one was. From almost the moment
Theo rolled over on topa me and taken my face in his big, damp
hands and started breathin on me thru his mouth and thru his
eyes, I knew we were gonna have to reinvent the wheel, maybe
even the whole world. And when he slipped up inside me, so
slow and so slippery and so warm and hard, I knew it was gonna
be so long oolong how long you gonna be gone—from the top,
from the beginnin, from letter A all the way to the cadenza. This
should all be in French, the way Danielle will carry on when she
starts tellin me in the late, late mornin, just before noon—if
she's had one of her Valiums—tellin me about her adventures
growin up, and can stretch it out, the way French people can and
will do, in those nasal honeybee variations on ooh-la-la!

It was that crazy new energy, tho, that young touch and that
slightly awkward touch and that dont-quite-know-just-how way
he had of doin it that got and kept me so excited he coulda
melted me right there in a butter dish and spread me on his toast
for breakfast or his bread for dinner, either side I'd spread. And

if he'da asked me, I woulda turned right around and licked every
bit of brown off that fine frame of his.

Oh, it got so I forgot all about Mamie Franklin. Mamie Franklin? Who was that? All Theo's squeezin and rollin was floatin me
right up outta myself, and I could watch me wavin bye-bye, goin,
"So long, Mamie."

Whoever it was wrestlin and tremblin and moanin on that
bed after that was a woman I hadnt laid eyes nor hands on in so
many years I couldnt hardly recognize her. She had pretty teeth,
I can tell you that much, gleamin, even teeth just like his. And
when she bit into his big musty, deodorized shoulder, Theo, he
didnt holler, didnt even whimper; he just went, "Hahhhh!!!"

"I didnt mean to hurt you," I exhaled in his ear, right away
lickin after where I'd bit, tastin him there with the whole fuzzy
flat of my tongue, which by then was almost as hard as his dick.
And when I slithered out from under him, hummin to myself,
and slid that very tongue in heart-swirled kisses and licks down
and around and all up and down that beautiful creature to the
place where he couldnt stand it no more, suddenly I felt him
tuggin, no, yankin on me easy, felt his hands tremblin at both
my armpits. He pulled me up and clamped his mouth around
mine so hard I peeped and saw the biggest flash of light thunder
up into his face and make his eyes go slack and brilliant like the
last we were gonna see of the sky with the sun burnin through
the burlap curtains of the bedroom window over by somewhere
far away, a place far away. And, unless I got this all wrong from
tryin so hard to get it right, Theo, my baby, squinched his eyes
tight and tears started fallin out of em right down onto me, all
drippin and salty. Or was it me doin the cryin?

I remember that lightnin in his face, those sky-drenched eyes,
crazy like happy eyes gone lazy-crazy, and I remember how all at
once he seemed to be twice as big up inside whoever I was, and
then it was like I was on Venus. Or was it Vesuvius? All I know
is, it was like I turned into maybe two or three dozen birds all at
once, a whole flock of em, and went to flying off thru the air,
straight into the sun, which was feelin so hot and delicious on

my feathery little limbs and wings until we all—the whole flock —started chirpin and screechin and singin and callin. There was fifteen minutes of blowin my top. Or was it fifteen years? Dont make no difference. I was gone. I wasnt there. Absent, somehow. Or maybe I was glued right there, wigglin and coolin down, maybe, say, in the presence of some kinda absence. I know that sounds ignorant, but that's exactly what it was like. Theo, look like, had to hold me down with all his might to keep me from flyin to pieces. It felt so real I didnt wanna stop there. No, never.

The first one to wake up and notice anything was me. I rose up outta the little snooze we'd drifted off into when the breeze from the window started turnin night-cold. In reality, I didn't wanna say anything or make any noise to disturb Theo. I wanted him to stay right there where he was, keeled over on his side with his arm flopped across me, all quiet and warm. But it'd already got dark, so I was startin to worry about him missin his art class.

Lookin back at it now, I can honestly say that I was layin up there in one of them moods you slip into when you first wake up. You know, when you aren't even sure whether you wanna go back to sleep or not. Figured I'd just lay there for a while and relive in my head everything that'd happened since Theo got to the house. A kinda warm secret feelin was swellin all thru me, and in my head I'd got up to the part where Theo was snappin my picture and I was posin for him with my hands on my hips and behind my head. And that's when I felt somethin vibratin, shakin kinda.

*Uh-uh*, I thought, *you startin to drift off into one of those double dreams, Mamie!* That's when your dreamin begins to mix in with whatever you happen to be doin at the time. I used to experience that when Burley first taken sick and I'd get insomnia. Some nights I'd wake up and have such a hard time gettin back to sleep until sometime I'd actually dream I was still sittin up awake when, in real life, I was asleep. Now, can you grasp that? Well, that's when the vibratin started, and there I was thinkin about bein in my own bed in my own house with this wonderful young man named Theo right there in Santa Monica.

Sometime it isnt easy to tell if youre dreamin or not, and I'm findin out that most of the time it doesnt matter, either. But the whole picture was funny; I mean, there was something about it that wasnt right. After all, I didnt hardly know Theo, and yet I felt like we'd just gotten to know one another in the most famil-iar sense, in the sense that they use that term in the Bible, the way Adam *knew* Eve, which all led up to *Carnal Knowledge,* with Jack Nicholson, Ann-Margret, Candice Bergen, and— what's his name, use to sing "Bridge over Troubled Water"— Paul Simon? No, the other one. You know.

Understand, I was bein careful to take close note of all this because in my thinkin, in my rememberin, I was at the part where Theo put the camera down and grabbed me. And now this memory was blendin in with a new feelin I was havin, some-thin that was causin some kinda flush to spread from my belly all up into my head. My breath got caught in my throat a little, and I could feel the bed rockin the same way Theo had rocked me to sleep in his arms. But then the bed started rockin harder, more like the kinda rockin the whole room'd been doin when Theo and I got down to basics. It even felt like I was back in that boat I'd been in up there at the Chryslers' the first time Burley popped back in on me from the dead.

I was breathin real slow and layin on my back, lookin up at that plaster spot on the ceilin, the one me and Burley use to study whenever we'd be layin in bed with nothin better to do. Burley always said that spot, where they smeared the plaster around for effect, looked like a rabbit. But I'm the one always thought it looked more like the state of Michigan. You know how when you look at Michigan on the map, it's like a raggedy rabbit jumpin sort of over a real raggedy glove?

Just when I was fixin to pinch myself and hold my breath— my stomach and forehead was gettin so hot it was like somebody'd come along and dashed scaldin water on me—that's when the whole bed started movin, and the floor underneath it.

And when I blinked to try and figure out what the next thing to do was, I saw the walls move too. And then I could feel the whole house goin wobbly and the yard sinkin down and, I swear, the entire block felt like one of those rides—like the Snake or the Dip or somethin—out at Disneyland, where youre just gettin comfortable when, *bloop,* the whole bottom of the thing's done dropped out from under you, only it keeps shakin around and comin back together and shakin around and comin back together. In the first place, you dont catch me out there on them things; I have enough trouble just makin it thru the car wash, much less payin good money to get so shook up it's all I can do to keep from pukin.

But this thing was growin on me, and my stomach wasnt doin so well. Right around the time I saw the rabbit actually jumpin over the glove, the lamps started jigglin and fallin off tables. Stuff was fallin offa shelves. I could hear glass breakin and shatterin from way out in the kitchen, and all thru the house I could hear rumblin and crashin. I even thought I could smell the oven still heatin.

Then all of a sudden, I sure enough got rattled. Out in the hallway where a lotta Burley's junk was stored, I heard somethin buckle over and—well, it sounded like it was somethin heavy enough to just go smashin thru the walls, like one of those big demolition balls they use to knock buildins down with. Lord, when I looked up, the rabbit had jumped clean over the glove and there was a big crack in the ceilin that was movin around and gettin wider. Out in the bathroom water was runnin; I could hear it, and the funny thing was I hadnt turned any water on. Then I realized the water wasnt comin from the faucet, but from someplace else. I looked over and Theo was still sleepin like a baby, but I knew he was gonna have to get up from there—and get up fast.

I sat up, tryna remember what it was they'd told us we were supposed to do: Go stand in a doorway, was it? Or get down under a table or go outdoors—or what? I couldnt remember. I'd been in so many little teen-einchy earthquakes before until I'd been kinda spoiled. But this one was different. Pictures were flyin off walls. The drawer fulla tapes I kept by the side of the bed, *that* flew out and all my movie soundtrack cassettes went flyin every which way! I started to cry. I was burnin up with fever, felt like, and I was cryin. Then I saw water runnin along the floor from under the bathroom door into the bedroom—and it was a whole *lotta* water! By then the house, every square inch of it, had somethin goin on. It was too much for me to be connectin with while I was still rollin with that ride too. I was gettin dizzy. The sound was deafenin; it was like when the garbage truck comes out on Friday mornins, except it was noisier than maybe a hundred garbage trucks. I didnt know what to do. I shook Theo, but the boy wouldnt budge. Then I tried to climb outta bed, but another round of shake-ups hit and knocked me back down. For one split second, sprawled there on the bed, it looked like I could see the floor buckin and rollin like it'd turned into an ocean wave made outta rugs and wood. And when the wave popped and wiggled over my way, back toward the bed, the force and the power and the strength of it was so tremendous it knocked both me and Theo clean out the bed and slammed us down on the floor.

I landed on my butt and was startin to groan and say somethin to Theo, when I looked around to hear where this cracklin noise was comin from. You know, it sounded the way a fallin tree will creak and crackle when it's about to fall, right after you holler *"Timber!"* Lo and behold, I felt some kinda powder or heavy dust fallin on my head and, Lord have mercy, looked up and couldnt believe what was goin on! The doggone ceilin was startin to split in two, and plaster and debris was breakin off and tricklin down like hail and snow. Now, that's when I froze, sure enough.

"Theo," I yelled, "let's get outta here! Do you smell somethin burnin?"

Theo was dazed, to put it mildly, and all he kept sayin was, "Why didn't you wake me?"

"Wake you! Lord knows I tried!"

"Where will we go?"

"I dont know," I said, doin a fast look-around. "Maybe under the bed. Do you remember what they say youre supposed to do in an earthquake?"

Theo's mouth fell open. "An earthquake?" he said. "Is that what this is?"

"What'd you think it was?"

"I don't know. I was having such a strange dream, I thought maybe this was merely an extension of it, or something. But now that I'm waking up—"

"Well, it doesnt matter if we're in a dream or not. We better get our butts someplace else before the roof caves in on us!"

We looked at one another. I could see Theo was *scared*. All at once, he went to reachin for his shoes under the bed. And that's when this big chunka ceilin swooped off and got him right in the forehead, right there up over his left eye. Blood started to trickle down. I screamed, and Theo went to rubbin at his head and groanin. Just as I was reachin for somethin to wipe the blood off, another slab broke off and got me smack in the neck and on one side of my shoulder. Aw, it hurt so bad I thought I'd been shot. But that's when I saw what had to be done. Rubbin at my neck, I grabbed Theo by the hand, kicked his shoes out of the way, and started crawlin.

"Quick!" I told him.

"What?"

"Under here, under here! Quick before we end up gettin crushed like those people in *Towerin Inferno*!"

Before Theo could ask any more silly questions, I tugged him toward the bed and underneath we went! Oh my God, and just in time!

Right after that, from where we lay shakin and breathin dust, it sounded like the whole roof was crashin down into the room, along with the walls, the chimney, the trees outside, and the resta the houses and buildins all up and down Celestina Street. I laid there in the dark, wonderin if maybe all those people with their predictions had been right after all. Jeane Dixon and Edgar

Cayce and them. Maybe the time *had* come for California to fall
off into the sea.

But, you know, it's funny what you actually catch yourself
thinkin about when it comes right down to Judgment Day. You
talk about shook up, as I laid there wipin blood off Theo's head
and squeezin his hand, two things were heavy on my mind. First
I wondered if I was ever gonna see my boy Benjie again. And
then, was my neck gonna stay paralyzed and hurt me like this for
the resta my life?

Under the circumstances, wasnt much either of us could do.
Like my daddy use to say, for the time bein it was every tub on
its own bottom. I didnt wanna say anything to Theo about it,
but my sacroiliac felt like it was outta whack too.

# 22

We didnt get to stay up under the bed for too long because, as the sayin goes, all hell broke loose. It started out with water.

"Are you feelin what I'm feelin?" I said to Theo.

"You mean, all this blood we're soaking in?"

"All what blood?"

"Mamie, I think I just might bleed to death if we don't get some sort of towel or something to stop the flow."

I let go of Theo's hand and ran a finger across the floor. Besides feelin dust, I felt a cool wetness, and it seemed to be spreadin.

"Oh, no!" I yelled. "Child, dont tell me we're layin up here in blood?"

Even in the half dark I could see Theo's eyes gettin big. "That's certainly what it feels like," he said, twistin around.

But it felt too thin to be blood, and there was too much of it spreadin all under my legs and belly and breasts and arms. Can you picture it? Me and Theo, both, butt-naked, all scroonched down under the king-size bed, with some kinda liquid seepin around and squishin us all up? And then I got quiet and could hear thru all the plaster collapsin and roof fallin down and the clatter of glassware and clinky things and all the resta the racket; I could hear water gurglin and hissin and roarin and carryin on. By mashin my face down against the wet, dirty floor—and that'll teach me to vacuum more carefully from now on—I could look out from under the bed across the floor and see where the water was comin from.

It was comin from the bathroom and, when I thought about it, I knew a pipe musta broke. Water started pourin out faster and faster and I thought to myself, *Uh-uhhh, Mamie! First you were afraid you were gonna get buried alive, and now the two of you better start worryin about drownin to death because that is surely what's certain to happen if you dont make another move.*

"We must get out of here!" Theo said it this time.

All I said was, "And we'd better do it fast and dont make any mistakes either!"

This time Theo got to pullin *me* by the hand. The minute we escaped from under the bed, we realized the plaster and stuff was still rainin down, so we couldnt stand in any one place too long.

"Where to?" I said.

"We'd better go stand in a doorway," he said. "That's what I was taught. Which way?"

I started pullin him toward the hallway leadin to the back door when, oh my goodness, I saw smoke issuin from the hallway and a flame flarin up in one corner. And—wouldnt you know it? —the damn smoke detectors werent registerin a thing!

"Would you look at that!" I told Theo, frozen in my tracks.

"As much as I'd like to, Mamie, I think we'd better keep mobile. The front door's back this way, right?"

"Yes, yes," I said. "Hurry up! I think this whole house is about to go up." I could feel myself changin as my throat was gettin choked up and the tears started to fog up my vision. All those precious things Burley had taken years to collect—there it all was gettin smashed and broken and thrown around! I couldnt believe what I was witnessin. It didnt seem right. Maybe all of this was a parta Theo's dream. I didnt have time to wonder about it, tho.

Just when we reached the front door, after dodgin around all the piles and stacks of debris that littered the livin room—like wreckage and disorder everywhere, and the chandelier'd fallen down and smashed that big china servin dish my grandmother passed down to me—I was just unlockin the latch and twistin the doorknob when it dawned on me that we needed to take a coupla seconds and think all this over.

"Whoa!" I said.

"What's the matter?" Theo looked like he was fixin to dissolve like ice cream on a cone. Either that, or he was gonna leap outta his skin.

"Look at us," I said.

"Mamie, there's no time . . . We've got to jam!"

"I don't know about you," I said, "but, earthquake or no earthquake, I'm not about to run out there with no clothes on."

The blood was all over Theo's face now, and some of it had already started to dry and cake around his mouth so that he looked a little bit like he had a full beard painted on, like we use to do when we were kids in kindergarten dressin up for a play.

"I never thought about that," he said. Then, without even battin an eye, he dashed across the room and snatched the tablecloth out from under the ruined plate and threw it around himself.

"And what about me?" I hollered at him.

"Oh," he said, "just a minute." And, lookin around the room real fast, Theo zipped to the sofa and grabbed up the quilt I'd been workin on all those years. I mighta been scared he was gonna get blood all over it, but even the thought of such a thing struck me as bein somethin only a genuine ninny could entertain, given all that reality that was closin in on us.

Theo draped the quilt around my shoulders, and I wrapped it the rest of the way around me like it was a beach towel. He adjusted the tablecloth, which kinda favored a toga, the way he got it to hang on his yummy body—and that's how we made our exit. Or maybe it was our entrance, dependin on which side of the door you wanna focus on.

I still wasnt crazy about bein out on my own front porch half dressed with somebody else in the same shape—and a young man at that, somebody that's strictly none of the neighbors' business. But push had obviously come flat down to shove.

"We might have been better off inside," Theo said all of a sudden.

"How come?"

"There's plenty that can fall on your head out here."

"How *is* your head?" I asked, noticin that the bleedin was subsidin a little bit.

"It hurts. Feels like somebody struck me with the flat of an ax."

"That's just how my neck feels. What did they teach you to do *after* the earthquake?"

"Well," said Theo, snugglin up close enough to study my neck. I don't know what he thought he was gonna see. "I think perhaps we'd better start worrying about shutting off the gas and water and—"

We slammed up against one another real hard when another tremor came rollin under us. I could look off down the block and see house after house tremblin on their foundations, and there were trees, little trees that hadn't been long ago planted, blown over to the curbs and in driveways. When I looked straight across the way at Sneaky Pete's, tho, who should I see but the man himself out there on his front porch in his underwear, lookin strange as could be. But I suppose he was thinkin the same thing while he looked across at me and Theo. I was barely registerin Monroe, when all the streetlights went out, along with what few house lights were still burnin. I couldnt help but wonder if the electricity at my place had gone out too. But that shock wave, I'm tellin you, was somethin else! I mean, you could see it by the way the house took a big dip and the sidewalk, look like, jumped up practically to eye level. Now, maybe it just seemed like that because I was too involved and caught up in the scariness of it all to be objective. The whole house went to wobblin and jerkin from side to side just like if you were to pass thru some child's playroom and bump up against a rockin horse that'd been standin still, mindin its own business until you came along.

Until the earthquake, I didnt have any idea of what'd been goin on in my life; how peaceful and orderly and stable and safe everything had been. But I'm gettin aheada myself. There I was clingin to Theo and him clingin to me and both of us half scared somethin was gonna fall again and hurt or explode on us or somethin. From where I was standin while that shock was rockin us, I could peep back thru the frontdoor window and see orange flames, yes, flames and smoke tearin loose inside the house.

"God," I opened my mouth to tell Theo, "we gotta do somethin drastic! This is awful! This is terrible!" But I started to cry; I couldnt help myself.

All off in the distance I could hear sirens whoopin and wailin. It was like the whole town had turned into some kinda testin grounds for police cars and ambulances. You could hear stuff bein blatted out thru loudspeakers too, but I couldnt make any of it out. In fact, the whole thing was rushin at me so fast and heavy I didnt have time to even consider that there was anything to understand or think about except to keep from gettin crushed or blown up or buried alive.

I could feel Theo's hand on the top of my head, and he was mashin on me, sayin, "Down, Mamie, get down!"

We dropped to the threshold and stayed hunkered down that way, me with my eyes closed the whole time, until the tremblin and the shakin stopped. The tighter I kept my eyes shut, the stronger the smell of the smoke got to be.

"Theo," I said, "do you think this stuff is ever gonna lighten up on us? Somethin tells me we better get away from this house!"

"How do you mean?"

"It's just this feelin I have."

When I opened my eyes and glanced around, I could feel smoke tinglin the insides of my nostrils and helpin make the tears flow even faster. And I could see it. I could feel that some odd and perfectly horrible event was about to take place—as if the earthquake itself wasnt horrible enough—but there was this little fraction of a millisecond too where none of it seemed to matter much, where the only thing that seemed worthwhile and essential was to hold on and to ride the moment. Maybe it was the same as when people talk about ridin a buckin bronco or the thrill they get when theyre zoomin down the freeway at a hundred twenty miles per hour, or the big rush Burley told me his boss Zaccharetti used to get when Mr. Z.'d drop ten grand on a roulette spin at Vegas. For some reason, that's kinda how I felt. It was like somethin inside me was sayin, *Well, Mamie, you know good and well that there is no way youre gonna come outta this without sufferin some damage, but if you play it right, you might come out with your life, which is all you ever had, anyway!*

"Quick!" I hollered from someplace deep down in my belly. "It's about to happen."

"What?" Theo shouted back.

"Never mind!" I screamed. "Just run, run, run, run, *run!*"

I kept yellin it even after we'd shot out from off the porch and were clippin across the yard thru the grass. I tripped on the hose, which I'd forgotten to roll up after gardenin that mornin, but Theo stopped and caught me by the hand and yanked me up, and off we went on racin, neither of us knowin where we were headed, yet somehow I didnt care. All I knew is that was what we had to do, and then it happened.

*BOOOOOMMM!!!*

That's not even the sound of it. It was more like a *fffft!* and then a tearin sound like a dozen sheets bein ripped at once and then a long hot thunderin sound like horses gallopin way far away on a lonely night in summer when youre sittin on the edge of some log, lookin at a grasshopper—or, as my cousin use to call em, a hoppergrass—chew tobacco, and then you feel the whole earth poundin and shakin with hoofbeats that go straight thru the nerve endins that lead from your ears down to the heart, and then you hear that soft explodin sound that's muffled at first before it goes up into pure flame and heat and boom and awfulness like the volume bein turned up on some heavy-metal music playin on a radio inside a car that's passin thru a quiet neighborhood in the dead of night.

By that time we'd made it across the street to Monroe's yard, and suddenly there he was gapin at us and stutterin somethin I couldnt make out, still right there in his raggedy underpants where I'd last glimpsed him, his eyes big as Susan B. Anthony silver dollars. In the darkness I could see flame and fire in Monroe's eyes, and all that was was the reflection from the sight of my house goin up in smoke, which I was too frightened for the moment to turn and face my own self. But I had to finally. There it stood, or there it *had* stood; it's still hard to talk about this. There the whole thing was, lookin like one of those brushfires you see all the time when it's summer in southern California. You're drivin thru Topanga Canyon, say, and look off and see a fire in the distance, even listenin to the newscasters tell about it on the radio while youre drivin, but it doesnt register. It's just sort of an idea, you know, until the tables get turned and it's you and your stuff that's gettin burned. Then you experience it different. Everything I owned in the world, except what little money I'd socked away in the bank, was in that house, and all I could think was how lucky I was to be outdoors.

"Mamie" I heard somebody yellin. "Mamie, that you?"

It was Monroe.

I shaped my mouth and lips and tongue and even wiggled my teeth into position to say somethin back, but the minute I opened my mouth nothin came out but big gulps of sadness and emotion and all the tears I musta been storin up for years.

"Mamie!" said Monroe, throwin open his arms.

I rushed into the hug he was holdin out, did it without thinkin. While I cried and cried and felt him holdin himself back from cryin, Theo stood back and watched us. The quilt was slippin away from me, but that didnt even seem to be important either.

Vaguely, I became conscious of Theo sayin, "Excuse me, but I think I'll race back over there and turn the hose on that fire until the fire department arrives."

Suddenly Monroe asked, "What makes you think the fire department's comin?"

"Oh," Theo said, startled. "I hadn't even thought of that. I
suppose we should call them, yes?"

I didnt know what to say. Nobody did. All along the block
people were out in their yards, standin around in robes and
nightgowns and slippers or whatever they'd been wearin when
the earthquake'd hit. It was pitiful.

"Mamie," I heard Monroe whisper in my ear, "you're the only
woman I love deep down. Dont worry about nothin. Dont worry.
You can always come and move in with me."

I didnt wanna say anything to Sneaky Pete, but to myself I
made a note that I hadnt heard him say that. Thru tears I
squinted across at Sweepea, my little Honda Civic, still parked
there all innocent and humble in the driveway. In some fuzzy
kinda way I knew that was probably gonna end up bein my home
away from home for awhile.

"There must be a telephone around here," Theo said, "so I
can call for a fire truck."

Monroe and I just looked at him. It was to the place where
anything you said sounded stupid and needless and senseless. I
could feel Monroe waitin for me to explain who this boy was
that I'd shot across the street with half naked, but I wasn't in no
mood to explain anything to anybody. What did it matter?

Without sayin another word, Theo walked quietly back down
the porch steps to the sidewalk, stopped and looked back at us,
then started crossin the street toward the house. Paralyzed, I
stood there watchin him, hypnotized by all the light from the
fire that was flickin and glintin offa him wrapped up in that
tablecloth.

"Hey, boy," Monroe shouted at Theo, "you aint spose to be
turnin no water *on* when it's an earthquake! What we need to be
doin is find us some wrenches and shut off the gas, electricity,
*and* the water!"

"But, mister," Theo yelled back from the middle of the smoky
street, "I can't stand to just watch Mamie's house burn down!"

I had to move my whole body around, my neck was throbbin so much and was so stiff, to see that Monroe was gettin embarrassed. I mean, it *was* a kind of a catch-22 situation—damned if you dont and damned if you do. When I turned back to look across the street, just when I thought I could sniff the aroma of my delicious coq au vin burnin in the breeze, I saw Theo fall out right there in the middle of the street.

Me and Monroe sort of waited a second to see if Theo had maybe just tripped accidentally, but the boy didnt show any signs of gettin back up, not right away, for sure.

"Monroe," I said, "we better get out there and see what's the matter with Theo."

Monroe just stood, lookin at me all stupid.

"Monroe!" I said. "Did you hear me?" I almost slipped up and called him Sneaky Pete to his face.

"Yeah, I heard you," he said. "And I reckon you right. But, Mamie—"

"What?"

"Who is he?"

"What you need to know that for?"

Monroe shrugged and tugged at his briefs. "Well," he said, "since we're gonna be out there pickin him up out the street, I was just kinda curious about who he might be."

"I'll explain later."

"You dont have to explain all that much," I heard Monroe mutter under his breath. "You aint exactly dealin with a fool."

"What was that you said?"

"Oh," he shot back, all clear and polite, "I was just sayin that on top of everything else, the weather's gettin a little cool."

I was still too choked up to say much of anything. We made our way to where Theo was layin. The heat from the fire caused me to break out into an instant sweat.

"Ummm," said Monroe. "It's a whole lot warmer over here, aint it?"

On bended knee, I pinched Theo's cheek. Right away his eyes

slit open and he said, "Mamie, I d-d-didn't feel g-good. I think I must have fainted."

There was so much to cry about now that I just let myself go crazy. I could feel the grief buildin up and buildin up, so I gave up tryna hold it back and keep it under control. Before I knew it, I let myself fall out across Theo and put my arms around him. I went to blubberin so hard until it actually felt at one point like all the liquids and fluids my body could retain were gonna get used up supplyin me with tears.

Monroe stood lookin down at us. I know he musta thought we'd both gone berserk. And we had. But I could hear other footsteps steppin and scuffin and scrapin over to where we were. By then I felt like my natural blood was what I was drawin on to keep the tears flowin, and, with Theo breathin heavy like he was about to choke on his own tonsils, I figured this had to be one of the pitifulest scenes to ever go down in Santa Monica history.

And just when I was thinkin this, just when the words were passin thru my head, I heard a deep, robust, unreal voice sweep down from I dont know where and say, "Well, isnt this somethin! Mamie, I'm just glad that trunk is safe and sound."

My neck had pretty much quit functionin by then, yet I did my best to strain and twist it around to where I could get another look at the flamin house thru all the legs of the people that was standin around us. Right there among the crowd, shinin and lookin like he'd just seen a—well, what do you say about a ghost that looks like he's been frightened outta his mind?

I wanted to get up and run to Burley, only I couldnt hardly even move.

# 23

But somethin was movin me anyway. The only way I know to even halfway describe it would be to say it was sort of the way things work inside your head when you lie on your back summer afternoons and look at clouds driftin by. There I was, flat on my back, didnt know where I was anymore, not payin too much attention to anything, when all at once it struck me kinda odd that clouds should still be around doin what clouds do, just floatin and moseyin cross the sky like an earthquake wasnt no real big thing. Not when youre the sky and got clouds hangin around you and draggin by all day and all night, goin all the way back to when the world first started. I lay there, meltin away and whisperin in my mind to myself about how funny it was to be losin everything—probably includin my mind—and there I was, lookin at the light from all the fire and flame, lookin what it was doin to the sky.

One cloud was puttin me in the mind of that very state of Michigan when my ceilin started splittin in two. Another cloud sorta favored Thelonious Monk, you know, in profile, with his little hat on and his goatee stickin out. And way over yonder, up over where my house use to be, there was this cloud that looked

like it was in a hurry to get to wherever it was headed. But then I
got to watchin real close, close enough to see somebody smilin
down on me before the top of his head started separatin out
from his face, and then the bald spot broke away from what little
hair he still had around the back of his head and ears. And for
the softest of moments I felt myself feelin like one of those
clouds, like that's all I'd ever been all my life. A cloud. Made
outta water. Or was it steam? Monroe was sayin somethin to me,
but I couldnt make out a word of it because his voice was all
clouded up. Now, I hadnt thought about that before—how
murky and smoky and foggy even voices can be. In fact, the
whole world wasn't nothin but a cloud, looked like.

While I was notin all this, another voice that wasnt Monroe's
spoke out from the inside of my ear and said, "It's like Al Smith
used to say"—and after that came a little bit of laughter—"no
matter how thin you slice it, it's still baloney."

"Who said that?" I said. I couldnt tell you if I'd said this out
loud, where Monroe and Theo could hear, or just said it to
myself.

Anyway, when the voice answered, I knew exactly who it was
this time. And, as bad as my neck was hurtin me and as confused
as I was, I caught myself feelin glad all over. From the pit of my
belly I could feel somethin loosenin. It was like the breathin I'd
been doin just dissolved all of a sudden and decided that insteada
stickin around with *me*, it was gonna slip out and do its own
thing, go on an excursion all by itself.

"Mamie," the voice said, "it's time you and I went for a stroll
and had a chat."

It scared me at first. You know, what's just happened couldnt
help but go down on record as one of the worst earthquakes to
lately hit the Golden State, and here I was listenin to voices and
tippin up outta my body. Picture yourself. Picture how it would
feel to be slidin away from your own body, your nerves all fluttery, and at first you stand there up over yourself, lookin down at
yourself, not believin it. Then after you walk around a little bit
and notice cant anybody see it's *you*, the real you, not that body

stretched out there on the sidewalk, then you get shook up. What I did was rush back inside my body, just to make sure I was still in control. But that didn't feel right because I could feel somethin nudgin me, a vibration or somethin, like when a truck go by at night and you be asleep but you can feel the rumblin it makes deep down inside your dreamin. This vibration was like a voice that wasnt makin any sounds, just quiverin like, say, the way a cat'll purr against your chest, all curled up in your arms.

I got confused. I could feel a coupla vibrations tuggin at me that way.

"Burley?" I said. "Is that you?"

"Yes," he said, "but it's somebody with me."

I decided to go on ahead and take a fat stab at namin who I'd figured the other voice'd belonged to all along because in my bones, or bonelessness, I knew I had to be right.

"Ben?" I asked finally, comin right on out with it. "Ben, is that you?"

The minute I said it, the whole picture started fallin back in place. That cloud with the bald spot and the nose and the eyes and the eyeglasses and the body with those funny clothes and stockins and button shoes—all of it shaped up real fast outta pure cloudiness. It was almost like if you were to run a movie of somethin breakin to pieces, then run the film backwards thru the projector and see those pieces fly back together all perfect.

"Indeed, Mamie," I heard him say. "Do mark how calamity will enter human affairs to roust us from our lulling and conceited dreams of calm."

"You dont say!" I'd been so used to lookin at Ben and thinkin about him that I'd forgotten what was apt to come outta his mouth once he was sure you were listenin. Oh, I cant tell you how good it felt to be up around him again.

"Mamie," said Burley, who was floatin there right along beside Ben, "what is this all about?"

Dont ask me where my answer came from because all I can tell you is what I said, which was, "Now, Burley, you know as well as I do that this is a pretty peculiar situation. The way I see it is we're all free spirits now and can do anything we want and go anyplace we want."

Burley turned and gimme that very grin of vexation he use to flash when he was in the flesh. "So tell me about it," he said, fannin his arms around in the hazy, colored glow that was kinda stickin to us the way light will hang around light after it's been rainin and you look out at a streetlamp or the moon and see how they be all ringed with light. That's what it was like: all three of us was drippin light. Oh, I'm tellin you!

"That's my problem," Burley went on sayin. "It's too much freedom out here and not enough limits. And"—Burley's eyes grew big— "Mamie, what you doin out here, anyway? And who *is* this man that's been trailin me around?"

"You dont know who this is?" I said. "You cant be serious!"

Burley stepped back and went to givin Ben the once-over. I like to died, lookin at the expression on his face. "You mean to tell me this is somebody I'm supposed to know?"

"Burley Cole, this is one of history's preeminent figures . . . One of the Founding Fathers of our republic . . . Our multifaceted scientist and humanitarian and diplomat. The man is a writer, a mathematician, a wheeler-dealer of the first order, a businessman, a comedian, an artist—among other creations, he's the one designed this greenback currency we love so much—aaannd—"

"Aw, Mamie, you know I wasnt all that good in history. Just cause you done read so much, that dont mean you got to go rubbin it in."

At this, Ben himself swung around in the light and took a nice, deep bow, the way folks was accustomed to doin in his time. "Please," he said, straightenin and facing Burley and me, "allow me to introduce myself. I, sir, am Benjamin Franklin, long retired tradesman and tinker, who has also been blessed to carry out appointments in service to my countrymen."

"Wait a minute!" Burley said. "Are you sayin what I think youre sayin? You the *real* Benjamin Franklin? The one that went out kite flyin and ended up inventin electricity?"

You shoulda seen Ben grin. "Sir," he said, "your generosity is endearing, for you attribute to me singular insights and innovations that clearly belong to no one mortal but, rather, to the ages. However serviceable I might be, I find that my services to humanity become every day of less importance as other hands improve in the business of harnessing nature's divine resources."

"You kinda got a way with words," said Burley.

"Cant he turn a phrase, tho?" I put in, glad to be around the man who'd been turnin up in my life ever since that night on the porch back in Mississippi when I first got onto how strange I really was, and how all of this spooky stuff seems to come so natural to me.

"You are so very kind. Ah, whom do I have the pleasure of thanking?"

"Oh," I broke in. "Ben, this here is Burley Cole. You remember I told you about him, the one that worked for the cheese company? We were livin together when you use to come to me in those trances down there in that very house."

Old Ben's face looked like it was fixin to go up in flames. "Ah, yes, indeed," he said, literally embarrassed to the skies. "How could I ever forget? The gentleman given to acquisitive serendipity. Or would serendipitous acquisition be the apter phrase?"

"Either way," I said. "Burley collected anything he could get his hands on, so long as it was cheap and he could haul it away in that truck of his."

"And look at it down there," Burley said suddenly. "Look like that's about the only thing this earthquake aint destroyed. Will you look at that! I just dont believe this shit!—uh, excuse me, Mr. Franklin."

Ben smiled and said, "Under the circumstances, I would urge you to extend your view even further. Disaster is without a doubt widespread. Not having sufficient comprehension of what has already been wrought, I find myself pondering the possibility that the U.S. Geological Survey might have already drawn up an account of the devastation this subterranean spasm has caused."

"Ben, you dont miss a thing, do you?" I hoped I wasnt lookin too sappy while I was sayin it, but I did have to lean forward and express myself at this point. "You mean, you still keep up with the Geological Survey and all the stuff they got around here today?"

"My dear Mamie, it is only proper—do you not agree?—that I take sensible measures for obtaining understanding of so dire a development."

"You never cease to amaze me," I said.

That's when old Ben moved up close and I could see and feel him lookin directly into my eyes. At the same time I was blinkin, blinkin hard, partly to squeeze out some of the water I thought was fuzzin up my eyesight and partly to get a better look at what was goin on. This wasnt no everyday occurrence, after all, and there was this powerful feelin buildin up at the backa my brain that kept sayin, *Mamie, are you dreamin, or what?*

"Uh-uhhh," I heard Burley say. "Looka yonder! Watch out now!"

"Watch out for what?" I said.

All Ben did was touch his hand to his lips to cover up a big grin that was bubblin up.

I looked down over the neighborhood to see what Burley was talkin about, but all I could see was fires here and there, fire trucks squealin to the scene, and people bunched up in pajamas and nightgowns and blankets. And I could make out all that rubble and damage and the busted-up streets and sidewalks and little children jumpin up and down and the wind blowin the branches of the trees all this way and that.

"Show me what *you* see!" I hollered at Burley.

"Indeed," said Ben, "let Mr. Cole lead us to where we might be able to observe at close hand precisely what it is that he perceives."

For the first time it hit me how off-the-wall the whole setup was. I mean, it scared me so bad I couldnt hardly speak. And what I was most afraid to ask was the most obvious thing that'd been tickin away inside since I'd risen up there with those two. Even after realizin what I wanted to ask, I still couldnt say it. All

I could say was, "Uh, how exactly, Ben and Burley, do we move in for this close-up view?"

This got Burley to laughin so loud I thought everybody in Santa Monica coulda heard him.

"Wh-what's so funny?" I cried.

"Here," said Ben, reachin out his hand. "All you need do is stand fast by Mr. Cole and myself while we descend for an intimate view of the spectacle that seems to have brought him and me both such incomprehensible amusement."

In a twinklin there we were back down on the ground, or so it seemed. The truth is that when I looked around me, I couldnt really tell you where I was situated. And when I looked at what was before me, I couldnt help but gasp. Was I losin it all? I knew I'd done already lost my mind, but what I saw wasnt makin too much of a case for what few wits I still liked to think I had about me.

There, laid out at the curb, was none other than Mamie Franklin! Yes, me! There I was, flat on my back and, except for that quilt, I was nekkid as a rainbow trout. And there Theo was, stretched out right there beside me—only the tablecloth he'd wrapped around himself had slipped a little bit so that some of his stuff was stickin out. Aw, poor child! Since I was hoverin close enough to actually breathe on us, I reached out my hand to flip up one corner of tablecloth so the boy wouldnt have to be layin up there sufferin from indecent exposure.

"Might as well save your energy," Burley said. "It might look like you can touch things from where we are, but I swear it wont work."

"Wait," I said, "let's get somethin straight before I go all-out crazy. Does my bein here with you two mean I'm dead too, or what?"

While I was waitin on one of em to answer me, my eyes kept pullin me to what was goin on with the other me laid out cold. Here come Sneaky Pete, Monroe, down on his hands and knees, straddlin me, got his face down over mine, gettin ready to clamp his mouth to my mouth. I hovered there, wherever I was, lookin at Monroe real close, and at the same time wonderin what Burley musta been thinkin. It's a funny thing when you catch yourself standin outside yourself lookin at yourself. You didnt hear me laughin, tho. No, it wasnt funny that way; it was funny the other way. And it was all gettin to be too strange.

I spun around, still waitin on Ben and Burley to answer my question about was I dead or not, but all I could see was their faces. Then even their faces went to fadin, and it was only Ben's voice I could hear.

"Mamie," he said, "I had, on the whole, abundant reason to be satisfied with the knowledge you displayed of your deeper self, even though it has been largely dormant these many vexsome human years. Now I must needs beseech you to explore that hidden side in all its beneficent amplitude. There you shall find all the answers your frightened heart seeks."

"B-but where you goin, Ben? Where's Burley? What is this? Dont leave me here by myself! Please dont leave me here alone!"

"Aint nothin to worry about," I heard Burley say. "We'll be back. At least, I'll be back. I dont even know myself where this Benjamin Franklin dude is comin from."

"We are all proceeding from the same source," Ben's voice said. "Mamie, I hasten you to befriend once again your secret self, to listen attentively to your secret voice, and to abide by your secret vision. That way perhaps you shall be reminded of the many powerful, peace-bestowing truths we have both befriended from the earliest times of our fond association. Need I remind you of Egypt, Athens, England, France, the Colonies, Philadelphia . . . ?"

"But, Ben"—I hollered out into the emptiness—"dont abandon me now! I need you! Burley! Please, dont go away. I've known for a long time my days were numbered. Does this mean theyve finally come to a close? Ben? Burley? Please come back . . . *please!*"

"Baby," I heard Burley's voice say, "you can contact me anytime you want."

"Indeed, Mamie, my friend," old Ben said, his voice trailin off real thin like Burley's. "All you need do is change the frequency of your receiver anytime you so desire to attune yourself to this plane."

"But," I said, "you havent answered my question. Am I dead or alive? Answer me, somebody!"

The only sound that came to my ears after that was a swishin sound. Was it leaves I was hearin? Was it the wind? I didnt mind where it was comin from because at just that moment, for almost forever, look like, this little rhyme started whisperin itself out to the sound of the wind. I mean, it was what the swishin wind was sayin:

Tell my mourners
Dress in red—
Aint no sense
My bein dead.

It said that over and over and over again until I could hear it bein whispered from my own parched lips. Even tho I needed a drinka water or somethin wet real bad, all I could do was repeat that rhyme, which seemed like the only thing left for me to hold on to, because the rest of my world had drifted and shifted into thin air.

# 24

The air mightve been thin, but the lips pressin up against mine were anything *but*. They were very definitely human lips, and not only human—Afro-human. I couldnt figure it out. I even peeped out from under my lids at the crowd around me to see if everybody or anybody was dressed in red. Except for a little girl —Marcie from up the block whose mother, I suspect, was traf-fickin in dope—this didnt seem to be the case. There was a good-size crowd mullin around, tho. Now, where was I? It was hard to accept that I was goin thru yet another change of mind, or whatever you call it.

"What's he doin to her, Mommy?" I heard Marcie say.

"It's all right, honey," her mama said. "He's givin her artificial respiration."

"What's that?"

"That's when someone's lost their breath and another person tries to breathe some of their own breath into them so that they will live."

"But, Mommy, what happened to Miz Franklin?"

"Shhh, be quiet, Marcie . . ."

That did it. Now I had a bead on where it was all comin from.

I remembered the look on Mr. Puckett's pudgy face while he was fingerin my paper on Benjamin Franklin, just about to hand it back to me. There he stood in the sun, light streamin thru the window like there wasnt any tomorrow. He was proud of me, I could tell, and I knew I was gonna do all right in everything connected with his class after that; everything connected with school. Mr. Puckett liked me after that. I was never gonna have to ask him if I could have a swat. And there I was up in fronta the class, recitin a poem. We all had to recite a poem by heart— and you werent allowed to do anything by Edgar A. Guest, and Mr. Puckett had put a ban on Joyce Kilmer's "Trees" too. So I'd picked Langston Hughes, not just because he had a lotta short ones, but because I knew deep inside that his piece called "Wake" was tellin the truth about somethin. It was still whirlin around inside my head. I could see the mourners all dressed in red, flamin red, and I *knew* there wasnt no sense in my bein dead. Dead? What was that? If winter died or summer died, then how come they always came back again and again, right on time, the followin year? Pretty soon I'd be in the ninth grade, the tenth, the eleventh, the twelfth. But I could tell it wasnt in the cards for me to go to college, not right away anyway.

I remembered Chance and Harry and bein tireda travelin and the day Burley died and Benjie so sweet and strong and intelligent and all the light sweepin straight down from out the sky, makin no noise at all, none whatsoever, and there was Theo all squiggly with light and the way he'd made me fly clean up outta my lonesome skin and the shakin and the crashin and the scared way we got the hell outta that house and hauled ass for our lives and Monroe out on his porch across the street, and Monroe . . . and Monroe . . . and Monroe . . . and—

Well, I'll be doggone! That's whose lips it was! Monroe's lips! And he was smackin and lickin and fumblin with my mouth like a puppydog, right there in public, right out there on the street with all those people crowded in close. This wasnt no artificial respiration he was givin me! Not the way he kept jammin his tongue all up inside my mouth and up against the insides of my lips. Dry as my mouth was, what I needed was somethin cool to drink—not somebody breathin their old gin breath and slobberin on me.

Finally there wasnt anything left to do but what felt right, so that's what I did. I bit Monroe, bit him on the tongue, not hard enough for it to hurt or anything—or so I thought—but all the same he raised up off me, and I could hear him go, *"Owwwww!"*

"Hold it," somebody hollered, "looks like youve done it! She's movin! The woman is alive. She's goin to live!"

"Hey," I said, catchin my breath and pushin Monroe away. "I cant breathe with you all up in my mouth like that. Back off!"

Monroe sat up and blinked and looked at me like I was a fallin star that'd just dropped at his feet, which maybe I was. I still felt confused. "Mamie," he said, "is that you?"

"Who else could it be?" I said. "What do you call yourself doin?"

Monroe was shaken. "Nothin," he said, "nothin. I was just tryna get some life back into you. We'd pretty much gave you up for dead."

"Well, I'm not," I said, strainin to sit up. The back of my neck was still hurtin me, tho. My head rolled over and I caught sight of Theo. "And what about him? What about Theo?"

"W-we can see *he's* still breathin. Botha yall musta suffered a concussion or somethin. What was that you were mumblin, Mamie?"

"Mumblin? Was I mumblin?"

"Yeah," said Monroe. "Sound like you were halfway tryna sing, too. Somethin about 'aint no sense in me bein dead.' My artificial respiration musta worked, huh?"

"Monroe," I said, "I can go along with the artificial part. But, you ask me, you were puttin out more perspiration than you were respiration. If I didnt know any better I would call the law on your behind."

I sat up anyway, even tho the kink in my neck was like a butcher knife cuttin at me from the inside now. I knew somethin was wrong and that I'd better not try to move around too much. When I looked out at the crowd and told em I was gonna be all right, that I wasnt among the fatal casualties, they all grinned and a few of em clapped. I wasnt crazy about havin that much attention lavished on me, more especially since there was a genuine, broad-scale disaster goin on.

Little Marcie came forward, looked down at Theo and asked me, "Is he goin to be okay, Miz Franklin?"

I took a good long look at Theo before I said anything. And while I was lookin, somethin interestin was takin place. I could see that not only was Theo gonna be all right but, as a matter of fact, when he did come to he was gonna be better than ever. The best part of his life was truly just beginnin. Now, how did I know this? I'm afraid I cant answer that; it's too complicated to explain. It's easy to do, once you get the hang of it, but it's hard to explain, especially to people who arent use to dealin with spookiness. Dont get me wrong: there's nothin strange about it. It's only a matter of slippin into that frame of mind, lettin yourself go and not bein afraid to deal with what comes to you straight from another parta yourself. I can say all this now, but it actually taken me some time to get to where I could tune in and tune out whenever I wanted to.

All I said to Marcie was, "Yes, sweetheart, the man's gonna be just fine. He's sufferin from shock more than anything else."

"Mamie," said Monroe, "I dont think you should move!" He was still squattin there beside me.

"Monroe, honest, I'm intact. My neck is killin me, but other than that, I'm all right."

The look on Monroe's face told me he thought differently. It was someplace between disbelief and amazement.

"Mamie," he said, "for somebody that's just been thru what you been thru, I just dont see how you can be smilin like that. Here, lemme help you get up."

"I dont need any help," I told him. "I can manage by myself."

But Monroe insisted on positionin himself in back of me and liftin me to my feet.

"You sure youre okay, Miz Franklin?" Marcie's mother said.

She was a brownskin woman who looked like she might have some Mexican in her. She stepped forward to take my hand and I could feel how hot and sticky her fingers were. Without warnin, the woman placed a hand on each of my shoulders, looked at me funny in the saddest way, and as if her eyes werent already red enough, she broke out cryin.

I wrapped my arms around her and squeezed her tight, even tho that caused the quilt draped around me to go to slippin some. And while she was pressed up against me like that, I could feel all the sadness jammed up inside her wantin to come out.

"Mommy, Mommy!" Marcie squealed. "Mommy, what's the matter?" The little girl grabbed ahold of her mother's leg and hugged it like the world was comin to an end, which it did seem to be doin.

"You dont know me," Marcie's mother blubbered in my ear, "but I've lived down the block from you for five years now and I dont think I've ever so much as said hello. I'm Robin."

"Ah, Denise," I said, "I know your daughter Marcie."

"I know. Y-your late husband use to always give her money and tell her to stay out of trouble."

"Is that right?"

"Yes, he was such a wonderful man. I never expressed it, but I felt so sorry for you when he died. I—I just couldnt take the time to tell you that. Dont ask why."

"Well, I wont ask you anything, Robin. You just go ahead and have yourself a good cry. Let it all pour out."

"Oh, Miz Franklin, what on earth are we going to do? This is awful, what's happened, awful!"

"Mommy," said Marcie in her red pajamas, "dont cry! Please dont cry!"

"It's okay for your mother to cry," I told her, restin a hand on her tiny head. "I need to be doin some cryin myself."

"Then why dont you, then?" said Monroe, who was busy takin all this in. He looked as if the fate of the entire western world was pretty much restin on his shoulders.

"Monroe," I said over Robin's shoulder, "I know I need to be cryin, but I just dont have it in me to do that right now. Maybe I'll do my cryin later."

Monroe shook his head and said, "I dont understand you one drop. I mean, at least my house and mosta the other houses still standin, and everything you own done gone up in smoke, right on down to Burley's truck. And, Mamie, here you are consolin somebody else, plus you arent even actin like you."

I didnt hear the rest of what Monroe was tellin me. It got drowned out by all this racket from the fire trucks and paramedics and police cars, and I dont know what-all, that came shriekin up Celestina Street. I just held on tight to Robin and little Marcie and thought how pitiful it looked up and down the block with everybody mopin and roamin around and all sleepy-eyed and scared and edgy and loud. The sireens and horns musta had some effect on Theo too. All of a sudden he shot bolt upright and grabbed his head in both hands and started yellin, "Help, help, help us, somebody!"

You talk about pathetic! All of it was too much for me or anybody else to process. Glad as I was to see Theo comin back to life, it set off somethin sad in me. Now that he was up and stirrin, I let myself collapse up against poor Robin, who had already all but collapsed on me. Tears started skeetin outta me like fire-hydrant water at a block party. Me and Robin both was tremblin.

"MAY WE HAVE YOUR ATTENTION PLEASE!" the voice blastin outta one of the police-car loudspeakers was sayin. "THIS IS AN EMERGENCY. WE ARE EXPERIENCING A MAJOR EARTHQUAKE."

"Isnt this the shits!" Robin cracked. "We already *know* that. Why dont they tell us what we're supposed to do?"

"THE CITY OF SANTA MONICA SEEMS TO HAVE BEEN HIT HARDEST. I MUST ALSO WARN YOU THAT WE HAVE STRONG EVIDENCE OF A RUPTURED GAS MAIN IN THE IMMEDIATE VICINITY—"

"Uh-uhhh," I said, "and I'll betcha it's right up under my house too!"

"Shhh!" said Monroe. "I wanna hear!"

"BY ORDER OF LOCAL AND STATE AUTHORITIES, THE CALIFORNIA GUARD HAS BEEN MOBILIZED AND IS PRESENTLY ON ITS WAY TO CARRY OUT RESCUE WORK. THIS MEANS THAT THE ENTIRE AREA IS BEING EVACUATED AT ONCE."

You could hear people gaspin and groanin and moanin up and down the block. Little Marcie tried to climb up into her mother's arms, but Robin said, "Get down, girl, you've gotten too heavy for Mommy to carry."

"Here," said Monroe, "I'll hold your child."

"She doesnt need to be held."

"It's all right," I told Robin. "He's a strong man. Let him carry her."

Theo, who was sweatin like a mule, wiped his forehead with the backa one hand and said, "This wouldnt have been a good night for the art class, would it?"

Feelin devilish all of a sudden, I couldnt resist winkin at him. "Theo," I said, "if you'da gone in there dressed like you are now, you probably coulda made a colorful model."

At this, Monroe and Robin shot us funny looks, while Marcie clamped her tiny brown arms around Monroe's neck and stretched out her neck. All the while her head was bobbin around like the valve on a steamin pressure cooker. That child didnt intend to miss a thing.

"TO MAKE THE GOING EASIER, THE CALIFORNIA EMERGENCY MANAGEMENT AGENCY WILL BE WORKING WITH THE GUARD, THE RED CROSS, AND THE SALVATION ARMY TO ASSIST YOU WITH YOUR FOOD, WATER, AND MEDICAL NEEDS. PUBLIC SCHOOLS AND OTHER FACILITIES ARE BEING READIED AT THIS MOMENT FOR IMMEDIATE OCCUPATION BY THE HOMELESS. PLEASE DO NOT PANIC. ALL AGENCIES ARE WORKING AS DILIGENTLY AND QUICKLY AS POSSIBLE TO CLEAR UP THE DAMAGE THE EARTHQUAKE HAS CAUSED. I RE-

PEAT: WHATEVER YOU DO, DO NOT PANIC! AND
PLEASE LEAVE YOUR AUTOMOBILES PARKED
WHERE THEY ARE."

"Whoa!" said Monroe. "This *is* serious. I wonder if theyll let
us go back in the house to pack a few things."

"Yeah, Mommy," said Marcie. "Can we go back to our
house?"

"I dont know about that, honey," Robin said, lookin panicked.
"Maybe I'll ask and see what they say."

"I dont care what they say," Monroe said, suddenly puttin
Marcie back down on the sidewalk and turnin in his tracks toward his house.

"Monroe," I said, "what you got in there that's more important than your life?"

"Shoot, I got me a great big bottle of Southern Comfort in
there somebody at the shop gave me for my birthday last week,
and it aint even been opened yet. I figure if I'm gon have to clear
outta here I might as well take it along."

And before we even had time to react, Sneaky Pete was gone!

Theo still looked weak as he shifted the tablecloth he was
wearin this way and that. But I could see a feeble grin playin
around his handsome face. When I asked him what was so
funny, he didnt say anything; he just leaned over and started
singin in a low voice.

A couple of helicopters were just beginnin to move in over-
head and I had a hard time hearin what the boy was singin, so I
said, "How's that again, Theo?"

"Oh, nothin," he said. "Just somethin I remembered from a
Lambert, Hendricks & Ross record my dad used to play." Theo
was yellin this in my ear, which was makin me feel kinda light-
headed out there in the night with all that disaster pilin up.

"And how'd the song go?" I hollered back at Theo.

"It's a song about a wino," said Theo. "It's called 'Gimme
That Wine.' This wino's house is burning down and he's singing, 'So I can drink one toast/before I roast.' "

As kids will sometimes do, Marcie overheard Theo singin and

busted out laughin. Now, I don't know if she understood *why*
Theo was doin this, or what, but her laughter got me to laughin
and even Robin had to lighten up some—for a moment anyway.

"Mommy," Marcie said suddenly, "I want a piece of toast.
Can we go in the house and get some toast? And my teddy? And
the TV?"

"Excuse me," said Robin, chasin after the cops in the loudspeaker car, "Officer, officer . . . I have a question!"

And it seemed like everybody started crowdin around the poor
cop car at the same time. I stood there, feelin totally relaxed for
some reason. While the sirens and the helicopters and the fire-
trucks raged on, I decided to sit myself right down there on the
curb and try to catch my breath. Benjie was on my mind again.
Benjie and Charlean and the Chryslers and Nomo and Tree and
Chance—all the people I cared about. I even thought about
Kendall, Burley's boy, and I never hardly ever think all that
much about Kendall, except to feel sorry for him.

There was a tremblin at the backa my neck after Theo sat
down beside me on the curb and watched Marcie take off after
her mother. He was doin a lotta that deep, heavy sighin, the
kinda sighin I was doin a lot of after Burley passed on. It was the
same kinda sighin I'd done at Papa and Mother Dear's funerals
too—that soothin kinda sighin I'll betcha everybody does when
somethin big has come to the end, and youre sittin there havin a
hard time figurin out if youre the one that's gone or the one
that's left.

Careful to keep his tablecloth on straight, Theo flopped that
lean, wonderful arm of his across my shoulder and said, "I'm
sorry, Mamie, I truly am. I hope you wont remember me as the
bringer of dark luck."

"Dark luck?" I told him in as low a voice as I could manage,
considerin all that racket. What strikes me funny, now that I
look back on it, is how the phrase itself was soundin to me. *Dark*
luck, I thought. Now, that sounds worse than *bad* luck. It was
the way Theo said it, tho, that struck somethin deep. "How
could I ever think like that?" I said. "I mean, you are one hell of

a lover, Theo, but even I would be hesitant to flat out say you made the earth move." But then I stopped and thought about it some. "On the other hand," I added, "I'd be scared anymore to tell you what I think. It's like . . . it's like I'm no longer even doin the thinkin."

"I'm afraid I don't follow you, Mamie."

"Yeah," I said. "It's somethin like all this stuff is thinkin me. It's like I'm bein thought."

"Huh? Theo pulled his arm away and looked dead at me, stone serious. "Mamie, I'm sure there will be medics coming along real soon. I don't feel all that well myself. Perhaps it would be best if each of us got a bit of medical and psychological attention. It's possible we're both suffering from some form of emotional shock or trauma that even we aren't fully aware of."

Dont ask me why, but I broke out laughin.

"You find that amusing, do you?"

"No, not exactly."

"Let's just sit still until they take us to wherever we're going."

"Theo, arent you worried about your family, your folks or anything?"

"Certainly, I intend to contact them just as soon as I can get to a telephone."

"Hahhh!" was all I said, doin some sighin of my own. "Isnt this somethin!"

He put his arm back around me and kissed me on my achin neck. Just as sweet as he can be. I felt sorry for him and everybody else more than I felt sorry for myself.

"Fifty-five dollars and ninety-five cents for your thoughts," Theo said after we didnt say anything for a long time.

I squeezed his hand. "I'm thinkin about Benjamin Franklin," I said.

"Benjamin Franklin!" Theo said, once again pullin back from me and starin. "That's a rather odd thing to be thinking of just now." Then he smacked himself on the forehead and snuggled back up. "Forgive me, will you? You're talking about Benjamin, your son, right?"

"Sure," I said. It so happened I had pictures I was lookin at
inside my head where me and Ben and Burley were floatin up
over this whole scene, which kinda resembled a real-life film of
some kind. It had me feelin glad too. I cant explain it. All this
good, glad kinda electricity was bubblin thru my body like soda
pop in a can that's been shook up. In fact, I'd be lyin if I said it
was all I could do to keep the top of my head from flyin clean off.
I could even hear Happy Lucas—my old tonk-playin, co-com-
poser bass player buddy from band days—hear him goin, "Look
out now before you flip your skypiece!"

It was good to have Theo up next to me, strokin my neck. For
one thing, it helped me kinda ground myself for the time bein.
With him hunkered up that close to me, I could tell where I left
off and he began.

I was tryin my best to click back into bein sad again, like I was
suppose to be, yet even when the army trucks and jeeps started
rollin up to collect us up and carry us off, I couldnt help but
think about the way Papa and Mother Dear and the whole of
Hattiesburg use to celebrate V-day. Maybe Theo was right, I
thought to myself. Maybe I did need to talk to a psychiatrist.

For the time bein, it was all I could do to keep from gettin
crushed and mangled while people ran and jumped and pushed
and shoved and hollered and screamed and toted and dragged
stuff. They kept this up until a man and a woman on one of the
military trucks hauled out a big, new-style electronic loudspeaker
and got us to linin up in formation, just like you see in the
movies. And while they were helpin me up into the back of one
of the trucks, I could see Monroe runnin down his front steps
with a paper bag fulla junk and Marcie boodlin along in behind
Robin with her teddy.

"I think we need some medical attention," Theo said to the
young soldier in charge of packin our truck.

"Don't worry," the soldier said, "after we get you out of here,
everything'll be taken care of."

The soldier looked to me like he couldna been more than

eighteen or nineteen years old and, for some reason, that set me off wantin to cry all over again.

All the soldier did was shake his head and give me what musta been his most sincere and innocent look. "We'll get you fixed up," he assured us. "Get you some clothes and *everything*."

# 25

I sat there in the backa that army truck, crammed in with old folks and people my age and youngsters and kids I only halfway recognized, and we all talked off-the-wall and outta our heads the whole way. The woman from next door, Josephine Rackham, the one who never has anything to say to me except why dont I have this bush cut down or that tree cut down because it's pushin up against her fence or the leaves are fallin over into her yard—well, she was just as nice as she could be.

"Oh, Mamie," she said, "youve been such a good neighbor! It must have been devastatin for you when you lost your husband. Burley was such a thoughtful, considerate man."

I was sittin there next to Theo, thinkin, *Well, if all these people felt so sorry for me when Burley died, then why were they just now tellin me about it?*

But then Josephine came up outta her bag, as we use to say in the band. "Loneliness," she said, "is terrible, isnt it?"

It took me a few seconds to realize what Josephine was really drivin at. All she wanted to know was what was I doin sittin up there in that quilt, with this young man wrapped in a tablecloth?

I said, "Josephine, that's why you see me always out there in my garden every chance I get. It just consoles me to be around young and tender; growin things—squash and tomatoes and garlic and geraniums; bloomin and flowerin things."

Josephine's eyebrows musta shot a good inch up her forehead. But when her mouth fell open, not one single word tumbled out.

While the truck was toolin along, all of us were tryna peep out the canvas openin in the rear to see what'd been goin on; check what the earthquake'd done to Greater L.A. That cop musta been tellin the truth about Santa Monica bein hard hit. It was dark and mosta the streetlights were out, but from what I could see there werent that many buildins on fire. It was dark, tho, and I couldnt really tell much. But there were people out everywhere and we kept havin to turn to drive around big chunks of concrete and cement and bricks and damaged cars.

All along Sunset Strip the electricity was out and folks were burnin bonfires and shinin flashlights; yet even at that, I could see where a lotta the signs and billboards advertisin movies and records had either tumbled down or were just halfway hangin in place. For some reason, I got a little thrill outta this. No more business as usual—no way!

There was one man who was puffin away on a stomach-turnin cigar, a big fat man with blotchy, red skin who kept sayin things like, "First thing in the morning, I'm getting my attorney on the phone. Anybody else here interested in instigating a class-action suit?"

"What do you plan to sue for?" someone else in the crowd asked.

"Negligence. The amount of property damage we've suffered is practically incalculable. Those gas mains should've been in good repair. Hell, I pay taxes the same as you!"

"But in the event of an act of nature," a squeaky little woman said, "is it possible to file suit? After all, no one's responsible for an earthquake, are they?"

"When in doubt," the fat man said, "I always say sue the bastards!"

"Watch your language, please!" said a little old lady with a tot

on her lap. "My grandson and other children are present. We
Jehovah's Witnesses take a dim view of profanity."

"Aw, shit!" the fat man said. But the crowd, includin the
soldiers, showed that they were definitely on the lady's side.
Cries and mutterings of "pipe down" and "knock it off!" and
"give us a break!" shot around the truck.

"Oh, fuck!" the fat man groaned and reached into a canvas
sack he'd been grapplin with. Now that all the attention was on
him, with his obnoxious cigar, we all could watch him peel back
the canvas and pull out one of those miniature TVs, a Sony
Watchman. Personally, I never did understand why those sets
were so popular in the first place: the picture's so tiny you cant
even hardly see the people or make out what's goin on. But by
his breakin out the television set, the whole mood of the crowd
did a flip.

"Hey," the same squeaky-voiced woman said, "does that thing
really work?"

"No," said the fat man, real sullen and nasty-lookin, still tryna
smoke us out. "I just brought it along to use for a pillow. Shit,
yeah, it works!"

The minute he snapped it on, everybody crowded around him.
There was nothin on but news and special reports on the earthquake. What else would they be showin under these conditions?
And you know how the news people have themselves a field day
when it comes to reportin on crises and emergencies. That's all
they seem to live for.

*"For those of you just tuning in,"* a woman at a desk was sayin,
*"Los Angeles has been rocked by what authorities are calling one
of the most unusual earthquakes in recent California history . . ."*

Some youngster who'd wedged himself in between me and the
fat man said, "I wonder what it was on the Richter scale?"

*"Seismologists at the U.S. Geological Survey report that this
evening's jolt registered seven point four on the Richter scale.
Property damage and personal injuries are widespread, with forty-
four deaths reported thus far. The city of Santa Monica has been*

*particularly hard hit. Major gas and water mains in that community have been ruptured by the quake. Fires are raging out of control there. The president has declared southern California a disaster area, and both the mayor and the governor have called out the Guard to assist in emergency rescues and the evacuation of entire sections of Santa Monica. Seismologists believe that, once again, the movement of the San Fernando fault set off this evening's disaster. It was the movement of that same fault that brought about the 1971 quake that rocked southern California, claiming the lives of sixty-four persons. Tonight's quake has been felt as far away as southern Oregon. We have reporters stationed on the scene all over the area, and we take you now to—"*

Without warnin, the fat man switched to another channel, where another news special was runnin. I sat there, watchin the two news people tampin down their little stacks of paper, wonderin how come they make such a big thing outta that when all they ever do is read from the teleprompter. I was also wonderin why the fat man went on flippin from channel to channel, when he shoulda known there wouldnt be anything else on except earthquake news.

"What's the matter?" the nice soldier boy asked him. "Is it too much for you to stay with one station so we can get an update?"

The fat man gave the soldier a look that was icy enough to make a hockey player uncomfortable. "You forget," he barked, "it's my TV. I can look at what I damn well want."

Whoa, that was one edgy crowd on that army truck that night! I was glad when we finally got to where we were headed.

Hollywood High School was where the procession of trucks ended up. I've never seen anything like it before or since. They had blocked off all the streets and diverted traffic and set up big-beam lights so people could see. We climbed out the truck into that chilly L.A. nighttime air and, lemme tell you, there were soldiers and police and volunteers rushin around every which way, haulin cots and tables and chairs and food and boxes of first aid and medicine—everything you could think of.

"This is where you'll spend the night," one of the soldiers told us. "This is all makeshift and jerry-built, but it's a roof over your head and there'll be something to eat. We want you to form a line diagonally across the campus grass over there. As the line moves forward, you will be given instructions on what to do and where to go."

Theo, who still looked weak, squeezed my hand and said, "I wonder what would happen if I just figured out a way to make it back to my place."

"That might present a problem," I said. "Sounds like all the roads have been rerouted and tied up. Besides, it'll be mornin before you know it; then we can both figure out what to do."

"But I *must* make a phone call," he said, turnin to another of the soldiers. "Is there a telephone around here I can use?"

The soldier pointed to a public phone up the street.

"Excuse me, Mamie," Theo said. I watched him hurry off up the block and noticed he was limpin.

While I was makin my way to the tail end of one of the lines that was formin, up walked this woman with a microphone in her hand and a coupla fellows with mini-TV cameras followin her. Right away I got one of those deep-down hits you get when you recognize somebody that's halfway famous, even tho you have trouble callin their name right off.

"Excuse me," she said, comin right at me.

I stood there with my finger pointed at her, my mouth hangin open, while I tried to remember who she was.

She musta known what I was up to because all she did was sparkle and flash me one of those slow and easy celebrity smiles and say, "Brett Toshimura, *Channel 7 Action News.*"

"That's right," I said. "So they got you workin out here tonight?"

"No rest for the weary. That's the journalism business."

"You mean, show business."

"A little of both, I suppose. Do you mind if I interview you?"

"About what?"

"About the earthquake. You're one of the victims they just transported from Santa Monica, right?"

Now, here I was suddenly a "victim." Well, even tho I wasnt exactly dressed the way I woulda liked, I told her, "All right, but could you try to keep from zoomin in too close? I'm not exactly lookin my best."

"I understand. Don't worry." Then Brett turned to one of the camera people. He moved right in on top of us. "Does this look right to you, Larry?" she asked.

"Perfect," he said. "We'll shoot from over here."

With the cameras goin, Brett said, "Your name is—?"

"Mamie Franklin."

"And what were you doing when the quake struck Santa Monica?"

"I was, um, just relaxin at home and, well, you know, turnin in early so I could get an early start today."

"And what is your occupation?"

"I'm a psychic."

Brett wasnt ready for that one, I could tell. She started battin her eyes a little too fast and said, "Really? So, tell me, did your psychic mechanism manage to pick up on the possibility of a disaster of this magnitude?"

"Why, yes, Brett. It just so happened I'd taken leave of my normal mind just minutes before the first tremors were felt."

"This was at your home in—?"

"Right there at 222 Celestina Street in Santa Monica."

"And you experienced a premonition that this was going to happen?"

"Indeed, I did."

I'd be dishonest if I didnt admit that I was enjoyin just bein up there in fronta those cameras. It was like I was workin again. Startin out, I hadnt the slightest idea I was gonna react like that.

"How much time elapsed between the time your psychic powers discerned the prospect of impending disaster and its actual unfolding?"

"Like I say, Brett . . . it was only a matter of minutes."

"But obviously that wasn't enough time for you to prepare for the quake?"

"No, not at all . . . for, you see, I was dressed for bed. In fact, I was *in* bed when plaster began to crumble from my ceilin and rain down upon me."

"And then you must have known it was already too late?"

"Precisely," I said, ready to go into another round of ad-lib reactions off the top of my head. But then somethin unexpected happened. While I was talkin, my mind started to actually rememberin how I'd felt when me and Theo were doin our damnedest to get outta that house before it went up in smoke. Pictures of the water floodin in and the flames flarin up and all Burley's stuff catchin on fire and every precious thing I ever owned goin up in that fire while we got out the best we could— all this got magnified in my brain while I was up there performin and I lost control.

It wasnt only that I lost control, but for the first time, it began to hit me how double-minded I was about the whole experience. On the one hand, I was devastated to lose everything I treasured. On the other hand, there'd been this exhilaration buildin up inside me ever since I took that trip outta my body and hovered out there in space, wherever it was, with Burley and old Ben. I had the most powerful, gladdenin feelin that somethin indescribable, somethin wonderful, was on the verge of happenin to me.

And yet I kept wonderin if maybe I hadnt cracked up under all the stress and emotion I'd been sustainin, only still didnt know it.

In point of fact, what happened was, I lost my train of thought while Brett and the camera people were focused on me, and I just broke down and started cryin and blubberin and sayin all these incoherent things. All I could tell at the time is that they were comin straight from the center of my heart.

"It's just awful, just awful!" I do recall tellin Brett that much. "I dont know what I'm gonna do. Everything I have in the world is gone, and I dont even know where my son is in this city, and he's the only child I have."

The words didnt matter; it was all those feelins dammed up inside me that'd been pushin to get out.

By the time I got thru, Brett was cryin, along with the two camera operators, and just about everybody in the crowd that'd gathered around to watch the interview were wet-eyed or choked up. Brett personally gave me her card after she put her signature to it and wrapped up the take.

After the red lights on the cameras clicked off, Brett said, "Call me first thing in the morning and I'll write you a personal check."

Larry, the cameraman, up and pulled a coupla twenties from his pocket and pressed them into my hand. And I could see that somebody in the crowd had started passin a hat around.

Just then, up popped Theo, still wrapped in his army blanket. He looked as if his phone call had left him satisfied. He limped right up to where me and the television people were standin and said, "Any new developments while I was away?"

Then he looked around and saw how everybody was lookin so sad, includin me.

"Mamie," he said. "Something *has* happened, hasnt it? Tell me what it is."

All I could do was shake my head and squinch my eyes and hold on to him to ease the tremblin until the sadness was bawled outta me.

"Is this your long-lost son?" the generous cameraman asked me, lookin all hopeful.

After that, I'm tellin you, you couldnt beat em off with a stick. Media people came crowdin in on me from all directions. It was like they sensed somethin hot was goin on. It was all I could do to blurt my name out and try to hold down my place in line too.

"I'm from the *L.A. Times,*" one of em said. "Would you mind if we get a picture and chat with you?"

"I'm an *Examiner* photographer," said another one, "and a couple of shots of you is all I want . . ."

"Mamie Franklin?" said some bright-lookin young woman with a pad and pen in hand. "I'm a stringer for *People* magazine, and I'd be very much interested in talking with you, perhaps after you've gotten some sleep . . ."

"Mamie, I'm Chad Fox, *National Enquirer.* Any chance of my having a few words with you?"

"Would you have a few words for National Public Radio?"

And that's how it went until I started feelin dizzy and grumpy. By the time they got me to one of the classrooms where cots had been set up, there were so many people makin a fuss over me until the only thing I could think of to tell em was I needed some privacy and some special medical care, which was the truth. If I hadnt needed it when I got there, I sure enough needed it now. I was even beginnin to have fantasies about how nice it would be to curl up in Sweepea, my little Honda Civic and pull my blanket over me and get a halfway decent night's sleep like that. I certainly wasnt ready to go tryna wash up in the lavatory down the hall, which was already jammed up with "victims."

Somehow, word of my need got back to Brett Toshimura, who was still hangin out in fronta the school, talkin with people, and she came back to where I was to tell me she had a doctor friend who worked at the hospital up the street. She said maybe there'd be a possibility they could make room for me to stay there for the resta the night.

"And," she said, "we'll drive you there personally in the *Action News* truck."

# 26

At first the people at the hospital tried to act like I needed to go down to the emergency ward where, as you might imagine, people were piled on top of each other in the waitin room and crammed up all in the halls. It was somethin like the way I picture Bombay or Calcutta to be. I knew that wasnt gonna work out at all. To tell you the truth, I wouldve been just as happy drivin back home and goin to bed. But there wasnt any home to go back to, and you already know where Sweepea was parked. Brett Toshimura knew as well as I did that the emergency wasnt the place for me.

We put our heads together and tried to figure out how we might get this hincty receptionist to let us in to see Brett's friend —this Dr. Yamamoto—who I suspect was also her boyfriend, goin by the soft glaze that came over her face when she talked about him.

"He's given me strict orders that he's too busy to see anyone," the receptionist said.

"But, wait a minute," I said. "Do you know who youre talkin to?"

"What do you mean?" the receptionist woofed, her nose

lookin like it was gettin harder and harder while she was glarin at
us.

"Youre talkin to Brett Toshimura of the *Channel 7 Action
News.*"

"Huh?"

I could see some dim kinda light clickin on in her overtrained
brain.

"Gee, you do look familiar, come to think of it!"

That's when it hit me to have Brett go outside where the
truck was waitin and bring one of the cameramen in and have
him bring in her little microphone, the one she uses to interview
people on the tube.

The minute we brought that off, the receptionist started meltin like chocolate ice cream.

"Let me try Dr. Yamamoto one more time," she said.

I'm tellin you here and now that the media is not to be played
with! A camera and a mike and the sight of somebody people
been seein on TV—that can open more doors than a boatload of
keys.

"It's a new receptionist," Brett confided. "I never would have
had this kind of trouble with Gladys."

Brett and Dr. Yamamoto greeted one another with a polite
hug. But you know, you can always tell when people tryna keep
outsiders from knowin how they really feel about one another.
Somethin told me the two of em really wouldna minded clutchin
each other a little stronger, and gettin in some kisses, too. Anyway, it wasnt any of my business. All I wanted was to sit down
and give my poor feet a rest.

"What seems to be the problem?" Dr. Yamamoto turned to
me and asked Brett.

"This poor woman!" Brett said. Already I could hear her gettin choked up and fluttery. "She's been through hell and high
water—"

*Hmmm,* I thought, *that's actually true.*

"Her house in Santa Monica burned to the ground. She's
passed out from shock. She doesn't know where to locate her son

or any of her close relations. She seems to be experiencing extreme fatigue . . ."

I stood and listened to Brett pour it on poor Dr. Yamamoto, who really did look like he was overworked. His eyes looked big thru his rose-tinted glasses, and they also looked like they might could use a generous squirt of Visine.

"You must have a close look at her, Chris," Brett told him. "I know youre backed up with patients, but . . . as a personal favor to me?"

Dr. Yamamoto got real still. He listened close to everything Brett was sayin, then he got his little doctor smile together and hit his intercom for a nurse to come in and see me into an examination room.

After that, I dont know what he and Brett did because the nurse, a real friendly-lookin woman with red hair and green eyes and freckles, she pointed to the examination table, told me to strip down to my underwear, and then, just like she'd gone and shocked herself, I watched her freeze.

"I'm sorry," she said, lookin all embarrassed. "I don't suppose you're wearing any underwear, are you?"

I shook my head.

"Well, sit down and relax. I'll take your temperature and blood pressure."

All my life I have hated those doggone examinin tables. They arent all that bad if you got your clothes on, but have you ever had to sit nekkid on all that crackly paper they spread over it? Whew, I'm tellin you, it's hardly what you call fun. But then, bein at the doctor's in the first place isnt supposed to be fun, is it?

The nurse surprised me by feelin my pulse with her bare hand clamped around my wrist; then she took a good look down my throat before she put the thermometer in. And while she was adjustin the band they tighten around your arm to take your blood pressure and pumpin it up, I could tell she really liked her job. You get so use to these wham-bam nurses and doctors until somebody that'll actually take the time to check you out for real can make you feel about fifty percent better right from the git-go.

I liked this woman, so I looked at her name tag.EILEEN Mc-GILLICUDDY. You could tell they almost couldnt squeeze all the letterin on there. She looked a little sour after she read what the numbers told her about my blood pressure.

"Doesnt look all that hot, eh?" I said, gettin the jump on her.

"It's, well, it's running on the high side. Borderline, really." She jotted this down on her clipboard, then pulled the thermometer from my mouth and held it up to the light.

"You're running a slight fever, too," she said, still frownin. "I'll bet you're simply worn out. But I think the doctor will want to give you a good going over. You have health insurance?"

"Last I heard, I did," I said. "But now, what with the quake and all, all the forms probably went up in smoke and—"

"Never mind." She handed me another board with a form clipped to it. "Just fill this out," she said. "Your name, address, company insured with—that sort of thing. Dr. Yamamoto will be with you in a few minutes."

Eileen McGillicuddy started for the door but halfway there stopped and turned around. "I can't tell you how sorry I am about your misfortune," she said. "It is a horrible thing that's taken place. I have no trouble whatever placing myself in your" —she got quiet for a second while she looked, I suppose, at my bare feet—"your place," she continued. "I have no trouble putting myself in your place. We *are*, in reality—all of us—*connected*, whether we realize it or not."

Again, I was touched and thanked her.

"If there's anything I can do to help you—and this goes beyond medical help—you have only to tell me what it is."

The instant she said that, I knew she wasnt makin it up, wasnt just bein polite, but meant it. Kindness like that can make you lightheaded, especially if you arent used to it. It tickled me to be fillin out that form after she'd left. No matter how neatly I printed in my address, that still wouldnt make 222 Celestina

Street spring back to life. I sure wished it could, tho. All I wanted to do was lie down.

I filled in the last question—Name and address of nearest relative to be notified in case of emergency—by writin out Benjamin's name. Then, feelin more lightheaded than usual—or maybe it was because I'd finally got to sit down someplace where it was halfway quiet—I decided to stretch out on the examinin table and wait for the doctor. I wrapped my quilt and blanket around me all snug and laid there like a corpse. Dead tired.

Dr. Yamamoto was a nice man but the strain, I could tell, was gettin to him. He gave me a good goin over, all the while lookin over his shoulder or at his watch like he was expectin, or even *hopin*, to be interrupted at any minute.

Finally when he was done, he said, "Considering the kind of crisis you're experiencing and the losses you've suffered, you aren't doing badly, Mrs. Franklin. Your blood pressure's too high, however, much too high. I don't know if it's diet, lack of exercise, stress, or a combination of all three, which it usually is."

"But black people's blood pressure tends to run high, doesnt it?"

"Yes, that's true. But that doesn't lessen its importance as a risk factor. In all frankness, I think you're exhausted and need a good night's rest, two perhaps."

"But there's no way I'm gonna get a good night's sleep down there at that high school."

"Miss Toshimura and I are aware of that. That's why she insisted upon delivering you to me. It won't be easy, but with a bit of manipulation I think I might be able to come up with a bed for you here for the night. My opinion is that you need to be observed overnight. I don't like this high blood pressure and I'm going to ask the nurse to get blood and urine specimens."

"That Brett is good people," I said. "But I guess you know that."

Dr. Yamamoto's face got flushed. I decided not to tease him.

"I am quite fond of her," he said, lookin all lost. But he sure didnt lose any time snappin back into his doctor thing. "Please be patient," he said. "You have no idea how many other people I have yet to see."

"Yes, I do too."

"Under the conditions, you are exemplary in your patience and understanding. Miss McGillicuddy will come back to get those blood and urine specimens just as soon as she's free. I'll check back in on you after you've rested."

"Oh, Doctor," I said before he got outta my sight. "This pain at the backa my neck. Is there anything you can do for this?"

"Ah," he said, walking back to me. "Let's have a look at that."

I felt him feelin and rubbin and pressin on my neck until he hit the very spot that hurt. I let out a yelp.

"Were you hit on the back of your head?" he asked.

"Remember now, the roof caved in at my place."

"Then you will have to be X rayed," he said. "But I'll see that you receive medication that will help you rest before we put you through any other procedures."

And with that, the good doctor got outta there before I could bring up anything else that might be troublin me. I sat, waitin for the nurse to come back in with that bottle or that jar, or whatever it was gonna be, and that needle. The way I was feelin, I figured the nurse might coulda killed two birds with one stone, so to speak. I was feelin so bad and shot it wouldna surprised me if I peed blood.

# ⚞ 27 ⚟

Straight off the top, I knew the medication they gave me, whatever it was, didnt need to be that strong to send me off into dreamland. You must know me well enough by now to know I'm kinda halfway out there mosta the time anyway. Miss McGillicuddy said it was a mild sedative, like they always say, and I was just plain glad to be in a bed again in some real clothin, even if it was just a green hospital robe. Lemme tell you, after you been bounced around in an earthquake and standin on your feet and gettin jostled and transported here and there and poked and rubbed and jabbed and led around like you got a ring in your nose, you are perfectly ready for that hot shower and slippin into some kinda robe. The bed they put you in could be on Pluto, far as youre concerned. That it happened to be in a tiny room way off in some parta the hospital it felt like people didnt too often frequent, well, that was heaven enough for me. The room was so tiny, in fact, that it put me in mind of a closet—a large walk-in closet, maybe, but a closet all the same, one that'd been remodeled into a hospital room. But it felt like Buckingham Palace to me.

"This will relax you," Miss McGillicuddy said.

I was fadin already while she pulled the hypodermic out my arm and swabbed the puncture with an alcohol-soaked cotton ball. "I don't believe in unnecessary medication," she said in a tone that made me see for a glimmer that there was some kinda special understandin that existed just between the two of us. It's interestin when you get those little jolts off people.

I looked at her face in the bright light before she snapped it off and left just a dim little bedside lamp burnin for me to see by. She had some of the steadiest eyes I have ever seen: green and bright and steady like she was takin in everything all the time. Most people when you talk to em, their eyes—if they look at you at all—flit around in all directions. Not this nurse's. When she looked at you, you knew you'd been looked at.

"Unless you'd like to chat some more," she said, "I'll leave you to rest. I think it's nothing short of a blessing that Dr. Yamamoto came up with this single room for you. As long as I've been working here, I didn't even know it existed."

"I got my guardian angels," I said, bein cute.

Nurse McGillicuddy took me seriously. "I know you do," she said, blinkin at last. "And they are taking good care of you. I know." She rested the flat of her hand against my forehead and I could feel all that warmth spreadin across the topa my face on back to my temples and ears and all down into my throat.

"That aspirin seems to be taking your fever down," she said.

"You know what?"

"Yes, Mrs. Franklin?"

"You have healin hands."

"You think so?"

"Yes, I can tell."

"That's what I always wanted to do—help people heal."

"You just happen to be a nurse, and that's good. But with those hands of yours, all you'd have to do is lay em on people and—"

I didnt know where all what I was sayin was comin from, and somewhere, down around my throat or someplace, I could feel a whole new world of givin-up-the-ghost closin in. All thru me this meltin, buttery feelin was spreadin out the way it feels when you first settle down in a nice bathtub fulla hot water, only it was inside of me. Everything around me looked so pretty and perfect, exactly the way it was suppose to look. Includin the nurse. I reached out to touch her warm hand after she'd pulled it away, and the last thing I remember is the sweetness in her voice and the way she smiled when she said, "Good night, Mrs. Franklin."

I didnt move a muscle. I laid there feelin myself growin lighter and lighter until it seemed as if I was made outta pure moonlight and was travelin thru the atmosphere at one hundred eighty-six thousand miles a second. That's still how fast light travels, isnt it? At least that's what they taught us back in science class. Pretty soon that little cooped-up room was too tiny to hold me in it. I was gettin bigger and bigger and bigger—not my body so much as my real self, the part we cant see. And there didnt seem to be any trick to it. All you had to do was undo all your knots and catches and float—just let yourself float. The only thing I wasnt crazy about was I felt like I was more in control when it happened out there in Santa Monica earlier. Now I had to do more than a little bit of duckin to stay out the way of that medication, that dope, which seemed to have its own ideas about where it wanted to take me.

What was it I'd been worryin about, anyway? Did you say an earthquake? Losin everything I had, just about? Was it my son and all the people I knew? Feelin like I was alone in this world? Hard as I tried, I couldnt remember much about worryin and what it felt like to be scared. The crazy fear spasms that'd been terrorizin my stomach for the longest, they all dissolved like sugar in a hot cup of tea. Honest, I couldnt remember what I'd ever been afraid of or worried about all back thru my life. And that's sayin somethin! All I ever really wanted was inner peace, peace of mind.

But it had already started, that feelin of floatin free and weightless and light. Right after the quake it'd started. No, earlier than that. I couldnt remember. Maybe with Theo. If I strained a little, I knew I could recall when it'd started. Strainin

was outta the question, tho. It was impossible to strain or struggle at anything, least of all stuff I tried to retrieve from memory,
which seemed to be shut down anyway.

"Have you even so much as a glimmering as to why you have
traveled this route?"

The voice was as familiar as a tollin bell, and just as clear. But
I had to get my bearins before I could identify it. The only way I
know to translate it into everyday terms would be to say it came
at me like those voices from the past musta been comin at people when Ralph Edwards would get em out there to play *This Is
Your Life* on television.

"Could you say a little more?" I asked.

"Why, Mamie, it astonishes me that you, of all people, should
meet with any difficulty in recognizing me."

I could see all the stars and constellations and burnin space
around us, but I couldnt see who it was until I got quiet and quit
tryin.

"There," he said. Then the lights went on and I could see him
real clear, except I had two angles on it. One had him standin in
a field with me, a field made outta sun and light. In the other
one, he was right there in the room, by the bed. The two pictures were one and the same, but I would shift my perspective
from one to the other whenever the mood was right. The fact of
it was I didnt have all that much control over which picture I
was lookin at; it changed by itself, dependin on what we were
talkin about. We started out hangin out there in space someplace, but as the conversation developed it shifted more and
more to the hospital room. You gotta keep in mind, tho, that
when we would be in the hospital room, when I saw it from that
angle, then it was the same as if I was still sedated. That is, while
Mamie Franklin was asleep, not the real me. The real me was
made outta the same stuff as Burley and old Ben.

"Ben," I said, suddenly bustin out laughin. I mean, you do
have to keep your sense of humor, no matter what. "Ben," I said,
"you love to fool with me, dont you?"

"I can assure you that I do not come in jest, Mamie. I have been appointed to inform you forthwith of a matter that is of paramount importance."

"Hey, hold on a second!" I said. "Slow down, Ben. I meant to ask you this when we met out there after the quake. Tell me, where exactly are you comin *from*?"

"I am none other than a messenger," he said, "come to bid you welcome."

"Welcome to what?"

"To your higher self. Nothing more, nothing less. You, my friend, are in urgent pursuit of information, and I have been dispatched to provide you with it."

It was confusin. There I was all shiny and listenin to my friend Ben; but there I was sleepin, too. I looked at myself on the hospital bed with the blanket tucked up around me so cozy and comfy. Oooh, was I ever toasty, as my son use to put it. When he was little, Benjie would tiptoe into my room and say, "Mommy, arent you toasty?"

Lookin real close, tho, at myself asleep, I could sorta make out this bright silver cord that was shimmerin in the dark and curlin straight up and around from my solar plexus.

"What's that?" I asked Ben without even pointin.

Automatically he knew what I was referrin to, and he said, "That, Mamie, is the connection. That's how you know you cannot get lost. For as long as the soul inhabits that physical body, this connection will persist. To wit, it shall exist for as long as you are—as you so quaintly put it—alive."

"So this is a dream I'm havin, right?"

"Somewhat," he said and then began to chuckle in a way that made his eyebrows and the lines in his forehead bob up and down, which caused those crinkles I love so much around his eyes to start dancin around like little lines of electricity.

"In reality," he explained, "people habitually take leave of their bodies during sleep."

"But I've known that for the longest."

"Of course you have, my friend, and this is precisely the purpose of my presence in your life."

"Run that one by me again, Ben. And tell it to me real slow so I dont miss a drop."

Ben began to laugh out loud from the middle of his belly right on up to the centers of his eyes, which I could see were gettin wet. "Mamie," he said, "our speaking with each other is hardly more than a passing formality. It would certainly be possible, as you already know, to impart the information it has become my duty to present to you in an altogether wordless fashion."

"Yes," I said, "and—?"

Ben reached out and took my hands in his. I could feel sure enough current pulsin back and forth from him to me and back again; and every time it completed that circle, the electricity would get stronger and stronger. When it got to the place where I thought I might have to be grounded or somethin before I went up in sparks, that's when I lost sighta myself layin down there in bed. Everything around me and Ben changed. All those stars and all those planets and space and stuff that'd been hangin around us, it just sorta melted away. And when I quit quiverin from takin all this in, we were all of a sudden in some other place where it was some other time.

I tried to cling to Ben with my eyes. You know how in a dream youll be lookin at somebody and they be lookin one way, and then when you look at em close theyll change, right there in fronta your eyes, change into somebody else? Well, that's what Ben did; he went to changin on me. His skin blackened so much it was practically as dark as Burley's, and he was wearin these skimpy little clothes, a loincloth, and had this animal skin slung around him. On his head sat the most peculiar-lookin thing: it was like a shawl with stripes that hung down in back and had this graceful little thingamajig that popped out the front in the center where his hairline started. When he took it off, he was wearin a wig. And when he took the wig off, his head was shaved as slick and as smooth as the skin of a nectarine. I had to take a good look before it registered. Ben—whose Egyptian name wasnt Ben, by the way—kinda put me in mind of King Tut. You remember how they'd made this big fuss over King Tut back here some years ago, and everybody went crazy over it? It was King Tut this and King Tut that. Steve Martin even came out with this silly record called "King Tut" and made him a lotta money. Well, that's who Ben looked like, except he wasnt a king, but some kinda dignitary instead.

When I looked down at myself, it was clear I was an Egyptian too. And I wasnt female either; I was a teenage boy. At first it was hard to tell what we were doin, but after I calmed down good and just let it all happen, it wasnt any problem to see that we were sittin up cross-legged someplace. But where? It was night. The desert, that's where we were. We were sittin out in the desert someplace, and Ben was like a teacher to me. Ben couldna been all that much older either—maybe around, oh, in his early twenties.

But there we were, sittin out there, sittin straight up, and he was showin me somethin about how to breathe a certain way so as to get your energy to run up along your spine a certain way. I'm feelin excited to be learnin this because it was considered a privilege of some kind. Silently Ben is communicatin to me about how excitement of any kind will get in the way of my learnin what he's tryna share with me. Enthusiasm, yes, that's okay, he's tellin me, but be careful about excitement. I cant tell exactly who we are or what we're supposed to be. I like my little loincloth, tho, which felt like it'd been made outta rough linen. And it was so warm and peaceful out there. Wasnt no airplanes or helicopters or traffic noise tearin at you all over the place. I can tell how hard I'd been workin to earn these teachins, and I can tell Ben loves me, really loves me. It's like I'm an important part of him and his life, somehow.

The minute I begin to get interested in the desert, in what's goin on around Ben and me—like, maybe if I look hard enough I'll see me a pyramid in the background—then the whole picture starts breakin up. I can still feel Ben's hand in mine, and the electricity is still surgin back and forth. So I go to squeezin harder. When youre just hangin out there in space like I was, you really do need somethin for a reference. And, I mean, I needed somethin that was steadyin because exactly at that moment the desert sands went to driftin and shiftin on us. Sand went to blowin up and flyin around, until it got to the place where I couldnt see anything else but the whole black bowl of a sky was packed with it.

And when the sand cleared up, Egypt was gone. Then there I was, a woman again; and it seemed like my whole mouth and throat was on fire with garlic, which for some reason or other, I'd been chewin a lot of, and chewin it in a hurry. I was sittin in a garden. It was a little on the cool side, and off in the distance I could see daylight about to break. A couple early birds were chirpin and carryin on, but it looked like I'd curtained myself off by havin all that garlic in my system. I wondered what this was all about. Other than the garlic, however, I liked the way I was feelin. The breeze felt good and so did the smell of dawn. But I felt damp, sweaty. And when I thought about it, I understood why. I'd been up all night long makin love.

So far, so good. Then when I thought about that, it hit me that now, on my way back home, I had stopped here to sit in my cousin's garden to chew me some garlic so my husband wouldnt know what I'd been up to. It wasnt easy to figure out. I check my clothes to make sure I'm lookin okay, and I must tell you I was crazy about the dress I had on—it felt so free and loose. Underneath I wasnt wearin a thing and that felt good, too. I knew my hair wasnt lookin quite right, but I wasnt sure what to do about that. The first thing I needed to take care of was my breath. But why not just sit for a while and enjoy the cool and the singin of the birds? I was thinkin this and admirin my cousin's garden when I heard somebody's footsteps breakin twigs and dirt in backa me. It was my cousin, a handsome young man around my own age, twenty-two. And he was chortlin and snickerin under his breath so much, I whispered to him real loud, "What's so funny?"

That's all was ever said. The rest of it played like a silent picture. If I had to describe him to you, I'd have to say he favored Buster Keaton more than he did Douglas Fairbanks. But I wasnt no Billie Dove either. The rest of the talkin we did, the same as in Egypt, was done by means of our minds. But it was clear that my cousin was old Ben. I could see around the eyes especially, the same-looking eyes he's always had, right on down to right now. I really dont think the eyes ever change, do you? He thought it was amusin, as he put it, that me and my husband —who was some kinda big-time wheeler and dealer there in Athens—kept up this charade, when both of us knew what the other was up to.

This led to me feelin that what Ben was sayin was true enough, but, bein a man, it woulda been hard for him to understand how it feels to be rich and privileged and have servants and a big place and all like that and to still dont feel like youre loved. Then he went into his thing about the difference between real love and human love, which I practically knew by heart. And when I really thought about it, it wasnt all that kissin and huggin and lickin and joogin and rasslin and passion I was after in the first place; it was makin that connection, you know?

It was bein with somebody that could make you remember for a few charged hours that you werent just flesh and blood and ashes to dust, but you were made outta somethin that was capable of soarin straight out beyond the sky, farther even than birds can fly. That's why I kept slippin out to see this particular man. He didnt make me forget anything; he made me remember.

Ben was good-natured, tho, and after a while he calmly related that my husband wasnt back from his trip yet, so far as he knew, and that I could take me a bath at his place and freshen up and grab a nap. Then, when he put his hand on my shoulder, I understood by his touch that we had a special thing goin on couldnt anything interfere with. It had somethin to do with the kinda love he liked to philosophize about.

And on it went like that. The scenes kept flickerin by. We went from there over to England in what musta been medieval times. Old Ben was a nun and I was a monk, and that time

around we pretty much saw eye to eye, it seemed, on how important it was to live the spiritual life, but neither one of us cared
for the church all that much. Isnt that somethin!

Then it was France right after the French Revolution. Yes,
France! And this was back when bein French, or at least bein in
Paris, was a *real* big thing! At least, that's the way it felt. And,
lemme tell you, in spite of the Revolution, I wasnt feelin much
pain. I mean, they werent about to run any benefits for me and
my family because we were what you call the new wave, *la nou-
velle vague*, as Danielle Chrysler likes to say. The bourgeoisie was
comin into style *and* comin home to roost, and once again I was
right there in the thick of it. Comin from a rich merchant family, I'd inherited more francs than you could pull with a six-horse
carriage, and I wasnt exactly bad-lookin either.

It seems I was one of those rich widows you always hear about,
and even tho I enjoyed livin the good life and bein socially active, I still was on the lookout for somethin bigger than myself,
for somethin I could express my humanitarian sentiments thru.
Now, I didnt know all this while the picture was comin to me; I
pieced a lot of it together afterwards.

The main picture saw me gettin dressed up for the evenin,
with my maids and servants layin out my new clothes and makin
a big fuss over how I oughtta look. Since I had planned to play a
little harpsichord for my distinguished guest later on that night,
I had to be comfortable at dinner *and* at the keyboard. So my
seamstress had come up with this fabulous gown and a cocked,
feathered hat you shoulda been there to see. I wouldna missed
this episode for the world! And do I have to tell you who this
distinguished guest was?

It seems old Ben was over there in France tryna raise money
for the Colonies, a cause I sympathized with. Me and quite a few
other French folks, especially the women, look like. Ben blew
into town with his cute little fur cap; and I heard him talk at the
home of one of my good friends, and I just fell in love with the
man. I mean, he seemed to be everything rolled up in one—I
dont have to tell you—plus he was charismatic and as magnetic

as a lodestone. Every time he'd look at me, my heart would go to thumpin, and his French wasnt half bad either. It was like Moms Mabley use to say, Everytime he *parlez-vous'*d, it was all I could do to keep from goin *oui-oui* all over myself. Oh, that man excited me so!

But it was the cause of the new nation, naturally, that drew me into gettin involved with him. It was funny. From the first minute I laid eyes on him, it felt like we'd known one another forever. So when he put the touch on me personally for a contribution to the cause he was over there to promote and raise money for, my purse flew wide open. And then when he touched me, *oooh-la-la!*

I felt proud about bein able to help the Yankees get King George and them off their backs, the same as we'd later clean house on Louis the Sixteenth and his bunch. Times were changin. The Yankees ended up whippin up on the British so bad that the only way I know to put it would be to say they pitched a boogie!

But it was Benjamin Franklin and always Benjamin Franklin who won my heart. He was sweet and he was smart and he was deep and kinda on the wily side too, but in an honorable way everybody could appreciate. You see, there was a side to Ben that he didnt show the public—his profound side, where he studied things the average person wasnt ready for yet. Ancient scriptures, Rosicrucianism, the power of the mind, all such as that. Ben was always up to somethin didnt nobody but him know much about, and he got things done too.

So maybe he does come off as bein tight with a buck. I'd be the first one to defend him, tho. What Ben really understands is that money is a medium, and you can use it to express a lotta things, and you can multiply it. Most people are scared of money because they think that's your true wealth, but if you back up and read what Ben had to say about makin money multiply, then youll see where he wasnt lookin at it as just a material thing. And Ben oughtta know: he designed the stuff, the currency for the United States.

But bless his heart, Ben always could spin around on a dime.
He could come straight up outta some profound study and smile
at you real personal and be ready to sit down and pick and strum
on the guitar or the harmonica, which he invented, and he could
play that thing too! He wasnt no Sonny Terry, but he sure could
get around on a mouth harp!

It's like he himself once said, "Look round the habitable
world: How few know their own good or, knowing it, pursue." I
believe that's in the *Autobiography*, which he had to leave a
whole lotta stuff out of. And I can appreciate old Ben's discretion, when you look at how tacky and rough these coarse, no-
sense-of-shame life stories have gotten to be now. People will tell
you anything in their autobiographies now. Who needs to know
every intimate detail about somebody's private life right on
down, I swear, even to their privates? Ben wasnt like that. You
can read him now and still be learnin somethin. That he was
about the only Foundin Father that took a hard line on slavery—
Ben was flat-out against it—is pretty interestin, isnt it? And
when he turned up in France and got to workin his charm on us,
it was like a breath of fresh air. Oh, we came to love him so!

So, recallin all that, it wasnt easy for me to step outta the
vision I was enjoyin of him comin to visit at my Paris house and
greetin me with a big hug that had me tinglin all the resta that
night. But now I could feel the light droppin away, and pretty
soon there I was hangin out in pure space again with old Ben.
This time I wasnt scared; there wasnt any reason to be. There
was a feelin pourin thru me like warm coffee that told me I'd
been out before on these kinda excursions with Ben, plenty
times. I was relaxin into it the way you do after you step inside a
movie theater and that kid rips that ticket in half and you buy
yourself some popcorn and find a nice seat someplace and fade
into the dream of what's up there on the screen.

Even if you were to hook me up to one of those lie detectors,
I'd still have the hardest time tellin you how long we hung out
there and talked and carried on. For one thing, I dont remember
our sayin too much. It was like those scenes or cuts or visions,

whatever you wanna call em, from the past; none of what we talked about was communicated in chit-chat. But I can tell you this: I was ready for it. I was never readier to communicate with anybody as much as I was with old Ben that night.

"The time has come," he told me right off, "to inform you that your days on earth are severely limited."

"I had a notion you were gonna say somethin like that," I said. "It's somethin I've sensed for the longest. What I dont understand is why. Why is this happenin?"

"There is a time and purpose for everything, my friend."

"Just like it says in Ecclesiastes?"

"Indeed. And if I recall right, there is a popular song that has been set to those verses."

"That's right, a group called The Byrds put that out in the sixties. You mean to tell me you know about that, too?"

"Mamie, I have all of eternity to keep abreast of anything and everything I so choose. The essential thing to remember is this: You must make the most of the time that remains for you in this life."

"Ben, I get the feelin this is serious."

"Yes and no. But for your comprehension, may I suggest that you regard it as being of grave importance."

"Tell me, how much longer do I have?"

"Unfortunately, I have not been entrusted with that information."

"Entrusted?" I said. "That must mean youre carryin out somebody's orders, right?"

"Let us say that this is my mission. It is the friendship and camaraderie and the love we have shared during our rounds of earthly residency that bind us so closely together. Not everyone, Mamie, has the privilege of knowing that their time is not long . . . so to speak."

"So why is this happenin to me?"

"How many times must you learn this? You know as well as I do that each of us is the architect of what you would call personal destiny. Although you are given to blaming outside forces and others for whatever befalls us, particularly if it be of an ominous or displeasing nature, you have known the truth for centuries. It lies buried within your secret self."

"In other words, I'm here to get somethin done; and when I'm finished, then it's time to get back in the wind."

"I couldn't have expressed it myself with such breezy vigor and bite. Mind you, I cannot be with you much longer this visit. Another pressing errand awaits me."

"What's that?"

"It concerns your friend, your late paramour. Common-law husband is the term you use, I believe."

"You mean, Burley?"

"Yes. As sometimes happens, souls abandon the body without being at all prepared for their new existence. Your Burley is one of those. He is so earthbound that it is enormously difficult for him to take leave of all the people and places and things he cherished while he was still in the body."

"Is that how come he keeps hangin around?"

"Precisely. Burley is, in a word, lost. He has friends among the angels—and I hope you will forgive my recourse to metaphysical terminology, but I can think of no other term that would adequately describe my dispatchers—and these friends are eager to assist him in finding the rest he so needs to refresh himself."

"So youre gonna help guide Burley home?"

"Home is hardly the term I would use but, yes, I shall do my best."

"Ben, I dont mean to get personal and I dont wanna sound dumb either, but isnt there some way you might could explain where we are right now? I'm askin because when I wake up from this, which I know I'll have to do by and by, I wanna be able to understand what all went on while I was out here."

"Odd that you should look upon it as being 'out here,' Mamie. However, I do understand your orientation. Truth lies within us. The key is in your thinking. Thoughts are real; they are energy. Most of the time we labor under the delusion that we are doing the thinking, while in reality we are receiving thought. Truthfully, do you think that I, Benjamin Franklin, a mere human personality, could have thought up such a plentitude of novel inventions and ideas? Hardly."

Suddenly I got a flash. Me and Ben had sat down someplace a long time ago and had this same conversation, almost word for word, about where he got his ideas from. And this is where I was havin trouble. Even tho I'd gotten the idea from seein some form of myself with Ben in all those old scenes from Egypt and places, it was still hard for me to buy the idea that we keep goin away and comin back. I could accept it when it came to new moons and full moons and summery September tumblin into October, which was all the time breakin my heart with its beautifulness. But when it came down to people, well, that slowed me down some.

"And we have discussed this previously as well, I can assure you." Ben laughed as if he was readin my mind again. "But let us not tarry. You must, as I have said, make the most of your remaining time. I would hasten you to be completely mindful of three things."

Oh, I was lovin every moment of it as I asked Ben, "Which are . . . ?"

"First, bear in mind that 'now' is the only time there is. Live fully in this nowness, for in reality it is all we have."

"That shouldnt be so hard to do," I said.

"You might find it more demanding than you think," said Ben. "Secondly, let go of the idea that anyone else is separate from what you like to think of as yourself."

"How do you mean that, Ben?"

"Exactly as it sounds. Endeavor to be at one with everyone and everything around you."

"That's gonna be tough."

"Perhaps, perhaps. But give it a try, and observe the results."

"And the third thing?"

"Lastly, you must love."

"Love?"

"Yes, love, love, love, love!"

"Ben, would you care to go into that one a little deeper? That's one I always have trouble with."

"As much as I would like to, Mamie, I'm afraid I cannot. The time has come for me to leave you for now."

"Hey, wait a minute! This is just startin to get interestin. I need to know more about why youre tellin me this, and I wish you'd talk about this love thing some more. You cant leave now without fillin me in."

"But go I must. Burley will pay you one final visit."

"When?"

"Never you mind. Soon you will awake upon your bed of sorrow. But, as you shall shortly behold, it will not be at all sorrowful. I am happy, nay, joyous for you, my friend. Once again you shall begin to discover your true self, the self that until now has only whispered to you in lucid moments of receptivity."

"But, Ben, will I ever see you again?"

"All you need do is beckon."

"But how do I know that? I mean—"

"Forgive me, Mamie. I must be on my way. As even you yourself once said upon such seemingly dolorous occasions when we knew one another in another land, *au revoir, mon chéri, au revoir . . .*"

My throat didnt even have time to get choked up good before Ben had vanished into pure light, and it was light that gushed in all around me at that moment, a warm thread of light that somehow I knew instinctively how to hop onto and flow with all the way down from wherever I'd been back to the body of groggy old Mamie Franklin still laid out down there on the bed in that teeny little Lysol-smellin sick room.

I didnt know if I'd been gone away for minutes or for years. All I know is I was cryin so hard when I finally came to that Nurse McGillicuddy was fast by my side, holdin my head in her hands and sayin, "It's all right, dear. It's quite all right. I'm here, there's nothing to fear."

And while her warm hands were smoothin my head and face, I noticed how the pain at the backa my neck had disappeared and how there was somethin spreadin from my solar plexus all thru the rest of me. It was a happy feelin that had these tinges of sadness in it. It was still dark in the room, but when she wiped the sweat from my forehead and kissed me there the way Mother Dear use to do when I'd be sick, I slipped back to sleep and it was like a total blank, like a white screen pulled down, with no pictures to shine on it.

# 28

Tellin what happened after that isnt easy, since I always caught myself havin to back off from what I thought was goin on so I could see how much of it was me and how much of it wasnt. At least that's how I saw it at first. This had to be one of the things Ben musta wanted me to understand. How much of what we see is comin from us? That's a tough one. I could give you a slew of examples.

When I woke up all the way that Sunday mornin, Nurse Mc-Gillicuddy was goin off duty, but she wanted me to know I had a lotta visitors come to see how I was gettin along.

"Really?" I asked. "A lot of em?"

"It's as if the entire waiting room were waiting for you."

"Oh?" I said. "Like who?"

She handed me a clipboard and said, "Here, check for yourself. One of them's your son. I know that much."

Even tho I was feelin so good from my visit with old Ben, I didnt know what to do. The idea of Benjie finally turnin up safe and sound was like some soothin salve bein rubbed deep down into this mother's heart. Already I'd been havin a hard time holdin myself down to keep from floatin away, but now I was sure enough ready to do some serious floatin up there with the Goodyear Blimp. And you know how the message I'd be flashin would read? It would say: BLESS MY SOUL, I'M ON A ROLL!

And that's what I was on too—a roll so long and high and wide, until the last thing I wanted to do was come down. Later I figured out that, as wonderful as it felt, this wasnt always the greatest place to be perched when you needed to be takin care of business. For the time bein, tho, pretty much anything that happened was all right with me. And in case you somehow miss my point, the medication they'd shot me up with had long ago worn off. I wasnt all that sure it'd ever taken in the first place.

After I looked down the list of people on the clipboard, I was ready to ease right back out there with old Ben and them. I mean, sure, I couldnt wait to see Benjie and Tree and Nomo and the Chryslers, but the last person I needed to see was Kendall, Burley's son. You know how some people got a way of bringin you down, even when they mean well? That's how it was with Kendall and me. And what was that meddlesome Inspector Beaumont doin out there? Were my eyes deceivin me? You mean, Chance Franklin was sittin out there to see me too? Didnt anybody get affected by the earthquake but me? Poor Charlean, where was she? And you know I couldnt help wonderin what Theo was up to.

"What's been goin on?" I asked Nurse McGillicuddy.

"Restful sleep," she said. "That's what has been going on for you. How are you you feeling, dear?"

"I'm fine, but it's the earthquake I need to know about."

"Honestly, I've been so busy working, I've barely had time to keep up with developments." Then suddenly she broke out with the oddest smile. "I could snap on the TV, if you'd like."

Miss McGillicuddy looked tired all right, and standin over me, with the light shinin offa her hair and her face all crinkly soft with wrinkles and squiggly with life, she let loose with one of the most angelic sighs I have ever heard. It was like a cool gust of wind blowin into a stuffy, hot room on a steamy day. I could tell this wasnt any ordinary sigh.

"There's somethin you wanna tell me, isnt there?" I heard myself askin her.

"Yes," she said, her eyes all moist and shiny, "there is. But I don't know how you're apt to take it. Personally, I think you should cancel all of your visitors until you've gotten more rest."

"And what does the doctor say?"

"Dr. Yamamoto's gone off duty, and Dr. Roth hasn't been in to see you yet. I'm going merely by gut intuition."

"You too, eh?"

"That's how I'm beginnin to operate, more and more. By instinct, you know?"

Nurse McGillicuddy dragged a tear from the corner of one eye with her finger and said, "All I know is there's something special going on here . . . Something I don't think any of us fully understands. All day long I've had this powerful feeling that someone else has been present in this room."

"Do you get any inklins," I asked, "about who it might be?"

"None whatever. But you mustn't listen to me. I believe in all that crazy stuff. When I leave work here, I'm headed across the street for late-morning services at Hollywood Temple."

"What's that?"

"Oh, it's a church, but not exactly your everyday place of worship. I don't belong or anything; I just like to attend their services because they are so beautiful."

I didnt wanna get into a conversation about religion with the nurse. Not here in Los Angeles. I said, "Why dont you turn the television on for a minute while I'm gettin ready?"

"Anyway," she said as if she hadnt heard me, "you can't see anyone until Dr. Roth has checked you out." Then she stood there by the TV set and looked at me all strange, only I could tell it was friendly strange and not nasty strange. "Mamie," she said. Then, "May I call you Mamie? It's all right for you to call me Eileen."

"What is it, Eileen?"

"What on earth are you going to do?" And the tears went to dribblin down her cheeks. "You have nothing, absolutely *nothing!* Yet you sit here with this smile playing on your face, quite as if everything were simply fine. All morning they've been playing and replaying your story on television. I don't suppose there's a person in southern California who hasn't seen it at least once."

"I dont understand. What do you mean, my story?"

"Here," she said, punchin the power button, "I'll bet it's on again right now."

We sat next to each other on my bed and stared at the screen. I thought about all what musta been happenin on the soaps while we'd been busy slippin and slidin in that quake. And I knew that tomorrow, Monday, millions of people right there around L.A. would be tunin back in to *General Hospital* and *Days of Our Lives.*

They were playin that commercial where everybody that works out at the airport—from the skycap to the counter clerks —is lookin at this man's ticket and seein how much he paid for his round-trip flight cross-country, and snickerin and goin, "So long, sucker!"

"I like that one," I told Eileen.

"It's crazy, isn't it?" she said.

Then they went back into the continuous coverage they were doin of the earthquake and its aftermath. We sat there and looked at footage of buildins all crumbled and sidewalks torn up, cracks in the street and the freeway, shots of people bein herded up like cattle by these various rescue missions, cars all smashed up and turned over. Right then and there I knew that a lotta what'd happened probably didnt have so much to do with the quake as it did with people gettin into the act, even if it was an act of nature. As awful as it looked, tho, they were still talkin about how Santa Monica suffered the most.

I looked up and there was Brett Yoshimura sayin, "Last night's disturbance appears to be the latest in an unusual stream of California earthquakes that have been traced back to the beginning of the decade, and which seem to have recently intensified.

Yesterday's shock, which was connected with the forces that
have been raising California's Sierra Nevada range and towering
White Mountains on the Nevada border, struck at 10:52 P.M.
Channel 7 was there, and now we're going to cut once again to
the altogether remarkable testimony of one Santa Monica
woman.

"Mamie Franklin describes herself as a psychic. Mrs. Franklin
says that, before it happened, she sensed that the quake was
about to take place. Nevertheless, she did not succeed in saving
her home and her possessions before she had to flee, like thousands of other Santa Monicans, for her very life . . ."

Then they went into the tape from the night before out in
fronta Hollywood High. I couldnt believe it! There I was, cryin
my heart out for real, right there on television, and tellin people
how I didnt know what I was gonna do and how the future seem
hopeless and how everything I'd worked and strived for all these
years had been wiped out and, and—well, you can imagine how
that mustve affected people. And you know how it is; they
zoomed in real close on my face and got everything in, even the
tears, which they all but ran in instant-replay slo-mo. My neighbors were gathered around and lookin pitiful. I had that quilt
pulled up around me the best I could manage. They would cut to
the smolderin remains of the house and follow the smoke trailin
up into the sky. Boy, I'm tellin you, it looked so bad all I could
do was shake my head.

"So that's what youre talkin about?" I told Eileen.

"You're a brave woman, Mamie."

"Lucky to be alive," I corrected her.

Then I couldnt believe my ears. Brett was back on the tube
talkin about how the switchboard over at the station was so lit up
with people wantin to contribute somethin toward my recovery
that theyve had to open up a special number and postal box
where checks and clothin and other contributions could be sent.

"What?" I said. "What is she sayin?"

"Precisely what you heard her say, Mamie. And she made the
mistake of telling viewers that you were recovering from shock

and other symptoms here at this hospital, so the receptionists are telling me they're getting swamped with calls as well."

If I hadnt just gone thru my session with old Ben, I know I wouldna been able to handle any of this. I sat there. My eyes were still fastened to the screen, but I wasnt hearin anything.

Finally I said to Eileen, "So that's how everybody knew where to find me?"

"I'm sorry," she said, as if it had all been her fault. "Here, you'd better lie back down. I'll go out and make an announcement that you're not up to seeing them all. You tell me who you'd most like to see and I'll ask them to stick around until the doctor's examined you again." She stopped and studied me.

You didnt have to have too much of an IQ to see how confused I was about all of this.

# 29

It took Dr. Roth the longest to get around to seein me. After he got thru squeezin and pokin around and testin, tho, he said it would be all right for me to leave the hospital, seein as how they didnt have room for all the people who needed to be there more than I did. Then it looked like Eileen and I werent ever gonna quit huggin on one another.

"Remember," she said, "you are always welcome at my place. I'll come pick you up, wherever you are. Out in the Valley where I live wasn't as hard hit as Santa Monica, but I know I'd better get right home after services."

"Considerin all the quake damage," I said, "how can you be sure theyll even be holding services this mornin?"

"I'm not sure at all. All the same, I'd better start getting myself together."

"Remember," I told her, and I meant every word, "youve got forever to get your act together."

Eileen laughed and said, "But you have to decide right now whose care you would like to be discharged in. Right, Dr. Roth?"

Roth, with his thin gray hair and wire-rimmed specs, looked and acted like an old-time, no-nonsense doctor. "Mamie," he said, "when was the last time you had a complete medical exam?"

"I must admit, it's been quite a while. But, you know, I have been meanin to do that."

"You're going to have to," he said, lookin all concerned.

"Is there anything seriously the matter with me?"

"I don't know about *seriously,*" he said. "There are some heart palpitations you should have checked out. I know you're undergoing a lot of stress right now, like the rest of us, and being here under emergency conditions doesn't help. But promise me you'll check in with your regular doctor at the first opportunity."

"I'll do that, Doctor," I told him. "What I need to know right now, tho, is how am I gonna handle all those folks out there in the waitin room here to see me?"

Dr. Roth and Eileen McGillicuddy looked at one another.

"You say you want to be discharged in your son's care?" Eileen asked.

"Yes, I do."

"Then," she said, "I have an idea about how we should handle this."


I'm tellin you, it all looked so strange out there with all that rubble and drizzle and confusion goin on until I didnt hardly know what to do. What was amusin me, tho, was how fast you can adjust to a new situation when you dont have any choice. What if the weather man had come on the news Friday night and said, "Seismologists are forecastin a major earthquake which they estimate will hit the Santa Monica hills and spread eastward, beginnin at approximately seven-thirty Saturday evening, so be prepare." Do you think we woulda acted the same way? I know I wouldna. But now everybody was shufflin and rushin around, tryna figger out what to do next.

Like, you take me. There I was rared back against the head cushion of that Rolls of Benjie's. He and Nomo had been rentin that car for so long I was startin to think it *belonged* to em; I believe they thought that too. And I was still wearin my hospital

gown and the trenchcoat Inspector Beaumont had given Benjie
to loan me. There was still so much of that dog smell in it, I
wasnt sure which was worse—bein out in the rain with nothin
protective on, or chancin it in my Kaiser greens.

"Mom," Benjie was sayin, "considering your condition, don't
you think the wisest move to make at this point would be to get
you over to my place, where you can lie down and rest?"

"Maybe," I said, "but somethin tells me I need to go get
Sweepea. I miss not havin my own wheels."

"But I can take care of that."

"Benjie, it'll only take a few minutes."

"How do you know it hasn't been towed?"

"I just know, that's all."

For maybe the twentieth time, Benjie shot me that half-
scared-half-mad look. "Mom," he asked, "are you certain you
feel okay?"

"Dont I look like I'm all right?"

"No, you don't."

"Then how *do* I look?"

"Like you're not all there. Like something's changed."

"I think what's changed, son, is I *am* all here. For the first
time in my life I am *all, totally, one-hundred percent here.*"

Now it was my turn to take a look at Benjie, which I did the
same way you might look at some wax at the tip of your baby
finger you just dug out your ear or the same way you might look
at yourself in the mirror to see if that Noxzema you smeared on
your face last night has helped make that new pimple on your
cheek fade away. In the middle of my stomach, tho, this warm
glow was spreadin. Secretly I wanted to tell the child to pull over
and cut the engine and let's just sit here and talk it all out for a
while. From the minute he'd turned fourteen, I hadnt gotten
much opportunity to see him by himself anymore. Seems like
there was always somebody else hangin around with him, a
buddy or some girlfriend.

He handed me the big stacka notes and cards and letters and
even a few telegrams expressin sympathy and condolences. The

ones on top he'd collected from all the resta the people in the waitin room; the rest had been sent in care of the hospital after that interview I did with Brett Yoshimura went out over the air. I flicked thru em. There was somethin from everybody except Kendall.

"Did he say anything to you?" I asked Benjie.

"Who? I can't read your mind, you know."

"Sorry. Did you talk any with Kendall?" For a moment I'd actually forgotten Benjie couldnt read my mind.

"Yes, and thanks for reminding me. He asked me to give you a message."

"Which was . . . ?"

"It was rather odd . . ." Benjie said, lookin straight ahead all of a sudden, like it was time to get back to concentratin on drivin. There were a buncha people crowded around a taco stand somebody'd set up, right there on the sidewalk where Santa Monica and Lincoln and Michigan kinda crisscross one another. I watched a pitiful-lookin woman with a baby in her arms and six other tots millin around where she was sittin on the curb. She had a taco and was chewin off little pieces and grindin em up enough in her mouth to spit out feed to the baby. And, naturally, there was some little brother—looked like he was part Vietnamese—out there with his skateboard and one of those suitcase radios playin Lionel Richie and them's "We Are the World, We Are the Children" just as loud as the volume would go.

"What was odd about Kendall's message?" I finally got around to askin. Shootin all thru me was this picture of old Ben, tellin me to stay glued right close to the here and now, to stay right with it and not go driftin off into what-was or what-might-be or what-mightve-been. It wasnt easy to do, but I liked the way it felt when I tried it.

"Kendall said to tell you he loves you, loves you very much, and that he is sorry."

"Sorry about what?"

"That's all he said. Kept saying it over and over, and he said he'd come see you too."

"Does he know where to find me?"

"I told him he could check with me."

"But, Benjie, we dont even know yet where that's gonna be."

"Mom . . . ," he said, lookin all hurt and confused. We were only a little ways from the old neighborhood now. "I feel like saying let's pull over someplace and talk. There's a lot you're going to have to explain to me."

I knew perfectly well what was comin. I could even feel fear radiatin out from Benjie like fireplace heat; it stood out, quiverin all around him the color of the sky before the storm clouds break. Yet I felt calm, cool, and collected, like we use to say; and when I looked inside myself to really see how I felt, there was no fear there. For all of this boy's life I'd been duckin and dodgin and lyin to him. Scared he was gonna find out his true origins. Scared about how he was gonna view me, his mother, once he did find out. And now here it was Judgment Day, and all I could feel in my heart was love, a love I could practically reach out and squeeze in my hand, it was so real. Somethin had snapped— nothin scared me. Anything that went down was just fine with me. I felt the way Jimi Hendrix was singin about in that song he did to the soundtrack for *Easy Rider,* where he's tellin us that if the ocean was to fall off into the sea it wouldnt scare him, and if a six should turn out to be a nine, he dont mind. It was a feelin like nothin else I'd ever felt.

"Did you hear what I *said,* Mom?"

He was talkin in that I'm-about-to-blow-my-cool voice of his I'd been hearin since he was in kindergarten.

"Yes, I heard you, Benjie. Watch where youre drivin, okay? Let's get to the house and we'll talk."

"Damn," he said. "What's this thing you have about the house? It's all burned down. I think you need some psychiatric help. Really, Mom. And you've needed it for a hell of a long time!"

"Young man," I said just as firm as him, "I dont need to be hearin that kinda language from you, *ever.*"

But I could feel the hurt and confusion movin into all that

fear that was hangin around him, and I couldnt help watchin the light around his body get muddier and muddier.

Even when you know a place has burnt to the ground, sometime you still have to go back and see the ashes and embers for yourself. That's the way it was with me. I couldnt believe it'd actually happened. It was like that joke Nomo Dudu stole from Bill Cosby about the man who went down to and stuck his head on the railroad track the same time everyday and got his head cut off when the train came along. So when people asked him how come he keeps doin it, he tells em, "Because I cant *believe* it's really happenin!"

Benjie stood around with his mouth poked out while I walked around and even got down on my knees at one point to poke around in the rubble.

"You know," he said, "you're really embarrassing me. Why don't you just let me drive you back to my place, have something to eat, find you some nice clothes, and then I can bring you back over here, okay?"

In my mind, while I was eyein what remained of the bedroom, I was considerin Benjie's suggestion. It made sense. And the more I thought about it, the more sense it made. I even weighed it up against my emotions—lookin at the wet, charred remains of the bed and the mattress and what was left of the other furniture. Seemed like whatever the fire didnt finish off, the firemen did.

"You do have a point," I said, steppin around some debris to get to where the bedroom closet was. The door looked like it'd been hatcheted with a vengeance.

Benjie was right in behind me. He said, "Then c'mon, Mom. Being out here in this rain isn't funny."

"Hold on," I told him. "I just wanna see somethin."

He had to help me yank at the clothes-closet door, but once we got it open there were all my clothes. Most of em'd been ruined, but there was my lavender skirt—the one I'd got in Switzerland—and right there on the hangers next to it hung my print blouse and that burgundy head scarf. Isnt it funny? Everything around them was damaged, but there these pieces were completely intact, lookin exactly like they did the day I'd gone out to Celluloid City to lay it on the line with Harry. Now if I could only find my Gucci pumps, I'd have me an outfit to wear.

"Mom," said Benjie, "are you for real? What do you intend to do with those fancy clothes?"

"Why, I intend to wear em, what else? Here, help me tie a knot in this plastic so they wont get wet."

"Do you intend to crawl around here in this downpour until you salvage everything you can find?"

"Not at all," I said. "That's the very reason I wanted to come pick up my own car, so I wont need to be dependin on people for rides. Once the weather clears up, I'll cruise back over here and look things over." As if they had a mind of their own, my eyes pulled me up to the top shelf of the closet. There in a shoebox were those eggplant Gucci pumps.

"They worked all night getting that gas main repaired," said Benjie. "I was pretty sure the aftershock was going to finish blowing us away. But it wasn't that strong."

I understood that he was only makin small talk to keep from explodin right there on the spot. I knew our big moment was comin right up, but I didnt want it to be in those hospital clothes or anybody else's clothes but mine. Thinkin back, that seemed to be the only hang-up I felt strong about at the time. Whatever else happened, I felt like I could handle it.

Back in the Rolls, Benjie said, "I feel awfully lucky. The quake hardly touched our building. Tree's mother's place was devastated, though."

"It was? Aw, poor thing! Is she all right?"

"She and Tree are at her grandmother's place out in Burbank. I'm supposed to call her as soon as we get back."

Benjie didnt know and I wasnt gonna say anything to him about it right off, but I sensed he felt uncomfortable about my movin into his apartment, even if it *was* an emergency and I *was* his mother. I glanced again at the envelope layin on top of the

stack of messages Benjie had collected in the waitin room at
Kaiser. It was from the Chryslers and I'd already read enough of
it to understand that they were offerin me their beach house in
Malibu to stay in until I found someplace else to relocate. I
figgered I just might take em up on that offer. After all, I wasnt
about to become a burden to *anyone.* Least of all, my own flesh
and blood.

I looked across at Monroe's house and wondered where he
was. There were other people on the block, dashin in and outta
their houses. Most of em seemed to be doin what I was doin—
gettin what they could while the gettin was good. The little girl's
mother that I'd always thought was sellin dope drove past with a
strange-lookin man. They honked their horn and I waved at em,
but the rain was startin to come down so hard now all I said to
Benjie was, "Lemme just see if I can start Sweepea up, then we
can drive down to the pier and talk."

"The pier!" Benjie cried. "Now I *know* you've lost you mind!
Mom, let's just get outta here. These ashes aren't going anywhere. Please, Mom, let's just clear out! Please!"

The Honda started *right* back up. And even tho Benjie didnt
think it was a good idea for me to be drivin *any*place, I wasnt
about to leave that car of mine again, especially since I'd just
finished payin off the last note. You might can get away without
wheels back in New York or Chicago or someplace, and people
might even act like it's okay to be without em in L.A., but one
way or another they will make you feel like what they really think
you are—a burden on the community.

Like I say, I was henceforth layin every last one of my burdens
down.

## ᴬᴸᵉᵉ 30 ᶻ⁾⁾⁾

Stayin right with it, hangin right with the moment the way old Ben advised me to do wasnt easy. But just makin the effort seemed to be changin everything, tho. I was openin up to a new way of lookin at the world. Not even in my deepest flashes did I ever suspect how much I'd been missin from lookin but not seein what was right there in fronta me. I mean, I was use to havin my train of thought derailed, but payin close attention to what was happenin at the moment was like bein in a movie, like bein up there on the screen where the story's goin on *and*, at the same time, bein out there in the audience that's so busy lookin at the movie they forget theyre bein seduced by light.

Followin Benjie over to his apartment out there in Westwood near UCLA, for instance, was like Cinerama. Remember Cinerama, where they were always filmin in bigger-than-life locations to fill up that wide screen? Well, bein in Sweepea after flyin around with Ben and Burley was like that. It was science fiction or fantasy or, like I say, bein in a movie. Why would I say that? Because mosta the time we go around believin that what happens when we're wide awake is real and what happens when we dream is not. Dreamin and thinkin are real too. This professor on TV, Carl Sagan, said the difference between outer space and inner space is still a mystery. I know for a fact he's right too. Because the travelin I did with my ghost buddies felt more natural to me than tearin around on the freeway, honkin at sleepy drivers doin seventy miles per hour before they drift over into your lane and cause an accident.

And there were jet planes zoomin right above the freeway, comin in to land at the airport. I'd glance over at people in their cars on either side of me. Either they looked bored or else dreamy or depressed or out of it. I began to get the idea. Nobody was really payin attention to much of anything that went on. We were so use to rattlin around on automatic that we musta needed movies and show biz and wars and earthquakes and anything else dramatic you can name to shake us up. Just knowin I could slip in and outta that weary body of mine whenever I felt like it changed all that for me.

All I could do was stare at everything, which looked new and strange to me. By the time we got to Benjie's, I figured, I'd be ready to face the music with my son. All the same, I still felt a little twinge, a little throb of edginess right in the center of my abdomen, down under my rib cage.

Chimes were boingin, kinda like some church bell was tollin the hour or ringin out a message. I couldnt tell if it was comin from outdoors across the way or from down the hall or from somebody's stereo, or what. It sounded kinda like my man Milt Jackson, as if he mighta been layin down a soundtrack to this new movie I felt like I was playin in. After a while I didnt care where it was comin from; I just let it play on inside my head and got use to how good and real it was soundin.

Benjie had fixed us some Constant Comment and was leanin forward in his chair as if he might be leapin up any minute to answer the doorbell or the phone. "Well, Mom," he said finally, "are you comfortable?"

"I'm fine," I told him while I wiggled around on that old porch swing he'd rescued from the campus recyclin center and had painted and cushioned up to make himself a passable sofa. "So Harry telephoned you, huh?"

"Yes. It sounded as though he might have been calling from his car. I could hear all these car horns and traffic sounds in the background. And the signal kept fading in and out."

"That sounds like somethin Harry would do. And what'd he have to say?"

"We talked for quite a long time, maybe half an hour."

"Half an hour on a car phone?" I said. "That means he musta really been in a serious mood. Had he read your script yet?"

All this time, Benjie had been tryna keep up his gruff look. His brows were all furrowed and his mouth was turned down. But when I asked him about the script, I saw the corners of his mouth go to twitchin like they were tireda bein sad and wanted to curl into a grin. He was stubborn, tho. He'd gone into this thing determined to get me told—and I knew he needed to get me told—and so Benjie wouldnt budge. Even while he was tellin me what, under any other condition, woulda been considered good news, he managed to hang on to that gloomy look in his face.

"Yes, he read the script."

"And did he like it?"

"He loved it. He even mentioned Nixxy Privates and this new comedienne, what's her name?"

"Fiona Prince?" I offered.

"Yeah. Your boss Chrysler's been handling her, hasn't he?"

"I believe so. And what else did the great Harry Silvertone have to say to you, Benjie?"

Now I could hear the chimes growin louder. I didnt wanna tune out me and Benjie's conversation, but when I cocked my head to one side it sounded like somebody was playin the saddest and the most beautiful tune I'd ever heard on the vibraharp, and it was solo. I could hear the notes and tones just as clear, bouncin off the walls and echoin from up outta some canyon, sounded like, which all mighta been happenin inside me. It was still hard to tell.

When I looked again at Benjie, his whole face had started to
quiver and his eyes were glazed over. I knew he was growin
nervous because he started pluckin at some imaginary speck at
the tip of his nose, a habit I'd been tryna break him up from
since he was in the second grade.

"He told me what neither one of you has been able to come
right out and explain during my entire lifetime."

And there was no way I was gonna avoid meetin my poor son's
gaze head-on, even tho it caused googobs of goosebumps to pop
out all over my arms and legs. Right there in the pit of my belly
was this shockwave of fear that was so powerful that my first
inclination was to ask Benjie if he had a sweater or a jacket or
somethin I could borrow. Then, when I zeroed right in on it,
when I gave it every ounce of energy I had in me—and it really
did seem to require all that—somethin happened.

There I was face-to-face with my only child at last. All the lies
and fabrications about his daddy I'd been feedin him practically
with his earliest baby food were piled up and shinin all around us
like a truckload of barbed wire that'd been dumped in the middle of his disheveled apartment livin room and then trimmed out
in neon:

*You dont need to know anything about your daddy; the less said
the better . . . I really didnt know your father all that well before
I got pregnant by him, and he disappeared outta my life before
you were even born . . . Yes, he kept after me and kept after me,
kept sendin me flowers and cards and letters and telephonin until
I just about had to go out with him in order to get rid of him . . .
He was a handsome man, very handsome, and I thought maybe he
could do somethin for me because he seemed to have money and
connections . . . Besides, Chance and I werent gettin along so
fabulously at the time and I was lonely and, well, I'm ashamed to
say it, but that's the way it was . . .*

Oh, the lie grew richer and more complex as Benjamin grew
older. The problem, tho, was that he believed it, believed it right
on down to the detail I'd invented about how I'd learned of
Horace's death. That was what I'd named his dad. He and some

new gal he was seein had gone swimmin out on Long Island in
some waters where they werent supposed to be and the both of
them had drowned out there one night. Supposedly, the only
way I learned about this was thru an anonymous call I'd gotten
from some buddy of Horace's who happened to know he'd been
sweet on me. Lemme tell you, I'd rhymed the story up so good
until I almost believed it myself. There was a parta me, tho, that
knew good and well Benjie didnt buy the story completely, and
that was the part that hurt whenever I caught myself feelin like
breakin down and comin clean. For years I'd wondered about
how I sensed Benjie coulda known this. Now, sittin up with him
eye-to-eye, I understood the gist of what his namesake, old Ben,
had only recently slipped to me. Once you quit lookin on the
stuff of the world as bein somethin separate from yourself, then
you begin to comprehend how the truth might be parta that
closed-circuit reality that's a parta everybody and everything.

"Benjie," I said, "so now you know the truth. That makes me
feel better. Your daddy all along has been Harry Silvertone, one
of the most successful producers in TV and movies. I only hope
you can forgive me for . . . for—"

"For trying to protect me from the truth," he said.

"Uh," I said, "well, that's one way of lookin at it."

"What other way is there, Mom?"

I was shakin, and I was thinkin about how I'd checked into
the maternity ward all by myself, with only my sisters and Jolene
and Rosie—Alice always ran her mouth too much—knowin what
I was up to. Do you know what it's like to give birth all by
yourself in some lonesome hospital room, knowin that the father
has no intention of claimin any responsibility for the child? I was
doin my best to forget about the past when Benjie's deep voice
came whiskin down into my heart like some soft, swift wind in a
dream.

"How do you feel?" he asked.

"About deceivin you, or what?"

"In general."

"Like a liar," I told him. "I feel like I dont even deserve to be your mother."

Benjie sat still for a minute while he soaked that one up, then he looked at me different, like his whole mind was changin. He let the twitches around the corners of his mouth curve up into a bona-fide smile.

"Mom," he said. "Remember that night you told me to beware of evil expectations?"

"No."

"Well, I do. It's all coming true, just like you predicted."

The bell-like vibratin in my head was so tuneful and melodious now that it was all I could do to sit there rockin and pretend like I wasnt really hearin it. Hard as I tried, I couldnt come up with clue the first to what Benjie was talkin about.

"All this time," I said, "I called myself lovin you."

"I think I understand, Mom."

"You do?"

The telephone rang, if you can call it ringin the sound these wimpy new electronic telephones make when they need to be answered.

"Excuse me, Mom." He snatched the receiver which'd been crouched right there at the toes of his shoes like some pussycat use to havin him pettin her. "Tree? No, she's here now . . . We're talking . . . There's no point in calling them anymore . . . What? . . . That's right, I'm saying cancel . . . Cancel everything . . . Honey, I don't care what they say . . . I'm not kidding . . . I'll call you back . . . Yes . . . Yes . . . Uh-huh . . . Un-huh . . . No . . . Forget it . . . You're at home? . . . Then let me call you back in a few minutes . . . What? . . . It's all over . . . No, I don't know how . . . I love you too . . . *Ciao* . . . *Ciao, guapa* . . ."

Turnin back to me, Benjie said, "I know you aren't up to this, Mom, and there's a lot we still need to discuss. I'm very upset, but I don't want you to feel bad. I mean, it's awful, it's dreadful what you've done, the deceit you've kept up, but . . . I'm no angel either."

Curious, I said, "And what have you done, Benjie? Are you and Tree expectin, or somethin?"

"Nomo and Tree and I," he said, "we might be going to prison."

What's interestin about fastenin on to the moment is this: You cant help but see how that sucker is always changin, and I do mean *changin*. And if you intend to go to ridin this thing called *now*, then you better be ready to do some movin, too.

This talk about prison, I must admit, shook me a little; I wasnt that detached yet. "What are you sayin, Benjie?"

"I hate to tell you this—"

"Well, while we're layin all our cards on the table namin names, you might as well come clean too."

"Oh, Mom," he said, his voice all trembly in his throat.

It didnt take me more than a second to wrestle up outta that jerry-built sofa and step over there where he was sittin. It was a chair Burley had given him when he'd gone off to college. In fact, it'd been Burley's favorite easy chair. I sat down on the arm where I use to sit by Burley and took Benjie by the hand.

"Tell me all about it," I said. "You tell your story and I'll tell you mine. You know what a good listener I've always been."

Squeezin my hand, Benjie dropped his head and said, "It's crazy. Too crazy. I didn't realize we were even being watched until . . ."

The bells, wherever they'd been comin from, were slowin down now, almost as if whoever was playin em had decided it was time to see how much music you could get outta just one note. That's all I could hear now, just a single note—I dont have perfect pitch, but I'da bet fifty dollars it was B-flat—boingin and tollin and ringin in the distance like raindrops fallin on crystal.

And that was how the resta the evenin went. Benjie went to tellin me about how Inspector Beaumont had evidently been trailin him and Nomo and Tree around. Right off, I remembered the feelin I'd been havin that somethin wasnt quite right about all those videocassettes they were always haulin around. Now,

Beaumont was supposed to be checkin into the background of why those burglars were tryna get into my garage, and somehow or other he got to pokin his nose in Benjie's affairs. And when he found out they were bootleggin a lotta first-run movies, then I reckon the whole thing started to look real juicy to him.

Benjie and them, it turns out, were workin for some jackleg video operation called A to Z TeeVee, which I remember passin everytime I would drive over to the post office to pick up my check from Harry. It'd been there for years. They were some of the first people in town to start sellin those big old satellite antennas that's so popular now. Back then, tho, A to Z was always in the papers because HBO and some of the other pay networks accused them of sellin equipment that would allow people to get cable for nothin. Now, all this is comin from what I remember from readin all those little pieces they bury way in the back pages of the *Times*, back there with items about somebody in Latvia or someplace growin two sets of baby teeth, and all like that. So they were always bustin the kids that ran A to Z and haulin em into court. But the judge would end up cuttin em loose everytime because of this law that says the airwaves actually belong to the public, to the people, and not to the television networks and stations. All the same, the cable people had the sheriff's department out patrollin neighborhoods, lookin for these hookups that A to Z sold cheap, like for under two hundred dollars, on people's rooftops.

Benjie said he didnt know how the whole operation worked, just his part. He and Nomo and sometimes Tree would pick up the tapes and drop em off at various places around town. I still dont understand all of it, but Benjie had a whole collection there at the apartment, and did they ever look like the real thing!

Of course, that was a federal offense, which Inspector Beaumont knew. What he wanted was for Benjie and them to get me to actually drop the charges against the two thugs they had in custody. Why? I did not know. All I knew was that somethin had to be done fast. Up at the hospital, when they met up in the waitin room, Beaumont told Benjie he'd give em another week to fall in line. If they didnt, he was gonna order an investigation and close in for a bust.

Benjie was cryin and sweatin while he told me all this. I'm not ashamed to say it—I am his mother, so I wanted to do everything I could to keep him outta trouble.

I threw my arms around him and we cried together like that. "Why were you doin this?" I asked.

"The money was good," he said. "Nomo and I figured that if nothing else worked out, we were going to shoot a feature-length videotape of our script, cast it with actors we knew from the drama department and places, and take it around to the networks and studios. There's a kid who did that with a script he wrote, and now Warner Bros. is going to do it."

"I hear that's how that Richard Pryor's *Live on Sunset Strip* was made."

"Huh? Mom, what are you talking about?"

"They shot it on videotape, then transferred it to film."

"That isn't what theyre doing with this kid's stuff. They're going to reshoot it with a big-time cast. What I'm saying is, this is one way to go now. They check out your tape and then ask to see the script."

"I'm not surprised," I said. "I know how much them monkeys hate to have to read anything. That's all Carleton ever talks about . . . how he cant wait until Sony or IBM or somebody comes out with a script-readin machine."

We sat there, lookin at one another for the longest. When I stopped to think about it, it sorta made me wanna do some laughin along with my cryin. I mean, how bad could things get, anyway? My house and all my belongins were gone; there Benjie was up to his neck in scaldin water; the lie I'd been perpetratin about his father had played out and come right back on me; I had a crooked police inspector on my hands; Burley was gone; and maybe—if Benjie was correct—I was losin my mind in the bargain; the doctors were tellin me I needed a serious checkup; the Chryslers by now had to be sick and tireda me never bein on the job, look like; and old Ben was tellin me somethin I'd already suspected, anyway—that I didnt have all that much time left.

Under the circumstances, it seemed like the best thing to do was to hold tight to Benjie and wait for whatever there was left to say to surface.

"I forgive you," I said. "I forgive, I forgive you, I forgive you. Now let's see what steps we can take to see if we cant keep yall from goin to the slam."

"Mother," he said. "I forgive you, too." And then he didnt say anything for so long, I was beginnin to think he'd lost his voice. I listened to his breathin while the last bell tone sounded, this time soundin like it was comin from the apartment upstairs. "But that doesn't mean I'm not still pissed," he finally hissed. "We're really going to have to talk about this some more."

"You might wanna have some words about it with your father too," I told him.

# ⤙⤙ 31 ⤙⤙

"I was there," Burley was tellin me. "I was there when Benjie and Harry Silvertone got together."

"Oh, yeah?" I said. "And what was it like?"

He'd met up with me when I'd gone out for a walk to get some sun, but I got so tireda people jerkin their heads around to get a loada me talkin to myself until I'd doubled on back to Benjie's just so I could talk with Burley in private. I didnt think people paid much attention anymore to anybody talkin to themselves, especially not around L.A., but you know what they say about the proof of the puddin.

"How'd you know where they were gonna meet?" I asked.

Burley said, "Mamie, you forget that after you done died, you got plenty time, *plenty* time, to find out anything you want to. And you got all the time in the world to do things too."

"So what youre sayin is it's none of my business."

"No, I'm just sayin you gotta be in my condition to understand that you can stand away from the world . . . like this . . ." Burley broke off to show me how he could zoom himself, his shiny shell of a body made outta light, way up in the sky or anyplace at all in the blink of an eye.

"It just so happen I was floatin around Benjie after he got finished talkin with that damn cop. I didnt go for that clown one drop. Benjie needs to be tied up and whipped—and Nomo, too —for all them counterfeit tapes they been hustlin, but that doesnt give this cop the right to come around cuttin deals with him about lettin those two dudes go scot-free after they broke into the garage like that."

"So you do keep abreast of things, dont you?" I said. Havin just brewed up a pot of Constant Comment tea, I couldnt resist teasin Burley. "Betcha you'd like to sample some of this, wouldnt you? Doesnt it smell delicious?"

"Mamie, you know I cant taste or even smell."

"I still cant get over that," I told him, "because you sure use to could smell. I could smell you all thru the house."

"Corny, corny," he said while the light clouded up in his face. "But I wanna tell you somethin about Silvertone and our boy Benjie."

"What?"

"That boy's gonna turn out to be as good a businessman as his daddy. You know, I felt it really wasnt any of my business what they had to say to one another after all these years, but—"

"That didnt stop you from gettin nosey, did it?"

"Mamie, just hear me out. You know, they met out there at the man's *other* office; he wouldnt meet Benjie up at the Tower."

"Yeah, that still sounds like Harry. What time of day was it?"

"Day? This was at night. Well, around dinnertime. Ben said he was hungry, so Silvertone sent out for some Chinese food and while they were waitin for it to be delivered, Benjie rared back in this big leather easy chair, which was just like the one his daddy was sittin in, and musta spent five or ten minutes, look like to me, just lookin at Harry Silvertone."

"*Lookin* at him, Burley? That long?"

"At least."

"And what'd Harry do while Benjie was doin all this lookin?"

"Well, naturally, he was lookin at the boy right back. I mean, this thing was *deep*, Mamie. Here's this black kid that's never

known who his father was and then it turns out to be a white
man, and not just *any* white man. His daddy ends up bein *the*
Harry Silvertone. Now, to me, that's deep."

"And what were you doin while they were sittin there starin
one another down?"

"What you think? I was propped right up there next to em,
checkin em both out."

"Dont tell me you planted yourself on the desk again?"

"No, I was leanin on this antique clock Silvertone musta done
ordered but didnt know where he was gonna put it yet. You
know, one of those grandfather clocks. I kinda felt like Father
Time. Mosta the time, tho, I just would float, flow, and fly all
around em and check out their stuff from different angles."

"Burley Cole, dead or alive, you are still chock fulla jive!"

Burley had to laugh at that himself. Then he said, "So after a
while, Silvertone slid into one of those big grins he flashes when
he doesnt know what else to do and he says, 'This is crazy, isnt
it?'

"And Benjie said, 'Yes, it is. That's precisely what it is—
crazy.'

" 'So where do we start, Benjamin?'

" 'Can I begin?'

" 'By all means,' Harry said. 'Someone has to start.'

" 'I'd like to play a little word-association game with you, if
you don't mind.'

"Harry Silvertone hadnt been ready for that one; I could tell it
threw him off base a little. He said, 'Sure, whatever you want.'

"Benjie said, 'I want you to tell me the first thing that pops
into your head when I say these words, okay?'

"I even got more interested myself when Benjie proposed this.
Silvertone quit leanin back in his chair and suddenly sat up all
straight.

" 'All right,' he said. 'Shoot.'

" 'The first word I want you to respond to,' Benjie told him,
'is—'

" 'Wait a sec, Benjamin. How many of these are there going to be?'

" 'Oh, just three, and the first word I'd like feedback on is *fear.*'

" 'Fear'?

"I watched old Silvertone fidget around for a while before reachin in his pocket for a lemon drop. 'Well, fear is . . . I guess fear is—'

" 'Don't guess or think,' Benjie told him, 'just come back with whatever jumps up in your mind. Don't pause to mull it over. Be totally spontaneous. This is only a game.'

"Now, Harry Silvertone probably didnt have a spontaneous bone in his body, yet he did manage to come back to Benjie with: 'Integrity.'

"Benjie didnt understand. He said, 'Integrity'?

" 'Sure,' Silvertone said. 'The biggest thing I fear is losing my sense of integrity.'

" 'Oh? Is that why you never stepped forward and let me know who you were?'

" 'Now, listen, I always thought it was best for your mother and for you to not have the likes of me in your lives.'

"Benjie said, 'Was it that, or was it because you couldn't handle the embarrassment of having an illegitimate child by a black woman? Wouldn't that have been difficult to explain to your legitimate wife and kids?'

"Silvertone sat there squirmin. I was thinkin he'd probably give anything to be able to pull the kinda stuff I pull: slip right out thru the floor or up thru the ceilin if I feel like it. 'So what's the next word?' he said.

"Benjie said, 'The next word is *guilt.*'

"Harry's eyes commenced to gettin watery when Benjie sprung that one on him. And you know me. I drifted right down there in between em to where I could move in real close on Silvertone to make sure the tears was real."

"Aw, Burley," I said. "It sounds to me like you got carried away."

"Wouldnt you?"

"I dont know . . . Maybe. So what kinda answer did Harry have when Benjie said *guilt* ?"

"Not too much of one, really. He wiped at his eyes and I watched his lips twitch while his eyes were rollin up in his head, lookin up there for what to say, I reckon. Then he said, 'Guilty, sure I feel guilty. I *am* guilty. For over twenty years I've felt guilty, and I'm sick of it. I'm—I'm really tired of it. Goddamit! Guilt makes me think about guilt, that's all! And I've been swollen with guilt from the minute you were born.'

"Well, by then I was startin to feel sorry about bein there. I didnt wanna really see Silvertone break down and cry like a baby. But, do you know, that's exactly what he did."

"No! Burley, you mean, Harry Silvertone broke down?"

"Swear to God! He got to cryin so hard it look like to me Benjie was startin to become ashamed of him. Then Benjie asked him, said, 'If my being born was tantamount to disrupting your social well-being and familial equilibrium so completely—' "

I had to bust in and interrupt Burley when he told me this because that was Benjie thru and thru. He always had a way of trottin out all that bookish stuff when he was either indignant or sarcastic about anything. "That sounds like my boy," I said.

"Nobody else *but.* Benjie said, 'If that was the case, then I'm surprised Mom didn't undergo an abortion.'

"Silvertone said, 'She didn't want one, and I didn't want her to do anything she didn't want to do. I told her I'd take care of an abortion if she wanted one, but she didn't. Neither one of us did, really.'

"Benjie said, 'You mean, you didn't push it?'

" 'Of course not. I care too much about Mamie, even now, to not respect her decisions.' "

"And what did Benjie say to that?" I asked Burley.

"Hard to say. That's when the man showed up with the Chinese food, so they moved over to the desk and unbagged it and started to chow down. That stuff looked good, too, so good I got to wishin again I was back in my body so I could greaze right along with em. You know how crazy I was about that shrimp fried rice and those pork buns, yum!

"They kept talkin while they ate until they got to the place where they were beginnin to relax with one another, kind of, and then Silvertone talked about his wife and kids, said he use to try to figure out ways to break the news of their stepbrother to his children but, for the life of him, he just never could bring himself to do it. And then Benjie asked him why, if he cared so much for you, he never bothered to visit.'

"I betcha Harry choked on that one," I said.

Burley laughed. "Yep, that's exactly what he did. A piece of somethin got caught in his throat when Benjie came up with that and Silvertone commenced to coughin so hard he had to excuse himself and hit the john for a minute. But by the time he got back, he was all composed and calm-lookin again. He sat back down to finish up his meal and asked Benjie what his third word was.

" 'Love,' Benjie told him.

"Silvertone's face went pure white on that one. I mean, it went as pale as the underbelly of a toad. 'Benjamin,' he said, 'that's been the toughest part of all. I dont know why I haven't been able to deal with that.'

" 'Maybe it has somethin to do with your integrity,' Benjie told him.

" 'Benjamin, come on, lighten up.'

" 'You're operating out of a long, time-honored tradition, you know. You're aware of that, aren't you?'

" 'Sure, I'm aware of it—slavery, South Africa, the Great White Father and Conqueror. Believe me, I don't feel good about any of it. And, Benjamin . . . Benjie, I want to change.'

"Benjie asked him, said, 'How much do you want to change? Are you willing to accept me fully as your natural-born offspring? Are you ready to do that?'

"You can imagine what kinda pressure Benjie was layin on Silvertone. He was gulpin his food down in big bites, not even chewin it. 'Yeah,' he said, but I didnt believe he meant it for a minute. He said, 'I'm ready to own up to it, Benjamin. It'll be complicated and of course there has to be some preparation made, but—' "

"Did Benjie accept him at his word?" I asked.

"Wait," Burley said, "I'm not thru yet. So Benjie said, 'You mean, twenty years hasn't been enough time to get you ready for breaking the news that you've got a son born out of wedlock?'

" 'Now, hold your horses,' Silvertone was sayin. 'All I'm asking is that you give me a couple of weeks, that's all.'

"Benjie asked him, 'Two weeks and then what?'

" 'Two weeks and I'll have broken it to—to the rest of the family.'

"This kinda stopped Benjie in his tracks. His eyes got all big and he went back to lookin at Silvertone real hard and slow like he'd started out doin to begin with. 'Do you really mean that?' he said.

" 'Sure, I mean it. I have to be able to live with myself, and the years are flying by too quickly now for this deception to be maintained.'

"Then he reached over and put his hand on top of Benjie's. That's when I had to do some reassessin, Mamie."

"What kinda reassessin?"

"I decided that, dont care what people say and what they make up, nobody really knows what's gonna happen to anybody. I cant tell you if Silvertone was bullshittin or not. All I can tell you is that both of em were as emotional as I have ever seen grown men get.

"Then Silvertone went to askin Benjamin all about what he'd been doin in school and what he thought about the picture business and, well, first one thing and another. I sat there flabbergasted at how short a time it took him to get his daddy to agree to hire him a good lawyer to help him with his legal problems and, at the same time, practically in the same breath, he told him, lookin Silvertone straight in his eye, 'You know, it's ironic that all along you've been my all-time favorite producer.'

"Now, at that point, I couldnt tell who was butterin up who, but it didnt take long for both of em to start gettin crazy about one another. I mean, it was gettin goofy in there and embarrassin. And, you know, Benjie actually had some piece of paper he took out of his briefcase with the script in it that had *agenda* written at the top of it. Now, I *had* to peep and see what it said, so I eased round there and read it."

"So what'd it say?"

"He had written down there, *typed*, I mean, *Fear, Guilt, Love*. And then he'd typed, *Stay calm and don't leave anything unresolved, emotionally or financially*."

"Doesnt surprise me in the least, Burley."

"It doesnt?"

"Not at all. That's the Harry comin out in Benjie; he was born thinkin he was slick. And the facta the matter *is* Benjamin Franklin *is* a smart kid. I just dont want him gettin too smart for his own good."

"So how do you feel about all this? You think Silvertone's got the nerve to break all this to his wife and kids?"

All I could do was shake my head and say, "I really dont know. But I have to reserve judgment for the time bein. Everybody's capable of change, you know."

"Do you believe that, Mamie? Do you believe a white man like that can own up to somethin this sensitive?"

"How many black men you know with outside children that've flat-out told their wives and other kids about em?"

Burley did a couple of his *zoom-whooshes*, I call em, and when he settled back down, said, "Dont come lookin at me. My inside child turned out to be an outside child."

"There's time," I said, "and while there's still time, anything can develop. I'm just glad theyre finally on talkin terms. Me, I'm tired of lyin."

"Tired of lyin, Mamie, or tired—period?"

"I know one thing: I'm sure tired of time. I can tell you that much."

The way Burley was lookin at me, I kinda got the feelin he was

tired of time too. Here lately he was startin to glow in a whole
different way, like it was time for him to make a change too.
Sittin there, lookin at him before he disappeared again, I felt a
brand-new wave of peace go to washin over me.

# 32

It was all I could do to pay attention after that; everything started movin so fast, seem like. But I tried my best to hang in there, which wasnt all that easy, considerin I was tryna stay over there at Benjie's for as long as I could stand it. It wasnt that I didnt like bein around my son; it was more like I needed some room of my own. For somebody facin a felony, he was about as sweet as he could be. Always was, except when he was goin thru his adolescent years, when he didnt even wanna be seen with me.

It got so I found myself gettin antsy about all of it. The earthquake, Benjie's problems, hasslin with the insurance companies, tryna decide what I wanted to do about work, and the money they were sendin me. I havent even talked about that yet, have I?

They played that tape of me cryin and carryin on over television so much until people just naturally went to feelin sorry for me and wouldnt quit sendin checks and money orders and even cash over there to Channel 7. Every few days, somebody from over there at the station would get in touch with me and tell me they were fixin to send over some more money. The first round got up to around eighteen thousand dollars, which was almost as much as the Chryslers were payin me. The round after that came to eleven thousand dollars. Brett Toshimura, who was responsible for pushin it over the news and in the press, said she couldnt believe it, and I had a hard time believin it myself. There I was with close to thirty grand I hadnt counted on, hadnt asked for, and which I wasnt sure shouldnt go to somebody needier than me.

And all the while, there I was, hagglin with the insurance company about the fire, and, pardon my mouth, but they were bein real assholes about it. All that money me and Burley had been layin out for years, and now they were tryna get off the hook, talkin about how they didnt pay off on earthquakes.

After I told em they could kiss my you-know-what, Benjie decided I might not be all that demented after all. But he was on his way to Cloud Nine by then—Cloud Seven, at least—because he and Harry had started meetin and, besides gettin along about as well as could be expected, it looked like they might have some kinda deal cookin on Benjie and Nomo's comedy. And to top it all off, Harry offered Benjie the services of his own lawyers to help him outta the mess he was in. I personally thanked Harry for that.

That was what I'd been waitin for. The world could do anything it wanted to now; I'd finally gotten my boy and his daddy together. Where they took it from there on out was their business. I was still ridin high on whatever was goin on inside me. But I found I couldnt talk about that much; people just absolutely *hated* it! I'd hear em talkin about their relationships and nicks in their Porsches and Mercedes-Benzes and how theyre just havin the rottenest luck with their investment portfolios, and how life had dealt them a mean, sorry hand and surely they deserved better. And there I was, just glad to still be around.

I wanted to see everybody one more time, altho I knew that wasnt exactly practical. I probably couldve afforded to jet around the country and visit my sisters and other relatives, but I already had my hands full with all the moves I'd have to make to find myself a new place to stay. I did call everybody on the telephone and had long conversations with em about how I was doin and everything. It seemed like they had all seen me in that TV clip.

"Girl," my sister Rose told me, "why dont you fly out here to Chicago and stay with us for a while? I been tellin you you wasnt doin nothin but playin with fire all them years you been out there in earthquake country."

"Aw, Rosie," I said, "it wouldnt do me much good now. I dont think I could even take care of myself in Chicago."

"Take care of yourself? What you talkin bout, Mamie?"

"Well," I said, "I've been out here in California so long now until all I been doin is gettin dumber and dumber. If I was to turn up in Chicago now, the Negroes there would be so slick with the games theyd be runnin on me that I would actually be too dumb to know what they were doin."

Rosie laughed and said, "You seen much of Maxine lately?"

"I'm ashamed to say I havent."

"I already knew that," said Rosie, "because I been talkin with Maxine."

"Oh, yeah? And how's she doin?"

"Aw, Mamie, it sounds like the poor child might finally be comin to her senses. You know how kids are now. It use to be we had to know what we were doin by the time we turned sixteen or seventeen, but now kids are still tryin to get the basics together when theyre thirty or thirty-five years old."

I had to laugh. "I have been noticin that very thing, Rosie. But I promise you, I will stop by and see Maxine. You know, if you had to apply for a permit to be somebody's aunt, they woulda been done revoked mine years ago."

And that was how I talked up hundreds of dollars, like I'd always wanted to do, without worryin about it.

The first person I wanted to drop in on the night I got to doin my travelin was Maxine, just like I'd promised her mother. So, since I knew Benjie was plannin to spend that Saturday night with Tree, I had the whole apartment to myself, which wasnt sayin much but at least it was halfway quiet.

I got into bed and got real relaxed and rested before I slipped off into my travelin state. Then, just when I was on the edge of fallin asleep, that fraction of a moment before you jump off the divin board of bein awake and plunge headlong right down into sleep, I connected with where I wanted to be, like fixin your gaze on that cloud I told you about. Before I knew it, there I was, driftin outside of Chance Franklin's house. From the outside, it looked about the way it always did: one of those two-bedroom stucco houses like you see all over West L.A., where the colored people live. There was a light or two left on inside, but I could tell without goin in that Chance wasnt home. I mightve gone on and left it at that if it hadnt been for the music I heard pourin outta the cabin out back where Maxine stayed.

So I let myself float on back there to have a look. Now I could hear the music real clear. Dinah Washington. She was doin that number she recorded live with all those wonderful players—Clifford Brown and Maynard Ferguson on trumpet and Harold Land and Herbie Geller and them. Ooooh, they sounded so good! "You Go to My Head" was what was playin, and the funny thing about it was it had the same scratches in the same places as the album I used to listen to called *Dinah Jams.* That was the record made me kinda wish I'd learned more about jazz, even tho that definitely was not where the money was at.

Right there I almost changed my mind and chickened out, but somethin was propellin me to have a look inside, just one little peek. Now, what'd I wanna do that for? There was Maxine, dozin on the little sofa with a half-finished bottle of champagne there on the table beside her. And on that same table was a cake with white icin and pink roses and letterin all across the top. I had to lean close to make out what it said:

HAPPY BIRTHDAY, CHANCE
FROM MAXINE WITH LOVE

If she hadnt been all swished up in her black negligee and a flower in her hair, I probably wouldna thought much of it. But I could see around her eyes where her mascara was smudged and runnin that Maxine had been cryin. That was Chance's record she was listenin to: the same one I use to sit up and play. I knew it by heart—every word, every solo, every pop, and every place where it stuck. I still loved the part where Dinah went: "Like a summer with a thousand/a thousand/a thousand/a thousand/a thousand/a thousand/a thousand/a thousand . . ." You had to gently push the needle over for her to finish: "Like a summer with a thousand Julys."

And that was how I'd been feelin lately, like I'd been caught up in a summer with a thousand Julys; and now it was time to be movin on. I stopped and took a good look at Maxine. She truly had grown pretty since I'd seen her last. I dont know if it was the way she'd filled out, or what. She looked so sweet, I decided to try to get over and talk to her while there was still time.

At one point, tho, I swear Maxine could sense that I was there in the room, spyin on her. It scared me. She kinda blinked a little bit, then she sat up on the sofa and looked around all funny. I was hoverin up there pretty close to her too, so it felt like all she had to do was reach out and grab me. What's scary about bein out there in that kinda predicament is you think you might panic and not be able to slip back into your own body in time. Sleepin on the sofa bed in Benjie's little toy livin room wasnt exactly makin my blood race, but it *was* someplace to be. After I backed off, tho, Maxine quieted back down. I watched her get up and go to the window and pull back the curtain to see what was goin on either outdoors or in Chance's house, I guess. Then she checked her watch again, clicked on the TV to one of those ignorant, creepy, rock video shows, and fell back on the couch and pulled a blanket around her.

*Poor baby,* I thought before I caught myself. Poor baby, nothin! And then I got to wonderin if I still had the nerve to keep myself outta my body long enough to see if I couldnt find out what Chance Franklin himself might be up to. We'd gone

thru many a birthday together, and this wasnt the first time he
hadnt made one of his own birthday parties.

I backed off and headed for the Strip. I say "headed," but
technically that isnt the way it works. All you have to do is
picture where you wanna be and who you wanna see and—*bam!*
—there you are. I didnt even like bein on the Strip all that much
when I was in my body; now it really was a test. But findin
Crime and Punishment was a piece of cake. I didnt wanna stick
around; I only wanted to see what Chance was doin on his fifty-
eighth birthday.

To do this, I had to do the opposite of what you usually do.
You would think that concentratin real hard would be the way to
go into this stuff, but actually it's when you relax that it comes so
natural. So I relaxed to the place where I was right there in the
club, watchin Chance grin for the people while he knocked out
one of his George Gershwin medleys— "Someone to Watch
Over Me," "Strike Up the Band," "Make Mine Music," "I Got
a Crush on You," and all like that—all of it leadin up, you
understand, to "I Got Rhythm," which allowed him to slice
right into mosta what he knew. Oh, and he could tear em down!
I even got excited myself, listenin to him rattle off those old
Lionel Hampton "Flyin Home" quotes and country-soundin
bebop bluesy things with a taste of Fats Waller, and those cute
little Count Basie licks you do way up at the toppa the keyboard.
And Chance can make it seem so easy, like steppin right out a
window on the thirtieth floor, then turnin left.

Hangin there, listenin to him like that, I felt a little bit of the
thrill creepin back. Just enough to let me know there was no way
I would ever go thru puttin up with the likes of Chance Franklin. There was a pretty good crowd in there that night and, I
must say, there was no way you could criticize their generosity;
they clapped their hands raw. Then, while he still had em in the
palm of his hand, Chance lit right into "All God's Chillun,"
singin the words like he'd just set em down personally that
mornin fresh after he'd just experienced what he was singin
about. That's how he had taught me to do, and it still worked.

But what got me was the smooth way he slid right into "I Just Called to Say I Love You" and then did his *Casablanca* jokes and Humphrey Bogart, Peter Lorre, Sydney Greenstreet impressions before he modulated into another key to do "As Time Goes By."

After the set I stayed with him until he got over to the bar to greet some of his well-wishers, as he liked to call em. "Mamie," he'd always be tellin me, "be careful you dont become a slave to your well-wishers." People—stylish white folks mostly—were bunched and lined up to shake his hand and hug him and say one thing or another. The one who caught my attention, tho, was a strikin-lookin woman in a big white hat who waited her turn real patient at one end of the bar. There was somethin awfully familiar about her, the sure way she moved when Chance finally got to her and she spun around on her stool to give him a big slippery-lookin smack around the lips. And then she turned and all at once I understood why I'd had this feelin. I mean, if it mattered to me one way or the other, I could say it was straight outta *New Faces of 1952.* That's where Eartha Kitt sang this song, "Guess Who I Saw Today," remember? She's tellin her husband or else her boyfriend about this couple she saw that looked like they were so much in love and cha-cha-cha. And it turned out she'd seen the very man she was suppose to be singin to.

I looked at Chance Franklin and I looked at Danielle Chrysler huggin and kissin on one another like that, and saw em as just two people who happen to be fans of one another. Wasnt any of my business. All the same, I wondered some about it, especially when this serious-lookin woman came up on Chance from behind and said, "Is gude to see you becoming so popular, very popular, Mister Chance. Is gude for you, is gude for biziniss also."

I knew that had to be the boss. That just had to be this Natasha I'd heard so much about. From the look she gave Chance and Danielle, I could tell too that somethin deep was goin on here I wasnt sure I wanted to stick around for.

"Why, Natasha," said Danielle, stickin out her hand, "how wondairful it is to see you."

At that, those big blue eyes of Natasha's squinched a little as she gave Danielle the once-over. "Ahk, Danielle, dolling, it is you. Welcome back to Crime and Punishment."

Danielle didnt miss a lick. She closed right in on Natasha and hugged her too. "Natasha," she said, "we must talk. Carleton and Harry and your husband Irving, zey are all talking together about a project. And so I shall ask when you might be free to have lunch with me." And suddenly they fell off into talkin French, which made Chance look a little awkward, even tho he kept tryna break in with stuff like *c'est la vie* and *quel dommage* and *toot sweet* to make out like he was right in there with em.

French or no French, I could tell that the greetin Danielle had given Chance didnt exactly endear either one of em to Natasha. The American in me wondered what it must feel like bein over here from Europe and havin to learn how to bake and slice all this American pie. But the woman in me was pickin up on all too much to stay there eavesdroppin like that. Satisfied to have some idea of what was goin on, I wanted out.

I was slackin off, relaxin into withdrawin myself from that picture when my ears latched on to the scratchy sound of another voice, one I still sometimes missed.

"Mamie," it said, "what you doin out here again? Dont you know it's plenty people would give anything to be back in a body again?"

"Burley?" I asked. "Is that you?"

"No, it's the Great Houdini."

What made me nervous was I'd almost made it back to the me that was tucked into Benjie's sofa bed before I got interrupted. I didnt mind, tho. From what old Ben had told me, I didnt think I'd be seein Burley again so soon.

# 33

"What you doin out here this time?" Burley wanted to know.

"Just checkin out a coupla things."

"That's risky business."

"Why you say that?"

"Because of where you still happen to be situated."

"And where am I 'situated'?"

"You still situated in the body. Now me, I can run around and carry on and pull that kinda stuff, but youre takin a chance."

"Why?"

"Why do you think? You know, you could get stuck out here and not be able to get back."

"Ive thought about that," I said, "and it's worried me some. That's why I'm backin off from this scene I was just at now, so I can make it back home to Benjie's."

"How's that boy doin, anyway?"

"First-rate, as they use to say in Hattiesburg. You mean, you havent been around here spyin on us? I thought that was all spooks did."

Burley went to chucklin. "I aint that kinda spook," he said. "I havent been much of anyplace lately. Old Ben and a crew of other souls claim it's their duty to see me to my rightful new home. They say they cant quite carry out their duties until I get this last thing that's been vexin me taken care of."

"And what is it's been troublin you, Burley?"

"Kendall."

I felt awful that I couldnt tell Burley I'd been to see that son of his. "Kendall was at the hospital," I said, "and he sent me a nice note, too."

"Kendall sent you a note? What'd it say?"

"Told me he was gonna come visit me soon and that he loved me. I got a little bit shook up behind it. I never thought Kendall cared anything for me. Have you been in touch with him?"

"Been in touch!" Burley shouted. "How'm I gonna be in touch when I cant even touch anything over there in your world?"

"Have you even seen him at all?"

"Yea, and I dont like what I've seen, either."

"Like what?"

"Some of Frank Zaccharetti's people been talkin to him. That's how come I asked you to look out for him, Mamie. I knew you had these psychic powers, and I figured that if you and Kendall could get together after I died, then the both of you might benefit."

It made me feel bad to hear Burley say that. What was wrong with me? I coulda at least made the effort to look Kendall up. I still wondered how much Burley knew about what I'd been doin.

"Doesnt sound like youve been stickin around here in L.A. much at all."

Burley looked down at me all sad and confused-lookin. "Nope, I havent," he said. "More and more there's been this magnet that's been pullin on me to make myself at home over here."

"Over where, Burley?"

"Over here in this . . . I reckon you'd call it this dimension, or somethin. But there's some unfinished business I need to fill you in on before things get any worse."

"There's somethin you need in that trunk up at the Chryslers'," I said, gettin the jump on him.

"Baby, you almost read my mind. But it's a little more urgent than that."

"What is it, then?"

"I would like it if you could get it out from up there at the Chryslers' and take it someplace where you can go thru the contents in private."

"Burley," I decided to ask point-blank, "what's in that old beat-up trunk, anyway?"

"Papers and things, army keepsakes, souvenirs, records . . ."

I didnt live with Burley seven years without learnin by the tone of his voice when he was hedgin or holding somethin back from me. "And what else?" I asked.

"Some business stuff."

"What business stuff?"

"Zee's Cheese Products documents."

When he told me *that* he coulda stopped right there and I probably coulda figured out the rest, but I was anxious about swoopin back into my body before I lost my nerve.

"Are these papers that belong to Zaccharetti?"

"A few of em, yes."

"And what else?"

"Somethin for Kendall and somethin for Benjie."

"Tell me, Burley—what?"

"I want that to be a surprise. It's Zaccharetti's stuff you gotta dig up."

"Burley, what's goin on?" And when I looked at him real hard, even in his bodyless state, I began to understand somethin. "Did you cut some kinda deal with Mr. Z.? Is that it?"

"He gave me a buncha stuff to get rid of for him."

"And what'd you do with it?"

"C'mon, Mamie! You know me well enough to know how hard it is for me to get rid of *anything.*"

"And did he pay you to dump these papers?"

Burley nodded and started gettin all withdrawn.

"What are they, Burley, incriminatin files?"

"Search me. I didnt look at em. I didnt *wanna* know. All I know is this: There are people around who would do practically anything to get ahold of those documents."

"What do you want me to do with em after I take em out?"

"Send em to Kendall."

"Kendall! I dont get it."

"You aint got to get it, just get the papers outta that trunk and mail em to Kendall. He'll know what to do with em."

"But why didnt you do that before . . . before you passed?"

"That was what I meant to do. You see, that's why they say, 'Never put off till tomorrow what you can do today.' Now I'm able to appreciate that and all them other little sayins they use to have—'A stitch in time saves nine,' 'The early bird gets the worm,' and—"

"Burley, not meanin to cut you off, but would you get to the point?"

"How did I know I was gonna have a heart attack? Besides, I'd been carryin that secret around for so long that it scared me to even think about it, especially after I got low sick and started worryin about how you and Kendall and Benjie were gonna make it with me gone."

I was touched to hear this. I said, "Youre a good man, Burley. You always were. I'm sorry about all of this. But you coulda told me, you know. You didnt seem to have any trouble tellin me everything else."

"It only *seemed* like I told you everything else."

"So tell me this," I said. "Will sendin those papers to Kendall get him in any trouble?"

Burley sighed. "The truth of it is, the way things stand now, Kendall's havin that stuff will get him *outta* trouble." His voice grew tender. "Mamie, please dont ask me any more questions. Just take care of this, please."

"Dont worry," I said, "it's as good as done."

Relieved, Burley said, "Where you gonna be?"

"At the Chryslers' house in Malibu, I think. They offered it to me, anyway, to do some restin up."

"And then what?"

"I really dont know, honey, and I dont care much, either. I got more money than I've ever had in my life, and the funny part is I havent even been tryin to make any."

"You dont seem to believe in workin anymore," Burley said, "that's for sure."

"Are they talkin about the earthquake over there?"

"You know, Mamie, this 'over here' and 'over there' mess is gettin me confused. I mean, you *are* 'over here' right now, talkin about 'over there.' No, folks here aint too much interested in no earthquake. To us, hearin about an earthquake's about the same as if you was to say, 'It rained last night.' Night and day dont mean a thing to me, and you gotta have a physical body before somethin like an earthquake can have any meanin."

"Doesnt it bother you, tho, that the house is gone, your truck, all your belongins—everything?"

Burley just stood there in the middle of nowhere and shook his glowin head from side to side. "Not anymore," he said. "All I care about now are the people."

"The people?"

"That's right, the people I care about—Kendall, you, Benjie, and a few others."

"You know Benjie's gone and gotten himself in some trouble too?"

"I'm a little bit ahead of you on that one, Mamie."

"Huh?"

"The people that's been tryna get the trunk, they got to that cop."

"What cop? You mean Beaumont?"

"Whatever his name is, the same sucker that turned up at the house on your birthday."

"The day you . . ."

"The same day I died, Mamie. It's all right to say it. After all,

I'm *dead*, aint I? Well, Zaccharetti's people got Beaumont in their back pocket now."

"Hmmmm," I said, now that the picture was startin to clear up some. "Now, that would explain a few things. For somebody that hasnt been doin much gettin around, you seem to know an awful lot. Where'd you find all this out?"

"It's too dull to go into, Mamie. Get to the trunk, and this whole thing'll be just about done blown over."

"It's as good as done," I told him. "And, by the way, where's my friend old Ben?"

"I never know where anybody is around this place," said Burley. "You see, we dont all live together."

"So where do *you* hang out?"

"I'm supposed to be movin in with a community, I guess you could say, that's on my level, or somethin. Ben keeps tellin me, 'As ye sow, so shall ye reap.' Now, there you go—that's another one."

"So it's segregated, huh?"

"You askin the wrong person. Lemme get there first, then I'll tell you what it's like. Lord knows I'm sicka this shuttlin around from one spot to another down here on the earth. Just plain weary, Mamie, that's what I am. I just wanna let it all rest and maybe sleep for about a thousand years."

"Well, lemme tell you, I have been lettin it go."

"That's fine, but dont let it all go completely until . . ."

"Burley, I think I got the message."

Now that I was in his dimension, I reached to see if he was still good for a hug and maybe a peck on the cheek. But the instant my arms opened wide and I stepped forward, it all went kaput. The whole scene started evaporatin like fog that's been shined on by strong sunshine. And I was startin to see somethin about all these little crazy outlines I was havin; they were all like movies. Like, when youre dreamin—and I knew by then that all my dreamin wasnt necessarily done while I was asleep—and your eyes be movin. At least that's what they say, that you can tell if somebody is dreamin by the way their eyes move, even when theyre shut. Well, for eyes to see, there's gotta be some kinda light playin on em for them to see by. And that's what seemed to be goin on. Light, light, and more light—that was what it was. When I was a little girl and we'd go to the Grand Lux Theater, I'd get so wrapped up in what was goin on up there on the screen until it always shocked me to look back and see that fat, flickerin stream of light pourin steady thru that hole from up there in the projection booth. I would look at that light and understand how, some kinda way, none of what we were lookin at was real. Robert Montgomery hadnt died in that plane crash in *Here Comes Mr. Jordan* any more than Warren Beatty did in that remake they shot years later. All those murders and cars blowin up and people starvin and crooks and Indians and cowboys and lovers and people gettin snatched up in the nick of time before the guillotine whops down and talkin mules and train robberies and lions and tigers and elephant walks—none of that stuff was real. No more than that coyote that's always chasin after the roadrunner and then gettin dynamited or tied to a stone and pushed off a cliff. It was all done with light. And there people were, pullin every kinda low-down, evil stunt they could think of just so they could somehow get in the movies or make money offa movies or control the movies, or somethin. I wasnt any different; they'd fooled me too. Pretty much every last one of us was out here gettin seduced. And by what? Nothin but light, not a thing but light quiverin and makin patterns on a screen. Now that I wasnt worried about losin *anything* anymore, it was all startin to fall together.

"Burley," I yelled. "Burley, come here and let me kiss you. Burley? Burley, dont go!"

Suddenly I could hear myself yellin, and it woke me up. And the pillow I was huggin had gotten soppy wet from all that sweatin I musta been doin. I sat up, lookin around, and little by little it came back that I was at Benjie's and it was almost three o'clock in the mornin. No sooner did I start wonderin where he was than I heard his sleepy voice comin from the bedroom.

"Mom," he said, snappin on the light. "Are you okay? I think you must have been dreaming about Burley again."

When he kissed me and I smelled liquor on his breath, I said, "Where you been? What's goin on?"

"I was up with Harry—I dont think I'll ever be able to call him Dad—up until almost an hour ago. I tiptoed around to keep from waking you. You looked so . . . intense in your sleep."

"Oh yeah? What's Harry talkin about?"

"Good things, Mom, nothing but good things. I'll tell you about it in the morning. You'd better get back to sleep." He leaned over the sofa bed and took me by the shoulder. Even tho his kiss on the forehead smelled like some kinda mixed drink, I was moved by it. I went to cryin again.

"Oh, Benjie," I whined. "Please, please, please forgive me for what I did."

"I've already done that, Mom. It sounds as though you might be having trouble forgiving yourself."

"Oh, Benjie . . ."

He just looked at me and turned the light back off. "See you tomorrow."

"I'm movin out, you know."

"I know. You already told me. But wait'll you hear what I have to tell *you*!"

"Good night, Benjie," I said, then got real still while I went over everything that'd happened in my head. Try as I did to stick with the *now*, I felt myself really missin all my motion-picture soundtracks that'd been destroyed in the fire. I woulda given anything at that moment to be able to pop the music from *Diva* into my tape player, particularly that part where the opera singer goes out on a midnight walk around Paris with that young messenger was after her.

That's how I was feelin as I went back to sleep. Actually, tho, it wasnt so much a case of me goin back to sleep as it was sleep slippin up on me. Take it from me, all that flittin around in the ether will wear anybody out. I mighta been losin it, like Benjie and the others were always hintin and tellin me flat-out, but I still had some of those old yens and yearnins in me. Later that night it was Theo who came to me in a dream, except he was a combination of people—sorta like Chance and Burley and Theo all rolled up in one.

# 34

For the longest after that, everything made me cry. I cried when Benjie told me the next mornin that Harry thought his script needin some reworkin but he thought it was original, totally original, and that he'd like to do it either as a screen comedy or for television. Benjie was so excited I was afraid to ask him about his legal troubles.

"Harry told me not to worry about it. He's going to make some calls. It turns out that one of the companies filing suit was Silvertone Communications."

I cried when I pictured Harry again at that desk, the phone growin outta his head, chewin on that candy and makin faces. Here everybody wants to get into the movies and dont even realize theyre already in one of the strangest movies yet, a movie that's been goin on for billions of years—and that's still gettin made.

"Did he mention money yet?" I asked, like every uncool mother and wife you ever knew.

"He says if it works out I'll be comfortable."

"Sounds like Harry," I said. "Just dont sign anything without seein a lawyer of your own—even if he is your father."

I cried when Carleton and Danielle got Rodrigo and one of his gardeners to help load the trunk in Sweepea and then gave me directions how to get to their Malibu place.

"We've already told the neighbors you'll be there," Mr. Chrysler told me. "Danielle and I might drop by on the weekend just to see how you're getting along."

"And I am waiting," Danielle said, "for my big hug from you, *ma belle* Mamie."

They both looked so glamorous, standin out there by the garage in the early autumn light. Mr. Chrysler had a script and a copy of that paper, the *Spotlite*, where I saw the ad for that tear-gas pistol I'd ordered. I couldnt help likin em both.

"What in heaven's name are you going to do with that trunk, Mamie?"

"Just go thru it and sort out its contents," I told Mr. Chrysler.

"Well, when you are finished with zis," said Danielle, "you can come back and perhaps do some sorting for us."

Mr. Chrysler got his grave look and said, "Mamie . . . uh, have you made up your mind yet about the future? I understand that with all your good fortune you could probably buy and sell the two of us now, but—"

"That's one of the things I'll be thinkin about there in Malibu," I said.

"Don't think too much," said Danielle. "Remembair, you are going zere to rest."

Mr. Chrysler cleared his throat. "It would be good to know by the weekend, Mamie, if you're going to continue working for us. If not, we have to make other arrangements."

"I do understand."

I cried when Danielle and I hugged, and I cried when Rodrigo got me off to one side and thanked me for persuadin the Chryslers to keep him on. I hadnt done any such thing, but since it seemed to mean so much to him, I wasnt about to rob Rodrigo of the gratitude he felt, even if it was misbegotten. He was the kinda person who wouldnt like you messin up any big thank you he'd been practicin up to spring on you in English.

With his big straw Mexican workin hat pressed up to his chest, he said to me, "From the bottom of my heart, Señora, Meeses Frankleen, I am thanking you for your kindness." For a minute there, I thought Rodrigo was gonna break into a Billy Eckstine imitation, or somethin, he got to lookin so intense.

"Youre a good worker," I said, "and a sweet person too."

When he came up outta his bow, he said, "You have at your house a garden you like me to work in sometime?"

"Not any more," I said and explained.

Rodrigo looked more hurt about what the quake'd done than I did. I had to get outta there. I was sick and tired of cryin so much.

But the cryin didnt stop there. I cried at the way the light was fallin thru the Noxzema trees. I cried that the season was changin and there was nobody for me to curl up with in front of a fire and do my quiltin. I cried and cried and cried in traffic, at the way people looked all hostile and sad in their automobiles, blastin ugly music, guzzlin wine behind the wheel on the freeway, chompin on Big Macs while they drove, smokin and smokin and givin other drivers the finger—anything to try to get away from themselves. And since that meetin I'd had with Ben, my sensitivity to people had been changin fast, maybe too fast. Most of em were scared, I knew that much. But I'd already known that, goin all the way back to when I was three, maybe four. Scared and lonesome, that's what we mostly were. Scared maybe because we took the idea of light too lightly. And lonesome for somethin we couldnt always put our finger on. But I was finally startin to feel as if I was gettin there, that I was more or less gainin on it anyway. It's like when we were kids at Christmas and the whole family would start gettin ready for this day of days as early as August or September, Papa and Mother Dear would be talkin about layin aside somethin for Christmas and Mother Dear would start makin and sewin stuff for people and puttin up special jars of jam and stuff. And of course we kids dreamed about what it was gonna be like, dreamed all outta proportion perhaps. Then the sure-enough Christmas turned up, and there we sat with our toys and gifts and cakes and pies and turkey and that cornbread stuffin of Mother Dear's I loved so much and friends and relatives would fill up the house and we'd sing and play the piano and tell stories and carry on into the night. Before you knew it, Christmas would be come and gone and I'd be sittin on my bed, wonderin whatever happened to all the wonderful things that were gonna happen. You know what I mean? There's a yearnin beyond yearnin that we're always yearnin for. And it's all connected up somehow with light and imagination, like the way you play a picture thru a projector and get all those still pictures to actin like theyre really movin and doin somethin. It's like John Barrymore said in this book on actors actin I read around in when I was takin courses up there at the community college. I cant remember his exact words, but I believe they went somethin like this: *It's all imagination when youre actin. Like, you take a death scene. The audience knows you arent really dyin; you know youre not dyin. But you gotta play the scene as if your death is gonna affect everybody connected with you in your life. And that takes imagination.* I swear, that's pretty close to what he said. I remember because it caused goosebumps to break out all along my arm while I was readin it. Of course, it coulda been that it was a hot day too, and I was there in the college library where they keep the air conditioner turned up so high you could just about hang meat out there in aisles between the shelves, and you certainly wouldnt have to worry about no ice cream meltin.

Now, this is what old Ben musta meant when he told me to stay in the here and now. I'd gotten so busy zigzaggin around inside my own mind—trippin, like they use to say—that I wasnt payin much attention to where I was goin, not until I checked myself pullin off the freeway, headed for my old house again. It was a pattern, somethin like birds flyin south in the wintertime must be programmed to do.

I pulled over and wondered what was goin on. This big feelin was swellin up inside me again, and frankly I felt a little dizzy.

The only thing that calmed me down was lookin out at the day
—the sweet October light floatin out from the sun and coatin
everything so golden and bright. It was almost like you could
taste that light on your tongue. I knew it would be warm and
nectarish.

For no particular reason, I drove down the pier and parked
and cut the engine. Usually there weren't too many people there
in the middle of the afternoon. I could see where the earthquake
had jumbled everything up. There were still teams of workers out
there, pickin up debris and loadin it in trucks and diggin with
shovels and there was even a pavin crew settin up to get busy.

I missed all those folks who use to come down there on roller-
skates or skateboards with their big sails, and I missed that little
old lady that's suppose to be seventy-somethin years old who
would get right out there and skateboard with those kids. But
even with the work crews, it was still quiet enough for me to sit
and lean back and look out across the water, just let my eyes shut
and do what seagulls do. Coastin. I liked to coast all around in
the sky-blue air, except now I could do it inside my head, behind
my eyes. I could sail and sail that way until somethin friendly or
savory lookin turned up.

I thought about the time in East St. Louis when the Inklings
were playin this raggedy little club—a saloon with a piece of
stage, really—and I was sick as a dog, runnin a fever, didnt
wanna be there in the first place. But Chance and the band were
countin on me, since it was the kinda crowd that didnt go much
for jump numbers or tricky show-offy pieces as much as they did
slow blues. They went in for "After Hours" and "I'm Drinkin
Again" and bluesy ballads like that. Humble black folks who
didnt pull any punches. They were there to drop their little
scraped-together money, get mellow in their heads or lit-up
drunk, and listen to you sing their own life and the stuff they
knew about back to em. Everybody always wonderin what this
special thing is that Negroes have about certain songs and
rhythms and this blues thing. What it's about is relaxin into
somebody else tellin their story, which is almost always the same

as your story, or the story the song tells. It took me a lotta practice and experiencin to be able to do that. My voice wasnt exactly trained or all that beautiful, either. I found out that if youre experienced enough, then you can pretty much talk your story out and connect with people where they live, which is in their hearts.

I sat there in Sweepea in the gold of the sun by the blue of the sea and thought about the good times and the bad, and the bad didnt seem all that bad anymore. Because of them, I'd made it this far. Benjie was gonna be all right. As soon as I got those papers to Kendall, he'd get straight, accordin to his father.

There didnt seem to be anything else to do except go thru that trunk and rest. All the same, I had this sudden urge to go see Charlean Jackson. I knew she was at work and that her boss was outta town, but I figured I'd better first call the house.

# 35

Places can make all the difference, and not always for the better. At first I wasnt so sure I was gonna like the Charlean Jackson I found workin in that environment. Even with Nixxy not there, she still wasnt quite the Charlean I loved.

I wanted to talk with her while she went on about her business, performin her duties, but she insisted we sit out in the livin room—and, lemme tell you, Nixxy Privates got a livin room would make the Chryslers' look like the projects, or somethin you might run up on out in Watts or Compton anyway. But I understand how it is with us. After we struggle up and get a break and manage to get sure enough money pourin in, we can sometimes outdo the white folks at their own game. I mean, why should that be so odd or surprisin? After all, for the longest we were the ones takin care of their land, cookin and cleanin for em, raisin their children, teachin em how to relax and enjoy themselves, singin and dancin for em, makin em laugh. Everybody's so quick to forget that the Vietnamese and the Laotians and the Cambodians and Guatemalans and Haitians and the Nicaraguans—or Niggeraguans, as Nomo calls em—havent been here that long yet.

I didnt like the way Charlean wouldnt let me forget she was still on duty, even tho it was only the two of us up there in the house. For instance, everytime I'd get up to go to the kitchen for somethin or go to the bathroom, she would hop up the minute I left the room and go to brushin wrinkles outta the sofa or wipin up crumbs. I did the same thing when there was company at the Chryslers', and I wanted to be sure it looked to everybody like I was on my J. But all I wanted to do was holler at Charlean for a few minutes, catch up on each other, then be on my way. Why couldnt she just relax and be herself?

"Charlean," I said, no longer able to bite my tongue, "honey, youre gonna wear your poor self out, you keep on like this."

She'd just gotten back from the kitchen with a sponge and was wipin up some cream that spilled out the pitcher onto the glass top of the coffee table where we were havin our decaf.

"What was that, Mamie?"

"You oughtta check yourself out. You work too hard."

Charlean bucked her eyes at me kinda puzzled-like. Then some light bulb musta popped on deep back in her brain because she got that big smile she's famous for. "Oh," she said, "am I actin too domestic?"

"Relax," I said. "I'm the same way myself, so I know the syndrome. I didnt come over here to be waited on; just to see you."

"Sorry, Mamie. You know, Nixxy isnt the easiest person in the world to work for. He might act like he's goofy and wild and crazy and outta control when he gets on television or on film, but around here that joker dont miss a thing. I honestly dont believe there is a speck of dust that floats thru this house that Nixxy Privates dont personally observe and take note of." Charlean sipped from her cup and sighed. "Sometime, Mamie, I think you got the better deal."

"A flat deal," I said, laughin, "if there ever was one."

"No, I mean it. See, youre over there with the white folks, which is where I use to be. Now, I know for a fact they dont work you half as hard as Nixxy works me. Johnnie Mae Keyes use to tell me that Will Frisbee and Gardenia and them just about drove her and Fletcher crazy with the kinda scrutiny and close inspection they gave that house of theirs. She swore up and down that Gardenia use to come trackin in behind her with a magnifyin glass and would point out every toeprint and every spot of grease and fleck of lint."

"Yeah, girl," I said, "but you gotta take some of that stuff Johnnie Mae puts out with a whole shaker fulla salt. Dont forget, Friz caught those two with their hands right there in the till. I didnt only hear this from you; I heard it from Danielle too."

"Danielle!" Charlean looked amazed. "What's she know about it?"

"All I know is after you told me that, I came in one day and there Danielle was, goin on about how much she and Carleton appreciated me bein so trustworthy, that she'd heard Will Frisbee's help was stealin him blind."

"Unh!" Charlean's head went to bobbin. "You cant do nothin here in L.A. without it gettin all cross town, can you?"

"Honey, you know that's all these people around here do is gossip. Which reminds me. You heard anything new about Nixxy gettin together with Fiona?"

"Yes, indeed. Mamie, that Englishwoman came down here actin all proper and haughty. You know how these British artists can be sometime. But when she sat down over there at the table, she like to crack me up with all the things she was comin out with. Workin around here, I thought I had seen everything, but that Fifi Prince is *out* there. She is indeed some new kinda nut."

"Tell me about it. You know my story."

"That mornin you walked in on her over there with your boss, right? I remember. Well, it was hard to figure out what they had on their minds that night she was here. By me havin to work and do around in the kitchen and serve them too, I only got to pick up bits and snatches. They are plannin to do a picture, tho. All they lack is a script."

"That's what I'm hearin too," I said.

Without sayin anything, Charlean got up and walked real fast to the edge of the rug, another fancy Persian that people really ought not to be walkin on. She looked back at me like she was embarrassed and then stooped and used her fingers like a comb on the fringe at the edges of the rug.

"Well, it sure sounds like you have been thru the mill," she said, straightenin up.

"You dont know the half of it."

"It must be nice to have that load off your mind about your son and his real father."

"Yes, it is."

"I never told anybody this," she said, "but I can understand perfectly where you comin from with that. While I was over there in Montclair, workin for Dexter Shank, we had a few go-rounds, you know."

"And who won?"

"Wasnt nothin to win, wasnt nothin to lose. That's the way I saw it. I never did have all that strong a moral fiber. Shank made it so easy, I couldnt see much reason at the time for not givin in. But, like I was tellin your boy, Dexter Shank wasnt only a Red; he was a horse of another color. He was so smooth and convincin in whatever he did that after we hooked up a few times, I started gettin involved in passin out leaflets about keepin the Marines outta Lebanon and such, but did have sense enough to never join the Party. I'm just not a joiner. Never would join anybody's church, neither. I wonder how Silvertone will break the news to his family?"

I told her, "I've wondered the same thing. And I always fig-ured you and Shank had written a chapter or two."

All Charlean did was laugh as if to say: And that's the last youre gonna hear of it too.

The minute she sat back down, Charlean absentmindedly reached across the table and plucked somethin off my shoulder.

"That's an awful nice sweater," she said. "Where'd you get it?"

"This is the one I picked up at that clearance sale the last time we went shoppin."

"And how much did you pay for it?"

"It's a three-hundred-dollar sweater," I told her, "but I only paid nineteen ninety-five."

I thought Charlean was gonna choke. She went to coughin and sputterin coffee and tryna clear her throat and act cool all at the same time. "Mamie, youre jokin!"

"I am," I admitted. "This is one of the sweaters from the little stash of clothes I keep at the Chryslers'. There arent many, but I'm sure glad I had it. I bought this thing in New York more than twenty years ago."

"Well, it still looks in style. It's beautiful, really," Charlean sat way back in her chair and studied me. She surprised me again by askin me to stand up.

"What for?"

"I just would like to have a good look at you, that's all."

"But I dont get it," I said, gettin to my feet.

Charlean took her time lookin me up and down, squintin her eyes and shakin her head. "Mamie," she said finally, "it looks to me like youre glowin a little around the edges."

"Glowin?"

"Yeah, you look like youve taken off seven or eight years since I last saw you. What's been goin on with you, girl? I mean, *really* goin on?"

"Nothin, Ive just been tryna get myself back together since the quake and Benjie's trouble and all like I told you."

She just sat there blinkin and grinnin her secret grin. "If I didnt know you better," she said, lookin sly, "I'd swear you'd fooled around here and fell in love."

I tried my best to laugh. "In love!" I let out a grunt. "And who with, might I ask?"

Charlean said, "I dont know. It just looks to me like youre actin pretty perky for somebody that's been bogged down with all the tribulations you been havin to deal with lately."

"In love?" I said again, not believin Charlean had said that. "I cant even think of anybody I could even call myself in *like* with, much less in love."

"You been seein that cute waiter from the restaurant, havent you?"

I started to play dumb, but it no longer seemed to matter. "I saw Theo once," I told her. "It was the night of the earthquake."

And what'd I tell Charlean that for? She got to cacklin and slappin her thighs so hard I thought she was really gonna choke this time.

"Explain to me the humor of that, please."

"Girl, that earthquake was such a freakish thing to begin with, I knew it had to have some unusual causes. Now I know that you the ones behind it, right? Aw, Mamie, I'm just havin a little fun at your expense. You dont have to take it so solemn."

Charlean didnt know it, but I could laugh right along with her on that one. I'd been thinkin along those lines myself.

"But what a price to pay," I said, "just to experience a little tenderness."

"Mamie, love at any price is just as dear."

"Is that somethin Emily Dickinson said?"

"Naw," said Charlean, still studyin me. "I said that. Said it just now and it's true too. What more could you want, Mamie? You got you some money, you got you a honey, and youre fixin to start life all over again. For somebody from Hattiesburg, Mississippi, you have not done bad."

# 36

After a couple days by myself at their beach house in Malibu, the Chryslers wouldna known me and neither would anybody else. I got so calm, look like, until nothin rushed me or got me off kilter. Of course, it's easy to say somethin like that when youre out there sorta bein a hermit; it's a whole lot tougher when youre tryna pass for civilized.

It got so I could wash out a few things in the bathroom sink, hang em up to dry, and actually listen to the dryin goin on while I fixed myself a sandwich or some yogurt to eat. Food didnt interest me, and neither did what was goin on back in town. There was enough goin on right there around me to occupy my mind and my energy. For one thing, the hours got to meltin down like ice. In fact, I even took an ice cube out the fridge just to see if I had the concentration to watch it while it melted, and I did. Nothin I'd recommend to anybody else, tho.

One mornin I drove into town and put mosta that thirty grand in a savins account for Benjie. Whatever the insurance company was gonna pay me, I intended to put that in his name too. Finally when there was nothin else left to do, I got up in the middle of one night and took some paper and a ballpoint to write out my will. But the pressure had been buildin up so strong to go thru Burley's trunk that I figured, well, this is it. You might as well go on and get it over with.

The nice man who lived down the beach had helped haul it into the bedroom where I could work with it comfortably. It was kinda funny. I'd sit there, lookin at that old ugly trunk, then I'd look across the room and stare at that stone Buddha that Carleton and Danielle had set up in there. It was like both of em were kinda the same, somehow—old and mysterious and hard to penetrate. But I liked the Buddha better than I did the trunk. I remembered when the Chryslers went on that Zen kick of theirs. They just about wore me out with all their little stories and jokes —*ko-ans*, they called em—and every other weekend they'd be up there at that place in Tassajara, meditatin and takin those baths. I mighta had more sympathy for em if they coulda explained to me what the thing was all about. But it sounded to me like it was just one more experience to add to their collection. I think I liked Buddha because he reminded me of Nomo Dudu. I dont believe Nomo's got a serious bone in his body.

So this is what everybody wants to get at, I thought after I got thru wipin all the dirt off the trunk. I unlocked it and pulled back the top. It didnt look like any real big thing. On top there were all these papers and envelopes fulla photographs.

There were a lot of snapshots of Burley and his family: his folks and his grandfolks, and some nice ones of him and his first wife Cerise—his only legal wife, actually—and Kendall, who was kinda cute and jolly-lookin as a baby and a little boy. And there were shots of Burley in the army and him and Kendall fishin and at Disneyland and playin football, and stuff, and shots of Burley and me when we first met there in Vegas and I was thinkin pretty soon I was gonna *buy* this casino until my luck turned around. The ones that surprised me were the pictures he'd kept of him and Benjie and me. Benjie at fourteen, Benjie at fifteen, sixteen, and so forth. I could see from the look in their eyes in every single pose how much they really liked one another.

That set me to cryin again, so I stacked the photographs up

real neat off to one side on the floor by the bed and went on into the next layer. I never saw so much army junk in my life. Burley musta saved every piece of paper the army ever handed him. I mean old stubs from SRO shows and punched-up meal tickets— everything. Finally, finally, just about when I thought I was gonna fade back into Harry Truman times and get sent over to Korea myself, I hit a buncha file folders. I didnt even have to touch em to know what they were—and I started not to. But you know how it is with felines and maybe with females too. My curiosity just wouldnt let up.

I broke open the seal on the stack that was there and flipped thru one of the folders. What they were was mostly receipts and records of stuff, but the entries were all handwritten and the figures tended to run in the thousands and tens of thousands, all of it from a long time ago. And then I hit a picture of Mr. Z. himself; Frank Zaccharetti all duded up in one of those dark fifties suits and broad-brimmed hats with a necktie that made him look like Senator Estes Kefauver of Tennessee mighta been standin there just outside the border of the snapshot, waitin to haul Z. up in fronta his committee like they did Frank Costello and them. And for all I knew, that mighta happened.

But it was his teeny little wife, who looked cute and pitiful at the same time that made me do a double take. It was her standin there in the picture with him and their five children—all girls, except for the littlest—that made me put everything back. And as I was puttin the picture back, my eyes fell on another file which I honestly only peeked at for a second. It was all the old early jail and arrest records of Zaccharetti and his pals, which he had evidently bought up to get rid of. Now, why didnt Burley have sense enough to just dump that stuff in a river or a lake someplace? He coulda disposed of it anywhere, coulda even set it afire.

Isnt it curious how you can put off somethin for as long as you can, then when you finally do get around to doin it, come to find out how it never was all that hard to do—you were only makin a production out of it? That's how it was with those records. I found me a box, flopped that stuff of Zaccharetti's in it, found a big paper grocery sack, wrapped that around the box, looked up Kendall's address in my little book, made out the package to him, and decided I would find out where the closest post office was and take it over there sometime tomorrow.

Then I laid down, found me one of those easy-listenin stations, and pulled the covers up around me. I had this feelin, tho, that somethin had been left unfinished. Just as I was losin consciousness, it hit me.

I clicked the light on, got back outta bed, dragged the trunk over, and went inside it again. There at the bottom, under two big army overcoats of Burley's and a medal they'd awarded him, there were these two canvas bags look somethin like mail sacks. The things were so heavy I wasnt sure I could even lift em outta there. When I started undoin the straps on em, my heart jumped. I could practically smell what I was gonna find.

And sure enough, when I got the strap on the first sack loose, there it was. This time I shed a few tears of joy, and then I got scared. Oh, I was so tired of puttin myself thru those changes! All I could see pokin up at the brim under the flap of that sack was packets and packets of fifty- and one-hundred-dollar bills. Now you can understand why I would get frightened, even tho I got a kick outta seein old Ben again. What was Burley doin with all this cash? And why hadnt he tapped it when we were havin the hardest time financin his illness? I didnt get it.

And believe it or not, it was all too much excitement for me. I didnt even have much interest in countin out the money. Muhammad Ali, you know, use to get his big checks cashed so he could go home and count the money out on his hotel bed. *Bam!* One hundred fifty grand! Or whatever it might be. It was all too much. What I wanted was some sleep so I could wake up fresh and get that package off, so they would leave both our sons alone.

It all worked out. I even called Kendall to make sure the package had gotten there all right. He sounded relieved. I still didnt understand how the whole thing worked, but we made an agreement to get together when I got settled someplace. I didnt tell him about the money; I didnt tell anybody about that. It hurt my head to even try to figure out what I oughtta do with it. If I tried to deposit it in a bank, that would draw suspicion. And if I tried to be reasonable and give Benjie and Kendall their share —which I estimated roughly at a third apiece of whatever the amount—then that might open up another can of worms. This was one case where I didnt wanna be the early bird.

And so I decided to finish writin out the will I'd started. I put in the will that Benjie would get one bag and Kendall the other. I intended to sit down and count the doggone money just to see how much it was. I cant describe the feelin that came over me while I was busy gettin that straight, gettin it straight to myself, that is. Here Benjie was gonna have the kinda financial security he'd always envied about those kids he went to school with, and I didnt have Harry, his daddy, who was rich, to thank for that. It was Burley, who never did have anything but stuff and more stuff, that'd make this possible. I went out and made copies of the will, which wasnt at all what you'd call fancy, and addressed one to Benjie and one to Kendall. Then I put both of those in a bigger envelope with a little note and a hundred-dollar bill and addressed it to Charlean Jackson, c/o Nixxy Privates. *DONT OPEN UNTIL XMAS,* I wrote on the front. While I was out takin care of things, I took out a safe-deposit box at my bank and put the original will in there.

I thought about Mother Dear with her sayin about how life was like an onion, and I felt like I hadnt been doin anything but peelin back layers and layers for days. The days and nights were startin to close in on one another—a few daytime hours, a couple nighttime ones.

When I turned on the TV and all the programs started makin me cry, even down to somethin like *Sesame Street,* I asked myself: Now how can *Sesame Street* make anybody cry? Or *Donahue* or *Oprah Winfrey?* Or old *Wonder Woman* reruns?

I knew then that I was the one with the problem. Maybe I'd

look for an apartment someplace. Maybe I wouldnt. Maybe I'd
go back home to Mississippi and visit those people. Or maybe I'd
go to Africa or Brazil or visit Europe again like I'd always
thought I wanted to do. If I hadnt already been feelin like the
wealthiest woman in the world before all this money dropped
into my lap, maybe it woulda been different.

Since I didnt have any address or phone number for Theo, I
stopped by at the restaurant to see if he still worked there. He
did and he told me he'd come out to see me again on his day off.
He didnt quite look the same; there was somethin different
about him now. I think it musta mostly been sadness.

"I wanted to get ahold of you," he said, and I believed him,
"but I didn't know how. The hospital wouldn't give me any
forwardin information, and neither would the television station."

"You went to the station?"

"I called them. I even made a twenty-dollar cash contribution
to that fund. I felt sorry for you."

"Sorry for me? You were in pretty bad shape too."

"I know, but I'm still young and you're—no, I didn't mean
that. When I saw you on the news it made me feel so bad, so
strange . . ."

"It's all right," I said. "Here we are now, and I'm glad you
could stop by."

"What a great place," he said.

"Cute, isnt it?" I looked at the big flat-lookin portfolio he was
carryin and said, "What you got there?"

"Oh, just some drawins of mine. I thought you might like to
see what my work is like."

"You mean, I'll one day be able to tell people 'I knew him
*when*'?"

I was amazed myself at how fast we kinda floated into bed.

I took his face in my hands and started givin him little kisses.
"You have such gentle skin," I said. "Do you even shave?"

"Yes, but I've never had much need for a razor. Nobody in my
family is all that hairy."

"Sounds like you might have Indian blood. They say Indians dont grow much body hair."

"I don't know," Theo said, wrappin his arms tight around me. "That reminds me . . . my folks are coming down to visit next week."

"Are they up in Canada?"

"Washington State. Dad bought some property there. That's a great part of the country to buy up right now, if you have the money."

All my life I'd been hearin people say stuff like that—if only you had the money—and now that I had the money, I knew it couldnt be any better than bein able to go anywhere you wanted whenever you felt like it—and without havin to drag your poor body around.

"Tell me," I said, "are you American, Canadian, or what?"

"I'm still Canadian," he said, "although I have considered taking out citizenship here. Mom and Dad regard that as unthinkable."

All I did was kiss the tip of his nose for an answer. I didnt even care that all that activator gel he'd plastered in his hair was greasin up the pillow somethin awful.

I said, "When I was singin with a band, we'd hit Ottawa and Montreal and Toronto sometime. I'm speaking strictly about gettin into town when the sun's goin down and gettin out before noon the next day. I always thought it would be nice to go up there to relax, for a change."

Theo sat straight up in bed. "You use to sing with a band?"

"Sure."

"When was that?"

"Oh, years ago, while I was still in my teens and early twenties."

"Interesting . . . Who'd you work with?"

"Outfit called Chance Franklin and the Inklings."

"Oh, so that was your first husband, eh?"

"Yes . . . for awhile. We already had the same last name. Franklin is really my maiden name, you know."

"Why'd you quit?" Theo was pullin the covers back up over us now, like he was fixin to settle in for a while.

"Well," I began to explain, not really anxious to touch on the subject, "we simply didnt get along too well. You see—"

"No, why did you get out of the music business?"

I had to laugh. "Oh," I said, "it got to be a hassle. Travelin around is aggravatin enough. It got to the point where I got tireda bein in places I didnt like. Always drunks, always smoke, and always there was somethin dangerous about to break loose. That can get old after a while."

"But didn't you miss it—the excitement, the attention?"

"No, not at all."

"What'd you do after you dropped out?"

It felt absurd layin up in my own bed—well, it felt like my bed —bein quizzed by a youngster about stuff I hadnt given much thought in so long I didnt quite know how to explain it. But I loved that it was Theo. Bein all tangled up with our arms and legs and bodies all cozy like that made me feel so authentic I mighta told him anything he wanted to know at the time.

"For a while," I told him, "I went back to school and got my high-school diploma. I'd married and gone on the road before finishin. It made my folks and relatives so mad and cut me off from the family so much I still havent regained the closeness. Then, while I was workin, I started takin night classes at a community college."

"What in?"

"First one thing, then another. I liked history a lot."

"Yes," he said, loosenin his grip on me. "I remember you had a lot of books on the subject and . . . and what's this thing you seem to have about Benjamin Franklin?"

I laughed so hard when Theo asked that—I was sure he musta got the idea that I'd nutted out on him. "Oh, me and Ben, we go back a long ways," I explained, knowin he'd never understand how far.

Actually it was the way he'd touched my belly just when he was yankin one arm out from under me that made me laugh so. I liked it just fine with his hand restin there, but when he touched my belly it tickled the stew outta me.

"You okay?" he asked.

"Yes, just ticklish right there."

"Oh, I'm sorry."

"For what? Theo, you can tickle me anytime, anywhere."

His lips grazed the nape of my neck in a kiss and he said, "I don't understand what happened."

And that's one of the things that made me crazy about him— all that youngish innocence. It shimmered all around him like starlight.

"So what happened after that?" he said.

"I'll tell you if you really wanna know."

"Mamie, I am a professional listener—that's what makes me such a good waiter. At least that's what they tell me at the Cross."

To tell the truth, I kinda wanted to leave it at that. But there I was and there Theo was, and I could feel him warm and alive next to me everyplace I focused.

So while he listened, I told him about how I fooled around the movie business, playin all these bit and two-bit parts Harry Silvertone was gettin me. Then it got kinda fuzzy, even in my own head, as years and years came rushin at me full force in ways I wasnt ready to face head-on yet. But I blabbed on, all the same, about how I didnt like the picture business either, and how Harry started likin me and wanted me to be his housekeeper, which was a joke that jumped serious.

This was where I had to do some fancy sidesteppin to keep the secret part of all that to myself, altho why I dont know, except it still didnt seem to serve any purpose to blab everything to this child at my side, tender as he was. Besides, it wasnt easy even then to tell about goin to work for Harry, never at his main house, but always at one of the other places he kept in town, where he could go off and be by himself, the same as he liked havin a lotta offices to work out of—that was just Harry. Couldnt stand bein pinned down, and Sylvia, his first wife—the one that favored Barbara Stanwyck—she use to complain whenever I'd see her or when she called over to the other house, that Harry hardly ever talked to her when he was makin a picture. Well, Harry didnt much care for any kinda talk except business and deals and deals and more deals. I coulda told Sylvia that, but never did. He'd hired me to keep his private places tidy and do a little light cookin and sorta play maid. I could tell he was doin it because he called himself likin me, but he was payin me pretty well. He didnt waste any time movin from bein an agent into producin. Everybody knew he was goin straight to the top and straight to the bank. He had that know-how, you know? Sylvia had it too, and she was behind him every incha the way, even if he did treat her funny. I wasnt surprised when years later they broke up and she started this blue-jean and trouser shop that's a nationwide success now—Both Feet In. You cant go anywhere without seein one of em now. But after I got pregnant with Benjie, I couldnt stand bein around Harry. That's understandable, isnt it?

I always suspected Sylvia knew all along Benjie was Harry's baby, but she never let out so much as a word or a funny look about it. Right away Harry got shook but promised to take care of the child and he kept his word. Every single month the check came, even tho he got a little sloppy about bein punctual as the years rolled by. I could count on a fat check from Harry. I never liked the situation, but I loved my baby; so I kept right on livin that lie, livin and dyin with it. We lived all right. Benjie always got the best. Daddy and Mother Dear came out a few times to see their grandchild, and I took Benjie back there a couple times when he was real little. But, aside from Rose—Maxine's mother in Chicago—I didnt hear much from the resta the family after I set down in L.A. They'd given up on me when I ran off with Chance. But Jolene and Alice stayed down there and raised their families. The both of them never liked white people, anyway; so for me to turn up with a child by this white man—and a Jew at that! Somebody I wasnt even married to, who in fact was already married—that just wouldnt do.

They didnt know how to deal with that, so they didnt deal with it. I couldnt much blame em, could you? But Rose was different. Rose was always a little like me and we both took after Maurice, my brother who died in Korea. Both of us were easy-goin and never took life all that seriously. I dont know where we got that from, maybe from Mother Dear, who spent more time chucklin over the world than she did worryin about it.

I always think about Ruby Franklin. Five-six times a day she'll come poppin up in my head. I always see her hunched over a hot cup of Lipton's and skimmin the newspaper. "Now listen at this," she might say. "Harry Truman is mad 'cause some critic wrote somewhere that his daughter, Margaret, cant sing. Here's one of the most powerful men on the face of the earth, and he cant stand for nobody sayin anything about his daughter's singin. Now think about that!" That kinda stuff was just plain funny to Mother Dear.

So after workin for Harry I got so I kinda liked doin domestic work, only it had to be on my terms. With me, you see, people werent just hirin a maid; they were gettin themselves a little extra, besides. Chance taught me that—to be good to yourself by regardin yourself as somethin special. He sure didnt have any trouble in that department. He always told me that the way you saw yourself and the way you acted toward yourself was the way other people were gonna act toward you, too. I was such a girl when Chance got aholda me, it took me years to undo all that programmin he'd done on me. But this part was true.

I always knew I had this gift, this psychic ability, whatever you wanna call it, but I never tried to do anything with it until I'd put in some time around L.A., long enough to understand that people out here on the Coast put more value in that kinda thing. It wasnt my style to hang out a shingle or to open up a shop, but I did let it be known I could do readins. Sure enough, word got around.

At first I had me more business than I knew what to do with, but after while I got tireda havin all these people traipsin in and outta my house, that is, when I wasnt sittin up at their places. It got so all the entertainment people wanted me to do readins on em. I did a right smart of that before I had a vision one mornin just before wakin up. This was *years* ago. In the vision an old Chinese gentleman, a man who use to run a grocery store I'd stop by, was dancin all around my house and keepin up so much racket that when I went out to see what was the matter he changed into a prince or royalty of some kind and, dancin and singin all the while, told me the best thing for me to do—for Benjie's sake—was to keep the use of my powers under control and to keep workin at somethin that was simple and steady until Benjie got grown and outta the house.

"Why?" I heard Theo ask, and it kinda scared me because I'd gotten so tangled up inside myself with relivin the years I'd almost forgotten I was tellin him all this and he was listenin. "Why do you think he would say something like that?"

"Because when you do readins on people, you run dead up against a lotta energy I can only call, well, weird."

"Weird?"

"I mean, just because you can channel other people's thoughts and experiences doesnt mean youre immune to bein affected by what theyre puttin out. Most people put out far more negative thoughts and energy than they do positive."

"I'm afraid you've lost me there," he said in a jovial kinda way. "I don't know what you're talking about. You're beginning to sound too much like these New-Age and New-Consciousness people I keep running into. You certainly have enjoyed a full, rich life. Mamie . . . would you sing for me sometime?"

"Why, yes, of course. I'd be happy to sing for you, but you gotta quit puttin stock in these labels they put on the truth."

"What? Oh, Mamie, are you crying again? Is it because I brought up singing?"

"No, no . . . It's just that no one's asked me to sing . . . not for years."

Theo looked at me all hard and said, "Who do you think you sound like? Are you as good as Whitney Houston?"

I grabbed him and smothered him with all the kisses I'd

stored up that'd been achin to be put on somebody, to belong someplace. And we made love and made love until I didnt think I could stand it anymore. It surprised me to discover I'd been in the world so long by then I could even tell by his hard lovemakin he musta been feelin guilty. About somethin. Maybe he'd found him a girlfriend, somebody his own age—but that was all right. That was as it oughta be. He didnt have to prove anything to me, but since it seemed like he wanted to anyway, I just fell in and went along with it. We got into stuff I hadnt done with anybody since I was just a beginner. And some of it took the breath outta me too; my poor spine just wasnt that flexible anymore. But it meant more than that, and I began to think while I was goin up in flames again for the last time—I'd lost track hours ago, looked like—I understood what Emily Dickinson had been tryna tell us on that sweatshirt of Charlean's. The brain *is* wider than the sky. Mine felt like it was ready to call it a day or a night, or whichever.

I collapsed and slept and woke up and slept and kept doin that until it was time for Theo to leave. He looked so gentle and kind, gettin up and bein real quiet about not wakin me up while he was gettin dressed. I kept thinkin, *Now, if he was as good with words as he is with drawin, maybe he'd be the one for me to channel my story thru.* There'd be somebody, I knew, when I got ready to tell it. Somebody was bound to be tuned to my frequency.

I played like I was asleep, but I could hear him unzippin his portfolio and takin somethin out. Then I heard the sound of his pen scratchin out a note. After he collected all his stuff, he leaned over me in the dark and kissed me so soft on the lips it wasnt funny.

The minute I heard the door click shut, I rolled over and snapped on the light long enough to take in Theo's neat calligraphy. *Mamie*, it said, *I don't think we need to see each other again, not as lovers. Perhaps as friends. I love you too much to ever hurt you. And I want to keep that way special forever. Love, Theo.* And then he gave his phone number where I could reach him.

I stretched out, thinkin about the song I wanted to sing for Theo. The ocean was churnin in the distance and I continued to play at bein asleep. After while I sat up and pecked out Benjie's number on the telephone.

"Hello, darlin," I said to his machine. "It's just me . . . Mom . . . You have no idea how much I love you, do you? Dont waste your time worryin about anything."

Then I got up, feelin a little dizzy and went into that giant bathroom of theirs and fixed me a nice hot bubble bath. I musta soaked in it for a good hour. It was so cozy and warm it seemed like I could feel every single one of those winkin bubbles personally pop against my skin. I took my time towelin myself dry, then slipped into a brand new nightgown I'd treated myself to the day before. I cant tell you how good it felt slidin over my head and down around my body—all silky and airy and light. It seemed like it might help to brush my teeth. While I was squeezin the toothpaste out on the brush, I looked in the mirror to check myself out. That was when my heart almost stopped and my hands started shakin.

I wasnt there.

I mean, there was no me in the mirror. No image, no reflection, no likeness—nothin. I turned on the light up over the mirror and looked again. Still nothin. I shut my eyes real tight a few times and opened em up and looked in the mirror again. I could see the wall in backa me with the towel rack and the towels and washcloth hangin on it, but still no reflection of me.

Oh, Lord! I got to rememberin all the times I curled up in the dark with my popcorn in theaters and looked at Bela Lugosi go thru this very scene. I stepped out the bathroom and went back into the bedroom and checked myself out in all the mirrors there. Nothin again. I pressed my face and hands up to the mirror, and it was like lookin clean thru a glass wall or a door. I wiped away the warm, wet tracks of my tears from the mirror and laid down in the bed to catch my breath. Surely I was exhausted, fatigued, worn out. Maybe if I played some more at bein asleep, then everything would straighten itself out and I'd wake up in my right mind. But just before layin down, I picked up the picture Theo had drawn of me from memory. I sat down on the bed and held it back, real careful not to smudge any of the dark charcoal, and looked at it until I thought the thumpin in my heart would cut off my breath. Far as I was concerned, Theo's picture beat any mirror image of me, anyway, anyday.

I propped the drawin up on the bureau and laid down to play like I was sleepin some more. But the playin turned into the real thing. It didnt seem to matter anymore. It wasnt long before there I was, watchin my real self freein itself from me myself, and there was Burley and old Ben and my brother Maurice all runnin toward me in what seemed to be the middle of a dream, and all I could feel was pure gladness and the satisfied feelin I'd done everything I wanted and everything I could. So all I had to do now was relax and be completely where I was, which felt like just the right place for me to be now.

I took my last breath and felt the top of my head openin, just like Burley had told me, and out I went, dissolvin into quietness. It was kinda like when I'd slipped out before to look in on people, except calmer—since this time I knew I wasnt goin back. I could see just as plain the room and the house and the rooftop, then the whole neighborhood, then Malibu by the ocean so blue, but there was no more blues to be singin or cryin. And pretty soon I could tell at last there was nothin left to see but the sea, and nothin left to do but keep on swimmin upstream in that sweet, bright river of light.